Mending Fences

SHERRYL WOODS

Mending Fences

MIRA®

Recycling programs
for this product may
not exist in your area.

ISBN-13: 978-0-7783-2895-7

MENDING FENCES

For questions and comments about the quality of this book please contact us at
Customer_eCare@Harlequin.ca.

www.MIRABooks.com

Printed in U.S.A.

Dear Friends,

I'm always being asked what sparks the ideas for my books, especially after more than 100 of them. A glimpse into how *Mending Fences* came about will give you some indication of the process that my sometimes quirky mind goes through.

For many years now I've worked with the same accountant, and during those years have also gotten to know his wife. Carl and Dianne Margenau are terrific folks, who've recently made a move from Miami to North Carolina, so much of our contact is now by phone. During one of those calls, Dianne mentioned how much they missed their longtime neighbors, how close the families had been over the years and what wonderful people they were.

So I began to think…. What would happen between two families who'd shared so many important events, so many hopes and dreams and such a deep friendship, if something tragic occurred with the potential to split them apart? From that conversation, *Mending Fences* was born. Please keep in mind that beyond making me wonder what if… there are no similarities between the Margenaus and their longtime neighbors and the characters in my book. Still, Dianne gets the credit for kicking my imagination into overdrive and Carl, as always, gets credit for keeping me out of financial hot water. I'm grateful to them both.

I wish all of you neighbors you can count on and friends who enrich your lives.

As always,

Sherryl

1

Grady Rodriguez had been a police officer for nearly twenty years, but he'd never gotten used to interviewing young women who'd been the victims of date rape. It wasn't quite the same as talking to those who'd been assaulted by strangers. For those women, there was little ambiguity about the attack. It was usually random, unexpected, violent and degrading. It could happen to any woman at any age who happened to be in the wrong place at the wrong time.

Date rape tended to happen to young, often inexperienced women who knew their attacker. They were left with a million and one questions about what they might have done differently, how their judgment about the guy could have been so wrong, why saying no hadn't been enough. He'd responded to too damn many of those calls, listened to too many brokenhearted sobs, seen too many injuries.

In either case, the women questioned everything about themselves. They dealt with unwarranted shame, sometimes made a thousand times worse by the well-meaning reactions of the people who loved them. In all instances, it changed who they were, made them more cautious, less trusting. Sometimes it destroyed relationships or even marriages.

From everything he could see as he and his partner, Naomi Lansing, walked into the off-campus Coral Gables apartment where tonight's attack had happened, Lauren Brown was typical. A pretty college student with shiny, long blond hair, she barely looked old enough to date. A kid that young shouldn't have had her innocence stripped away in a manner that left her eyes glazed with pain and disillusionment. Seeing her huddled in a corner of the bed in her room in tears, Grady wanted to punch his fist through a wall, but Naomi was cool and calm, the kind of soothing presence the situation required.

Naomi's compassion allowed him to remain in the background, to study the scene in a coldly analytical way. They were the perfect team for this kind of investigation, something he'd never have predicted back when they'd first been assigned to work together and every encounter had been a test of wills.

"She was like that when I came in," Lauren's roommate, Jenny Ryan, told them in an undertone. "Just rocking back and forth and crying. She said her date had hurt her, but she wouldn't say anything else. She asked me not to, but I called nine-one-one anyway. The creep shouldn't get away with this. I don't care who he is."

Something in her words gave Grady a chill, the hint that Lauren's attacker was well known, perhaps well-respected in the University of Miami campus community.

"You did the right thing," Naomi assured her. "We'll take it from here. Could you wait in the other room?"

For a moment, Jenny hesitated. "I'm not sure I should leave her."

Naomi sat on the edge of the bed, careful not to crowd Lauren. "You'll be okay, right? You're up to talking to me?"

Lauren's head bobbed once, but she didn't look up.

As Naomi began murmuring the most intrusive questions in her quiet, matter-of-fact voice, Grady studied the bedroom. Painted and carpeted in the bland beige of inexpensive rentals, it was decorated in a style that was too shabby to be chic. There were mismatched pieces of furniture, a few snapshots—family pictures, it looked like—stuck into the dresser mirror, a laptop computer next to a stack of textbooks and an antique rocker he would bet had been a prized possession from home.

Other than the tangled spread and sheets on the bed and a few pieces of clothing that had been tossed on the floor, the room was neater than most coed rooms he'd seen. Carefully gathering the clothes she'd apparently been wearing, he noted the buttons missing from her blouse, the torn strap of her bra and a rip in her panties, all consistent with someone intent on having sex, perhaps with an unwilling partner. He found three buttons scattered around the carpet and added those to the evidence.

Leaving it to Naomi to retrieve the sheets and spread and whatever trace evidence they might contain, Grady walked into the living room to join the roommate. "Any idea who Lauren was out with tonight?" he asked her.

"Evan Carter," she said without hesitation. "You know who he is, right?"

"Yeah, I've heard of him," he said, struggling to maintain a neutral expression.

Carter was a star football player at the University of Miami. Only a sophomore, there was already speculation about him becoming a top NFL draft choice before graduation. News reports, however, also cited his excellent grades, good enough for the career he hoped to have in the legal field representing professional athletes. He had brains, talent and charm—the kind of trifecta that made it easy for people to miss any hints of a darker side, the sense of entitlement and immunity that came with being a celebrity of sorts.

A local boy, Carter was already used to the spotlight by the time he entered UM. He'd been courted by both the Florida Gators and by Florida State Seminoles, top UM rivals. When he'd opted to stay close to home, there'd been a sigh of relief from the Miami fans, who'd followed his stellar high school career.

"Is that the crowd Lauren hangs out with—the jocks?" he asked Jenny.

"No way. To tell you the truth, Lauren's never dated much. She's basically pretty shy and quiet. She's here on a scholarship, so she studies a lot. Evan's the first guy she's really talked much about. They're in the same biology class—I'm in it, too—and they've been working on this project together for a couple of weeks now. When he suggested dinner and a movie, she couldn't believe this superjock had asked her out. She was so excited." Her lower lip quivered and her expressive dark eyes filled with anger. "Damn him for doing this to her!"

"Were you here when they left? Did you see them together?"

Jenny shook her head. "I had to go to the library to do some research for a paper that's due on Monday. I didn't get back till about two minutes before I called you."

"So you can't be sure they actually got together tonight," he suggested.

Jenny practically quivered with indignation. "Are you trying to say she made it all up or something?" she demanded. "Lauren would *never* lie about who she had a date with or about what happened. Lauren doesn't lie. Period."

"Maybe a girl who doesn't date much developed a crush on this unattainable guy, built herself a whole fantasy scenario," he suggested.

"No, absolutely not!" Jenny said emphatically. "She's the most honest, grounded person I know. Her dad's a minister, for goodness' sakes. She has this whole moral code she lives by. Most of the time the rest of us fall way short of meeting her standards, but she never judges any of us for that."

Satisfied, Grady backed off on any suggestion that Lauren could have exaggerated anything that happened with the Carter kid. Instead, he focused on what Jenny herself knew firsthand. "But you yourself didn't witness any part of the date, correct?"

She sighed. "No. I never saw them together, but I imagine there are plenty of witnesses in the building or on the block. It's mostly college kids living in this area, so there's always somebody going in or out, especially on a Friday night. And Evan's the kind of guy who attracts attention. He makes sure of it."

Grady knew the type. They thrived on being the center of attention, being recognized. They also thought they were above the law. Maybe tonight Grady would get lucky and that tendency would seal the case against Evan Carter.

"If Detective Lansing looks for me, tell her I'm going

to knock on a few doors, see what I can find out from the neighbors," he told Jenny. "I'll be back in a few minutes. You'll stay put, right?"

"Of course. I'm not leaving Lauren."

The white stucco building on the fringe of the UM campus only had four units, two upstairs, two down. He tried the downstairs doors to no avail, then loped back upstairs and knocked on the door across the hall from Lauren's. When it swung open, the sound of classic jazz flowed through the air. The long-haired kid wearing boxers, a T-shirt and flip-flops stared at him with blurry eyes and a bewildered expression.

"Is the music too loud or something?" he asked Grady. "I try to keep it low."

"The music's not a problem," Grady assured him. He showed him his ID. "Mind if I ask you a couple of questions?"

"Am I in trouble?"

The kid sounded nervous, which made Grady wonder what he was up to. Then he caught a whiff of marijuana and knew. That, however, was a problem for another night.

"No, no trouble," he assured him. "This is your apartment?"

"I have a roommate, but he's out on a date."

Grady made a note. "What's your name?"

"Joe Haas."

"And your roommate's?"

"Dante Mitchell."

"He plays football, doesn't he?" Grady asked, trying to envision the huge defensive tackle sharing a place with this skinny, unassuming kid.

"We're from the same hometown. His folks think I'm

a good influence on him." He shrugged, his grin self-deprecating. "As if he'd ever listen to me. Still, we get along okay."

"Have you been home all night?"

"It's Friday night," he said as if that was answer enough. "I've been here just chilling out."

"Seen anybody? Heard anything unusual?"

He stared at Grady with a blank expression. "Like what?"

"Anything that seemed out of the ordinary?"

"Did one of the apartments get robbed? Is that why you're asking all these questions?"

"No. I'm just trying to get a feel for what was going on around here tonight."

"I think everybody's out, except me. Dante left around seven. Jenny headed out about the same time with a bunch of books. She always goes to the library on Friday night. She says it's quieter then. The guys downstairs, they always head straight for happy hour after their last class on Friday. I don't think they've come in yet. They're usually pretty noisy, so I would have heard them if they'd come back."

"What about Lauren? Have you seen her?"

He shook his head. "I know she had a date with some jock, a friend of Dante's."

"Did she tell you that?"

"No, Dante mentioned it. He thought it was pretty hilarious for some reason."

"Why was that?"

"I guess because Lauren's really shy and this guy thinks he's some big hotshot."

"You know a name?"

Joe shook his head. "I'm not that into football. Dante probably said, but it didn't stick."

"And you never saw Lauren with this guy?"

He shook his head, then frowned. "Lauren's okay, isn't she? Nothing happened to her tonight, did it?"

Grady ignored the questions. "Thanks. If you think of anything else, give me a call." He handed him his business card.

Joe followed him back into the hall, his expression filled with concern. He bypassed Grady and headed straight for Lauren's door. Grady intercepted him. "Not tonight."

Alarm shadowed the boy's eyes. "I just want to check on Lauren. She's a sweet kid, you know?"

"Talk to her tomorrow, okay? She'll need a friend then." He leveled a look at the kid. "And you might want to lose the weed before I come around again. Next time I won't look the other way."

"Shit!" Joe said, his expression immediately guilt ridden. He all but ran back to his own apartment and shut the door.

Grady shook his head. For a fraction of an instant he was grateful he didn't have teenagers, but then he thought of his beautiful little Megan and his heart ached. She would have been sixteen now and he would give every last breath in his body to have his daughter back, no matter what sort of foolish mistakes she might make.

Tonight wasn't the night to travel down that dark path, though. Another young girl needed him.

Inside Lauren's apartment, Jenny was exactly where he'd left her, blindly thumbing through a magazine, her attention directed toward the room where Naomi was still questioning Lauren.

"Did anybody see anything?" she asked when she realized he was back.

"The kid across the hall was the only one home, and he confirmed she was supposed to go out with some jock tonight, but he didn't see him and didn't have a name. He says his roommate had told him that."

Jenny smiled. "Joe's a little spacey most of the time, but he's a good guy. It might not seem like it, but he's practically a genius. He's studying physics, but most of the time he's bored, because he knows as much as the professors. He puts up with a lot from Dante, who thinks he's God's gift to the universe. Will it help that Dante knew about the date, too?"

"It might," Grady conceded.

"What happens next?"

"We'll need to get Lauren to the hospital, get her checked out," he said. "Can you come along? It might make her feel better to have a familiar face around."

"If she needs me, I'm there," Jenny told him.

A few minutes later, Naomi emerged with Lauren and the four of them made the trip to the Rape Treatment Center at Jackson Memorial Hospital for the necessary indignity of a physical examination.

As they waited outside while a physician gathered evidence and offered counseling to Lauren with Jenny at her side, Grady sat beside Naomi and compared notes. "You think she'll go through with this? Will she press charges against the Carter kid?" he asked. "It's a tough road, especially with his high profile. The publicity could be pretty devastating, even if her name's kept out of it."

"She's scared," Naomi said. "But she's starting to get angry. If she weakens, something tells me her roommate will make sure she fights back."

He nodded. "Jenny's mad enough for both of them. I wish all the girls we come across had someone in their corner like that."

Naomi nodded. "Me, too."

"We need to do this one by the book," Grady said wearily. "I want an arrest warrant in hand before we go anywhere near that kid."

"That could take time," Naomi warned. "It's almost morning now and half the judges are going to be on the golf course and the rest are probably out on their boats."

"We'll call the state attorney's office and leave that problem up to them. I don't care how long it takes, I want that warrant before we say boo to that kid. The media's going to be all over this case and I'm not losing it because we didn't cross every *t* and dot every *i*."

Just then the weary-looking physician who handled for too many of these cases emerged from the treatment area.

"How's it going, Doc?" Grady asked Amanda Benitez.

"I'm starting to have a very jaded outlook on life in general and men in particular," Amanda said. "This guy roughed her up pretty good. He was smart about it, almost as if he knew how to go about it without leaving the kind of obvious visible marks that would call attention to what he'd done. Her stomach, her upper thighs have some nasty bruises, though. He was strong and he was mean."

Grady read between the lines. "He's done this before?"

"I'd say yes. You know the pattern as well as I do. It's not just about the sex. This is a guy who gets off on hurting women, the more innocent and defenseless the better. You have a name?"

Grady nodded. "And when this goes public, the shit is going to hit the fan."

It was well past midnight on Saturday and Marcie had just finished cleaning up the kitchen, putting every dish and glass back into place, polishing every piece of chrome and mopping the floor for the second time that day, when the doorbell rang.

Worried that it would wake Ken and the kids, she hurried into the living room to answer the door. Startled to see two uniformed officers and two other people in plain clothes outside at this hour of the night, she was tempted not to open the door, but weighed her caution against the possibility that they'd wind up waking her family by continuing to ring the bell. She finally opened the door a crack, the security chain still in place.

"Can I help you?"

"Pinecrest police, ma'am," one of the uniformed officers said. "We have two detectives from Coral Gables who'd like to speak to your son. Since they're out of their jurisdiction, we came along."

"I don't understand," Marcie said.

"You're Mrs. Carter?" the female detective asked. "Evan Carter's mother?"

Marcie's breath lodged in her throat. "Yes, why?"

"We need to speak to your son," she repeated. "Is he here?"

"He's asleep. What is this about?"

"I'm Detective Lansing," the woman told her. "And this is Detective Rodriguez. We need to talk to Evan. Would you get him, please?"

Though it was phrased as a question, Marcie recognized a command when she heard one. She tried to think what Ken would do. He'd probably tell them to go away and come back at a civilized hour, but Marcie had been brought up to respect authority. Four very somber police officers from two jurisdictions were more than enough to intimidate her.

"You'll have to give me a few minutes," she said at last. "He's a sound sleeper."

"No problem. We'll wait," the woman told her.

Reluctantly Marcie let them inside, then started to climb the stairs. After only a couple of steps, she turned back. "Maybe I should…" she began, her tone apologetic. "Could I see some identification?" She'd read stories about fake police officers, even in uniform, and home-invasion robberies. Even though she recognized the Pinecrest logo on the uniform and saw the marked car in the driveway, it was smart to be absolutely sure.

Without comment all four of them held out badges and ID, removing any doubt that they were exactly who they'd said they were. She almost wished she hadn't asked. Until that instant, she'd been able to hold out a slim hope that this was all some hoax or maybe a case of mistaken identity.

Evan was a good kid. He always had been. Oh, he had a mouth on him. He was like his father that way, but he'd never given them any trouble. He'd never so much as put a ding or dent in the car, never gotten into mischief the way some of the other boys in the neighborhood had. His dad had seen to that. Ken was a stern disciplinarian and both her kids showed him a healthy amount of respect.

Thinking about that made this whole scene feel surreal.

Once again she hesitated. "Why do you need to see Evan at this hour? Is he in trouble?"

For the first time, Detective Rodriguez spoke. "Ma'am, could you just get him? We'll explain everything then."

Filled with a sense of dread, she climbed the stairs. At the top she debated waking Ken but decided against it. Who knew what he would do or say? He had a quick temper and a sharp tongue. He tended to act first and think later. He might wind up making a bad situation worse. If Evan needed him, there would be time enough to wake him then.

Inside Evan's room, she found him sprawled face-down across his bed with a sheet barely covering him. Sometimes when she saw him like this, it caught her by surprise. In her heart, he was still her little boy, not a full-grown man with broad shoulders and muscles toned by hours of training at the gym. His cheeks were stubbled with a day's growth of beard and his blond hair, usually so carefully groomed, stuck out every which way. Seeing him reminded her of the way Ken had looked when they'd first met, way too handsome for his own good.

"Evan," she murmured, her hand on his shoulder. "Wake up! Evan!"

He only moaned and buried his head under the pillow, just as he had for years when she'd tried to wake him for school. Marcie knew the routine. She yanked the pillow away and then the sheet, averting her gaze from his naked body as she did so.

"Wake up!" she commanded, shaking him.

"Wha...? Go 'way."

"Get up now," she said urgently. "There's someone here to see you."

He blinked up at her. "What? Who?"

"They're police officers, four of them. Two local and two from the Gables."

"Shit, oh shit," he muttered, raking his hand through his hair.

Something in the panicked expression that flitted across his face terrified Marcie. Had there been an accident? Had he left the scene? Or drugs? She knew there were kids at college who used them, but Evan had always been smart enough to steer clear. He'd wanted his football career too much to risk messing it up by experimenting with drugs or steroids. Ken had hammered that lesson home years ago.

"Do you know what this is about?" she asked. "Should I get your dad?"

"I'll handle it," he said, grabbing a pair of jeans and yanking them on, then snatching up a T-shirt from the end of the bed and pulling it over his head. "Don't come downstairs, Mom, okay? I'll take care of this."

Marcie fought to stay calm. "I don't like the sound of this, Evan. I think someone should be with you. Do I need to call a lawyer?"

"I said I'd handle it," he snapped. "Go to bed."

Marcie winced at his tone. She should have been used to it by now. Ken used that exact same tone when he spoke to her, but it was relatively new coming from Evan.

"You're not going down there alone," she insisted. "Now either I come with you or I get your father."

"Whatever," he said belligerently.

Marcie followed him downstairs. At the bottom of the steps, the two detectives stood in his path.

"Evan Carter?" Detective Rodriguez asked.

"Yes. What the hell is this about?" he demanded, his voice radiating antagonism.

Again, he sounded so much like his father, it gave Marcie goose bumps. Instinct kicked in. She was about to try to smooth things over with the detectives, but realized they were oblivious to his attitude and totally focused on their own mission.

"You're under arrest for the rape of Lauren Brown," the woman said quietly. "Anything you say can and will be used against you…"

Rape! Marcie was incredulous. This simply couldn't be happening. As the detective read Evan his rights, Marcie fought back the bile rising in her throat and ran upstairs to wake her husband. She couldn't shake the sound of the word *rape*. It kept echoing in her head.

"Ken, get up now! The police are arresting Evan. They say he raped somebody."

She didn't have to say it twice. Ken bolted out of bed with a curse and ran for the stairs, Marcie right on his heels. She heard Caitlyn's door open and knew that her daughter had been wakened by the commotion as well.

"Mom, what's going on? Why is there a police car outside?"

Marcie couldn't bring herself to explain. "It's all a terrible misunderstanding," she said. "I'm sure that's all it is. Your father will straighten everything out, but I need to go with him."

"Go with him where?" Caitlyn asked, her eyes wide. "It's the middle of the night."

"To the police station. I'm going to call Emily and see if you can go over and spend the night at their house, okay? I don't want you here alone."

"Who's been arrested? Is it Dad?"

"No, sweetie, it's your brother, but like I said, it has to be a mistake." Her hand shook as she picked up the phone and hit the number on the speed dial for Emily.

Her friend and neighbor answered on the first ring, instantly wide awake. "Marcie, is everything okay? I saw the flashing lights on a police car turning onto your street, but I never heard a siren. What's going on?"

"I can't explain now. Can Caitlyn stay with you?"

"Of course," she said at once. "Send her over. Is there anything else I can do?"

"Pray," Marcie said, her voice catching on a sob. "Pray that the police have made some horrible mistake. My boy…" She couldn't even finish the sentence.

"They came for Evan?" Emily said, sounding as shocked as Marcie felt.

"Yes. Please, just watch out for Caitlyn. She's on her way. I don't know how long we'll be gone. I'll tell you everything tomorrow."

"Go. Don't worry about anything here. Just promise that you'll call me if there's anything else I can do."

Marcie sighed as she hung up. She wondered if Emily would sound half as supportive once she found out what Evan had been accused of doing. There were some things even a best friend could never understand or forgive.

And if there was any truth, any truth at all to the charges, Marcie wasn't entirely certain she'd ever understand it, either.

2

Ten years earlier

Dinner was going to be another rushed affair. Emily Dobbs had spent two hours in a tedious, unproductive teachers' meeting after school, then picked up her husband's dry cleaning, run by the post office for stamps, stopped by the drugstore for her prescription for birth control pills—not that she'd needed them lately—and spent fifteen minutes at the market trying to figure out what she could fix for dinner in the twenty minutes she had left after she'd picked the kids up from the sitter's. Spaghetti with salad and garlic bread had been the quick and easy answer. She supposed that was a step up from stopping for fast-food burgers or ordering pizza, something she'd resorted to way too many times recently.

Every week she vowed to come up with nightly menus and a shopping list, rather than improvising every meal at the last possible moment. So far, she'd failed to follow through, despite her good intentions.

Lately everything in her life felt as if she were doing it on the run. Maybe she should have waited to go back into teaching, but she'd missed being in the classroom after Josh and Dani were born. As soon as Dani had started in preschool, Emily had sought out and gotten a position teaching high school English just a few miles from home. Derek hadn't been overjoyed when she'd told him, but he was traveling so much for business, he'd hardly been able to complain that she would be neglecting him or their marriage.

The kids, however, were another story. When it came to her son and daughter, she was assailed by guilt on a daily basis. They were growing so fast and she was missing some of it. Josh was a strong, athletic nine-year-old now with a well-developed mind of his own. Dani, with her long dark curls and her preference for dresses and tea parties, was a seven-year-old princess, ruler of the second grade.

As Emily stopped in front of Linda Wilson's house, she watched her two precious children race outside and across the lawn. Well, Josh raced. Dani walked as sedately as if she were on a fashion runway, at least until her brother called back some taunting remark that had her sprinting the rest of the way.

"Hi, Mom," Josh said, jumping into the front seat as Dani climbed more demurely into the back, then stuck out her tongue at her brother. Josh rolled his eyes, then directed his attention toward Emily. "Guess what?"

"What?"

"We've got new neighbors in back, and they've got kids. Mrs. Wilson told me that Evan's the same age as me and he plays football and soccer and baseball. There's a girl, too," he added, as if that were of far less consequence.

"Her name's Caitlyn," Dani said, "but she's just a baby."

Josh rolled his eyes. "She's five."

"That's too little to be my friend," Dani said with a dramatic sigh of disappointment.

Emily bit back a smile. "Are you sure about that, sweetie? I bet she'd love to come to one of your tea parties," she suggested. "You were five when we started having them, remember? Maybe she's never even been to one and you could show her how much fun they are. In fact, since she's just in kindergarten, there are probably lots of things you could teach her."

Dani regarded her solemnly. "You think so?"

"You could ask," Emily said.

Dani was silent for a long, considering moment, then nodded. "Maybe I will."

And so it began…

The kids pestered Emily all day Saturday to let them go play with Evan and Caitlyn Carter. They both knew that there was one rigid rule in their house, that they were never to go to another child's home unless she knew the parents, and she had yet to meet their new backdoor neighbors.

Exhausted from cleaning and grocery shopping and with a stack of English papers still to grade, she knew there would be no peace until she gave in.

"Okay, fine. Let's take a walk and see if they're home," she agreed eventually.

The neighborhood in southeast Miami was shaded by pin oaks and giant banyan trees with their gnarled, twisted trunks that looked as if they belonged in a horror movie rather than in some pleasant, suburban neighborhood. Most of the well-landscaped yards were surrounded by hedges of bougainvillea in colors ranging

from purple and fuchsia to red or white. The prickly
vines with their profusion of brilliant flowers served as
something of a security barrier without the need for
fences or gates, though high wrought-iron gates had
started to appear at the end of a few driveways as
property values went up, along with the crime rate.

Only a few blocks from the waters of Biscayne Bay,
Emily thought she could detect traces of salt in the air,
along with the lingering scent of night-blooming jasmine.
It was enough to remind her how much she enjoyed being
outdoors at this time of year, when the Miami air had less
humidity and the sky was a clear, vivid blue. She and
Derek needed to get back into the habit of taking a walk
after dinner the way they had when they'd first moved into
their dream house. Back then, they'd pushed Dani in her
stroller and Josh had ridden along beside them on his
tricycle.

A few years ago, they'd also known all their neighbors in this well-established area, but as prices had
soared, many of their older neighbors had sold out and
moved to more manageable condos or retirement com-
munities. Lately the turnover had been so frequent that
there were only a few familiar faces left from those early
years…the Wilsons down the block, the Delgados on the
corner and Janice Ortiz and her elderly mother on the
next street.

"Mom, hurry up!" Josh said impatiently. "Can't you
walk any faster?"

Emily grinned at him. "I can, but I'm enjoying the
fresh air."

He regarded her blankly. "Why?"

"Someday you'll understand," she said, ruffling his
brown hair.

"It's like stopping to smell the roses," Dani said. "Grandma Dobbs tells Dad he needs to do that." She wrinkled her forehead. "I'm not sure what she means, though."

"She means your dad works too hard," Emily told her.

"No joke," Josh said with disgust. "He's never around anymore to play ball with me."

"He has an important job," Emily reminded him, feeling the need to defend Derek, even though Josh was expressing a dissatisfaction that she often felt herself. Then, as a reminder to herself as much as to her son, she added, "We should be grateful that he's such a hard worker. That's why we're able to live in such a great house and you kids get to go to wonderful schools."

"I'd rather be able to play ball with my dad," Josh grumbled. "Dad doesn't even come to my games half the time anymore."

Emily resolved to remind Derek that he needed to get some balance back into his life, that his son needed more from him than a fancy house and every hot electronic game to hit the market, all purchased out of guilt over his too-frequent absences and a string of last-second disappointments.

As they approached the sprawling, Spanish-style house with a red-tiled roof that the Carters had just moved into, she hunkered down on the sidewalk in front of the kids. "Now remember to be on your best behavior," she instructed. "The way you are when we visit Grandma Dobbs and Grammy and Poppy, okay?"

Josh was practically bouncing with excitement. It had been a long time since there had been a boy his age living close enough for him to hang out with. "Come on," he pleaded, then made a dash for the pretentious wrought-iron gate that was new to the property. He tried to turn the handle, but it wouldn't budge. He regarded it with dismay. "It's locked."

Emily was as startled as her son, but she spotted a buzzer next to the gate. "I think we probably need to push that button," she told her son, and watched as he gave it an eager punch.

"Yes?" The disembodied voice sounded far away.

"I'm Emily Dobbs, your new neighbor. My kids and I just wanted to welcome you to the neighborhood."

A long buzz sounded and the gate swung open automatically. Josh stared at it, then grinned. "Cool!"

Dani wasn't as enthusiastic. She eyed the gate warily and reached for Emily's hand. "What if we can't get out again?" she whispered.

"I'm sure it only keeps people out," Emily reassured her. "It's not meant to trap anyone inside."

"Are you *sure?*" Dani asked.

"I'm sure, sweetie."

By the time they'd walked along the curving driveway, two kids were racing in their direction. They skidded to a stop.

"Wow, this is so great," the boy said. "I didn't think there were any kids in the whole neighborhood. I was really bummed. I'm Evan. My sister's Caitlyn."

"I'm Josh," her son told him. He added grudgingly, "That's Dani." Focusing his attention once again on the boy, he said, "I heard you like to play ball."

"Any kind," Evan confirmed. "You want to throw some passes out back? Football's my favorite. I'm gonna go pro someday and play for the Dolphins."

He said it with such absolute confidence that Emily had to fight to hide a smile.

Josh looked up at her. "Is it okay, Mom?"

"Sure," Emily told him, then looked back to see that Dani was eyeing a dainty little girl in orange shorts, a purple T-shirt and tiny sneakers with dismay. The outfit, with grass stains and streaks of dirt, was a stark contrast to the pastel flowered dress and patent-leather shoes that Dani had chosen for the visit.

"How come you're all dressed up?" the child asked Dani with a puzzled look. "You been to church?"

Dani regarded her with disdain. "I like to dress up. I like to read books and I like to have tea parties, too."

"I play ball with my brother," Caitlyn said. "But only 'cause there's nobody else around." Her wistful gaze shifted to follow the direction in which the boys had disappeared. Then she sighed. "My mom just baked cookies. You want some?"

Obviously the thought of home-baked cookies was enough to overcome Dani's reservations about Caitlyn. "Sure." Then she glanced hesitantly toward Emily. "You're coming, too, right?"

"Absolutely," she said, and followed the girls up the walkway.

When she spotted Marcie Carter waiting in the doorway, Emily couldn't help smiling at the irony. In her fashionable linen slacks, silk blouse and expensive jewelry, she looked as if she ought to be Dani's mom, not Caitlyn's. Her makeup was flawless, every highlighted hair on her head was in place and her French manicure didn't have a chip in it. Emily immediately felt as disheveled as little Caitlyn, but unlike the child she found herself apologizing.

"I'm sorry I'm such a mess, but the kids were so anxious to come by, I didn't take time to change. I hope you weren't getting ready to go out."

"No, indeed. I've been baking cookies. Come in and have some. You'll have to excuse the chaos, though. We've barely finished unpacking."

Emily glanced around, looking for some evidence of chaos, but as near as she could tell this house was already a hundred times tidier than her own. There was a faint lingering scent of paint in the air, mingling with the far more appealing aromas of sugar and chocolate. The tile floor in the foyer had been replaced since she'd been here for a neighborhood cocktail party a couple of years ago. All of the carpets looked brand-new, as well. Every piece of furniture was in place, the pillows were plumped, fresh flowers filled huge, oversize vases in each room. If this was chaos, she wanted to know how to accomplish it.

"Do you mind sitting in the kitchen?" Marcie asked. "I'll be able to keep an eye on the oven. I still have a few dozen cookies to bake for a PTA fund-raiser on Monday. The girls can take some cookies and milk onto the patio."

"That sounds perfect," Emily said, following her through the house. In the kitchen, she had to keep her mouth from dropping open. It looked like something out of a design magazine with its expensive cherry cabinets, black granite countertops and professional-grade stainless-steel appliances. Serious stuff must happen in this kitchen. It wasn't meant for someone who threw a meal together at the last second, stuck frozen dinners into the microwave or baked cookies from refrigerated dough from the grocery store.

"How did you get roped into a bake sale when you've barely moved in?" she asked Marcie.

"I always volunteer at the kids' school," Marcie replied as she put chocolate-chip cookies onto a plate, poured milk into two tall plastic glasses and artfully arranged it all on a tray. "Here you go, girls. Do you need any help?"

"I can carry it," Dani told her, reaching for the tray.

"I can take my own," Caitlyn countered, almost tipping everything onto the floor in her eagerness to grab a glass of milk.

"Maybe I'd better get them settled," Marcie said, taking the tray from Dani, carrying it outside, then returning. "I don't know if you've noticed, but my Caitlyn has an independent streak. She spends so much time with her older brother that she doesn't know her own limits." Her expression turned wistful. "I wish she was as much of a little lady as your Dani."

"Something tells me they'll balance each other," Emily said. "I'm so glad Dani finally has someone close to her age nearby and Josh was over the moon when he found out you had a son his age."

"How long have you lived in the neighborhood?" Marcie asked as she efficiently scooped up perfectly rounded balls of dough and put another huge sheet of cookies into the oversize oven.

"About seven years now. Josh was two when we bought the house and Dani was still a baby."

"You like it here?"

"Love it," Emily said. "And it's a great school district."

"I can tell that already," Marcie said. "I made it a point to meet Josh and Caitlyn's teachers before we made the final decision to move. I wish the class sizes were a little smaller, but unfortunately unless you send the kids to private schools, you won't find that anywhere anymore. That's one of the reasons I like to volunteer. I figure the teachers can always use some extra help."

"I can vouch for that, though most of the parents at the high school where I work are too busy with their jobs to get involved," Emily lamented. "I have to struggle just to get them to take time off to come in for parent-teacher meetings."

Marcie seemed surprised. "You teach at the high school?"

"Yes. I teach English," Emily confirmed. "I was teaching when I got married and I went back to it once both of my kids were in school. Do you work?"

"Ken—he's my husband—and I think being a mom is a full-time job," she said, a faintly defensive note in her voice.

Emily wasn't about to quibble with her choice. "It's great that you're able to do that, if it's what you enjoy," she said sincerely. "I almost went stir-crazy during the years I was home with the kids. I need that added stimulation of working and I enjoy teaching. It's hard, though. I have to admit there are days when I feel as if the kids aren't getting nearly enough of my attention, especially with their dad out of town on business so much."

"Your husband doesn't object to you working?"

"To be honest, he wasn't overjoyed when I went back to work, but mostly because he was afraid it would be a reflection on him. He thought maybe people would get the idea that he wasn't a good enough provider. Derek had a tough childhood, so image is important to him. He's a real workaholic."

"Now that I get," Marcie commiserated. "Ken's just as bad. He'd work twenty-four hours a day if he didn't require at least some sleep."

She retrieved the baking sheet of cookies from the oven and slid another tray in. "There, that's the last of them. Now maybe you and I can relax and you can tell me the scoop on everyone in the neighborhood. Any good dirt?"

Emily laughed. "I'm afraid there are no desperate housewives around here, though I think Adelia Crockett might have a crush on one of the deliverymen...or maybe she really is addicted to QVC and that's why there are so many packages coming to her house all the time."

"Adelia Crockett? I don't think I've met her yet."

"Three doors down from you. She drives a bright red convertible. She moved in about a year ago. I met her once at a neighborhood barbecue, but mostly she keeps to herself. She's in her forties, I'd say. Doesn't work, so either she divorced well or she has money of her own."

"Is she going to show up on my doorstep needing help with a leaky faucet one of these nights?" Marcie asked wryly.

Emily grinned. "Last I heard, she was more likely to show up with a toolbox and offer to help with *your* leaky faucet. She seems pretty self-sufficient, but like I said, I don't know her that well."

"Any other gossip? Is there a neighborhood borrower who never brings anything back? Someone who throws outrageously noisy parties? A complainer who calls the cops about everything?"

Emily stared at her. "Where on earth have you been living?"

Marcie chuckled. "Actually it was fine and the neighbors were all really nice, but you never know what you're getting into when you move. The real estate brokers might warn you about an anticipated bump in real estate taxes, but they won't say a word about the neighbors who cause everyone grief."

"Well, rest assured, everyone around here is pretty quiet and friendly. You're going to like it, unless you were hoping for a little excitement. About the wildest thing that happens is Eddie Delgado doing karaoke at the summer barbecue. The man has the voice of a frog with laryngitis."

For an instant Marcie looked taken aback, but then she put a hand over her mouth and giggled. "I'm sorry. I met Eddie the other day. I can't even imagine…" Her voice trailed off and she giggled again. "I like you, Emily Dobbs. I think we're going to be good friends."

"Even though I don't even know what half the appliances in this kitchen are for?" Emily said, surveying the array of intimidating stainless steel. It appeared Marcie owned every cooking aid showcased in the Williams-Sonoma catalog.

Marcie patted her hand. "I know, and that's all that matters. You make sure our kids get out of school with a basic knowledge of grammar and literature and I'll make sure we're all well fed."

"Now there's a plan I can get behind, but let me be the one to welcome you with a barbecue. I'll invite all of the neighbors over next Saturday. Derek has figured out how to use the mammoth grill he insisted we needed and I'm capable of making a salad and a few side dishes."

"Only if you let me bring dessert," Marcie said. "There's a chocolate cake with fresh raspberries I've been dying to try. If I make two, will that be enough?"

"That depends on whether one of those is meant just for me," Emily told her, not entirely in jest.

Marcie grinned. "I'll bake three. We'll share the third one over coffee when we get together afterward to dissect the party."

"Let me retrieve my kids and I'll get out of your hair," Emily told her.

"Oh, let them stay, please," Marcie said. "I'll walk them home later, say around four."

"Are you sure?"

"Positive."

Grateful to have a reprieve so she could grade papers in total silence, she seized the offer. "If they give you any trouble at all, just call me or bring them home." She jotted down her phone number and address for Marcie, who immediately stuck the paper onto a bulletin board by her phone.

"They'll be fine," Marcie assured her.

"Then I'll say a quick goodbye and remind them to be on their best behavior." When she returned from speaking to Dani and Josh, she impulsively gave Marcie a hug. "I'll have peace and quiet to grade papers. I can get it done in half the time it usually takes. You have no idea what a miracle that is! I'll call you with the details about next Saturday."

"Don't be a stranger, okay? Promise me."

"You bake. You offer to watch my kids," Emily said. "Are you kidding? I'm ready to adopt you."

The Saturday-night barbecue to introduce the Carters to their neighbors was the first of many occasions the two families shared during that winter and spring. For the first time in her marriage, Marcie actually felt as if she were a part of the community around her. She liked knowing everyone on her block and the next, being able to exchange greetings with people and ask about their families and jobs, rather than living in isolation the way they had in their old neighborhood.

She'd never told anyone, not even Emily who would surely understand, about the early financial struggles she and Ken had had in their marriage. She felt as if it would be a betrayal of her husband. Ken had worked hard to rise above their past. They'd scraped by and saved until they could afford an impressive house in a well-to-do area, but even before they'd moved, he'd insisted they strive for a certain image. Sometimes he worried more about the image than the substance of their lives, but Marcie understood. She knew he wanted only the best for her and their kids. He was single-minded about it. If he was impatient with her when she tried to get him to slow down or questioned his priorities, well, he'd earned the right to have things his way. She'd long since reconciled herself to that.

Oddly, though she and Emily had become extremely close, Derek and Ken didn't get along all that well. She didn't understand it. Derek was a great guy. He was warm and funny, the kind of dad who showed a real interest in all of the kids and actually listened when they spoke to him. He and Ken should have had a thousand things in common, but there was a wariness between them that sometimes cast a pall over their get-togethers. If they'd been a couple of kids, she would have described it as some kind of rivalry, but they were both mature adults.

Still, it was plain that Ken was always trying too hard to impress Derek and Derek knew it. It was happening again tonight as they ate by the pool at her house.

"You should have seen it," Ken boasted. "I had those guys eating out of the palm of my hand. The best wine. Steaks so tender you could cut 'em with a butter knife. Then Marcie here has to go and ruin it all by bringing in these little cups of pudding." He rolled his eyes. "I don't know what she was thinking."

"It was chocolate mousse with shaved white chocolate on top, not pudding," she said defensively. "And in case you didn't notice, they ate every bite and asked for seconds, so I'd have to say it was a hit."

"They ate it to be polite," Ken scoffed.

"I'm sure it was delicious," Emily said loyally. "Marcie knows more about entertaining than most people will ever know."

"Thank you," Marcie said, feeling her cheeks flushing at the praise. Or maybe it was from embarrassment that her husband was demeaning her in front of their friends.

"I don't suppose you have any of that mousse left," Derek asked wistfully. "It's one of my favorites. Needless to say, Emily never makes it."

"Yes, needless to say," Emily said, shooting him a grateful look. "I did make instant pudding a couple of weeks ago."

Ken frowned at both of them and their attempt to elevate Marcie's efforts.

"I still think some fancy soufflé would have impressed them more," Ken grumbled, then brightened. "The bottom line, though, is that the next day they signed on the dotted line. Biggest account I've reeled in yet. I'm telling you that vice presidency is mine."

"You've worked hard enough for it," Marcie said, relieved that he'd dropped the topic of her cooking. "You certainly deserve it."

"Damn straight," Ken said. He looked at Derek, and for an instant there was none of the usual bluster in his voice, when he said, "Maybe you can give me some pointers on how to handle the boss to make sure I get the job. You've been a vice president at Jankovich and Davis for a while now, right?"

"A couple of years," Derek said. "Only thing I can tell you is to work hard and do your job. Go above and beyond whenever the opportunity presents itself. In the end that's the kind of thing that gets their attention."

Ken looked flustered. "You didn't spend a lot of time schmoozing with 'em, telling 'em you were the right guy for the job?"

"Not really," Derek said, then added diplomatically, "but they're two different companies, Ken. I'm dealing with international sales. You're dealing with public relations. You know how things work with the people in charge where you are. You have to use the tactics that work under those conditions."

Ken nodded. "Flash and dazzle, that's what works with my boss," he said confidently. "In PR, it's all about the sizzle, you know what I mean?"

Derek grinned. "I know exactly what you mean."

Marcie sat back and relaxed for the first time since the discussion had started. For once it seemed the two men were on the same wavelength. With any luck that would last through dessert.

And tonight she'd been smart enough to bake Ken's favorite cake with caramel frosting. It had taken forever to get the caramel just right, but it would be worth it if he ended the evening with a smile on his face.

Sometimes it seemed she spent as many hours of her day trying to please her husband as Ken spent trying to win the praise of his bosses. In that regard, they both had tough jobs.

There wasn't a chance in hell she'd ever admit it, but sometimes she envied Emily, whose identity clearly wasn't all tied up in gaining her husband's approval. There'd been a time when Marcie had actually known exactly who she was—a pretty girl from a modest background who was smart, but far from brilliant, and more interested in cooking and baking than the corporate world. She'd also known what she'd wanted out of life. She wanted to marry an ambitious man with potential, have a family and enough money to buy not only the things they needed, but the things they wanted. She'd thought she'd won the lottery when she married Ken, but lately she wondered if she hadn't given up more than she'd gotten.

She glanced over at Ken and wondered what had happened to the handsome guy who'd pursued her with the same single-minded determination he now used to chase down new accounts at work. He was still good-looking, still driven, but increasingly it seemed he was taking her for granted. Maybe that's what happened after ten years of marriage, but sometimes she longed for the days when he couldn't keep his hands off her, when he used his charm on her, not on everyone *except* her.

She sighed and focused her attention on the conversation, which had returned to football as Derek and Ken debated the Dolphins' chances for making the Super Bowl and lamented bygone days under Coach Don Shula. She glanced across the table and saw that Emily was just as bored as she was.

"Time for dessert?" she inquired brightly. "It's chocolate cake with caramel frosting."

"From some can?" Ken asked in a scathing tone.

She gave him a chiding look. "Have you ever known me not to make it from scratch?"

His expression brightened. "Okay, then. I'll take a piece. A big one."

"Me, too," Derek said just as eagerly. "Nobody bakes the way you do, Marcie."

"Certainly not in our house," Emily agreed unapologetically.

Marcie marveled at the exchange. Derek's tone hadn't held even a hint of implied criticism of his wife and Emily's response had been just as easygoing. Why couldn't Ken speak to her or about her the same way? And why couldn't she make herself speak up if his attitude bothered her so much?

Knowing she wouldn't find an answer to that tonight, she pushed the topic aside and went inside with Emily to cut the cake. At least she'd gotten that right.

3

"Mom, can Caitlyn spend the night?" Dani asked Emily on Friday. "Please. It's not a school night and her mom says it's okay with her if it's okay with you."

Emily thought of her plans to try to bring some order to the chaos around the house. She'd even had some crazy idea about enlisting the kids to clean up their own messes before their dad came home tomorrow after two weeks on the road for business. She gazed at Dani's hopeful expression and sighed.

"Sure, why not?" she said. "We'll order pizza."

"And we can watch videos and have popcorn?" Dani asked.

"I assume that means a trip to choose the movies," she said, resigned to going back out on the hot, humid evening. Late September was just as bad as July when it came to the Miami weather.

Dani grinned. "Uh-huh. She gets to pick one and I get to pick the other one. That's what we decided."

Emily shook her head. Dani always had a plan and it was always fair. "Fine. We'll go as soon as Caitlyn gets here."

Dani threw her arms around Emily's waist. "Thanks. You're the best! I'll call her now."

Emily watched her daughter race up the stairs. She was nine now and she'd overcome all her reservations about being friends with a girl two years younger. She and Caitlyn were as close as sisters. That they chose to spend most of their time here, rather than in the Carters' far more organized household still bemused Emily, but she had to admit that most of the time she enjoyed having all the kids underfoot. Caitlyn and Evan were both polite and well behaved. They set a good example for her own kids.

She glanced out the back door and saw Josh and Evan horsing around in the pool. Sliding open the back door, she called to her son, who trotted over.

"Caitlyn's spending the night with Dani. Do you want to ask Evan to stay, too?"

"Awesome," Josh said at once. "Hey, Evan, Caitlyn's staying over and Mom says you can stay, too, if you want to."

"Count me in," Evan called back.

"Ask your mom," Emily reminded him. "As soon as Caitlyn gets here we're going out to get videos to watch. You guys can come, too, and pick your own."

"Thanks, Mrs. D," Evan said. "I'll be right back."

Already tall for his age, Evan pushed himself out of the pool with an athletic grace that Josh didn't possess. Much as her son enjoyed sports, he didn't have the raw talent that Evan had. Thankfully, though, the two boys weren't especially competitive. Josh just enjoyed playing the game, whatever it was on any given day, and was happy enough to see his friend excel at it. Josh seemed to have inherited her laid-back personality, rather than his dad's competitive, ambitious one.

As she stepped back inside, Emily heard the phone

ringing. Before she could reach it, Dani apparently grabbed it upstairs, then shouted, "Mom, it's for you! It's Mrs. Carter."

Emily picked up the portable phone and sat at the kitchen table. "Hey, Marcie. How are you?"

"Fine, but wondering why on earth you'd let yourself in for having Evan and Caitlyn over after working all week. You must be exhausted and sick to death of kids."

"I don't mind. And your kids are never any trouble."

"You're sure you weren't trapped into going along with this? I know how persuasive Dani can be when she's on a mission."

"Absolutely not. What are you and Ken up to this evening?"

"Ken has a business dinner, so I'm on my own."

"Then come on over with Evan and Caitlyn. You and I can watch our own movies and drink some wine."

"Really? You're not too tired?"

"To watch a chick flick that Derek would rather eat worms than see?" Emily asked. "Never." Besides, she'd heard the note of loneliness in Marcie's voice and recognized it all too well. She'd learned to cope with Derek's absences, but Marcie was completely at sea when Ken was out of the house. She'd tried to talk to her once about finding some interests aside from Ken and the kids, but Marcie always claimed she was perfectly content and had more than enough to keep herself occupied.

"Where is Derek, by the way? Won't he object to all the commotion?"

"He's still in Brazil. He won't be home till late tomorrow."

"Great!" Marcie said. "Gosh, that sounded awful. I

know you miss him. I meant it was great that we can have an evening to ourselves. I'll bring the chocolate. I baked brownies today. A lot of brownies. I was bored."

"Good luck for me," Emily said with enthusiasm, though the further evidence of Marcie's discontent struck her once more. "See you soon. You can come with us to the video store to pick out the movies."

By the time she'd hung up, Emily already felt rejuvenated. Movies, wine and chocolate with a friend and her kids and their friends upstairs. What could be better than that? It would certainly be a huge improvement over the lonely evening she'd been anticipating, one in a long string of lonely evenings that had become the norm as Derek's job kept him away for longer and longer periods of time. She might have adjusted to the stretches of being on her own with the kids, but that didn't mean she liked it. And unlike Marcie, she knew that sooner or later she was going to have to do something about fixing it.

"What on earth are you doing?" Emily demanded a few weeks later when she found Josh in the backyard with a pair of hedge clippers attacking the bougainvillea that separated their yard from the Carters.

"Evan and me need a path," he explained.

"Evan and I," she corrected automatically.

He looked up at her, his expression blank. "Huh?"

Emily sighed. It was a wonder she kept her job, when she couldn't even get her own kids to speak proper English. "Why do you and Evan need a path? You can walk around the block."

"It's too far. We've been trying to crawl through the hedge, but this stuff has thorns."

"So you decided to chop it down without asking permission?"

"Dad said it was okay," he replied, snipping away more of the thick hedge with its brilliant fuchsia flowers that thrived in the South Florida heat and humidity.

She doubted Derek had any idea what he'd agreed to. He'd probably been on the computer or absorbed in paperwork, which was how he spent the few days he was at home anymore. Whatever he'd said to Josh was more conversation than she and her husband had had lately. She was growing tired of feeling like a single parent most of the time, only to have her authority usurped the moment Derek made a rare appearance at home. It was something they needed to discuss, but she couldn't even figure out how to manage that when he rarely came to bed before midnight and fell asleep the second his head hit the pillow. They hadn't had a night out on their own for months now. If he'd been a different kind of man she'd have wondered if he was having an affair, but she knew his work was his only mistress. Accepting that didn't seem to stop the increasing resentment she was feeling.

She took one more look at the gaping hole in the hedge and shook her head. On the bright side, it would take her less time to wander over to sit in Marcie's pristine kitchen with a cup of her special-blend coffee and a slice of her homemade key lime pie. Lately that had become her refuge from the emptiness she felt every day when she got home from school and faced one more night on her own.

On her bad days, she envied Marcie. She was everything Emily was not. She thrived on being a housewife, a room-mother in her kids' classrooms, an officer in the

PTA. Her spotless house could have been a designer showcase. There wasn't a speck of dust that Emily had ever seen, much less a magazine out of place, a dirty glass in the sink or smelly socks or sneakers tossed on the floor. By comparison, the best that could be said of Emily's home was that it looked lived in. The last time she'd baked, she'd burned the chocolate-chip cookies. Dirty clothes overflowed the baskets in the laundry room and dishes were left wherever anyone set them down until Emily rounded them up.

Back inside, she headed for Derek's office and found him punching numbers into a calculator. When she spoke, his head snapped up and he muttered a curse at the interruption.

"Sorry," she said. "I thought maybe we could talk."

"I'm in the middle of something."

"You're always in the middle of something. Do I need to make an appointment to get on your calendar?" She couldn't seem to keep the sarcasm out of her voice.

It hadn't always been like this. When she and Derek had met in college, she'd admired his drive and ambition. They'd spent long hours talking about his goal of owning his own company someday, not just some little mom-and-pop business, but a corporation. Her parents had been impressed with his single-minded determination, as well.

"He'll go places," her father had told her when she'd announced their engagement. "He'll be a good provider."

And he had been. He was vice president of sales at a multinational corporation based in Coral Gables. Their home off Old Cutler Road was in a neighborhood known for its lush landscaping, architectural diversity, upper-income families and good schools. She and their kids wanted for nothing.

If she longed for the kind of conversations they used to have or for the passion they'd once shared, maybe she was expecting too much. Maybe this was the way things were supposed to be after twelve years of marriage.

Then she thought of the affection still evident in her parents' marriage after more than thirty years and knew she was wrong. She and Derek were missing the best years of their lives. They were occasional roommates, not partners.

"Let's go out to dinner tonight," she suggested impulsively, draping her arms around his neck from behind and leaning down to press a kiss to his cheek. He smelled faintly of his favorite musky aftershave. "Just you and me. I'll see if the kids can stay with the Carters."

"I'm beat," he said, linking his fingers through hers. "I don't feel like going out. Invite the Carters over for a barbecue instead. We'll throw some steaks or some salmon on the grill, hot dogs for the kids. It doesn't have to be a big deal."

Emily barely managed to contain a sigh. It wasn't the evening she had had in mind, but it was a concession, especially since she knew Derek wasn't all that crazy about Ken Carter. Truthfully, she wasn't either. She didn't like the way he put down his wife at every turn, mocking her devotion to him and the kids and their home, a devotion he himself demanded. She and Derek had discussed their mutual dislike of the man, but agreed to put it aside in the interest of neighborly harmony. Still, more and more they were keeping the contact to a minimum. She had her friendship with Marcie and the kids had their bonds, but recently the families maintained a more careful distance.

Sometimes she worried that Marcie was aware of how

she and Derek felt, but it was the one subject they'd never discussed. She figured if Marcie had found some way to tolerate her husband's demeaning behavior then it wasn't Emily's place to criticize him, any more than it was her place to question Marcie's decision to build her entire life around her family, rather than building a separate identity of her own.

"If you're so tired, are you sure you're up to dealing with Ken tonight?" she asked Derek point-blank. He usually had little patience with him when he was in a great mood.

"I'll just let him talk and tune him out," Derek said. "Ken gives speeches. He doesn't have conversations. That pretty much takes the pressure off me."

She grinned at him. "Sometimes I wonder how Marcie can stand the man, but she seems blind to his faults."

"Or maybe she's learned to tune him out, too," Derek suggested, a twinkle in his eye.

Emily chuckled. "You are so bad."

"But you love me, anyway, right?" he said, turning to meet her gaze.

"Yeah, I do," she said. Lost in the depths of his eyes, for a moment she remembered all the reasons why…his wicked sense of humor, the way he could make her feel with just a glance, the solidity of his devotion. "I really do. That's why I wanted to spend the evening out with you."

"Another time, I promise. When I get back from this next trip, things should slow down."

She accepted the promise, because she had no choice. "I'll hold you to that."

"Go call the Carters, then, but tell them we'll need to make it an early evening, okay?"

"Sure," she agreed, feigning enthusiasm. "I'll see if they can come at six. Do you want time for a shower or should I just let you know when they get here?"

"I'll run up in a little while and grab a shower and be down in time to start the grill," he promised. "Then you can sit back and relax."

Emily thought of the trip to the market she needed to make to pull off this impromptu gathering, the preparations required to stock the patio bar and have everything ready for the grill. She wasn't Marcie, who could entertain at the drop of a hat. In her case, relaxation didn't enter into it.

At least, though, she could look forward to some adult conversation, even if it wouldn't necessarily be with her husband.

Marcie was on edge, though she couldn't have said why. She was as comfortable at Emily's as she was in her own house. Tonight, though, there was some kind of tension in the air that seemed worse than usual. Ken was trying too hard, as always, and Derek seemed to have less patience with him than ever. She'd even caught Emily rolling her eyes once behind Ken's back. She'd almost called her on it, but she hadn't wanted to start a discussion that might cause a real rift in their friendship.

There were times when she felt almost as competitive with Emily as Ken obviously did with Derek, and she felt petty for feeling that way. Despite everything Marcie did to create the perfect home, it was evident that her own kids preferred being over here. They didn't seem to notice the clutter or care that the meals were more often takeout than homemade.

Right now they were all in the pool, shrieking at the

top of their lungs as they played some silly game they'd
devised, mainly to torture the girls as near as she could
tell. Ken had told them to pipe down twice now, but
Derek and Emily seemed oblivious to the noise. She
figured the shouts would last another two minutes before
Ken blew a gasket and ordered Evan and Caitlyn out of
the water and spoiled things for everyone.

In an attempt to avert a scene, she stood up and
walked over to the pool. "Evan, Caitlyn, you heard your
father," she said quietly. "Settle down."

"We're just having fun, Mom," Caitlyn said, wiping
her wet hair out of her face and looking up.

"You can have fun *quietly,*" Marcie said.

Evan scowled up at her. "Who put you in charge?" he
asked belligerently. "We're in Mr. and Mrs. D's pool."

Behind her, Marcie heard a chair scrape back. She froze,
terrified that Ken was about to cause exactly the kind of
commotion she'd been hoping to avoid. Instead, though,
it was Emily who came up and slipped an arm through hers.

"Evan, that's no way to speak to your mother," Emily
scolded gently. "And the decibel level is getting pretty
loud. Maybe you guys should take a break and go inside
for a while. We picked up a bunch of movies earlier
today. Josh, why don't you make some popcorn?"

"Sure, Mom," he said with easygoing acceptance. He
immediately climbed out of the pool and wrapped
himself in a towel. "Come on, Evan, I got that action
movie we missed."

Evan gave Marcie one last scowl, but he followed
Josh inside.

"Thanks," Marcie said, when the kids were gone. "I
don't know why he listens to you but ignores everything
I say."

"Most kids would rather obey any other adult than their own parents," Emily said. "I see it at school all the time. They'll be sullen and unresponsive with their mom or dad, then turn right around and be sunny and polite to me."

Marcie hesitated, then asked, "Evan's never sassed you, has he?"

"Never," Emily said.

"If he ever does, I want you to send him straight home. Don't tolerate it, okay?"

"I will, but it's never been a problem. I swear it. You're a good mom, Marcie. Don't ever question that. And both your kids are terrific."

Marcie forced a grin. "Do you think if kids are this much trouble now, we'll survive their teenage years?"

"Of course, we will. We'll still be bigger and stronger—for a while anyway—and we'll gang up on 'em," Emily assured her. "Come on. Let's go inside and put together that strawberry shortcake you brought over. My mouth's been watering since you got here. I love strawberry season, don't you?"

Marcie finally relaxed. "I drove down to the fields to get these. They were huge and sweet as candy." She leaned in and confided, "I had a fresh strawberry shake while I was there."

Emily laughed. "If you're going to make that drive then you have to have a shake. It's a rule. Maybe we can take the kids down to the Everglades next weekend and go for a hike on one of the trails. We can stop for a shake on the way back."

"A hike?" Marcie asked warily. "Won't there be bugs?"

"Not this time of year. Just alligators," Emily teased, trying and failing to hide a grin.

"Is that supposed to reassure me?"

"Come on," Emily said. "The boys will love it."

"And the rest of us?" Marcie asked, still skeptical.

"Will survive by thinking about the strawberry shake we'll have afterward."

"Aren't men supposed to take their sons on outings like that?" Marcie asked.

Emily merely stared at her. "Derek and Ken? You have to be kidding."

Marcie gave in to the urge to laugh. "You have a point, though I'd pay big money to see it."

"Me, too," Emily agreed, handing her two dishes piled high with shortcake topped with huge strawberries and a mound of whipped cream, then picking up a tray with the other bowls herself. "Let's go sweeten them up with dessert. Who knows what we'll be able to talk them into after that."

Paula, Emily's favorite coworker at school, had just undergone breast cancer surgery and it had all of the female teachers jittery. There was a sudden interest in breast self-exams and a flurry of appointments being made for mammograms.

Shaken more than she liked admitting, Emily came home from visiting Paula at the hospital and headed straight for Marcie's, where the coffee was waiting, along with a sympathetic ear.

"How is she?" Marcie asked.

"Scared to death," Emily told her. "The surgery's almost the least of it. They want to do both radiation and chemo. She's looking at a long, tough road with unpredictable results."

They both fell silent.

"Did you call and make an appointment for a mammogram?" Emily asked eventually.

"First thing this morning," Marcie told her. "My appointment's for next week. You?"

"I'm scheduled to go in next week, too. I thought we were too young to be worrying about this. We're only thirty-two, for crying out loud. I thought we had years before we had to start getting tested, but Paula's only thirty-three. If she hadn't found that lump, she'd never have known. She teaches the health and PE classes at school, so she's the one woman who's on top of these things." She frowned. "I just hope to God it wasn't too late."

"Don't even think like that," Marcie admonished. "She's going to be fine. She's tough."

Emily nodded. "And her husband's been a real rock so far. Dave's been by her side every step of the way, bless him, and I don't see that changing."

"I knew I liked him when you had them over for dinner last year during the holidays," Marcie said. "And I've enjoyed getting together with Paula at your house to talk about books. She and I have the same taste and she always knows when the good books are being released and gives me a heads-up. I'm so glad you introduced us."

"Maybe you could return the favor while she's recuperating, take her a few books from time to time. She turns her nose up when I try to get her to read the classics."

"Probably because she had to read them all in school. Now a good mystery, that's always fresh."

"Murder and mayhem, you mean," Emily said. "I've seen your to-be-read pile. I don't know how you sleep at night after you read that stuff."

"Oh, for goodness' sakes, I'm not reading thrillers about serial killers," Marcie retorted. "They're cozy mysteries with amateur sleuths. Hardly a drop of blood anywhere. It's all about solving the crime."

"Whatever," Emily said, grinning at the defensive note in her voice. "I love teasing you about your reading material."

"Really? Don't think I don't know about the stash of romance novels you have hidden under your stacks of Charles Dickens and Jane Austen," Marcie countered.

Emily flushed. "How do you know about those?"

"Caitlyn, of course. She and Dani have been sneaking them to read."

"I swear, I am going to kill my daughter," Emily grumbled. "As my child, she's supposed to be reading great literature."

"She's ten," Marcie noted, her lips twitching.

"Well, there are plenty of great children's books for that age."

"Obviously her taste is as varied as her mom's. Just be grateful she's reading at all."

"I should be, shouldn't I?" Emily said, then sighed, her thoughts returning to their sick friend. "Can you think of anything else we should be doing for Paula?"

"Besides being there for her?" Marcie said. "I imagine that's what she needs most—friends who will stick by her, take her to appointments, whatever. If you see her again before I do, tell her I'll do that, by the way. I'm free most days. I can take her anywhere she needs to go."

"She'll appreciate that, I know. Now I'd better get home and think about getting dinner on the table."

"I knew you'd be running late today, so I made an extra lasagna, if you want it."

"Have I mentioned lately what an angel you are? What would I do without you?"

"Starve?" Marcie inquired wryly.

Emily grinned. "Not as long as half the restaurants in the neighborhood deliver, but you do give my children an opportunity to experience a home-cooked meal from time to time. For that, I am eternally grateful."

Marcie chuckled. "So are they. Dani asked me the other day if I could teach her to boil water so she'd know more than mommy."

"Ha-ha," Emily retorted. "Very funny."

"Well, she did," Marcie insisted. "Seriously, both girls want me to give them cooking lessons."

Emily shrugged. "Then by all means, go for it. Let me know if Dani's any good at it. If she is, maybe I'll be able to stay out of the kitchen altogether."

"You hate cooking that much?" Marcie asked, her expression incredulous.

"I hate most things I'm lousy at. Cooking tops the list. Sewing's a close second with household organization right on their heels."

"All my favorite things," Marcie said. "How on earth did we ever become such good friends?"

"Proximity?" Emily suggested. "And the fact that you're one of the nicest people I've ever known."

Marcie grinned. "Ditto. Now let me get you that lasagna."

She handed Emily a baking dish big enough to supply dinner for at least three nights.

"Are you sure you didn't confuse my family with Josh's Little League team?"

"You'll have leftovers for another night," Marcie said. "Want some cookies for the kids' lunches?"

"Good heavens, no! I still have the ones you sent home with me yesterday. You need to take a day off from baking."

"And do what?" Marcie asked with an expression that said she honestly had no idea what she'd do with herself.

"Spend the day with Paula," Emily suggested at once. "And take a few dozen cookies to the nurses, so they'll treat her right."

Marcie's face lit up. "I'll do it first thing tomorrow."

"Give her another hug from me and tell her we miss her at school. Let her know I'll stop by the hospital after work with all the gossip."

Marcie walked outside with her. "She's going to be okay, you know."

"I know," Emily said automatically as she slipped through the opening Josh had cut in the hedge between the houses. She just wished she could believe it.

4

Emily had barely left the house, when Marcie heard the garage door open and realized Ken was home, hours earlier than usual. Her stomach immediately tied itself into knots. Whatever had brought him home at this hour couldn't possibly be good. Still, she took a quick look at herself in a mirror to check her hair and makeup, then plastered a smile on her face as she waited for him.

When he finally came inside, his tie was askew, his collar open and, if she wasn't mistaken, he'd been drinking. Her smile immediately faltered.

"Ken, what's wrong?"

"The bastards fired me, that's what's wrong," he said, immediately going to the liquor cabinet and splashing several inches of Scotch into a glass, then taking a gulp that clearly wasn't his first of the day. "I've worked my butt off for those jerks for how many years now? Fifteen? And now I'm history."

"Did they tell you why?" she asked hesitantly, knowing as soon as the words were out of her mouth that it was exactly the wrong thing to ask.

His face flushed an even brighter shade of red. "Because they're idiots, that's why. One little mistake and none of the accounts I brought in, none of the work I'd done for them mattered."

Marcie smothered a desire to point out that if the mistake had been so small, surely they would never have done such a thing. Ken *had* worked hard for them for years. She might not know a lot about the corporate world, but surely they wouldn't have fired him over something insignificant. Had she said such a thing, though, Ken's already precarious mood would have turned even darker. She doubted she'd ever hear the whole story. Ken never admitted his failures. It must be killing him just to confess he'd been fired.

She also had to swallow all of the questions she had about what came next, whether they'd offered him severance at least. There was little use in admitting to her own panic at the thought of him being unemployed. Underneath all of Ken's bravado, she was sure he was fearful enough for both of them. Nor was he likely to have any of the reassuring answers she wanted to hear. It was too soon. Her role, of which she was very much aware, was to boost his self-confidence, not to add to his troubles or make him feel worse.

Although she was silent, he scowled at her as if she'd voiced her thoughts. "Well, don't you have anything else to say? I'm sure you think this is my fault."

"I never said that. You've given a lot to that company and it's their loss that you're gone. Another company will snap you up, I'm sure of it."

"Aren't you just little Mary Sunshine," he said sarcastically.

Despite his nasty attitude, she was determined to think positively. That's what he needed from her. "I just think it's important to be optimistic. This is the opportunity you've been waiting for, Ken. You could finally open your own company. You have more than enough experience to do that."

For the first time since he'd walked in, the anger seemed to fade from his eyes. The fear Marcie knew he was trying to cover drained away as well. He sank into a chair at the kitchen table and regarded her with a bewildered expression. "How'd I make such a mess of things? I blew off one meeting. I didn't think it was a big deal, but apparently it was to the client. They were nervous about our campaign and me canceling the meeting made their anxiety escalate. They told my boss I was unreliable and that since they obviously couldn't count on me, they'd go elsewhere. If it had been any other client, it might not have mattered, but this was our foot in the door and I destroyed our chance to get more work."

Marcie couldn't believe that after years of missing family occasions for work, Ken would skip out on an important business meeting. "Why, Ken?" she asked, not even trying to hide her frustration. "Why would you cancel a meeting? You never do that."

"I was wooing another potential client. He wanted to play golf. I thought everything would work out fine."

"Did the new client sign with the firm?"

He shook his head, looking utterly defeated. "No, so it was all for nothing. It was a judgment call and I blew it. What the hell are we going to do now?"

Falling into her familiar role as cheerleader, she stood behind him and massaged his tense shoulders. "It's not a disaster, Ken. It's not."

For several minutes it was so quiet that Marcie could hear the ticking of the clock on the wall, but eventually Ken rested a hand atop hers.

"I'm sorry for yelling at you. None of this is your fault. I just wasn't expecting this, you know."

"I know," she said, moving around to sit in his lap so she could meet his gaze. If ever there'd been a time when he needed her support, this was it. "This isn't the end of the world. I have so much faith in you, more than you have in yourself, I think."

His lips curved slightly. "You always did, even way back when we first met. Nobody'd ever believed in me like that. I know I don't always tell you how much I appreciate what you do around here, but I do. I don't know what I'd do without you in my corner."

The rare praise warmed her heart. Sometimes she wondered if he even noticed her at all, much less appreciated her. And his careless words had the capacity to cut her to the quick. A moment like this, though, reminded her of the gentle, sensitive man she'd married. All too often she feared he'd gotten lost along the way in his frantic climb to the top.

She looked into his eyes. "What do you want to do next?" she asked. "If you could choose anything, what would it be?"

He gave her a lopsided, boyish grin. "Take you upstairs to bed?"

Her heart skipped a beat, even though she doubted he could even make it up the stairs on his currently unsteady legs.

"Besides that," she said, careful to keep her tone light so he wouldn't take offense at the apparent rejection.

He scrubbed a hand over his face. "Hell if I know," he murmured sleepily.

"Well, we'll figure it out tomorrow," she assured him. "Why don't you lie down in the den and rest before the kids get home? I'll let you know when dinner's ready."

"Probably should take a shower, sober up," he muttered. "Don't want them to know I've been drinking."

"Good idea," she said, relieved that he was thinking that clearly. "I'll run up and bring down a change of clothes for you and you can use the shower in the guest suite." In the doorway, she hesitated, then said, "And let's not tell them what's going on just yet, okay? Let's wait till we have a plan."

"Sure," he said, stumbling past her. "You always know the right thing to do, Marcie. Always right."

At his words, which didn't sound at all like a compliment, tears stung her eyes, but she had too much pride to let them fall. This was the way things went with Ken. One moment he was sweet as could be and the next he could cut her heart out.

Dani studied Caitlyn's scared expression. In the five years she'd known her, she'd never once seen Caitlyn scared, not even when they'd ridden this totally awesome, terrifying roller coaster on a trip to Disney World. Because there was a two-year age difference, Caitlyn tried hard to act as grown-up as Dani. Sometimes Dani even forgot she was only ten. At other times, Dani felt that two-year age difference was as vast as the ocean. She felt grown-up at twelve, almost a teenager, and sometimes like now, she felt responsible for the younger girl.

"You okay?" she asked when Caitlyn, who was never silent for more than a minute, hadn't said a word for way longer than that.

Caitlyn shook her head. "Something's going on at my house."

"Like what?"

"I don't know. Every time I walk into a room my mom and dad get real quiet, like they don't want me or Evan to know something."

"You think they're getting a divorce?" Dani asked, her own voice trembling and barely above a whisper. That was her own biggest fear, that her mom and dad would wake up one day to the fact that they hardly ever saw each other and decide to split for good. She'd never heard them fight, but she knew being apart that much couldn't be good. Moms and dads were supposed to do stuff together. Even though Mr. Carter worked all the time and could be a real jerk, the Carters still did more things together than her own mom and dad ever did.

Caitlyn's eyes widened at the question. "No!" she shouted, then promptly burst into tears.

Filled with regret for making the suggestion, Dani moved to her side and draped an arm around her shoulders. "It's probably not that," she insisted. "I was just guessing. They probably just had a fight or something."

Caitlyn shook her head. "I think maybe my dad's sick."

Dani frowned. "Why would you think that?"

"Because he's been home every day this week."

"Couldn't he be on vacation?"

"He's *never* taken a vacation. He didn't even take a day off to go to Disney World with us, remember?"

"Still, that doesn't mean he's sick."

"Then what could it be?" Caitlyn asked.

"I don't know," Dani admitted. She looked at her friend. "Maybe you should just ask your mom."

Not that she wanted to ask her mom if she'd ever thought about divorcing her dad. For one thing, her mom would probably tell her it was personal and that she didn't need to know, which was bogus. A divorce might be between her parents, but it affected her, too. And Josh, though he was oblivious to what was going on right under their noses. Plus he was fourteen, which meant he was oblivious to everything except sports and girls.

Beside her, Caitlyn sighed. "I don't think my mom will tell me anything. She probably thinks she and my dad are doing a great job of keeping this, whatever it is, from me and Evan."

"What does Evan think?" Dani asked.

Caitlyn gave her an incredulous look that was wise beyond her years. "If it doesn't involve a ball or a bat, he doesn't think about it at all."

Dani grinned. "Yeah, I know exactly what you mean," she commiserated. "Brothers are a pain, huh?"

"A royal pain," Caitlyn agreed.

Silence fell and, once again, Dani was the first to break it. "I'll bet things will be okay any day now and you'll have done all this worrying for nothing."

"Probably so," Caitlyn said.

But Dani could tell, looking into her eyes, that she wasn't buying it.

For the first time in forever, Emily went for a couple of weeks without catching more than a glimpse of Marcie. What little spare time she had was spent with Paula, who was not only sick as a dog from the chemo, but showing signs of depression. Emily and her other friends from school were spending as much time with her as possible trying to lift her spirits and take care of some of the household chores. Emily did laundry during her visits, others brought casseroles, and any one of them dusted or straightened up if the house needed it. Marcie was driving her to appointments, which were mostly in the morning, so they rarely crossed paths.

Paula's kids were tiptoeing around the house trying to be quiet, trying to be brave. It broke Emily's heart every time she saw them.

"Why don't you let me take the kids home with me tonight?" she suggested to Paula. "You and Dave can have an evening on your own."

"To do what, stare at each other and avoid the one topic neither of us wants to talk about?" Paula responded.

Emily regarded her with surprise. "If you want to talk, then you probably need to take the lead. I suspect Dave is trying not to upset you."

Paula sighed. "No, the truth is we've run out of things to say. I mean, really, it's not as if anything's changed. I had surgery. Now I'm doing chemo. No one knows how any of this is going to turn out. What is there to talk about? Funeral arrangements?"

"Stop that!" Emily said, dismayed. "You'll be old and gray before you need to worry about that. Maybe what you need to tell your husband, though, is that you're scared. You have a right to be, you know. This is scary stuff."

Paula's eyes suddenly welled with tears. "When the doctor first told me and we came up with this whole plan, it was, like, okay, good. There's a plan. I know what to do. Then all of a sudden, I realized, I could actually die…" She frowned when Emily started to interrupt. "No, you know it's true. Why deny it? There is no guarantee in this plan that I won't die." She choked back a sob. "My kids aren't even in high school yet, and I could miss seeing them graduate or get married. I could miss having grandkids."

"But you're not going to miss anything," Emily said. "You are going to beat this. I insist on it."

Paula chuckled, then swiped at her damp face with a tissue. "God, you sound just like Marcie. You spend too much time together. You're starting to sound alike."

"Are you kidding? She's much more refined than I am," Emily said.

Paula gave her an odd look. "Why would you say that? Because she spends a fortune on clothes and you don't? Because she bakes cookies and makes gourmet meals? None of that makes her one bit better than you."

Emily sighed. "I'm sorry. I sound as if I have a bad case of petty jealousy, don't I? And I don't, not really. I adore Marcie."

"Me, too," Paula said. "She's been a godsend with all these appointments." She frowned slightly. "Have you noticed that she seems a little off lately?"

Emily regarded her with a puzzled expression. "Off how?"

"I'm not sure I can explain it, just not her usual upbeat self, as if there's something weighing on her."

"To be honest I haven't seen her for a couple of weeks, but she was okay last time we were together."

"Maybe you should give her a call. I asked if everything was okay, but she blew me off. You two are much closer. Maybe she'll open up with you."

"I'll call her the minute I get home. Thanks for saying something. Now you just need to say something about how you're feeling to your husband. I've never seen a man more devoted to anyone than Dave is to you. Don't shut him out, Paula. Let him be there for you."

"I just feel he's had to accept so much already," Paula said. "The mastectomy, me starting to lose my hair, being sick all the time. It pretty much destroys the mystique that marriage needs to stay alive."

"Or maybe it puts it on a whole new footing," Emily suggested, giving her hand a squeeze. "Talk to him, okay?"

"I'll do it tonight, bossy," Paula said. "Thanks for being one of my biggest morale boosters."

"You'd do the same for me," Emily told her.

As she drove home, it wasn't Paula's low mood that was on her mind, though, it was her observation that something was going on with Marcie. As soon as she walked in the door, she picked up the phone.

"Hey," she said when Marcie picked up, "mind if I run over for a minute?"

To her surprise, Marcie hesitated, then said, "Why don't I come there instead? Five minutes, okay?"

"Sure," Emily said, then slowly hung up, trying to recall the last time Marcie had wanted to stop by her house for a late-afternoon visit, rather than having Emily come over.

She waited until she saw Marcie coming through the hedge, then called out, "How about lemonade? I just bought a carton at the store yesterday and I don't think the kids have been into it yet."

"Sounds good. Did you see Paula today?"

"Just left her," Emily confirmed as she went inside and took the carton from the refrigerator.

"Was her mood any better than it was this morning? She was pretty down."

"The same this afternoon, but we talked a little and I think she felt better by the time I left." She poured the lemonade over ice and put the glasses on the table, then sat down to join Marcie. "So, how are you? We haven't had a minute to catch up for a couple of weeks now. How'd your mammogram go?"

"It was fine. Yours?"

"Okay, thank goodness, though I am not anxious to repeat the experience anytime soon." She studied Marcie's face and thought she detected a shadow of worry in her eyes. "Everything else okay?"

"Sure."

"Really? You look as if something's on your mind."

Marcie's smile seemed forced. "Not at all. I've just been very busy. Ken's going out on his own, which means there are a thousand and one details for me to follow through on."

Emily regarded her with surprise. "He's opening his own company? When did that happen?"

Marcie avoided her gaze. "Oh, he's been thinking about it forever and the time seemed right."

Emily wasn't buying it. There was something Marcie wasn't saying, but obviously whatever it was she didn't want to share it with Emily. "That's great," she said with feigned enthusiasm. "He must be excited."

"And more demanding than usual," Marcie said, her expression wry. "We've been looking at office space and picking out furniture. I could do all of that for him, but he insists on second-guessing every decision I make."

"You're not thinking of going to work for him, are you?" Emily asked.

Again, Marcie avoided meeting her gaze. "Just for a few weeks till things settle down."

"Oh, Marcie, are you sure that's wise?" she blurted before she could stop herself.

Marcie stiffened. "What do you mean?"

"Just that he can be awfully hard to please."

"Don't I know it," Marcie agreed, visibly relaxing. "But it will only be for a little while, then he'll find someone permanent."

"Not if you do the same superb job for him at the office that you do at home," Emily commented.

For the first time since she'd arrived, Marcie's smile was genuine. "Honey, don't you know by now that I am smart enough not to let that happen? I've lived with the man for more than fifteen years. I know exactly how to get him to replace me when I'm ready to go."

Emily laughed. "That's good then."

"Everything okay around here?" Marcie asked. "The kids say Derek has been gone for a couple of weeks now. That's even longer than usual, isn't it?"

Emily's good mood faded. "Yes, and it's getting really old. I hardly feel as if I'm married anymore. Josh is getting to the age when he needs his dad around more than ever, but I can't even catch up with Derek half the time to tell him what's going on with his son, much less get his advice on how to handle it. Then when he is here, the kids have figured out how to play us off against one another because they know we never have time to come up with a joint plan. And Derek will always agree to whatever they ask, because he feels guilty about being gone. I'm sick of having to be the bad guy all the time."

Marcie frowned. "I've never heard you say a word against your husband before."

"I've never been this frustrated before," Emily admitted. "I think watching Dave hover over Paula has made me realize what's missing in my marriage. Derek is a wonderful man in many ways, but he and I simply don't have a real partnership. I wanted that from my marriage."

"What are you going to do about it?" Marcie asked. "Have you told Derek how you feel?"

"More times than I can count. He just keeps saying things will get better. I'm rapidly losing patience."

"You're not thinking about divorcing him, are you?" Marcie asked, her tone hushed as if she hated to even speak the word.

Emily sighed. "I honestly have no idea what I'm going to do," she said. "But I'm getting really tired of the status quo."

And if Derek wasn't motivated to change it, one of these days she would have to.

"What about a trial separation?" Marcie asked. "Maybe that would be just the wake-up call he needs."

Emily shot her a look filled with irony. "We're separated all the time as it is."

"This would be different," Marcie insisted. "But, okay, what about counseling?"

"I suggested it, and Derek even agreed to consider it, but every time I scheduled an appointment, we had to cancel because of one of his business trips. When I pointed out to him that that was exactly the problem with our lives, he accused me of not supporting his career the way he's supported mine. Then he had the audacity to suggest that if I hadn't gone back into teaching, I could have been traveling with him."

"Maybe he had a point," Marcie suggested.

"Oh, please, have you forgotten we have two children?" Emily retorted, as irritated now as she had been when Derek had made his outrageous claim. "What

are we supposed to do with them if both of us go galli-
vanting off all over the place? Park them with you?"

"You could have," Marcie said.

"No," Emily replied fiercely. "It is not up to you to
raise my kids."

Marcie reached for her hand and gave it a squeeze.
"Just don't do anything rash, okay? Derek's a great guy.
You know that."

"I do know," Emily said with a sigh. "That's why this
is so awful."

But more and more she was convinced that divorce
might be the only way out.

Six months later, when Josh was fifteen and Dani
thirteen, Emily finally called it quits with her marriage.
She'd tired of the loneliness, of Derek's long absences
on business trips. All the money in the world couldn't
compensate for the sense that she was the only one truly
giving anything to their relationship.

As she sat at Marcie's kitchen table, tears rolled down
her cheeks. It didn't matter that the decision was right.
It still hurt.

"I don't know what else to do," she told Marcie. "Am
I wrong for wanting more out of my marriage? Nothing
I've said has made one bit of difference with Derek.
Nothing's changed."

Marcie gave her a sympathetic look. "No," she said
softly. "But you're braver than I am. I don't think I could
face being on my own. What would I do?"

For an instant, Emily was snapped out of her own
troubles. "Are you and Ken having problems? You
always seem so cheerful." In fact, she'd often wondered
how Marcie stayed so upbeat when her husband was

such a jerk. Ever since Ken had opened his own office, he'd been worse than ever. Marcie had worked for him for exactly two weeks before she'd insisted on hiring her own replacement.

Marcie regarded her with a wry expression. "Cheerful is in my job description. Do everything around here, keep a perfect house, fix perfect meals, raise perfect children, and smile no matter what. Heaven forbid, anyone see a crack in the image of a perfect family."

It was the first time that Emily had detected even a trace of bitterness in her friend. "I had no idea you were so unhappy. I mean I know he drove you nuts at work, but I thought everything else was solid. I guess we've both done a pretty good job of covering, even with each other."

"Some things you don't share, not even with best friends," Marcie said. "And I'm not unhappy. Not really. I'm just having one of those days, I suppose." She waved off the comment before Emily could respond, then forced a smile. "Enough about me. Are you really going to ask Derek for a divorce?"

"Ask? No, I think this is one time when I'll tell him how it's going to be." She gave Marcie a rueful smile. "You know the really sad part? He'll be shocked."

"Then maybe that will give you a chance. You'll have his full attention."

Emily shook her head. "It won't be enough to make him change and since I can't change my expectations, it's too late. I just have to accept that it's over."

To Emily's regret, she was right. Derek was stunned when she told him she intended to file for divorce, but he didn't even waste his breath protesting that he would change when they both knew the words would be little more than empty promises. He just quietly packed his bags and moved to a suite in a hotel closer to his office.

The kids seemed to take it in stride, too, since little changed around the house. They'd grown accustomed to their father being gone on the most important occasions of their lives. He hadn't been in town for a birthday or school assembly or awards ceremony in years.

The divorce was accomplished with a minimum of fuss and hardly any lingering resentment. Perhaps that was the saddest part of all.

As she and Derek left the courthouse, she regarded him closely for any sign that he regretted the dissolution of their marriage as much as she did. Instead, he looked as if he were in his usual hurry to be somewhere else.

"I don't suppose you want to go somewhere for coffee and talk about this," she said.

He studied her blankly for a minute. "This?"

"How our lives are going to change now. When you're going to see the kids. That kind of thing."

"I thought we'd work it out as we go," he said. "We don't need some sort of formal agreement, do we?"

Emily sighed. "No, of course not."

He gave her a distracted kiss on the cheek as if they were separating till dinner, rather than for the rest of their lives.

"I'll be in touch," he said. "Call me if you or the kids need anything."

She watched him stride off and tried to remember how she'd ever fallen in love with a man capable of such a total lack of emotion. The last time she'd seen Derek's eyes shine with excitement or enthusiasm, he'd been talking about some deal he'd made, not looking at her or the kids at all.

She told herself she was well rid of him, that her future was brighter without him, that she could cope with raising the kids on her own since she'd been doing it that way for years anyway.

By the time she got home, she'd convinced herself that she was just fine. She threw her purse on the kitchen table, walked outside and crossed the yard and went straight to Marcie's back door. It opened before she could knock and Marcie held out her arms. Emily stepped into the embrace and burst into tears.

"It's over," she whispered. "In the blink of an eye, it was just over, almost as if it didn't even matter."

"Of course it mattered," Marcie said fiercely. "You and Derek had some good times, you know you did. And you have two amazing kids. How could that not matter?"

"It doesn't to Derek," she said with a sniff.

"I doubt that."

"He walked away without a second glance. He was already thinking about his next meeting."

"Which is exactly why you divorced him," Marcie reminded her. "But that doesn't mean it was always that way. You're allowed to mourn the good memories, even while you curse his black soul for making you so miserable."

Emily grinned through her tears. "Curse his black soul? Where'd you come up with that one? Did Caitlyn sneak one of my historical romance novels over to you? Besides, he hasn't made me miserable. He left me feeling nothing and that's a thousand times worse."

"I'm sorry," Marcie said, then gave her a hesitant look. "I baked a cake for the occasion."

Emily laughed. Leave it to the ultimate planner to

have thought of that. "Of course, you did. Are we having a party, too?"

"I have half-a-dozen people on standby if you want one," Marcie said. "Should I call them?"

"What the hell," Emily replied. "Somebody needs to mark the occasion. Make those calls." She hesitated. "What about the kids?"

"Paula and I have that covered. Dave's taking all of them out to a ball game and pizza after. We thought it would be a good distraction for Dani and Josh. Okay with you?"

"What would I do without friends like you guys?"

"Have a pity party all alone?" Marcie suggested.

"Probably," Emily agreed. "But there wouldn't be cake."

5

Marcie was at her wit's end. If Ken had been obsessed with work before, he was now a thousand times worse. Hardly a night passed when he didn't have a business dinner and even weekends were spent playing golf with clients, then hanging around the club to have drinks.

At first, she'd anticipated that she'd be as busy as he was, entertaining the way she'd always done, but to her dismay he took his clients to restaurants. It was rare that he even thought to include her. It left her at loose ends and with the kids getting older, she had fewer and fewer demands on her time. Neither Evan nor Caitlyn appreciated a gourmet meal, when they could grab a burger with their friends. She'd even cut back on her baking, since she was almost the only one eating the cookies, cakes and pies. She still kept something on hand for Emily's visits, but lately both of them had started worrying about their weight. More and more, brownies, lemon bars and decadent chocolate cake were guilty pleasures reserved for special occasions.

Today, though, she simply didn't give a darn about any of that. She'd baked a key lime pie, her personal favorite, and if she wanted to sit at the kitchen table and eat the whole thing, then who was going to stop her? She was on her second slice when Emily walked in.

"Uh-oh," she said, observing the pie. "What's wrong?"

"It has just dawned on me that I am obsolete," Marcie told her, taking another bite of pie.

Emily frowned at the comment. "By whose assessment?" she asked as she poured herself a cup of coffee from the fresh pot Marcie had brewed a few minutes earlier.

"Mine."

"Okay, let me get this straight. You're a wife, a mother, an active volunteer in the school and yet somehow you've decided you don't matter?"

"Pretty much," Marcie said, shoving the remaining three-quarters of the pie across the table. "Help yourself."

"I don't think so, because obviously some ingredient in that pie has addled your brain."

"No, hear me out," Marcie told her. "Ken's completely consumed with work and he doesn't even need me to entertain his clients anymore. Evan's either playing football, practicing football or chasing girls. He manages to find sufficient time in there to keep his grades up, but the only things he needs me for are laundry and the occasional infusion of cash."

Emily nodded. "Okay, I do recognize those symptoms. Josh is almost as bad, though he does expect me to get breakfast on the table for him and to keep the refrigerator stocked with milk and the cupboard filled with bread and peanut butter. Under duress, he will actually hold a conversation with me that consists of more than monosyllables and grunts."

Marcie gestured with her fork. "See, I told you. You're only marginally better off than I am. The big difference is that Dani still needs you and you have your job."

"Well, I'm sure Caitlyn still needs you. She's fourteen, even younger than Dani."

"In Caitlyn's case, she's fourteen going on thirty. She's convinced I know absolutely nothing of value. I suspect she talks to you more than she does to me."

Emily flushed.

"See, I knew it!" Marcie said.

"Well, Dani probably talks to you more than she does to me," Emily countered. "That's typical. It hardly means you're obsolete."

"Well, what am I supposed to do with my time? It's not as if they're looking for room-mothers for the seniors, or even for the eighth-graders. I offered to chaperon a field trip the other day and Caitlyn pitched a fit. She said she would be totally humiliated if I did that."

"And you interpreted that to mean what?" Emily asked. "That she was rejecting you? Embarrassed by you?"

"Both of those," Marcie said.

"She's just struggling to find her independence," Emily corrected. "It has nothing to do with you, so don't take it personally. Trust me, at that age none of the kids want their parents to chaperon anything, which is why teachers end up doing it."

Marcie knew she was probably right. Emily had a lot more experience dealing with teenage angst than she did. That still didn't give her a clue about what she was supposed to do with all this time she suddenly had on her hands.

"Okay, I'll concede that I'm probably overreacting," she said finally. "But I honestly have no idea what to do to fill my days."

"Get a job," Emily suggested.

"Please," Marcie scoffed. "Doing what?"

"Anything you want to do. Get a real estate license. Take classes and get licensed as an interior designer. You'd be great at that. Open a catering business or a bakery. There are probably a thousand things you could do. You just have to choose something that excites you."

"Other than a few years working retail when we were first married and the two whole weeks I worked for Ken, I don't exactly have a stellar résumé."

"Which is why opening something of your own would be ideal," Emily said enthusiastically. "Ken's business is on a solid footing now, isn't it? You could afford to take a risk."

"I suppose," Marcie said, but with little conviction. She'd never been much of a risk taker. She'd liked being a housewife and mom. It had been challenging and rewarding. Any other work sounded like drudgery.

Still, Emily wasn't letting up. "Talk to Ken," she prodded. "See what he says."

"I know what he'll say. He'll tell me I already have a job running this house. The possibility that he might have to remember to take out the trash or call the plumber would horrify him."

"He'd want you to be happy, though, wouldn't he?"

"Of course," Marcie said a little too quickly, then added candidly, "as long as it doesn't inconvenience him." She met Emily's gaze. "The thing of it is, I already *know* what makes me happy. I just don't see any way to get it back again without getting pregnant and having another child."

Emily stared at her as if she'd suddenly grown two heads. "You wouldn't!"

"Believe me, I've considered it," Marcie said. She jabbed her fork into the pie and stuffed another bite in her mouth.

Emily studied her worriedly, then grabbed the remainder of the pie and dumped it in the sink.

"What are you doing?" Marcie cried out, appalled.

"Getting rid of this before you kill yourself with an overdose of sugar," she said as she turned on the garbage disposal.

Apparently satisfied that she'd rid Marcie of temptation, Emily faced her with a stern expression. "Tomorrow morning I expect you to get out of this house and volunteer for something."

Marcie stared at her blankly. "What?"

"Doesn't matter. Anything that will make you feel useful and get you out of this mood. And tell your kids they're having dinner at home tomorrow night and at least three nights a week from now on."

"They'll hate it."

"They'll deal. Tell Evan he needs good nutrition at least that often to keep his body in shape for football and tell Caitlyn she's expected to be here because you say so. Be tough. Tell them neither one of them gets a dime for spending money if they don't follow house rules. That ought to whip them right into shape."

Marcie bit back a grin, her mood lifting ever so slightly.

"I can do that."

"Of course, you can. I'll be back tomorrow for a full report. The kids might be growing up, but there's no reason you need to let them go one second sooner than you absolutely have to. They still need to know that their mom and dad are in charge." She gave Marcie a curious look. "Think Ken will back you up?"

"He will if he expects to have sex anytime in the next twenty years," Marcie said, then chuckled. "God, I feel better already."

"Then my work here is done," Emily said, giving her a hug. "Call if you need backup."

"Just knowing I have it should do the trick," Marcie told her.

Maybe she wasn't quite obsolete, after all.

Dani couldn't recall a time when she hadn't been in and out of the Carter house as if it were her own. Caitlyn was her very best friend. They shared all their secrets, excluding the fact that Dani had a crush on Caitlyn's big brother. It was something she would never in a million years have told her mom or her own brother. And it had seemed totally weird to tell Caitlyn.

She wasn't entirely sure when she'd first looked at Evan and realized what a hunk he was. For a long time, he'd been like a brother, in other words a nuisance most of the time. Then one day she'd seen him with a bunch of girls at school and taken a good long look at him. He was hot! His body had filled out with muscle. He had the most amazing brown eyes, like chocolate, she thought dreamily. They were such a contrast to his blond hair, that turned really, really pale after he'd been outside in the sun for days on end. She didn't care that much about football, which was his passion, but she knew enough to know he was good. Really good. She'd clipped half-a-dozen articles from the local paper about what a hot college prospect he was. She kept them in an old jewelry box under her bed, so no one in her family would see them.

After she'd pretty much been hit by some bolt of lightning, she couldn't stop thinking about him. She started getting these fluttery sensations in the pit of her stomach whenever he was around. She started doing dumb stuff, hoping he'd notice her, wearing the skimpiest bikini her mom would let her get away with, doing cannonballs in the pool, hanging out at football practice or at the Carters' even more than usual. Evan could usually be found in the den watching movies once his homework was done. More than once she'd convinced Caitlyn to join him and hang out.

Unfortunately, Caitlyn had picked up on Dani's interest, not Evan. The other day she'd called Dani on it.

"Do you have a thing for my brother?" she asked when they'd been in the Carters' pool for hours and Josh and Evan had gone inside to grab snacks for all four of them.

"Quiet," Dani said, mortified. "Do you want Evan to hear you?"

"Sorry, but you were acting all goofy. You've been doing that a lot lately when Evan's around."

"Well, you have to admit your brother's pretty cool. Why wouldn't I notice him?"

"You and every other girl," Caitlyn said. "He must get, like, a hundred calls a night on his cell phone. I don't get it myself. He's a pain."

"That's just because he's your brother. He's cute and he's smart."

"And older than you. You're wasting your time getting hung up on him. He thinks of you like a kid sister, same as me."

Dani couldn't deny it, but she still harbored hope that one day he'd wake up and notice her. After all she was underfoot all the time. Just last week he'd taken her and Caitlyn to the movies and decided at the last minute to see it with them. He'd even bought them drinks and popcorn. It had felt almost like a date. She'd put the movie stub into her treasure box with the clippings.

Afterward, though, Josh had gotten all weird when he'd heard about it. He'd come charging home and confronted her.

"I hope you're not thinking about hanging out with Evan," he said heatedly. "If you are, forget about it."

"What difference does it make to you?" she demanded. "You're not my keeper."

"No, but I am your big brother. It's my job to look out for you. Evan's too old for you."

"He's eighteen," Dani retorted. "Same as you."

"And you're sixteen."

"I'm old enough to date."

"Not Evan," Josh repeated, his expression grim. "I mean it, Dani. Stay away from him. He's trouble."

She had no idea what he meant. The two of them hung out all the time. "That's not a very nice thing to say," she said. "He's supposed to be your best friend."

"It's one thing to hang out with a guy. It's another thing to let him spend time with your sister. Take my word for it, okay? Evan's too experienced for you. Forget about him."

"No, it is not okay," Dani said stubbornly. "I'll hang out with any guy I want to."

Josh flushed. "If you don't listen to me, I'll talk to Mom. She'll make you listen. Are we clear?"

Since having her mom find out that she was crazy

about Evan was the last thing Dani wanted, she promised Josh she'd steer clear of him. He didn't need to know that she'd kept her fingers crossed behind her back when she said it.

Now Caitlyn gave her the same dismayed look that Josh had given her.

"Forget about him, Dani," she said with surprising urgency. "He's not good enough for you."

Dani regarded her with a puzzled expression. "How can you say something like that about your own brother?"

"Because I know him better than you do," Caitlyn said. "He's not always this nice guy, superjock, the way he pretends to be around your house."

"You're just saying that because he thinks you're a pest," Dani accused.

"No," Caitlyn said emphatically. "Besides, it would be weird if you were dating my brother. Find some other guy to date and forget about Evan. Please."

But of course, all those warnings accomplished was to make Evan more intriguing than ever. And luckily, because Evan and her brother still hung out together almost every day, there were plenty of opportunities for Dani to spend some time with him and find out for herself if he was the terrific guy she thought he was. Getting time alone with him was trickier, but one of these days she'd accomplish that, too.

It was the final football game of the season and the last of Evan's high school career. Everyone at school was speculating that he'd have offers from the University of Miami, Florida and Florida State, but the coach had predicted he'd also be sought after by some top-notch out-of-state schools.

"Are you going to the game tonight?" Paula asked Emily that afternoon.

"Of course. I'd probably go anyway, but the fact that it's Evan's last game means that the Carters are making a big deal out of it. They're having a party for the team afterward at their house. Marcie's in her element. She's been planning it for weeks. She went over the menu with Evan so many times, he finally told her to just order pizza, because she was making him nuts."

Paula winced. "How'd she take that?"

"Oh, she brushed it off, and just made the next five versions of the menu on her own with a little input from Josh. He came home scratching his head one day and asked me what the hell pâté is. When I told him, he made a gagging sound and told me to call Marcie and tell her absolutely not, no way was she to serve anything that disgusting, to stick to chips and dip. I think she's concluded that both our sons have no class whatsoever."

Paula laughed. "It ought to be an interesting party."

"I'm just glad that Marcie found a good excuse to throw one. She was really down there for a while, thinking that no one needed her anymore."

"Doesn't she get how much everyone counts on her, me included?" Paula said. "I will never forget how good she was to me when I was going through all those chemo and radiation treatments. And it wasn't even that we were best friends, the way the two of you are. She just saw something she could do and she did it."

"Well, if you ask me, one reason Marcie doesn't value her own worth nearly enough is because of Ken," Emily said, breaking the vow of silence she'd always taken on the subject of Marcie's husband. Maybe it was because she'd overheard him snapping at her over nothing last night while she and Marcie had been on the phone. Her patience with his behavior had worn thin through the years and suddenly she couldn't keep her low opinion to herself a second longer.

"How so?" Paula asked.

"He's always dismissed what she does as if it were of no consequence," Emily explained. "But I know he'd be the first to blow a gasket if she stopped doing it."

Paula gave her an odd look. "You don't like him much, do you?"

Emily hesitated, then shook her head. "No, mainly because of how he treats Marcie. She's this wonderful, totally devoted wife and he demeans her every chance he gets. It's taken everything in me over the years to bite my tongue and not call him on it."

"Obviously he must have some good qualities for a woman like Marcie to stay with him all this time," Paula suggested.

"I suppose," Emily said, not even trying to hide her doubts.

One of the best things about her divorce was that for the past two years she'd hardly spent any time around Ken. Without Derek in the picture, Ken saw no need to waste his time trying to impress some high school teacher and they'd all but stopped doing things together as families. Tonight she was going to have to put aside her distaste and tolerate him, but with any luck she could escape from the Carters' after an hour or so. The party was really for the kids, anyway, and her presence there— as Josh's mom and a teacher from their school—would be a damper. She figured it was the perfect excuse to sneak away the second she'd had her fill of Ken's bluster and ego.

* * *

Emily had done her best to steer clear of Ken all evening. To his son's embarrassment, he was busy boasting about Evan's game-winning touchdown in an increasingly boisterous way. Evan had repeatedly begged him to stop, but Ken had had a few drinks and was past listening.

Emily had retreated to the kitchen, planning to tell Marcie she was going home, when she overheard crying coming from the downstairs bathroom. Her instincts as a mom had her moving in that direction. She tapped on the door.

"It's Mrs. Dobbs. Is everything okay?"

Her question was met with a loud sniff, but no response.

"If there's anything I can do to help, I will," she said. "Please talk to me."

"Go away," a girl murmured, her voice too thick with tears for Emily to be able to recognize it. "There's nothing you can do."

"I can listen," she said.

"Just go away," the girl pleaded. "I'll be okay."

Emily finally retreated and went in search of Dani. She found her by the pool, her adoring gaze locked on Evan. She shook her head. She'd figured that sooner or later Dani was going to develop a crush on their neighbor. Thank goodness it hadn't happened till he was almost ready to leave for college. She was doubly thankful that Evan seemed to be oblivious to Dani's infatuation. Though Evan had always been polite to her and was well liked in school, for some reason she didn't think he'd be a good match for her daughter. She'd never been able to put her finger on why, other than those rare instances when she'd heard him being disrespectful to his mother. He'd sounded a little too much like his dad. Fortunately, he'd shelved the attitude at home and was always on his best behavior at school. Apparently he was wise enough to understand that teacher evaluations and good grades might be as important as athletic prowess when it came time for him to get into college. He made it a point to turn on the charm for most adults, in fact.

When Emily finally located Dani, she pulled her aside. "I need to speak to you for a second."

Dani tore her attention away from Evan and followed Emily through the hedge to their backyard. "What's going on?"

"Have you noticed anything happening tonight that might upset someone?"

"Like what? Who's upset?"

"To be honest, I don't know, but I overheard a girl sobbing in the downstairs bathroom. I tried to get her to talk to me, but she wouldn't."

Dani looked horrified. "Well, Mom, what did you expect? You probably freaked her out. What did you do, stand outside the bathroom door and interrogate her?"

Emily winced. "Something like that."

"Jeez, Mom. How humiliating!"

"Okay, I get that it wasn't the coolest thing in the world to do, but I'm still concerned."

"Maybe one of the couples just broke up or something. We're all practically grown-up. We don't need our mommies trying to fix things."

Duly chastised, Emily backed down. "Okay, I'll let it drop, but keep your eyes open. There may be somebody over there who could use a friend, that's all I'm saying."

"If I see anybody bawling their eyes out, I'll give them a tissue," Dani promised, then hugged her. "You can't be a mom to the whole world, you know."

"I suppose not," she agreed. "Just as long as you know that you can always come to me, no matter what."

"Like I have any big problems," Dani said, her expression lighthearted.

Emily cupped her daughter's face in her hands. "Make sure it stays that way." She pressed a kiss to her forehead. "Go on back to the party. Have fun and don't stay too late. You still have curfew, even though the party's at the Carters'."

"Couldn't I spend the night with Caitlyn?"

"Not when there are likely to be football players sprawled all over the place for most of the night."

"But that's why it would be so cool," Dani said.

"And so out of the question," Emily said. "Be home at midnight and not one second later."

Dani gave her a resigned look. "Yes, ma'am. Does Josh have to be in at midnight?"

"He's got a one a.m. curfew tonight, since he's not driving."

"That sucks."

"Take it up with the court of appeals in the morning," she suggested.

"Who's that?"

Emily grinned. "Me."

If she could get her kids through the next few years with their hearts and limbs in one piece and their minds at least halfway well educated, she would consider herself lucky. She thought of the brokenhearted sobs she'd heard earlier and amended the thought. She was already darn lucky.

6

Present

The whole scene at the police station was totally surreal.
Marcie felt as if she were caught up in a nightmare. All
she wanted to do was grab her son and run. She'd
declared him innocent until her throat was raw, but no
one was listening to her. The two detectives had pointed
her to a hard chair and told her to wait. She'd watched
helplessly as they'd taken Evan off. He was still in handcuffs, and still berating them loudly and with language
that made her cringe. Though she understood the fear
and anger behind his outburst, she doubted his attitude
was helping.

Across the squad room, Ken was on the phone
trying to reach their attorney, who only handled civil
matters, but might be willing to come to the station in
the middle of the night to help them straighten out
this mess. Every chance he got, Ken was also insist-
ing that there be an immediate arraignment so he could
take Evan home.

"Sir, that's not going to happen before morning," Detective Rodriguez told him. He had to raise his voice to

be heard above Ken's nonstop demands. "Why don't you and your wife go home and get some rest?"

"I'm not leaving my son here so you can railroad him into confessing to something he didn't do," Ken snapped.

"We're not going to railroad him into anything," the detective responded, his tone growing increasingly impatient. "He's asked for an attorney and until he has one, we're not asking him a thing."

"Yeah, right," Ken said, getting in his face. "I know how guys like you operate. You want to write this up and get it off the books so you can move on to the next case."

Marcie saw a muscle working in the detective's jaw and guessed he was rapidly getting to the end of his rope. She crossed the room and put her hand on Ken's arm. He jerked it away and scowled at her, clearly furious about her interfering. For once in their marriage, she refused to back down.

"Have you found an attorney?" she asked quietly. "Is Don coming in?"

"No, but he recommended somebody and said he'd give him a call. He told me to call back in a few minutes. He said he'd have another name if this guy wasn't available. I was about to do that when this joker tried to hustle us out of here."

Marcie avoided Detective Rodriguez's eyes and focused on Ken. "Then don't you think you should concentrate on getting in touch with Don again? Evan needs legal representation as quickly as possible, so we can put this behind us. The last thing he needs is us making a scene that will make things worse for him."

"Okay, okay," Ken said, shooting another lethal look at the detective before dialing the number for their longtime business attorney.

Marcie turned to the detective. "Could I see my son?"

He hesitated a moment, then nodded. "I don't see why not. Come with me."

He led the way to an interrogation room. The pretty, dark-haired detective whose name Marcie had forgotten was sitting outside the door, her presence a disturbing reminder that Evan was in custody.

"Let her spend some time with her son," Detective Rodriguez said.

"Sure," the woman said, giving Marcie a look filled with surprising compassion. "You doing okay, ma'am?"

"I've had better nights," Marcie told her.

"I imagine so." She looked as if she wanted to say more but, instead, she merely opened the door for Marcie.

Inside the nearly bare, sterile room, Marcie found her son seated at a table with his head resting on his arms. When he glanced up, she saw the fear in his eyes for a split second before he managed to hide it behind the bravado of a boy trying desperately to prove himself a man.

"Mom, what are you doing here?"

"I came with your father, of course. Are you okay?"

"What do you think?" He blinked back a traitorous tear that threatened to escape. "You should go home. Dad's got everything under control."

Marcie knew better, but she didn't say that. Resisting the desire to rush around the table and hug Evan, a move she knew he'd despise, she sat across from him instead and reached for his hand.

"Tell me what happened, Evan. Explain to me how the police could have come to this horrible conclusion."

He frowned at her. "What, are you working for the

cops now? You want me to make some big confession so they can use it against me?"

Marcie stared at him in shock. "Of course not. I just want to help. How can I do that if I don't understand how this happened?"

"It's not your problem," he said. "Dad will get an attorney over here and I'll be out in a few hours. This will never stick." His cocky expression faltered. "You believe me, right?"

"You're my son and I have faith in you," she said, not entirely certain why she couldn't put any more conviction in her statement than that. Surely this whole thing was a lie. She wanted to believe that her son was incapable of raping anyone. No, she *did* believe it! Evan simply couldn't do such a thing.

Unfortunately, Evan heard the note of doubt in her voice. "You'd believe the word of some lying little slut over mine?" he asked incredulously.

Marcie immediately sat up a little straighter and looked him in the eye. "No son of mine will ever refer to a woman—any woman—in that way, do you understand me? And if you expect anyone to believe you about this, I suggest you drop that disrespectful attitude at once. It won't serve you well."

Evan blinked at her harsh tone, probably because he hadn't heard it in years. "Sorry," he mumbled. "But, come on, Mom, what do you expect? She says I raped her."

"Did the two of you have sex? Can they prove that?"

Evan's cheeks flushed with embarrassment, but Marcie knew this was no time to mince words. She had to be strong and get to the bottom of this, if only for her own peace of mind. "Did you?"

"Yes."

"Then there's no question about that much," she said, her tone matter-of-fact, her heart aching. God, could this be any more of a disaster? "But you're saying it was consensual."

"Damn straight, that's what I'm saying. I know when a woman wants to sleep with me."

There was an arrogant note in his voice that made her wince. "Oh? How do you know that?"

He faltered at the direct question. "I can just tell, okay? Come on, Mom. Do you really want to discuss this? It creeps me out talking to you about my sex life."

Marcie wasn't overjoyed about the conversation either, but she knew his answers were too important to back off just because the topic made them both a little squeamish. "What if she says no? Is that enough for you?" she asked, cursing herself for leaving this kind of conversation to Ken. Who knew what he'd taught his son about sex, probably that a man could get whatever he wanted with enough charm and determination.

Evan pushed away from the table so quickly that his chair tumbled backward and crashed on the floor. The door to the room immediately opened and Detective Rodriguez walked in.

"Everything okay in here?"

Marcie forced a smile. "Certainly. Evan stood up too quickly and the chair fell. It was just an accident."

He didn't look convinced, but he retreated.

Marcie returned her attention to her son. "You haven't answered me, Evan. Do you take no for an answer?"

"I'm not talking about this with you," he said tightly. "Go home where you belong and let Dad handle everything. At least he's on my side."

Marcie paled at the hurtful remark, but she refused to

back down. "I'm on your side, too, but I'm also a big believer in facing facts. Having a woman claim that you raped her is a very serious thing, Evan. It's not just going to go away. You might be able to talk your way out of a speeding ticket, but not this. This could destroy your life, do you understand that?"

"You're just full of good cheer, aren't you, Mom? Go home, okay? Dad will fix this."

Her gaze clashed with her son's, but in the end she was the one to look away. The cocky self-assurance she saw there made her want to cry. She would stand beside Evan no matter what, because he was her son, but in that instant she knew she couldn't believe a word coming out of his mouth.

Emily was as stunned as everyone else when the rumor that Evan had been arrested for date rape spread through the school by mid-morning on Monday. According to the headlines splashed across the local page of the morning paper, an unidentified freshman at the University of Miami had accused him of the attack, saying that rather than leaving after their date, he'd insisted on coming in and then demanded sex. When she'd turned him down, he'd raped her.

During her first break, Emily read the article with a sense of disbelief, especially since Marcie had been deliberately vague about why the police had come for Evan. In fact, their only conversation after she'd called to ask if Caitlyn could stay with Emily had been a request that Emily keep Caitlyn for the rest of the weekend.

"There's too much going on over here right now and she doesn't need to hear any of it," Marcie had said, sounding completely drained.

"Caitlyn can stay as long as you want," Emily assured her. "Shall I come by for her things or send her over?"

"No," Marcie had said quickly. "I'll pack a few things and drop them by."

"She has a lot of questions," Emily had warned her.

Marcie sighed. "We all do."

Finally Emily understood the hint of desperation she'd heard in Marcie's voice and her rushed visit to drop off Caitlyn's clothes. She'd barely said a word beyond thanking Emily for taking care of Caitlyn and being sure she got to school on Monday.

Now, as Emily scanned the morning paper in the teacher's lounge, she tried to imagine the way she'd feel if this had been Josh who'd been accused of such a thing. She also wondered what on earth Marcie had been thinking by allowing Caitlyn to go to school this morning. A sensitive fifteen-year-old girl wasn't prepared to cope with the stares and whispers and intrusive questions about her brother that were bound to hound her during the day.

Taking her cell phone from her purse, she dialed Marcie's number. To her dismay it was Ken who answered.

"Ken, it's Emily. Is Marcie there?"

"She doesn't have time to talk now. We're in the middle of a crisis here, in case you haven't noticed."

"I know. That's why I'm calling. The news is all over at school. I'm worried about Caitlyn."

"Caitlyn will be just fine," he snapped. "She's not the one in trouble."

"But—"

He hung up before she could utter the protest, once again proving that in his eyes Evan was the only child in his family who mattered. Emily had seen it before, had seen Caitlyn struggling to get her father's attention, but beyond his frequent reprimands, it seemed he was barely aware of her presence. It was clear all his hopes and dreams were tied up in his son. But even if Evan was at the center of this current crisis, it didn't mean that Caitlyn wasn't affected, too.

There was a hesitant knock on the door of the teacher's lounge and Dani stuck her head in. "Can I come in, Mom?"

"Of course. What are you doing out of class?"

"I told Mr. Litchfield I needed to see you. It's about Evan. Have you heard what they're saying?"

Emily nodded as she tried to read Dani's expression. Whatever she was feeling about this was well hidden behind a carefully neutral mask. She patted a place next to her on the sofa.

"The story was in the paper," she said, drawing Dani close. "Did you see it?"

Dani shook her head. "I just heard the kids talking. I don't think we should have dropped Caitlyn off at school," she said worriedly. "This is going to freak her out."

"I thought the same thing," Emily replied. "I just tried to reach Marcie, but Ken said she couldn't talk now. I'd go take Caitlyn out of school myself, but not without their permission."

Dani regarded her urgently. "But you're on the list, right? Mrs. Carter put you on a long time ago, so you could pick Caitlyn up in an emergency. I'd say this qualifies, wouldn't you?"

Emily nodded slowly, considering what was best for Caitlyn. "You're absolutely right," she said finally. She thought of how angry Ken was likely to be but decided it didn't matter. It would be irresponsible to abandon Caitlyn to deal with this on her own. "Let me go make some arrangements for someone to cover for me." She studied Dani. "What about you? How are you doing with all this?"

For a moment, Dani tried to put on a brave face, but it quickly faltered. "I hate it," she whispered. "Kids have been in my face all morning. I don't know what to say to them."

"I'm sorry. If I'd known about all this before we left the house, I'd have kept both of you home today. By tomorrow, hopefully the talk will have died down."

"Yeah, right," Dani said skeptically. "This is the biggest scandal ever to hit anyone from this school. We'll be lucky if the talk dies down by next year."

Emily winced. "You're probably right," she admitted. "You wait here, while I get things settled in the office. Then we'll both go to get Caitlyn. I'll call Marcie on her cell phone and tell her. Even if she doesn't answer, I can leave a message that Ken can't intercept."

Dani gave her a shaky grin. "Devious. Way to go, Mom!"

"I'm not sure that's a trait I want to encourage," Emily said sternly, but it didn't wipe the grin off Dani's face.

Thankfully, her principal was totally understanding. "I'll take over your classes myself. I know you have a work plan, so I should be able to muddle through for the rest of the day." She winked at Emily, her expression mischievous. "And just think of the advantage I have over most substitutes. The kids are already scared of me."

Emily laughed. "Not just scared," she said. "You

terrify them. Heaven knows why, though, because we all know you're basically a softie."

Valerie Granville winced. A statuesque black woman who dressed in black slacks and bright tunics made of African-inspired fabrics, she had a steely, direct gaze that some found intimidating. "Hush. We can't let that get out. The inmates will take over the asylum. Now, go. If you see Mrs. Carter, tell her we're all thinking about her and about Evan. That boy never gave anyone a lick of trouble during the time he was here, and that's what I've been telling all these reporters who've been calling all morning. I expect the police to be sniffing around before long, too, and I intend to tell them the same thing."

"Thanks for letting me take off at the last minute like this," Emily said. "The girls really do need a break from all the talk."

"I'll call over to the middle school and tell Mr. Jacobs you're on your way for Caitlyn."

"That would be great," Emily said, then went to retrieve Dani.

Ten minutes later, they were parked in front of the middle school. "Back in a flash," she told Dani.

Inside, she walked into the office and started toward the desk, only to be intercepted by a sobbing Caitlyn, who threw herself into Emily's arms.

"Oh, sweetie, don't cry," she whispered, holding her tight. "Everything is going to be okay."

"It's not," Caitlyn said with a sniff, wiping her eyes with the tissue Emily handed her. "It's not going to be okay. Dad's probably freaking out and blaming Mom. That's what he always does. It's probably why they didn't want me around yesterday."

When she lifted her eyes to Emily's, they were filled

with betrayal. "They should have told me. I'm part of the family, too. They shouldn't have let me walk into school this morning not knowing. It was just plain mean."

Emily agreed, but she wasn't about to say it. Instead, she said, "I'm sure they're so upset that they weren't thinking clearly. If I'd known, I would have told you myself, but they didn't say a word to me, either. And obviously the media didn't pick up on it till sometime last night since it didn't hit the newspaper or TV till this morning. I'm sure your folks thought they had time to tell you before the news got out."

"Yeah, right," Caitlyn said sarcastically. "Was it their idea for you to come and get me?"

Her need to know that she mattered to her parents nearly broke Emily's heart. "I know this is what they'd want."

Caitlyn's shoulders sagged. "That means it was your idea."

Emily kept one arm tight around her shoulders. "Actually it was Dani's. She's waiting in the car. Let me sign you out and the three of us will spend the rest of the day doing something fun that will get our minds off all this."

Don Jacobs emerged from his office just then and gave Caitlyn a sympathetic look, then turned to Emily. "I'm glad you were able to pick her up. It's been a little rough around here this morning. I've had her in here since right after homeroom."

"I can imagine," Emily said, knowing how cruel and unthinking kids could be.

"I called the house, hoping to speak to her parents, but I couldn't reach them. If Caitlyn needs the rest of the week off, I'm sure we can arrange to get her assignments to her so she won't miss anything."

Emily appreciated his understanding and the carefully worded suggestion. "I'll speak to her parents and let them know that," she promised him.

At the car, Caitlyn scrambled into the back seat.

"You okay?" Dani asked, looking over her shoulder.

"Today really sucked," Caitlyn said. "But it's better now. Thanks for telling your mom to get me."

"No problem," Dani said, then glanced at Emily. "What are we going to do now?"

Good question, Emily thought. She imagined that the Carters' house was in chaos. In fact, given Evan's football celebrity, the entire neighborhood was probably swarming with media. Neither girl needed to deal with that.

"How about lunch and a movie and some shopping?" she suggested. That ought to keep their minds off what was happening to Evan.

For the second time in the past hour, Dani beamed at her. "Mom, you're the best."

Emily shook her head. She now knew that the way to achieve maximum regard in her daughter's mind was to practice deception and help her play hooky from school to do her favorite things. Those were probably not the best lessons for her to be imparting. Then again, she couldn't think of a single time when breaking a few rules was more called for.

"Lunch at The Falls," she suggested, mentioning the nearest shopping center, which also had movie theaters and some of their favorite stores.

"TGIFridays," Dani said at once. "Okay with you, Cat?"

From the back seat, Caitlyn finally mustered a faint grin. "Awesome."

"Then that's what we'll do," Emily said. "I'll call your mom and let her know where we are. Maybe she'll even be able to get away to meet us."

"She won't," Caitlyn said, her grin fading. She regarded Emily worriedly. "Maybe this is a bad idea. Maybe it's wrong for me to be having fun, when Evan's in trouble."

"Sweetie, there's nothing you can do to help your brother right now. As long as your mom and dad know you're safe, they'll be able to concentrate on fixing this."

"I suppose."

Emily left another message on Marcie's cell phone, then drove to the mall, but by now both girls were subdued and some of the fun had obviously gone out of the stolen day. They picked at their food, barely exchanging a word.

When they'd finally finished, Emily studied them. "Would you rather skip the movie and shopping?"

"It's up to Caitlyn," Dani said without enthusiasm.

Caitlyn cast an apologetic look at Dani. "I want to go home."

"Yeah, me, too," Dani admitted.

"Then that's what we'll do," Emily said, leading the way back to the car. Inside, she glanced in the mirror at Caitlyn. "We'll go to our house, though, then call to see if it's okay for you to go home. Or if I can't get your mom on the phone, I'll go over and check in person."

Caitlyn nodded.

"You will get through this," she assured Caitlyn. "I promise. I know it seems pretty awful now, but you're strong and so is Evan."

"I guess," Caitlyn said, though she avoided Emily's eyes.

Emily glanced over at her daughter and saw that she was staring out the window. She looked as if her last reserves of energy had drained out of her, but it was the lone tear tracking down her cheek that made Emily's heart turn over in her chest. For the first time all day, she thought about how much Dani idolized Evan. Despite that, she'd put Caitlyn's feelings first, because that was the kind of kid she was. Now, though, it was evident that this was too much for her.

What had started as a crisis for the Carters was clearly going to have a ripple effect on all of them.

By the time Emily drove into their neighborhood, it was awash in television news vans and satellite trucks just as she'd feared. She was able to park in her own driveway only after maneuvering around some guy who kept trying to stick a microphone through the car window and into her face. Beside her in the car, Dani's complexion was ashen and Caitlyn was hunkered down in back looking scared to death. Emily regarded them worriedly.

"Think you can make a run for it?" she asked as she cut the engine.

"I don't want to talk to them," Dani said. "And I don't want to be on TV."

"Me, either," Caitlyn said with a shudder.

"You don't have to say a word. Just get out when I open your doors and hang on to me. I'll get us inside, okay?" she said, though she had no idea how to accomplish that. Nothing in her past had prepared her for running a gauntlet of microphones and cameras.

Both girls nodded. When Emily rounded the car for her daughter and grabbed her hand, it was like ice. Caitlyn's was no better. "Pretend you're rock stars avoiding the paparazzi," she instructed, drawing a faint smile from her daughter, but nothing from Caitlyn.

"Okay, girls, let's do it," she said, shielding them as much as she could as they dashed toward the house. Infuriated by the reporters' persistence, she batted away the microphone of the one reporter who got too close.

"You should be ashamed," she said, using her sternest classroom voice. "I doubt badgering teenage girls is in your job description."

Inside, she gathered both girls close for a fierce hug. "I'm sorry."

Dani jerked away. "I'm going to my room," she said.

Caitlyn stared after her, looking hurt.

"I'm sure she didn't mean you couldn't come, too," Emily told her.

"It's okay. I should probably go home anyway."

"Give me a minute and we'll go together," Emily said, then went into the kitchen and called the Carters.

This time Marcie answered.

"Oh, thank goodness you called again," Marcie said at once. "Is Caitlyn okay? I got your messages. I would have come to meet you, but I couldn't get away."

"We're at my house now. The girls weren't up to a movie or shopping. Is it all right for Caitlyn to come home? I think she really needs to be there."

"Sure," Marcie said. "Ken's gone to the office to try to work out some kind of PR plan for dealing with things. I think you can sneak over the back way. I haven't seen anyone lurking in the bushes back there."

"We'll be right there, then," Emily said, then hesitated. "Marcie, are you okay?"

"I honestly don't know."

"We'll talk when I get there," Emily promised.

She turned to find that Caitlyn had followed her into the kitchen. She gave Emily a resigned look.

"They don't want me home, do they? Mom just wants to see you."

Emily gave her a quick hug. "Don't be silly. Your mom said to bring you right over."

Caitlyn's expression brightened ever so slightly. "Really?"

"Really. You ready to make a dash for it through the backyard?"

"Uh-huh," she said eagerly.

"Let me run upstairs for one second to check on Dani and then we'll go."

She found Dani facedown on her bed. She didn't look up when Emily sat down beside her and touched her hair. "You want to come with us?"

"No."

"Do you want to talk about what's going on? I can take Caitlyn home and come straight back."

"No."

She sounded so lost that, for a moment, Emily debated staying with her. Dani had to be shaken up over this. She probably needed to talk, whether she wanted to or not. But one thing she'd learned about her daughter through the years was that Dani only talked when she was ready to. Trying to force her only led to frustration for both of them.

Besides, right this second, Marcie probably needed to see a friendly face. Emily could only imagine how alone she must be feeling with her son at the center of such a scandal.

"I'll be back in a little while. I'll take my cell. Call me if you need me."

"Whatever."

Emily sighed.

Downstairs, she found Caitlyn waiting just inside the back door.

"Okay, sweetpea, let's go."

Slipping through the hedge, they ran across the Carters' well-manicured back lawn. The sliding door was locked, the blinds drawn. Emily tapped lightly and Marcie peeked through the blinds, then opened the door, her relief evident.

She gathered Caitlyn close and tried to quiet the sobs racking her daughter. "Oh, baby, I'm so sorry you had to find out about this in such a horrible way. I should never have let you go to school this morning. I just wasn't thinking straight."

"It's not true, is it, Mom? Evan didn't do what they're saying."

"Of course not," Marcie said, looking at Emily over Caitlyn's head. Though her words were firm, there was little conviction in her expression.

"Come and sit down. I'll pour us some tea," she said, keeping her worried gaze on Caitlyn. She filled three glasses with ice, then poured the tea, but when she went to put cookies on a plate, she suddenly burst into tears.

Emily rushed to her side. "What is it?"

"There aren't any cookies," Marcie whispered, her voice choked.

"It's okay. We don't need them."

"But there are always cookies," Marcie said, clearly distressed. "That's what I do. I bake and I cook and I keep this place perfect and now it's all falling apart."

"No, it's not," Emily reassured her. "You'll have everything back on track in no time. Now, sit and drink your tea."

Caitlyn was staring at her mother with dismay. "Mom, you never cry."

Emily watched Marcie struggle to gather her composure.

"You're absolutely right," she told her daughter. "I don't cry. I fix things." Her hand trembled as she picked up her tea and took a sip. "I just don't know if there's any way to fix this."

7

On his way into the station, Grady wove his way through a sea of reporters who were shouting out questions about the Carter case.

"Do you really have enough to make this stick?" the reporter for the morning paper called out.

Grady regarded Jim Halloran with an expression of disbelief. "How long have you known me, Halloran?"

"Ten years, maybe longer," the older man replied.

"Have you ever known me to make an arrest if I didn't think I had enough to take the case to court?"

"You saying that on the record?" Halloran asked.

"If I hadn't been, it would be a little late to take it back now," he said, gesturing to the microphones from a dozen different local radio and TV stations and at least one network news crew. By afternoon, he expected the rest of the media vultures from around the country to be on this, too. The arrest of a star collegiate athlete on a felony charge was big news in certain circles.

"Anything else you can tell us about the victim?" a young woman asked.

"Yeah, is she in the habit of making false charges?" some guy in the back yelled.

Grady recognized him as a local sports anchor. Obviously he had an agenda. He was already biased in favor of the athlete. It didn't surprise Grady, but it did disgust him.

"I guess you'll all have to draw your own conclusions from the evidence," he said.

"Is Evan Carter getting out of jail today?" someone else asked.

"Attend his arraignment and find out," Grady suggested. "I have no control over that."

He shoved his way through the crowd and went inside to find Naomi waiting for him. She gave him a wry look.

"Having fun yet?"

"Not so much. How'd you get past them, kick them in the shins?"

"I snuck in the side door. No one's staking it out. Since you're smart enough to have done the same thing, why didn't you? Were you hoping to make a point?"

He shrugged. "If I didn't give them a comment, no matter how inane, the chief would. They're like a pack of hungry sharks. They won't leave without being fed."

"An apt analogy," she commented, then handed him a cup of real coffee from the Starbucks a few blocks away. "Thought you might need this. The chief wants to see us. I believe the word *immediately* was mentioned."

Grady sighed. "I figured it wouldn't take long before he started feeling the pressure."

"If he hadn't been deep-sea fishing in the Keys all weekend, it would have started first thing Sunday morning about the time we walked in the door with Carter in tow. We should probably count our blessings."

"I'm not feeling all that blessed at the moment," Grady said. "You?"

"Not so much." Her eyes lit up. "We could take a call and make a run for it. Nobody could question us for simply doing our sworn duty, right?"

Grady nodded in the direction of the chief's office. "Too late. He's coming this way and he doesn't look happy."

Chief Mike Miller had a gray crew cut that accented the sharp angles of his face. With his perpetual tan, piercing blue eyes and commanding manner, he'd won over the community in the PR wars, but it was his honesty, fairness and his willingness to stand by his officers that everyone in the department respected.

"In my office," he said tersely.

"Already on our way, sir," Grady said as he walked past him.

As he and Naomi sat down opposite the chief's desk, Miller closed the door, then sat on the edge of the desk in front of them. The better to intimidate them, no doubt.

"Okay, what the hell hornet's nest have the two of you stirred up while I've been out of town?" he asked.

"I imagine you already know the answer to that," Grady responded.

"But I would love to hear what you have to say," Miller said sarcastically. "And while you're at it, maybe you could explain why I had to read about it in this morning's paper, instead of getting a call from one of you to give me a heads-up."

"You were away," Naomi ventured. "And we had things under control."

"Really? Under control? That's what you call finding a bunch of damn reporters camped on my front lawn at home this morning? To say nothing of finding twice that number waiting here? All of them were expecting me to have some sage comment on the case of a superstar jock being hauled in for rape. Until I read the paper, I didn't even know there was such a case in my jurisdiction, much less the kid's name."

His eyes cut straight through them. "Do you have any idea how much I hate surprises? Ask my wife. Surprises, even the good kind, give me hives. I don't like them. And I especially don't like them when it means I'm going to walk in here and find a hundred messages from the mayor and every damn person I've ever met from the university calling to tell me we'd better be damn sure we've got the goods on this kid."

"Sorry, Chief," Grady said, and meant it. "We thought we'd have plenty of time to brief you before this got so out of hand."

"How naive are the two of you?" Miller demanded. "You a couple of innocent cops handling your first high profile case?"

"No, sir," Naomi said, leaning forward. "But we have what we need against this kid. I guarantee it."

"I hope you do," he said. "Because people in this town don't like to see their athletes falsely accused of serious crimes. It tends to make them jumpy. It tends to piss them off." He leveled another icy look at them. "It sure as hell pisses me off."

"Yes, sir," Naomi said.

The chief sat back. "Okay, then. You still think you want to pursue this case?"

"Damn straight," Grady said. "The kid is guilty, the State Attorney's office agrees, and as long as the victim doesn't get scared off, he's going down."

Miller nodded, his expression solemn. "Detective Lansing, you make sure this young woman doesn't change her mind."

"I'll do my best," she promised.

"And I want everything you've got on my desk in the next hour. If I'm going to tell all these important people to take a hike, I want facts at my fingertips, so I can do it with confidence."

"Done," Grady told him.

He and Naomi rose and started for the door, only to have Miller stop them.

"One more thing," he said, waiting till they'd turned back. "Good work. Only thing that makes me sicker than surprises is the kind of guy who'd do a thing like this."

Outside the chief's office, Naomi released a deep breath. "How long do you think he'll run interference for us?"

"For as long as he believes we have a solid case," Grady said. "Which means we need to get out of here and make damn sure we do."

When Emily got home again, she found Derek pacing in the living room. "I don't suppose I need to ask what you're doing here," she said, leading the way into the kitchen and pouring them both glasses of iced tea. "You heard about Evan."

"It's been hard to miss. You'd be amazed how people, who have absolutely no facts, take sides in something like this. I was ready to bash in a couple of faces myself, and I don't even know what's going on. Do you believe what they're saying?"

Emily hesitated. "God, I don't want to, because the whole idea that Evan is capable of such a thing makes me sick."

Derek nodded. "A few years ago, I'd have said absolutely no way, but lately? I don't know."

She regarded him curiously as she sipped her tea. "What changed?"

"Evan changed," he said simply. "He's gotten more and more like his dad."

Emily frowned. She'd seen the same thing, but hoped she'd been wrong. She wanted Derek's take on the changes. "What do you mean exactly? How's he changed?"

"Haven't you noticed how he talks to Marcie? He sounds exactly like Ken."

She sighed. "I've noticed it," she conceded. "But I figured it was a phase, like a lot of teenage boys go through."

He lifted a brow. "You ever heard Josh talk to you like that, even on his most belligerent days?"

"No, but our son is perfect," she said, smiling.

Derek grinned. "True enough, but you know you wouldn't tolerate it and neither would I." His expression sobered. "I'm just saying that the way Evan treats Marcie could be indicative of how he treats other women."

"I don't want to believe that," Emily said firmly. "And it's a huge leap from mouthing off to his mother to raping a co-ed. I'm withholding judgment till all the facts are known. You should too. We've known that boy almost his whole life. I love him as if he were one of our own. He and I have probably had more heart-to-heart talks than Josh and I have. I always had the sense that he was growing up to be a basically decent guy."

"I know. Me, too," Derek said. "But, like I said, lately he's been saying some stuff to his mother in a tone that gives me chills. I called him on it once and he got really defensive, told me it was none of my business."

Emily cringed. "He actually said that to you? He always looked up to you, asked for your advice."

Derek nodded. "I know. It caught me off guard, too, but it's one more example of how he's changed. Maybe it's all the attention he's been getting lately. Maybe it's given him a false sense of his own importance. Some kids just can't handle the kind of celebrity that's come his way now that he's playing ball for the university."

"But Evan's been preparing for this practically his whole life, at least as long as we've known him. He was a superstar in high school sports, too."

Derek shrugged. "Not the same. He's interviewed on ESPN practically every weekend now or on the sidelines by whichever network is broadcasting the UM games. Could be it's gone to his head."

Emily shook her head. "I just don't see it. He still wanders over here for an afternoon snack or to hang with Josh by the pool. Since they're both still living at home where there's some parental influence in their lives, I actually convinced myself that he was staying pretty grounded. Josh is."

"Maybe because Evan *is* underfoot over here all the time, you haven't noticed the changes the way I have. I only see him once in a while when I get together with Josh, and Evan tags along. To me the change has been dramatic and unpleasant."

"I suppose," Emily said. The whole conversation was making her uneasy. Had she missed some important clues about Evan, as Derek was suggesting? Had she just locked in on the polite, sweet boy he'd been and turned a blind eye to the man he was becoming? The possibility was disconcerting.

"Were you with Marcie when I got here?" Derek asked, interrupting her thoughts.

She nodded.

"How is she?"

"She's a mess."

"What about Josh and Dani? How are they taking it?"

"Dani's upstairs. She was really upset by the talk at school. She practically begged me to go take Caitlyn out of school, so I did."

Derek looked surprised. "Marcie let her go to school today, knowing what she'd be facing?"

"I don't think she even stopped to think," Emily said.

"What about Josh? You talked to him about this?"

"Josh hasn't gotten home from school yet. He should be here soon. I didn't see him before he left this morning and I doubt he looked at the paper, but I'm sure he's heard all about it by now. The news must be all over campus."

Derek regarded her with an unfamiliar helpless expression. "How the hell could something like this happen?"

"We don't know that it's true," Emily reminded him again, still clinging to a slim shred of hope. "Right now it's just an accusation."

"Still, do you really think a young girl would put herself through all this, if it weren't the truth?" he asked. "Come on, Em. Put yourself in her place. It would be a helluva lot easier to say nothing."

Emily knew he was right, but she simply wasn't ready to admit it. Instead, she asked, "Are you going to stay for supper?"

"If it's okay," he said.

"Of course."

"I just thought I ought to be here for the kids, you know, in case they want to talk or something."

She gave him a wry look. "That's new."

"What?"

"You worrying about the kids."

He frowned. "I've always put their best interests first," he said, looking injured.

Emily sighed. In his own way, she supposed he had. It just wasn't her way. He hadn't been here day in and day out the way she'd been. Ironically, now that they were divorced, he probably gave the kids more of his undivided attention than he had before. He'd been religious about keeping the plans he made with them.

"I'll get dinner on the table," she said.

"While you do that, I have some calls to make," he said. "Mind if I use the phone in the den?"

"No. I'll let you know when dinner's ready."

As soon as he'd walked away and as she was pulling hamburger from the freezer, Josh came in the kitchen door. "Is that Dad's car in the driveway?"

She nodded. "He's in the den."

"I guess he heard about Evan."

"Yes." She looked at her son as he took a gulp of milk straight from the carton, a habit she'd tried unsuccessfully to break for years now. "Do you know the girl involved? I know her name wasn't in the paper, but I'm sure everyone on campus has figured it out."

"Oh, yeah," Josh confirmed. "I have a class with her. She wasn't there today."

"What's she like? Could she be lying? Trying for a few minutes in the spotlight?"

"Lauren? No way. She's kinda quiet. I don't even think she dates that much. I was surprised when I heard she'd said yes to Evan, but I guess nobody turns him down."

"Have you spoken to Evan?"

Josh shook his head, his expression grim. "And I don't want to, either."

Surprised, she met his angry stare. "Why?"

"Because I saw this coming a long time ago," he said. "When it comes to women, the guy's a bully, Mom. Just like his dad. I wish to hell I'd warned Lauren. She didn't deserve this."

A strangled gasp in the doorway had both of them turning just in time to see Dani take off.

"What's with her?" Josh asked.

"This whole thing has really upset her. She always had a crush on Evan, I think."

Josh got a strange expression on his face. "You sure that's all it was?"

Emily felt her stomach clench. "What are you saying? Do you know something I don't know?"

Josh shook his head. "I don't *know* anything."

"She never went out with Evan," Emily protested. "I'd know if she had."

"But she hung around over there plenty," Josh said.

Just then Derek appeared in the doorway. The color had washed from his face. "Are you saying you think that boy might have hurt Dani?" he demanded. "If he laid a hand on her, I'll kill him myself."

Emily reached for her ex-husband's arm, felt the muscle clench. "No," she said. "Dani's fine." She simply refused to believe anything else. She would know if Evan had ever hurt Dani. She would *know.*

"If she isn't, Dad's not the only one who'll be in line to make Evan pay," Josh added in a tone that sent a chill down Emily's spine.

Dani was looking out her bedroom window when she saw Caitlyn slip through the hedge and make a run for their back door. Caitlyn was the last person Dani wanted to see right now. Her mom had been wrong earlier. She hadn't wanted Caitlyn to come upstairs with her. She'd been relieved when she'd gone home instead.

Caitlyn knew too much, things Dani had never told another human being, things about which she was totally ashamed, things involving Evan and what had happened between the two of them. Most of the time she worked hard to forget, but today had brought it all rushing back. Spending time with Caitlyn earlier had been awful. She hadn't even wanted to look her in the eye for fear one of them would give something away.

Still, there was nothing she could do to hide. Her mom would never lie and tell Caitlyn she'd gone out and it was too late to sneak out the front door before Caitlyn could catch her. She steeled herself as she heard the soft knock on her door.

"Come in," she called out reluctantly.

Caitlyn came into the room and went straight to the chintz-covered chair she always claimed. After a silence that seemed to stretch out forever, she cast an accusing glance at Dani. "I've been calling your cell phone ever since I left here this afternoon and you haven't taken any of my calls. I know you're avoiding me on purpose and I know why," she said, her tone filled with hurt.

"Don't," Dani said. "I won't talk about Evan with you. Not now."

"Why not? It's not as if we don't know what's going on. Everybody's talking about it. You're supposed to be my friend. If I can't talk to you about this, who can I talk to?"

"I *am* your friend," Dani said. "I got my mom to get you out of school, didn't I? That doesn't mean I want to talk about this with you. We'll just get in a fight, the same

way we did when I tried to tell you what had happened
last year."

Caitlyn stared at her in dismay. "You think he's guilty,
don't you?"

"Don't you?" Dani retorted.

Caitlyn looked down. "My dad says it's just a bunch
of bullshit, that they'll never make the charges stick," she
said. "He says girls like to make up things about athletes
so they can feel important. He says this will never go to
trial." She faced Dani with a stubborn set to her chin. "I
think he's right. It's all bogus."

Dani stared at her in shock. How could Caitlyn be so
blind, especially with everything she already knew about
her brother? "You can't be serious. You actually think
that's what happened, that this girl made up the whole
thing? Come on, Cat, you can't possibly be defending
Evan."

"I can, too," Caitlyn said. "He's my brother."

"That's not what matters now. Just because he's
family doesn't mean he can't do something awful. Think
about that poor girl. Do you honestly want him to get
away with this? I know you love him, but what he did is
wrong."

Caitlyn flushed. "He didn't do it," she said fiercely.

Dani held her gaze. Eventually Caitlyn blinked and
her eyes filled with tears.

"It might not be true," she whispered.

"You know it is," Dani said fiercely. "You have to know."

"Not for sure," Caitlyn insisted.

"You *know*," Dani repeated. "You know because he
did the same thing to me. I know you didn't want to
believe me then, but now you have to see that I was
telling the truth, because it's happened again."

And if she'd spoken up, if she hadn't been so ashamed, so sure it was all her fault, maybe it would never have happened to another girl.

She knew her mom thought she was upset because she'd discovered that her perfect Evan might have a pretty major flaw, but that wasn't it at all. She'd known just how badly flawed he was for a while now and she'd kept her mouth shut. Now she'd have to live not only with her dirty little secret about what he'd done to her, but with the guilt over what her silence had cost someone else.

Emily was thoroughly subdued when she got to school on Tuesday. Dani had told her she had a stomachache. Emily knew it wasn't true, but she'd let her stay home just the same. She'd had a hurried conversation with Marcie, who was keeping Caitlyn home as well. She'd promised to keep an eye on both girls, though Dani had flatly refused to spend the day at Marcie's house.

There were several teachers in the lounge having their morning coffee before classes started. They all fell silent the minute she entered, which told her that Evan's arrest was the hot topic of the morning once again.

Paula was the first one to speak. "We've been talking about Evan," she admitted. "None of us can picture him doing anything like this. You know him better than we do. Do you think the charges are true?"

"I really don't think I ought to be speculating," Emily said. "This is serious stuff and it's not as if I actually know anything about the case."

Paula regarded her curiously. "I thought you'd be the first to leap to his defense. He grew up next door. He and

Josh are like brothers. Do you have doubts about his innocence?"

"Honestly, I don't know what to think," Emily responded. "Evan has been in and out of our house since he was nine. I thought I knew everything there was to know about him. That said, I doubt the police would arrest him without solid evidence. All I really know is that I'm sick about what's happening. I'm worried about Evan, but I'm worried about Marcie and Caitlyn and the toll this is taking on them, too. Even if the charges prove to be false or he's acquitted down the road, right now they're paying a really high price."

"Then you do think he's innocent?" Paula persisted.

"Okay, so maybe I do. Or at least, I want to believe that." She faced her colleagues. "Come on, you guys. You know Evan, too. Was he ever anything but polite and respectful in class?"

"He was great in my class," Paula said, her expression turning thoughtful. "And I never heard any gossip about him mistreating his dates, either. That kind of thing can come up in health class, maybe not in front of everyone, but girls will come to me privately and ask what they should do about guys who won't take no for an answer. None of the girls who went out with Evan ever hinted at anything like that, not to me anyway."

Elena Perez, a popular math teacher who'd only been at the school for a couple of years, had been quiet up till now, but she finally spoke up. "I think we can never know what goes on between a boy and a girl unless we are with them," she said, her voice strained but passionate. "And I think when a girl makes a claim like this, it takes a lot of courage and she should be believed, rather than trying to find excuses for the boy."

Emily was surprised by the vehemence in her voice. "We're not saying anything against the girl, Elena. Not at all. But we're talking about a boy we all know, a boy who's never been in any sort of trouble. Rape is a very serious accusation. His entire future's at stake."

"So is hers," Elena retorted, her voice quivering with outrage. "She could spend the rest of her life feeling as if she were the one who did something wrong, as if she somehow encouraged this attack. A rape by someone she trusted could forever change the way she views relationships. It could destroy her faith in men."

Suddenly getting it, Emily crossed the room to sit beside the younger woman. "You're talking from experience, aren't you?" she asked gently. "This happened to you?"

Elena's eyes filled with tears as she nodded. "I was in college, as well. I had come from a very strict background and had done little dating in high school. I had been out with the boy only a few times, when he began to push for things I didn't want. Nothing..." She swallowed hard. "Nothing I said or did could stop him."

"I am so sorry," Emily told her. "You're right. The rest of us are fortunate not to have been through anything like this. None of us can imagine how devastating it must be for the woman. I would never try to excuse Evan's behavior if he did this. If he's guilty, he deserves to be punished, even though my heart aches for him and his family."

"Save your compassion for the victim," Elena said, then rushed from the lounge.

Paula, Emily and the two other teachers who'd remained exchanged glances.

"I had no idea, did you?" Emily said, heartsick.

"No, but it explains a lot," Paula said. "Haven't any of you noticed that she never stays in the lounge when she might be alone with one of the men? And even though she's beautiful, she never talks about dating. She always comes to our parties alone, if she comes at all."

"And an incident like this, involving a student she knows, must bring it all crashing back on her," Emily said. "Something tells me this whole mess is going to have repercussions none of us have anticipated."

"Have you seen Marcie?" Paula asked.

"Briefly, yesterday afternoon. We couldn't talk too much because Caitlyn was there and she really needed some time with her mom. I'm going to stop by again later."

"Tell her I'm thinking about her, okay? I'll call in a few days when things settle down a bit. If she needs anything at all, though, tell her all she has to do is call me. I owe her big-time."

"I'll tell her," Emily promised.

Paula sighed heavily. "I can't even imagine what she's going through. This must be hell for her."

Emily thought of the bleak expression she'd seen in Marcie's eyes the day after. "Something tells me hell doesn't even begin to cover it."

8

Grady wasn't satisfied to have Lauren Brown's testimony and the rape kit evidence. He wanted to nail down enough hard facts to ensure a conviction when Evan Carter went to trial. He and Naomi were already catching a lot of personal flack over the high-profile case. Once he'd appeared on the news and people were able to put a name and face to the arresting officer, he'd been deluged with calls. No one wanted to believe that a seemingly clean-cut, upper-middle-class kid like Carter with the whole world spread out under his nimble feet was capable of such a crime. They preferred believing that Lauren Brown was a consummate liar.

Ken Carter was doing his best to make it easy for them. The guy had put all of his public relations skills and contacts to good use, starting a subtle smear campaign against the girl that as near as Grady could tell was based solely on carefully worded innuendo. Unfortunately, nothing was so blatantly inaccurate that Lauren could have sued him or the media for libel. Not only did it sicken Grady, but Lauren's friends were justifiably outraged. Her roommate had called not ten minutes ago and asked him what they should do.

"Paint a different picture of Lauren every chance you get," he'd told her. "Tell the reporters about the studious, responsible young woman you know."

Jenny had scoffed. "Like the media wants to hear anything good about her. As soon as I start saying what a great girl she is, the microphones shut down. What I don't get is how they found out who she is. I thought victim names were supposed to be kept secret."

"The media usually respects that," Grady says. "But it doesn't mean they won't try to find out and make contact. And Ken Carter has made it easier for them. I'm sorry. Remind Lauren that it isn't the court of public opinion that counts. It's what happens when we go to trial."

"I've tried telling her that, but she just wants all of this to go away," Jenny told him. "She won't even show her face on campus. She hasn't been to class since it happened. If she winds up flunking anything, she'll lose her scholarship. I'm worried about her, Detective Rodriguez. I'm afraid she'll back down and let the son of a bitch go free."

"Want me to send Detective Lansing over to talk with her? Or set up a session with a rape counselor?"

Jenny sighed. "No. For now, I'll handle it. I just needed to vent, you know. She's the victim, but people are treating her like she's the criminal. And even though the media isn't reporting her name, everyone on campus knows who she is because Evan Carter and his dad are putting it out there every chance they get. It would be hard on anybody, but it's really hard for someone like Lauren who isn't used to the spotlight. And she's worried sick that her folks will find out. Her dad's a minister and she's convinced he'll blame her, just the way everyone else is doing."

"Believe me, I get that," Grady said. "Hang tough, both of you. She's lucky to have you on her side and if Detective Lansing can help, all you have to do is call."

"Thanks, Detective."

The conversation had strengthened Grady's resolve to make sure the case was airtight by the time it went to court. He recalled what the doctor at the rape center had said, that Carter had most likely done something like this before and gotten away with it. Grady walked through the squad room in search of Naomi. He found her flirting outrageously with a new patrolman who was still wet behind the ears.

"Robbing cradles again, Lansing?" Grady inquired.

"Bite me," she replied sweetly, then winked at the kid. "See you, Kevin."

"Yes, ma'am," he said, looking dazed.

As Grady and Naomi walked away, he struggled to hide a grin, especially when he noted her disgruntled expression.

"Did you hear that?" she demanded irritably. "He called me *ma'am*. How old does he think I am?"

"I'm sure he was just being polite to a superior officer, not making a statement about your age," Grady consoled, then added, "Grandma."

Naomi scowled at him. "It's going to be one of those days, isn't it? Who twisted your knickers into a knot?"

"Jenny Ryan."

Naomi immediately sobered. "Oh?"

"She says Lauren's wavering under the weight of all this attention."

"I'll go see her," Naomi said at once.

"Jenny says she can handle it for now, but we need to find some backup. You heard Dr. Benitez say Carter's probably done this kind of thing before. If he has, we need to find the women, establish the pattern."

"Let's do it," she said at once.

"Where do you think we should start, the kid's high school or his neighborhood?" he asked her.

Naomi looked at her notes. "I have one name here that could kill two birds with one stone. Emily Dobbs teaches at the high school and lives right behind the Carters. According to Evan's mother, the families spend a lot of time together. She's seen him under a lot of different circumstances over the years and could provide a character reference, according to Mrs. Carter."

Grady nodded. "Which means she's probably biased in his favor, but let's start with Mrs. Dobbs and see where that gets us."

Three emergency calls kept them from getting to the school. It was already four-thirty when they pulled up in front of the Dobbs' Spanish-style home with its climbing bougainvillea, well-manicured lawn and brand new Lexus SUV in the driveway.

"Fancy car for a teacher," he commented as they crossed the lawn.

"Her ex-husband is some corporate type who's paying generous alimony and child support," Naomi told him.

"And you know that how?"

"The Internet is a wondrous thing. I find out all sorts of fascinating facts while you're getting snacks from the vending machines at the station." She gave him a once-over. "You really do need to change your diet, Rodriguez. The chips and peanut butter crackers are starting to ruin those six-pack abs of yours."

"Butt out, Lansing," he commented as he rang the doorbell. "I gave up cigarettes, thanks to your pestering. Leave my diet alone."

When the door was opened by a dark-haired woman

with a tentative smile and eyes as blue as the sky over Biscayne Bay, he actually suffered a momentary pang about that last bag of chips. If they'd had teachers this gorgeous when he was in school, he might have studied a little harder. At least he'd have been happier about being cooped up inside all day.

"Emily Dobbs?" he asked.

"Yes."

"Detectives Grady Rodriguez and Naomi Lansing. We're investigating the allegations against Evan Carter. Could we have a few minutes of your time?"

Her expression hardened ever so slightly. "I really don't think there's anything I can tell you," she said, not budging from the doorway and pretty much confirming Grady's fear that she was staunchly in the boy's corner.

"You have known him most of his life, haven't you?" Naomi said. "And you work at the high school he attended, right?"

"Yes."

"Then you really could be helpful," she said. "It won't take long."

"Okay, fine," she said tersely, and stepped aside to let them in. "I hope you'll make it quick, though. My daughter's already upset about this and I'd prefer it if you were gone before she gets home."

"How old is your daughter?" Grady asked as she led them into a living room that was decorated in bright, cheery colors. A scattering of open books and magazines suggested this room was lived in, though he didn't notice a television anywhere. There was a family portrait in a frame on top of a baby grand piano. Obviously it had been taken before the divorce, since the husband was in it, along with two kids, a boy who was probably about the same age as Evan Carter, and the daughter Emily Dobbs was worried about.

She apparently noticed the direction of his gaze. "My daughter's only seventeen," she said. "And before you get any ideas, I will not allow you to talk to her, not without a warrant or whatever it is you need to speak to a minor without the parent's consent."

Grady saw the mother-hen ferocity in her eyes and backed off. Still, it was an intriguing twist. If the two families were close, the daughter might have noticed something in the Carter kid's behavior around girls that the adults wouldn't have seen. He wouldn't mind talking to the son, either. If the two boys hung out together, the Dobbs kid had probably seen how Carter treated the women in his life.

"What about your son?" he asked. "He's around the same age as Evan Carter, right?"

"Yes. They've been in school together for about ten years now."

"Nineteen, then?"

"Yes."

"Best friends?" Grady asked.

There was an unmistakable hesitation before Mrs. Dobbs nodded. It had Grady wondering if the two boys had had a recent falling out and, if so, why.

"Is he around?"

"Actually he goes to UM, too. He's at school now."

Perfect, Grady thought. "Name?"

"Josh."

"I'll make arrangements to see him later," Grady said. "I assume you won't have any objections, since he's old enough to speak to us without your permission."

Emily Dobbs's expression tightened, but she didn't

argue. She just scowled at him as if she wanted to cut his heart out. Naomi wisely stepped in.

Unfortunately, though, it appeared that whatever Emily Dobbs might know herself, she didn't intend to share with the police. Her loyalty to her friends ran deep, which kept her answers terse and to the point. It was an admirable trait in a friend, but Grady couldn't help wondering if the pictures of Lauren Brown's injuries would be enough to change that. No mother could look at those without envisioning the same thing happening to her child and being sickened by the thought.

"Thanks for your time," Naomi said eventually, when it was evident that they weren't going to get anything more, at least not on this visit.

Grady saw the relief in Emily's blue eyes and decided to rattle her just a little. "We'll be in touch," he told her.

"I've told you everything I know that might be relevant," she insisted.

He smiled at her. "Possibly, but it's amazing what people sometimes remember during a second or third interrogation."

Her chin shot up. "Wouldn't that constitute harassment?"

He shrugged. "Matter of interpretation, I suppose."

She frowned at that. "Do I need a lawyer?"

"Not unless you were in the victim's apartment last Friday night," he replied, his gaze steady. "Or unless you're withholding something relevant to this investigation."

"I don't know anything about what happened that night," she repeated, then added with a touch of defiance, "assuming anything did."

Grady lost patience. "Oh, it happened, Mrs. Dobbs. We have photos of the damage that boy did to her, as well as the testimony of the physician who examined her that night."

She paled visibly. "Damage?"

"Bruises, bite marks. He was rough with her, Mrs. Dobbs."

The remaining color drained out of her face, but Grady wouldn't allow himself to feel sorry for her. Maybe she knew something more, maybe she didn't, but she was defending a kid who didn't deserve it.

"Like I said, we'll be in touch."

Outside, Naomi regarded him with amusement. "She got to you, didn't she? Is it because she was holding something back or because she looked at you as if you were pond scum?"

Grady grinned. "Maybe both. You know me. I love a challenge."

Dani cut her last three classes. She'd gotten tired of all the speculation about Evan, when nobody knew anything, not really. Heck, some of the kids who were talking the loudest and making the most outrageous comments hardly knew him at all. The worst part was knowing they expected her to defend him and not being able to do that without gagging on the words. Nor could she publicly turn on him without stirring up too many questions she definitely didn't want to answer.

Once she was safely off the school property, she wasn't quite sure what to do next. She'd never done anything like this before, partly because she knew her mom would kill her and partly because she honestly liked school. She was probably some kind of nerd or something, because she got excited about learning new stuff. If what had happened with Evan was her biggest secret, then this was her second biggest. Nobody who wanted to hang out with the popular crowd wanted anyone to know that they actually liked classes and studying.

She had enough money with her to take a cab home. Or she could sneak off and go to a movie, but that didn't hold any more appeal today than it had when her mom had been willing to take her and Caitlyn a couple of days ago.

She could call Josh to come and get her. He'd leave class if she asked him to, but then he'd probably ask way too many questions about why she'd decided to play hooky. He thought being older gave him the right to boss her around. He'd been even worse since their dad had moved out, like he'd been left in charge or something. Besides, ever since this mess had started, she'd seen the way Josh looked at her, as if he wanted to come right out and ask her if Evan had ever laid a finger on her. She didn't think she'd be able to stand seeing the disgust in his eyes if she told him the truth.

Walking aimlessly as she debated where to go or what to do, she wound up at Fairchild Tropical Botanic Garden. As she stood outside the entrance, she wondered if she'd subconsciously headed here. Her mom had brought her and Josh here about a zillion times. They'd walked the endless grounds, touching all sorts of rare and exotic tropical plants and learning their proper Latin names. Dani knew her mom had been hoping that they'd take an interest in all the incredible flowers, succulents and palm trees in the gardens that spread over several acres, but she'd also brought them because it was peaceful with its winding pathways and small lakes.

Dani paid for her ticket inside the visitor center and

walked outside, then began to wander, gravitating toward the orchids. One day she'd like to grow orchids, maybe even go all over the world in search of rare specimens. Sometimes she thought maybe she'd even study horticulture and own a nursery someday. Could anything be more wonderful than helping people to create serene or vibrant gardens around their homes? Her mom and dad had planted hedges of bougainvillea years ago, but that was almost the extent of the landscaping around their house aside from a few palm trees and this giant banyan tree. Dani was the one who'd insisted on going to the nursery every year. She always brought home way too many flowers to fill the giant containers on the back patio with color. She was the one who knew which flowers needed sun, which ones preferred shade and which ones would come back year after year. Her mom and dad were clueless, but her mom, at least, had encouraged her interest in gardening.

Walking through the formal gardens here, she found a bench in the shade and sat down, then opened her backpack and took out her dog-eared copy of *Romeo and Juliet.* A lot of kids in her class thought it was wildly romantic, but she'd never gotten that. They'd *died!* And they were barely in their teens. If that wasn't tragic, what was?

Besides, what kid at fourteen knew anything at all about love? Oh, she'd thought she knew all there was to know when she'd gotten that crush on Evan, but look how that had turned out. She'd never seen beyond the fact that he was good-looking and smart. It just proved that no matter how long you knew someone, you could never see inside to the person they really were unless they wanted you to. The whole experience had pretty much scared her off dating.

Ever since she'd picked up *Romeo and Juliet,* she'd been thinking about the whole idea of feuding families. Right now her mom and Marcie were pulling together, but Dani knew that would all fall apart if she told anyone about what Evan had done to her. She didn't want to be responsible for her mom losing her best friend. And she liked Marcie, too. She'd been like a second mother. Sometimes Marcie was even easier to talk to than her own mom. She must be dying inside right now.

Because she didn't want to think about any of that, Dani opened her book and started to read. Soon, she was lost in the story and time slipped by.

When her cell phone rang, she was jarred back to reality and noticed that the sun was riding low in the western sky. Digging the phone out of her backpack, she winced when she saw that it was her mom.

"Hey, Mom," she said cheerily. "How are you?"

"I'm fine, but you are in more trouble than you ever dreamed of," her mother responded in her sternest voice. "Where are you?"

"On my way home," Dani said, standing up and shoving stuff into her backpack so it wouldn't be a total lie. She knew instinctively that her mom's mood didn't have anything to do with her being late. Even though she hadn't said it, she was ticked off because Dani had skipped school.

"Ten minutes, young lady."

Dani winced. She'd have to take a cab to make it that fast, but she could tell her mom had run out of patience. "Sure. Ten minutes," she agreed.

As soon as she'd hung up, she called for a taxi and went to wait at the front gate. Fortunately, the cab arrived in five minutes, which gave her about two minutes—give or take—to cover the three miles to the house. If she was lucky, maybe her mom wasn't sitting in the kitchen staring at the clock while she waited.

She had the driver let her out a few houses down the block, then ran the rest of the way home and breezed in the door. Sure enough, her mom was in the kitchen and she glanced at the clock when Dani came in and planted a kiss on her cheek.

"Sorry I'm late," Dani said. "Dinner's not burned or anything, is it?"

Her mother rolled her eyes. "With my cooking, a few minutes more or less won't make that much difference, which you know perfectly well."

"Then what's the big deal?" Dani asked, sitting down at the table, which was set just for the two of them. "Where's Josh?"

"He's eating on campus, then going to the library."

"Yeah, right," Dani scoffed.

Her mother frowned at her. "At least he called."

"I said I was sorry," Dani reminded her.

"So you did," her mother agreed. "But so far you've neglected to mention why you weren't in your last three classes today."

Dani winced. She'd known her mom would find out, though she'd hoped it wouldn't happen quite this fast. The teachers might not report Dani to the principal for skipping, but they would tell her mom. She'd rather take whatever punishment the principal dished out any day over seeing the look of disappointment that was in her mom's eyes right now.

"I didn't feel good," she said, improvising.

"Yet you didn't see the school nurse. I checked."

"It wasn't that bad. Just a headache. I needed to get out and get some air."

"And it never occurred to you to simply get a pass and come to my classroom, so I could give you an excuse? It was easier to play hooky?"

Dani flushed guiltily. "I didn't want the aggravation."

"No, what you didn't want was to take a chance I'd say no and send you back to class," her mother said, her expression unrelenting.

"I suppose."

Instead of looking furious, her mom looked worried, which made Dani feel even worse.

"Sweetie, can't you talk to me? I know this has something to do with Evan and everything that's going on with him. It must be really hard on you to hear what's being said about him."

It was, but not for the reason her mom thought. Dani merely nodded. "It basically sucks."

"The talk will die down," her mother said. "Things will get back to normal soon."

Dani stared at her. "How can they?" she asked incredulously. "He did a terrible thing. He could go to jail."

Her mother gave her an odd look. "If he's convicted, yes. But he might not be."

"How can you say that? The girl accused him. The police have evidence or they wouldn't have arrested him."

"Maybe their case isn't as solid as they've led everyone to believe," her mother said.

"What makes you say that?"

"The detectives were here today."

Dani's heart began to pound so hard her chest hurt. "They were here? Why?"

"Seemed like a fishing expedition. They were asking if I'd ever noticed anything in Evan's behavior suggesting he would be capable of something like this."

"And that's all?" Dani asked, the pressure inside her easing slightly. For a minute she'd been terrified they'd figured out the truth about her and Evan. Caitlyn was the only one who knew, but she might have slipped up. Then, again, why would the police even be talking to her?

Her mom regarded her curiously. "What else could they want?"

Dani forced herself to calm down. "Nothing, I guess. They aren't coming back, are they?"

"They might."

"Why?"

"I honestly don't know," her mother said, sounding annoyed. "I told them that I'd given them everything I knew, but I'm not sure they believed me."

"What was it like?" Dani asked. "You know, being grilled by the cops?"

Her mother's lips twitched. "I wouldn't say they *grilled* me. They asked a lot of questions about Evan and about how often we spent time with him, stuff like that. They were fairly nice about it—at least the woman was. The man was a little intense."

"Good cop, bad cop," Dani concluded.

"What?"

"Like on TV. One cop is all sweet and tries to be your friend, and the other one gets in your face, so you get all rattled and spill stuff."

Her mom laughed. "Well, I didn't know anything to spill, and he annoyed me, so he'd be the last person I'd ever tell anything, even if I did know something."

Dani thought she saw a faint blush on her mom's cheeks. That was interesting. "Was he cute?"

"Who?"

"The detective."

Her mom looked more flustered than ever. "I didn't notice," she said.

Dani grinned. "He was cute. I can tell. And he was into you."

"Oh, for Pete's sake, he was not."

"Was, too. You're blushing."

"I think we've gotten way off track here," her mother said. "You're grounded for a month. School and home, that's it. You'll go with me in the morning and ride home with me in the afternoon."

"But you go in too early and you never leave on time after school," Dani protested. "What am I supposed to do while you go to your meetings or grade papers or whatever?"

"I know it may seem like a novel idea, but you could study," her mother suggested. "No phone privileges, either, by the way. You'll turn over your cell phone when you walk in the door every afternoon."

"Mom!"

"Skipping school is serious, kiddo. We don't do that in this house. You know that."

Dani opened her mouth to argue, then clamped it shut again. If she was grounded, there was less chance she'd slip up and say something she didn't mean to. And she would have a legitimate reason to avoid Caitlyn. Seeing her right now was too uncomfortable. Maybe this was a good thing, after all.

"Whatever," she mumbled, because she knew her mom expected some sort of reaction. "I'm going upstairs to study."

Despite the tension between them, her mom grinned. "Now you're just trying to get back in my good graces."

Dani grinned back. "No, I'm just trying to avoid whatever it is that's burning in the oven."

Her mom dashed across the room and yanked open the oven door. Smoke poured into the kitchen as she pulled what had once been an actual chunk of meat from the oven. She dumped the disaster into the sink, then faced Dani.

"Pizza or Chinese?"

"Kung po chicken," Dani said at once. "Call me when it's here."

"You sure you don't want to stay here and talk to me till it gets here?" her mom asked.

Dani shook her head. "I really do have homework. I'll probably just eat in my room when the food comes."

Her mom frowned at that. "I don't think so."

Dani shrugged. "Whatever."

Before she could make her getaway, her mom suddenly pulled her into a hug.

"I love you. You know that, don't you?"

"Sure."

"No matter what," her mom said, giving her a look that rattled her.

Dani shuddered as she walked away. What if her mom had found out somehow?

No way, she told herself staunchly. If her mom knew what had happened with Evan, she'd confront her. No, she might suspect, but she didn't *know* anything. Only Caitlyn knew and she'd never tell, especially not now when it might land her brother in even more hot water than he was already in.

So, her secret was safe for the moment. She should have been relieved, but oddly, she felt more scared and alone than ever.

9

Marcie had had a pounding headache for two straight days. She'd never been under siege like this before in her life. Ken knew how to handle the media, but she didn't, so she ignored the phone and the doorbell, both of which rang constantly.

Meals, once her favorite time of day, had turned into torture. Evan refused to come to the table or even to look her in the eyes, when he was home at all. Ken was out of the house more than he was home. She and Caitlyn sat in the kitchen making an effort at small talk and trying to avoid the one subject that actually mattered.

Marcie wanted to reassure her daughter, tell her that this would all be over soon and things would get back to normal, but she couldn't. Unless this girl—this *bimbo,* according to Ken—recanted her story, the media attention would go on until there was a trial and Evan was exonerated.

He *had* to be exonerated, she thought, a panicky feeling sweeping through her. Her sweet, handsome boy couldn't possibly have done what they were accusing him of doing. She simply couldn't accept even the possibility that he had. She'd read a graphic description of the girl's injuries, which had left her feeling queasy and disgusted. Whoever had done that to her deserved to go to jail, but it hadn't been Evan, she told herself.

As bad as having the media camped on her doorstep was, as awkward as meals with Caitlyn had become, the worst part of this was the isolation. She hadn't seen Emily for a few days now and their conversations on the phone had been rushed and unsatisfying. She'd returned calls to the handful of friends who'd called to offer support, but those conversations had become awkward once they'd gotten past the pleasantries. She needed to sit down with her best friend and pour out all of the confusing emotions she was dealing with right now.

Across from her at the antique oak kitchen table where they'd started eating to avoid the emptiness of the big, formal dining room, Caitlyn was pushing food around on her plate. Marcie studied her, wondering whether she was really as okay as she claimed to be. She'd been abnormally quiet since this whole mess had started, but she'd refused to discuss her brother or her own emotions.

"Honey, you're not eating. Would you like me to fix you something else?" Marcie had been obsessing about meals, trying to fix Caitlyn's favorites, but nothing seemed to tempt her.

"I'm not hungry," Caitlyn responded.

The words were stunning from a girl who, until recently, had grabbed a handful of cookies the instant she walked in the door after school, then followed that with a full meal only a couple of hours later. She especially loved the old-fashioned comfort foods Marcie prepared from time to time—mac and cheese, meat loaf and mashed potatoes, roasted chicken with dressing—though she had never turned her nose up at the gourmet fare that Ken preferred.

"Don't you feel well?" Marcie asked, regarding her with concern.

Caitlyn gave her an incredulous look. "How can you even ask me that? No, I don't feel well. I'm never going to feel okay again." Her voice rose. "Do you have any idea what the kids at school are saying about Evan? Do you have any idea what kind of stuff they say to me? And you know the worst part? I can't even defend him. I can't even say they're liars, because the cops think he did it and they must know or they wouldn't have arrested him. Besides…" She clamped her mouth shut, biting off whatever she'd been about to add.

"The police make mistakes," Marcie insisted. "The girl could be lying. She has to be. Evan would never do something so…" She searched for the right word. "He would never do anything so degrading, so wrong."

Caitlyn sniffed, her eyes shimmering with unshed tears. She regarded Marcie with an almost pleading expression. "Do you really believe that, Mom?"

"Of course, I do. I have to."

"Why do you have to?" Caitlyn demanded, her voice rising in a sudden burst of anger. "Because you're his mother? Shouldn't moms and dads have to admit the truth, too?"

Marcie stared at her in shock. "Do you believe your brother did this?"

Caitlyn swiped at her tears, her expression defiant.

"Do you?" Marcie persisted.

Caitlyn's expression finally faltered. "He could have," she whispered.

"Why would you say such a thing? He's your brother, Caitlyn."

"That doesn't make him a saint."

"You're just starting to listen to all the gossip," Marcie said. "No wonder your faith in him has been shaken. Maybe I should keep you out of school for a while. I could get your assignments and teach you here. Under the circumstances, I'm sure the school would allow it."

"No!" Caitlyn stared at her with dismay. "That would make me more of a freak than ever."

Marcie backed down at once. "Okay, fine, but can't you at least try to tune out all the talk?" She held up a hand when Caitlyn was about to protest. "I know that's easier said than done, but try. If the subject comes up, just walk away."

"And by the end of the year, I won't have any friends left," Caitlyn said with weary resignation. "What Evan did is all they want to talk about."

"You'll still have Dani," Marcie responded, and thanked God for that.

Caitlyn muttered a response Marcie couldn't hear.

"What was that?" she asked.

"I said she's grounded," Caitlyn replied, though it was evident to Marcie that she was lying about the earlier comment. "She can't even talk on the phone."

"Why on earth is she grounded?" Marcie asked, deciding to focus on that, rather than the sarcasm she'd heard in Caitlyn's tone even when she couldn't decipher the words. Next to Caitlyn, Dani was the most responsible, best-behaved kid she'd ever known.

"She skipped school," Caitlyn said, then cast a defiant look at Marcie. "Who can blame her with everything that's going on, but Mrs. D was really, really ticked."

"Yes, I imagine she was," Marcie said, then gave her daughter a pointed look. "I would be, too, so don't get any ideas."

Caitlyn just stared at her. "Can I go to my room now?"

Marcie wanted to insist that she stay here, that they talk some more about how Caitlyn was feeling and what Marcie could do to make things better, but she knew she wouldn't really have any answers for Caitlyn anyway. "Sure," she said at last. "If you get hungry later, come down and I'll fix you a snack."

Caitlyn rolled her eyes. "Mom, I can fix my own snack."

"But mine are better," Marcie teased, trying to lighten the mood. It killed her to see her daughter this upset and to be unable to do anything to fix it.

Caitlyn's lips twitched in response. "Mine don't involve sugar and chocolate."

Marcie grinned. "Like I said, mine are better."

Her daughter paused in the doorway. "Mom, maybe you should fix a plate of those brownies you baked today and take them over to Mrs. D. You haven't been out of the house in days. Aren't you going stir-crazy?"

Marcie wanted to seize on the suggestion, but she hesitated. "You'll be okay?"

"Mom!"

"Okay, I'll go, but don't answer the door or the phone. Understood?"

"As if," Caitlyn said. "Tell Mrs. D I said hi. And if you see Dani…" She hesitated. "Well, tell her I miss her."

"Will do," Marcie said, though again she had the uneasy feeling that Dani's punishment wasn't the real issue keeping them apart, that there was some sort of rift between the girls.

Five minutes later, she was slipping through the hedge and rapping on Emily's kitchen door. When Emily slid it open, she immediately enveloped Marcie in a hug, almost squishing the plate of brownies.

"I've been thinking about you so much," Emily said. "You doing okay?"

"I'm okay as long as I don't read the papers or turn on the TV or talk to another living soul," Marcie said. "I brought brownies. Do you have any coffee made?"

"Of course. Sit down and I'll pour it." She studied Marcie critically. "Or would you rather have a glass of wine?"

"The chocolate will have the same feel-good effect," Marcie assured her. "Coffee's fine. Will you promise me one thing?"

"Anything."

"For the next hour can we talk about anything and everything except my son?"

"If that's the way you want it, of course we can," Emily said at once. "You know what I've been thinking?"

"What?"

"Maybe this would be the right time to take the girls away somewhere for a couple of days. It would be a good break for all of us."

Marcie immediately brightened. "Really? You could get away?"

"Of course."

"Have you thought about where we could go?"

Emily's expression turned thoughtful. "Disney? Key West? Sanibel? Wherever we want to go."

"Let's go to Sanibel," Marcie said eagerly. "I would kill for a couple of days doing absolutely nothing but walking on the beach and sitting on a balcony at night and listening to the waves crashing on the shore."

As soon as the words were out of her mouth, she frowned. "Is that terribly selfish of me? The girls would probably rather go to Disney where there are things to do every second."

"Let's ask them now," Emily suggested. "Unless you want to talk it over with Ken first."

"He won't care. His entire focus is on Evan these days. He'll be glad to have Caitlyn and me out from underfoot." She regarded Emily curiously. "Is this a good time to go away? I thought Dani was grounded. Caitlyn mentioned it."

Emily shot her a rueful look. "I think I can make an exception for something like this and it's not as if she'll be without supervision. Of course, she might view a weekend on Sanibel with nothing to do as extreme punishment." A glint appeared in her eyes. "In fact, let's just plan that. This trip is about us as much as it is about the girls, right? We deserve some real R & R."

"Will Josh be okay here?"

"He's in college. I'm just an annoying nuisance who forces him to check in from time to time and keeps the refrigerator stocked so snacks are readily available. He'll be ecstatic to have the house to himself." She grinned. "And I'll remind Derek to check on him about a million times. That ought to keep him from doing anything too outrageous."

"You really do have a diabolical streak, don't you?"

Emily looked surprisingly pleased by the comment. "I never thought about it. Maybe I do."

"So we're definitely on for this weekend?" Marcie asked.

"If we can get reservations, yes."

"I'll get on it as soon as I get home," Marcie promised.

"Or we could go on the Internet right now."

"No, please, let me handle it. It'll give me a project

for tonight while I'm waiting for Ken to get home." She checked her watch. "I'd better get back over there. I left Caitlyn alone. She promised not to answer the phone or the door, but the reporters can be awfully persistent."

"The attention will die down soon," Emily reassured her.

Marcie sighed. "I doubt it, but thanks for offering me some hope. I'll be in touch about the weekend." She grinned. "And as soon as we're all set, I'll start cooking. We won't have to do a thing once we get there except chill out."

"Sounds perfect. I'll stock up on our favorite wine and sodas for the girls."

At the back door, Marcie hesitated. "Thanks for sticking by me," she said, her voice thick with emotion. "You have no idea what it means to me. This is the worst…I just never imagined…" Her voice broke.

Emily crossed the kitchen to hug her. "I know," she said gently. "I know how I'd feel if I were in your place. I'd want my best friend in my corner and you'd be there."

"I would be," Marcie said, even as tears filled her eyes and spilled down her cheeks. Determined not to fall completely apart for fear she'd never pull herself together again, she backed away. "Sorry. Let me get out of here before the flood gates open and I drown you in tears."

"It would be okay," Emily said quietly.

"I know, and just knowing it makes me feel better. I'll call you later."

She ran across the yard, her mood improved by at least a hundred percent. For a little while, her problems had faded into the background and the prospect of a few days away had given her something to look forward to.

Maybe she'd get through this terrible time, after all. If she did, Emily would be a huge part of the reason why.

"Thanks for giving me a heads-up about Dani yesterday," Emily told Paula when she arrived at school the next morning.

"Did you find out where she went when she skipped classes?"

Emily stared at her blankly, then slowly shook her head. "What is wrong with me? Obviously I was so rattled by being questioned by the police that it never occurred to me to ask where she'd been. I was just relieved to have her back home."

Paula's eyes widened. "The police questioned you? When did that happen? What did they want to know?"

Emily was about to respond when the door to the teacher's lounge opened and the very people in question stepped inside.

"Mrs. Dobbs," Detective Rodriguez said politely. "Nice to see you again."

Emily scowled. "I wish I could say the same. I have nothing more to say to you, Detective."

His lips twitched, which showed off a surprising dimple in his cheek. With his olive complexion, dark hair and brown eyes, he was the epitome of someone's idea of a sexy Latin. Not hers, though. Definitely not hers, she thought even as her stomach did a traitorous little flip.

"Then it's a good thing I'm not here to speak with you, isn't it?" he said mildly.

Taken aback, Emily tried to cover her surprise by turning to pour herself a cup of coffee from the pot that was kept filled all day long. Her hand shook so badly she spilled more than she got in the cup.

"Are you Paula Mason?" Detective Lansing asked. "Could we have a few minutes of your time?"

"Of course," Paula said.

"I'll be going, then," Emily said, trying to edge past the two detectives, who were still blocking the doorway.

Detective Lansing stepped aside, but Detective Rodriguez stood there like a statue, a frown carved on his face. He waited until she finally risked looking directly into his eyes.

"We'll stop by your classroom before we leave," he said. "I wouldn't want you to feel neglected."

"Believe me, I could happily go for years without ever seeing you again," she said.

"Now that hurts," he replied with feigned dismay.

She forced a smile. "Good. Paula, I'll speak to you later."

Paula gave her an odd look, then nodded. "Later."

Emily waited till she reached her classroom before she released a heartfelt sigh of relief. She wasn't sure why she let Detective Rodriguez get under her skin so badly. The man was just doing his job. Sure, he was trying to convict a boy she thought of as a son, but her reaction went deeper than that. He made her nervous, the way a man made a woman nervous when he was blatantly interested, but that was absurd. Detective Rodriguez wasn't interested in her in that way. He was pursuing a lead, nothing more. She needed to keep reminding herself of that.

After all, a guy that good-looking probably had a wife and kids at home. And he was teamed up with a partner who was no slouch in the looks department. Detective Lansing could easily have modeled for some swimsuit calendar featuring female cops. As if that weren't intimidating in its own way, she had kind eyes, too, which was more than Emily could say for Rodriguez. He had penetrating dark brown eyes that saw too much.

God, what was wrong with her? Why was she thinking about the man's eyes? Why was she thinking about him at all? Obviously she'd gone too many months without sex. Without a man in her life at all, for that matter.

A bell rang and suddenly her room was filled with chattering students, which finally distracted her from her disconcerting thoughts. When a second bell rang, she forced a smile.

"Good morning. Has everyone finished reading *Moby Dick?* Shall we talk about Melville's theme?" she asked her advance placement students. These were the honor roll kids, the best of the best, which made it her favorite class of the day.

Marty Jacobs, the class clown, waved his hand in the air. "It was a whale of a good story," he joked.

Emily grinned despite herself. "Very insightful," she commented. "Anyone have anything more illuminating to offer?"

To her delight, several of the students had actually done more than read a summary of the book online. The discussion that ensued was lively enough to fill the entire hour and to keep her mind off the man just down the hall who was diligently trying to lock away her best friend's son.

Her next class, unfortunately, was less diverting. Just when she was ready to scream in frustration or order them all to get out the book and actually read it aloud right here and now, her classroom door opened and Detective Rodriguez beckoned to her. For once, she was actually grateful to see him.

"Open your books and read chapter one," she instructed her students. "We'll start with that when I get back."

She stepped into the hallway. "I'm in the middle of class," she informed Detective Rodriguez. "Can't this wait?"

"Will there ever be a really good time?" he inquired.

"Probably not," she conceded. "But I do get paid to fill young minds with knowledge, not to chat with the police."

"Didn't sound to me as if those young minds were all that interested in learning anything," he commented.

She sighed. "They're not, but that doesn't mean I don't have to try. Just tell me what you want so I can get back in there."

"To be honest, we're a little frustrated," Detective Lansing confided. "All the teachers we've spoken to claim that Evan Carter was a perfect student, a perfect gentleman."

"Maybe they've said that because it was true," Emily said impatiently. "Evan was always a good kid."

"No teenager is perfect," Detective Rodriguez said. "It goes against nature. Take your son, for instance."

"Josh?"

He nodded. "You'd be biased in his favor, right?"

"Of course."

"Can you tell me in all honesty that he's never made a mistake, gotten into mischief, done anything to make you want to throttle him?"

Emily was about to say just that, but she couldn't bring herself to utter the lie. "He's never done anything criminal," she said, "but yes, he's made his share of mistakes."

"And Evan Carter?" he said. "There's not one time in all the years you've known him when he's been anything less than perfect?"

"Nothing I could point a finger to and say that's where he went wrong," she insisted.

"You're either lying or wearing rose-colored glasses," he said, not even trying to hide his impatience. "I can't believe the mother of a daughter would sympathize with a guy capable of doing what the Carter kid did to this young woman."

Emily knew he was trying to push her into reacting, hoping she'd say something condemning, but she refused to fall into the trap. "*If* he did it, I would be disillusioned and angry, but you're asking me if I've ever seen any sign that he's capable of doing such a thing and I'm telling you, for probably the tenth time, that I haven't. You can ask me a hundred more times, and I'll tell you the exact same thing."

He sighed. "You keep count and let me know when we break the hundred mark," he said. "Maybe then I'll have worn you down enough that you'll finally tell me the whole truth."

He turned and walked away.

"Dammit, I am telling you the truth," she shouted after him.

He merely waved, but Detective Lansing gave her a sympathetic smile. "Don't mind him. He takes these cases personally. It makes him a great cop, but it's a little hard on people he thinks are holding back."

"But I'm not," Emily said in frustration.

"You don't *think* you are," Naomi Lansing said. "See you, Mrs. Dobbs."

Rattled by the suggestion that she might be inadvertently lying to the police and even to herself, Emily stared after the two of them as they exited the building. Why wouldn't they believe that she was being as candid with them as she possibly could be? She might be a reluctant source, but she was being truthful. Wasn't she?

She thought of Derek's belief that Evan was starting to take after his father and her own observations along that line. She hadn't mentioned any of that, and she wouldn't. She'd persuaded herself that it wasn't really relevant. To be honest, she suspected Detective Rodriguez would disagree.

Before she could think too long or hard about what her silence implied, she heard a commotion in her classroom and opened the door to find that chaos had ensued in her absence. Sucking in a deep breath, she walked into the room and shouted for silence.

The quiet that followed was rewarding, but it was only a tiny victory. Still, on a day like today, she'd take it.

Grady was in a foul mood as he and Naomi left the school. He knew that the teachers he'd spoken to knew more than they'd said. He just wasn't asking the right questions.

"Stop beating yourself up," Naomi said, regarding him with sympathy. "You know it's possible that none of them are lying. Evan might be the kind of kid who's capable of putting on a great show in front of adults. This crime is something that happens in secret and involves kids his own age. They're the ones we need to speak with. And when we do, we'll put the pieces together to lock him up. Even if there's no one other incident we can point to, the forensics alone in this case ought to be enough."

"Possibly, but you know how it goes in court. A good defense attorney can rattle Lauren, make her seem like a less than reliable witness. Evan will claim it was all consensual, that she likes it a little rough. I want that pattern, Naomi," Grady said. "I know there are other women out there. But how the hell are we supposed to find them, if everyone keeps looking at us as the enemy?"

"Everyone, or Emily Dobbs?" Naomi asked. "You seem a little obsessed with her. Are you sure it's all about her connection to the case? Or is it personal?"

He frowned at her. "She's a witness."

"I haven't seen you let a lot of witnesses rile you up the way she obviously does."

Grady knew Naomi was right. He could lie and say it was all about Evan Carter's case, but there was more to it. Something about Emily Dobbs got to him. Under the circumstances, though, it was best if he ignored the attraction.

"I don't have time to think about anything except getting this kid convicted," he told Naomi.

"Then let's forget the school for now," she suggested. "Maybe we can find Josh Dobbs on campus if we head up to UM."

Grady was too frustrated to seize on the suggestion. "There are thousands of kids on that campus. How are we supposed to pick him out?"

"Oh, ye of little faith," she mocked. "Give me ten minutes in front of a computer, fifteen tops, and I'll bet I can find his class schedule. Then we plant ourselves outside of his classroom and wait."

"How much time do you spend on that computer of yours anyway? And what the hell ever happened to privacy?"

"I spend enough time on it to be intimately acquainted with what it can and can't tell me," she said. "If you weren't a technophobe, I could teach you."

"Old-fashioned legwork has always been good enough for me," he grumbled.

"Which is why we're a good team. I understand that we're no longer in the Dark Ages and you have the persistence of a pitbull."

"You get that kid's class schedule and I'll buy lunch," he promised. "We can even go to that vegetarian place you like. I'll suck it up and order a soy burger."

She regarded him with justifiable astonishment. "You swore the last time I dragged you there that you would never, ever eat anything that disgusting again."

Grady grinned at her. "Which should prove the depths of my gratitude if you get that schedule."

"I'm on it," she said as they pulled into the lot beside the station. "Give me ten minutes. You coming in?"

"Nah. I'll wait here."

She regarded him suspiciously. "Here? In the parking lot?"

"That's what I said, isn't it?"

"You sure you're not planning to bolt down the street for a corned beef on rye from John Martin's the second my back is turned?"

"Never even crossed my mind," he declared innocently. Now, a burger and fries from McDonald's he could grab and finish before she ever knew he was gone.

10

Walking into the building where Josh Dobbs was taking a class in political science snapped Grady right back to his own college days. It hadn't been the best time in his life, at least not at first. He'd gone to school filled with simmering resentment. He'd wanted to go straight to the police academy, but his dad had insisted he needed a college degree if he ever hoped to advance beyond being a patrolman. He could still hear his old man.

"A good education is never wasted, son. If you don't listen to me for once, you'll live to regret it. Don't let that stubborn determination of yours to defy me at every turn make you let this opportunity slip away."

Eventually Grady had let himself be persuaded, mainly because his uncle, a career police officer and the man he really looked up to, agreed with his dad for practically the first time in Grady's memory. The two sons of Cuban immigrants—one an overachieving, by-the-book engineer, the other a jovial, dedicated street cop with no driving ambition—rarely agreed on anything, so it was worth taking note when they did.

Grady's first semester at community college had been flat-out awful, filled with classes he was convinced were a waste of time. By the second semester, when he was finally able to take a course in criminal psychology, he finally started getting the value of being in school.

And then he'd met the woman who would become his wife. Kathleen Donovan, with her red hair and flawless complexion, could have stepped into a pub in Dublin and been right at home. She had the friendly effervescence that Grady lacked. All it took to brighten his mood was the sight of her smile. And Kathleen was always smiling, right up until the day the smile was wiped from her face forever. Knowing he'd done that would haunt him through eternity.

But for a few years there, they'd been good together, their Irish and Cuban backgrounds blending surprisingly well. Both came from large, boisterous, Catholic families, and if one side spoke Spanish at home, well, they figured it would be great for their children to be bilingual.

His mother had embraced Kathleen as the daughter she'd always wanted in a houseful of boys. Even his father had adored her. Marrying her was the first thing Grady had done of which Miguel Rodriguez totally approved. When things had gone so tragically wrong, they'd taken her side over his. Not that he blamed them, but it had hurt just the same.

"Hey, where'd you go just then?" Naomi asked, digging an elbow into his ribs.

"Long ago and far away," he said. "How much longer till class gets out?"

"Five minutes," she told him.

"We don't even know if he's in there," Grady groused. "We could be wasting our time."

She gave him an odd look. "You have any other leads we could be pursuing?"

"No."

"Then let's just see where this one takes us." She gave him a long, considering look. "And wherever you went a minute ago, don't go there again."

Grady sighed. If only that were possible...

Ten years earlier

Grady had been on duty for nearly twenty-four straight hours. He'd taken a double shift to bring in some extra cash so he could buy Kathleen a new car. Hers was being held together by wishes and paper clips, or darn close to it. It had broken down half-a-dozen times in the past month and the repairs were getting more and more expensive. It didn't make sense to patch it back together one more time.

She needed something solid and reliable. She had a forty-five-minute commute to work every morning and she was out of the house before dawn. He didn't want her on the road at that hour in a car she couldn't count on.

Unfortunately, they'd depleted their savings to make the down payment on their first house. It had the pool that Kathleen, an ex college swimmer, had wanted. They'd probably overextended themselves to get it, but Grady knew she'd given up a lot when she chose him over some of the MBA guys who were destined to make a fortune in stocks and bonds or in their climb up the corporate ladder.

Between the need for cash and his willingness to take on extra shifts because he loved the adrenaline rush of being on the job, Grady worked too much. Kathleen had started complaining about it lately, but he'd rationalized his workaholic tendencies by citing her need for a new car.

When he'd crawled into bed this morning, exhausted down to his bones, she'd nudged him back awake.

"Don't forget you're picking Megan up from school

today," she reminded him. "It's a half day, so you need to be there at noon."

Grady groaned. Their six-year-old was a handful on her best days. He adored her with every fiber of his being, but she could get on his last nerve quicker than anyone he knew. Then she'd crawl into his lap and give him a smile that he swore turned on the sun.

"Why isn't she going to the sitter's?"

"Because Becky's having a root canal done. Remember, we talked about this, Grady," she said, her tone impatient. "I offered to call your mom, but you said you wanted to spend the afternoon with Megan."

He had a vague recollection of the conversation. "Right. Noon. I'll be there."

"And don't take her for a burger and fries for lunch," Kathleen warned him. "I've left tuna fish for both of you."

"Oh, goody," he said, making a face.

"It's good for you."

He pulled her down beside him and planted a lingering kiss on her lips, then said, "Which is why Megan thinks I'm the fun parent."

"I can live with that," Kathleen said. "Get some sleep, sweetie. I'll be home by six-thirty."

"You work too hard."

"So do you, but it's all for our future. Love you."

"Love you, too," he murmured, his head already buried under the pillow.

He woke at eleven thirty, but only because Kathleen had been wise enough to set two alarms, one beside the bed, the other across the room. They jarred him out of a sound sleep and had him cursing as he stumbled to shut off the particularly shrill alarm she'd placed out of reach.

A half hour later he was sitting in front of the school

waiting for his daughter. When she bounded down the sidewalk and saw him behind the wheel her eyes lit up.

"Daddy, I forgot you were getting me today! Can we go for ice cream?"

Grady grinned. Obviously he'd carried the indulgence thing a little too far. Then he thought of the tuna fish waiting at home.

"How about pizza instead?" Kathleen hadn't said anything about pizza, had she? So it wasn't like he was breaking his word.

"I *love* pizza!" Megan declared, her dark auburn braids bouncing. She had her mother's creamy complexion and green eyes, but her hair was a combination of his brown and Kathleen's red.

Grady grinned at her. "Me, too." When she was settled into her car seat in the back, he glanced at her in the rearview mirror. "How was school today? Did you learn anything exciting?"

"Ricky Johnson said a bad word and the teacher gave him a time-out."

"Now, that *is* exciting," Grady said. He decided against asking what the offending word had been. "But I was wondering more about arithmetic or spelling, something like that."

Megan frowned. "The teacher wrote some stuff on the board, but I already knew it."

"Really?"

"I could spell cat and dog a long time ago," she said with pride. "Mommy taught me."

"What about me? Have I ever taught you anything useful?"

She giggled. "You taught me to tie my shoes and to burp."

Grady grinned. "Well, at least one of those is useful."

Megan's smile faltered. "Mommy says ladies don't burp."

"That's true, but you have years and years before you have to worry about what a proper young lady should or shouldn't do. But believe me, when the time comes, Mommy is the one to listen to about things like that."

"Daddy?"

"Hmm?"

"Can we have ice cream after we have pizza?"

"Let's see if you have room for it," he said, not ruling it out.

"I'll have lots and lots of room," Megan assured him.

"Then we will definitely fill it up with ice cream," Grady told her.

"I love you, Daddy."

"You, too, *niña*."

She and her mom were his reasons for being.

Present

Students were spilling into the hallway. Grady had his eyes peeled for Josh Dobbs, hoping he'd recognize him after that one brief glimpse of his picture when they'd interviewed Emily Dobbs. Naomi was watching intently as well.

Just when he was convinced that the last student was gone and they'd wasted the trip to campus, he spotted the young man. He looked more like his mother than Grady had noticed in the photo. And in a happy coincidence, he was deep in conversation with Jenny Ryan, Lauren's roommate.

He and Naomi exchanged a look. She nodded in unspoken understanding and stepped into the couple's path.

"Jenny, I'm sorry to interrupt, but could I have a word with you?" Naomi asked.

Jenny's attention shifted from Josh Dobbs to Naomi and her expression faltered. "Detective Lansing, is everything okay? Lauren hasn't withdrawn the charges, has she?"

"As far as I know, she's sticking by her statement, but I thought we could talk about how you could make sure that doesn't change."

"Sure, no problem." She looked at Josh. "You don't mind, do you, Josh? This is important."

The boy had been watching the scene in wary silence, but he nodded. "No, go ahead. I'll catch up with you later."

Grady watched Naomi and Jenny walk outside and head for a nearby bench in a grassy area beneath some towering royal palm trees. Josh stood staring after them.

As Grady approached, the kid seemed to stiffen, as if sensing that Grady was with Naomi, even though they hadn't exchanged a word in his presence.

"Josh Dobbs?" Grady asked.

Alarm flared in his eyes. "Yes."

"I'm Detective Rodriguez. Could I have a few minutes of your time?"

The kid frowned. "You're the same cop who came to the house to talk to my mom, aren't you?"

Grady nodded.

"She told me about you."

"I'm sure she was filled with glowing praise," Grady said wryly.

Josh grinned. "Not so much, to be honest with you. Why do you want to talk to me?"

"Because I imagine you have a very different perspective on what's going on than your mother might have."

"My mom's pretty smart. She's around kids all the time. I think she knows how to read them."

"Probably so, unless they're intent on hiding their behavior."

"I suppose."

"Was it like that with Evan Carter?"

In an instant Josh's open demeanor shut down and he gave Grady the same kind of defiant look his mother had. "I don't know what you mean."

Grady grinned at his attempt at evasiveness. "Oh, I think you do. You're a straight-A student. Your mom bragged about that. I think you can follow my line of thinking. Does Evan Carter have a side that he doesn't let most adults see, especially your mother or his parents?"

The kid looked torn. Grady just waited as he struggled to decide between honesty and loyalty.

"Look, I really don't think I'm the one you ought to be talking to," Josh said.

"Why is that?"

"Evan and I have been friends since we were kids."

"So you're loyal. I get that. But loyalty should only go so far. Evan's committed a crime. And what about Lauren? Since you obviously know Jenny, I'm sure she's told you how tough things are for her roommate right now."

Josh looked even more distressed.

Grady pressed harder. "I'll ask you again, is Evan always the clean-cut, all-American kid that everyone thinks he is?"

"Look, I know what you're really asking me," Josh

admitted finally. "You want to know if I ever saw him mistreat a woman. The answer is no, not physically, anyway."

Grady seized on the loophole he'd left. "Verbally?"

Josh nodded with obvious reluctance. "But he didn't hide that from his folks. He treated his mom the same way. My parents would have grounded me for a year if I'd said some of the stuff to my mom that Evan said to his on a regular basis." He regarded Grady earnestly. "It's because of his dad. Mr. Carter talks to his wife the same way, like she doesn't have a brain in her head. It's like she's his personal slave or something, not a woman he's supposed to love and respect."

Grady heard the disgust in the boy's voice and thought to himself that Emily Dobbs and her ex-husband had done a good job with him.

"And you heard Evan speak with the same disrespect to women he was seeing?" Grady asked.

Josh nodded. "I tried to talk to him about it, but he just blew me off as if I was some kind of jerk for thinking it was wrong. I kept thinking that word would spread and women would start refusing to go out with him, but I miscalculated about the jock factor. He was a big man on campus and he knew it. A lot of girls will put up with just about anything if the guy is some big wheel."

"Did you ever have the sense that it went beyond verbal abuse, that he might get physically abusive behind closed doors?"

"It wouldn't surprise me," Josh admitted, "but we didn't double-date a lot. It was bad enough listening to him brag about all his conquests the morning after. To tell you the truth, that was one of the reasons we haven't been as close for the past year. I didn't much like being around him."

"You ever heard any complaints from women he'd been out with, any hints that he'd pushed too hard for sex?"

He shook his head. "Like I said, he's a star athlete. A lot of girls are so thrilled that he's paying attention to them at all, they'll just go along with whatever he wants. To be honest, I was surprised that he even asked Lauren out. She's not a groupie. She didn't hang all over him."

"Maybe that made her a challenge," Grady suggested.

"I suppose." Josh met his gaze. "I feel really bad about what happened to her. She's a nice girl. I just wish I'd warned her, you know."

"This isn't your fault," Grady assured him. He glanced toward the bench where Naomi and Jenny were still talking. "You dating Jenny?"

He shook his head. "I didn't really know her till the other day. We have this class together, but I didn't even know she was Lauren's roommate till she came up to me after all this started. She got right up in my face," he said with admiration. "She wanted to know where I stood, if I believed Lauren or if I was going to stand by Evan. She'd apparently found out we went way back."

"What did you tell her?"

He hesitated for a long time, apparently struggling once again with friendship over integrity. "That I wouldn't jump on the bandwagon to take Evan down, because I wasn't there that night, but that I didn't doubt Lauren's word, either."

"I admire your loyalty," Grady told him. "I just hope it's not misplaced."

"Me, too," Josh said.

"Thanks for talking to me." Grady handed him a card. "If you think of anything else or if you run across any of the girls Evan's been out with who are suddenly remembering that he mistreated them the same way, let me know, okay? Or just pass along my number."

"I will," Josh said.

Grady had started to walk away, when Josh called after him.

"Detective, did my mom mention anything to you about my sister?"

Grady froze in place. "Such as?"

"For a long time, she had a crush on Evan. None of us think it went any further than that, but with all that's happened, we're worried about her. Or at least I am. Dani did her best to keep our folks from guessing just how crazy she was about him, but I knew. I even told her to back off, but I'm not a hundred percent certain she did."

"You don't think your mom has talked to her about this?"

"About what happened to Lauren, sure, but not about whether he'd ever done anything to Dani. I think Mom's almost scared to find out the answer."

"Why?"

"Because she'd feel awful if Dani had gone through something like that and she hadn't even known about it, I guess." He gave him a rueful look. "And because she knows my dad and I would beat the crap out of Evan, if he'd ever touched Dani."

"I'm not the person you should be saying that to," Grady advised him. "But, believe me, I understand the sentiment." He wished he knew what to tell Josh. It wasn't his place to suggest he take matters into his own hands and talk to his sister. Emily Dobbs would probably resent the hell out of him if he did. And rightfully so.

Still, this was another indication that Dani Dobbs might be important to this case. He needed to speak to her, but her mother wasn't going to permit that unless he had enough evidence to convince her—or a judge—that the interview was necessary. He doubted that Josh's concern for his sister would take things to the right level of urgency.

"Keep an eye on your sister," he finally said. "If anything leads you to believe that something inappropriate did go on between her and Evan Carter, tell your parents or tell me."

"Dani won't tell me anything," Josh confessed. "I warned her away from him, so she's not going to want to risk hearing I-told-you-so from me."

Grady grinned at the admission. "If the opportunity arises, you could make it clear that you won't say that, no matter what."

Josh shook his head. "She won't believe me. I *always* say I told you so when she ignores my advice and messes up."

"I have a couple of kid brothers, so I understand the dilemma. Still, when it's this important, I think you could probably convince her that you're willing to break the pattern. And it is important, Josh. You know that. If Evan did hurt her, she has to be struggling with a lot of conflicting emotions, especially with all the publicity about what he did to Lauren. She may even feel guilty for not speaking up and maybe preventing this."

"I know you're right. I'll see what I can do. Thanks, Detective."

"Anytime."

"You think the other detective is through talking to Jenny by now?"

Grady nodded.

"Then maybe I'll go ask if she wants to grab some

coffee. Maybe she can give me some advice about what to say to Dani. Women are an enigma, you know what I mean? Even sisters."

"Believe me, I do," Grady said. He almost regretted not being able to ask the kid for a few tips on how to win over his mother, but that would be inappropriate...and pretty darn pitiful, when it came right down to it.

There was a message from Marcie waiting when Emily got home from school that afternoon.

"We're set for Sanibel," she said. "A two-bedroom suite right on the beach. It sounds heavenly. Let me know what time you think we can get away on Friday."

Beside Emily, Dani stood frozen. "You and Marcie are going away?"

"The four of us are going away," Emily said. "Marcie and Caitlyn and you and me."

Dani stared at her in dismay. "No way."

Emily frowned. "I thought you'd be pleased about getting out of the house for a couple of days."

"Not with them," Dani said heatedly, dumping her books on the kitchen table and storming from the room.

"Danielle Dobbs, get back here right this minute," Emily shouted after her.

In response, she heard her daughter's footsteps thundering up the stairs, followed by the slamming of her bedroom door.

This was not the reaction she'd been anticipating. Dani was usually eager to go anywhere at anytime. She and Caitlyn had always loved the mother-daughter trips the best. The four of them read books, played cards, pigged out and laughed till the wee hours of the morning.

Filled with an odd sense of trepidation, Emily slowly

climbed the stairs and went to her daughter's room. She tapped on the door, then opened it without waiting for a response, grateful that she and Derek had removed the locks years ago when Josh was small and Dani still an infant. Josh had accidentally locked himself in a bathroom and had screamed for a solid hour before they could get him out. The locks had come off that day. Later, when there had been grumbling about privacy, they'd turned a deaf ear to it.

"I didn't tell you to come in," Dani said, regarding her with a long-suffering look.

"I decided not to take a chance," Emily told her, crossing the room to sit beside her on the edge of the bed. "Want to tell me why you don't want to go away with Marcie and Caitlyn?"

For a minute, she didn't think Dani would answer, but Dani finally lifted her head, evidently troubled.

"Because all they'll want to talk about is Evan and what's going on with him and how unfair it all is."

"Actually I think that's the very last thing they're going to want to talk about," Emily reassured her. "The whole point of getting away is to think about something else for a few days."

"It won't happen that way," Dani insisted, her jaw set stubbornly. "You know it won't."

"Okay, let's say the subject does come up, don't you think that as their friends we should be willing to let them vent, if they need to?"

Dani scowled at her. "Why do you always have to be so fair?"

She said it as if being fair were the worst sort of crime.

Emily grinned, though she could see that Dani was in no mood for humor. "It's a good trait," she suggested.

"But I don't want to listen to them defending him," Dani said.

Emily's expression sobered. "I thought you'd be one of the first to jump to Evan's defense."

"Well, I'm not."

Emily knew she needed to word her next question very carefully. If she made too big a deal about Dani's response, she'd clam up. "Any particular reason?" she asked eventually.

Dani stared at the floor.

"Sweetie, is there some specific reason you don't want to talk about Evan?"

"I just don't, okay?" She gave Emily a pleading look. "Can't we just let it go at that?"

Emily didn't think they should. She tried one more time. "You know you can talk to me about anything, right? I've always told you that, and I meant it."

"There's nothing to talk about," Dani said, her expression shutting down. "If you want to go on a trip with Marcie and Caitlyn, go. I don't care. I'll stay with Dad."

"No, that's not the solution. Caitlyn needs your support as much as Marcie needs mine. You two have always been best friends and best friends stick by each other in a crisis." She gave Dani a hard look. "Unless there's some very compelling reason not to."

Dani leveled a tear-filled look at her mother. "You're not hearing me, Mom. I won't go. Period. I don't have to give you a reason."

Emily's stomach tied itself into knots. Dreading the answer, she said, "Yes, actually you do. If you'll tell me why you feel so strongly about this, I'll let you stay home with your father."

"I can't explain," Dani insisted.

"Can't or won't?"

Dani heaved a sigh. "Does it matter?"

"I think maybe it does," Emily said gently. "Talk to me, sweetie. Please."

She waited, but Dani only shook her head, looking miserable.

"Okay, I'll go on the stupid trip," Dani said grudgingly. "But I'm hanging out on the beach by myself."

Emily wanted to scream that the trip was no longer the point, that what mattered was whatever Dani was keeping bottled up inside, but she let it go. Badgering her would only create more resentment. It wouldn't get to the bottom of things.

Resisting the urge to sigh, she stood up. "I'll go call Marcie and tell her we'll be ready to leave right after school on Friday. It's only a half-day session, so we should be able to get on the road by one."

"Whatever," Dani mumbled, burying her face in a pillow. "Go away. I'm tired."

"You have homework," Emily reminded her.

"Have I ever once not done my homework?" Dani demanded. "You don't have to bug me about that, too."

This time, Emily did sigh as she closed her daughter's door behind her. This trip might not be starting off the way she'd envisioned, but she couldn't help thinking it was a good thing they were getting out of town. She and her daughter really needed some bonding time. Maybe then Dani would finally open up about whatever was troubling her regarding Evan. And even if Emily wasn't one bit sure she wanted to know the answer, she knew she needed to insist on getting it.

11

Emily had barely made it back downstairs, her thoughts still troubled by her conversation with Dani, when the doorbell rang. Since she was on her way past it, she opened the door without thinking. Detective Rodriguez was on her doorstep, alone.

"Detective," she said warily. "I thought we'd established that I have nothing more to say to you."

He gave her an unrepentant grin. "Had we? I seem to recall that I have at least ninety-eight more chances to annoy you before you finally cough up everything you know about Evan Carter." His grin spread. "Ninety-seven after we finish talking this evening."

"You won't go away if I just ask nicely, will you?" she inquired, unable to keep a wistful note from her voice.

"I'd rather not," he said. "How about a cup of coffee? Or some iced tea? Maybe a little friendly conversation? There's no harm in that, is there?"

"If I thought I could get you out of here simply by giving you something to drink and sharing a little small talk about the weather, I'd do it in a heartbeat," she told him.

"Well, then, that seems like a good way to start," he said cheerfully. "Ten minutes, fifteen if we discover we have something in common."

She gave him a wry look. "You mean beyond me telling you if Evan has a birthmark or is allergic to dairy?"

"Yeah, beyond that."

She stood aside. "Fine. Ten minutes. The kitchen is this way. Don't expect homemade cake with your coffee. I leave all the baking to Marcie."

"Evan's mother?" he said.

"Yes."

"You two are close, right?"

He pulled out a chair and sat at the kitchen table, looking too masculine for the cheery red decor with its ruffled curtains at the window over the sink and matching tablecloth splashed with a strawberry design. As she handed him his cup of coffee and sat down opposite him with her iced tea, Emily wondered why she'd never noticed the same stark contrast when Derek had been living here.

Maybe it was because Detective Rodriguez looked a little rough around the edges with the faint scar over his right eye, his dark brown hair a little long as if he'd simply forgotten to have it trimmed, and that sexy shadow of a beard that some men could pull off, though she had a feeling again that it wasn't intentional with him. His clothes—a pin-striped dress shirt and Dockers—which had most likely started the day neatly creased and pressed—had wilted in the Miami humidity. He'd stripped off his usual tie at some point and his collar was open. She had a feeling he'd be more comfortable—and even sexier—in jeans and a T-shirt.

"Have you always been a teacher?" he asked, surprising her.

"In terms of a profession, yes. I took some time off when the kids were small, but as soon as Dani started school, I went back to it."

"Must be tough these days."

Emily nodded. "Some classes are more rewarding than others, but I don't mind a good challenge. If I can get a few kids excited about literature or writing, it makes the rest bearable."

"Was Evan Carter one of the good students?"

She smiled. "I knew we couldn't go the whole ten minutes without his name coming up."

He shrugged. "It's my job to find answers."

"I don't have any." He leveled a doubting look into her eyes that made her want to squirm. "I don't," she insisted.

In an attempt to change the subject, she said, "What made you want to be a detective?"

"My favorite uncle, who came here as a child from Cuba, is a cop. I grew up listening to his stories and admired his dedication."

"What about your dad? You didn't want to follow in his footsteps?"

He gave her a rueful look. "My dad is an engineer. He was already in college, well on the way to his degree, when they fled. He was so single-minded about mastering English and finishing his education that he didn't have time to sit around and chat with my brothers and me." He grinned. "Do you know anything about engineers?"

"Not really."

"They're very good at building bridges or high rises,

but not so great with communication. Unless he was telling us to be quiet or disciplining us for misbehaving, he hardly knew we were around."

Emily studied him curiously. "Just how bad were you in an attempt to get his attention?"

He looked surprised that she'd guessed that. "Pretty bad. Nothing criminal, just nonstop mischief. It was my uncle, not my dad, who sat me down and told me that if my behavior escalated much further I was going to be crossing a dangerous line and he wouldn't be able to protect me. I respected him for that, for not being willing to bend any rules for me."

"And so you chose him to be your mentor," Emily said.

"Something like that. He was happy being a street cop, intervening with other troubled kids like me. He focused on crime prevention in our neighborhood. Me, I wanted to solve the big crimes. I like the puzzle, putting the bad guys behind bars."

"Evan Carter's not one of the bad guys," Emily said impulsively.

Detective Rodriguez regarded her with a disappointed expression. "If you spoke with his victim, I doubt you'd say that."

She didn't even try to hide her exasperation. "You've been saying all along that you want my impressions of him. Now that I've given you one based on having him in and out of my home for ten years or so, you've dismissed it. That's not a very unbiased attitude, Detective."

"Because I have hard evidence that contradicts your feelings," he said. "And your son thinks his sister might have a different experience with him, as well."

That one, simple sentence contained enough distressing information to stir her temper. She clenched her glass of iced tea so tightly she was surprised it didn't shatter. Putting aside his speculation about Dani, she focused on the fact that he'd made contact with her son.

"You spoke to Josh? When?"

"Earlier this afternoon. I ran into him on campus."

She didn't even try to hide her skepticism that the meeting had been as innocent as he seemed to be suggesting. "It wasn't an accident, I'm sure."

"No, Detective Lansing and I went looking for him." Again, his gaze locked with hers. "He's worried about his sister. What about you? Are you concerned about your daughter?"

Troubled by his persistence, especially after her own disturbing conversation with Dani earlier, she hedged. "I'm concerned about both of my kids. What mother isn't?"

He gave her a chiding look. "Come on, Emily. We both know what's at stake here. Do you think your daughter might have had any sort of inappropriate sexual encounter with Evan Carter?"

Just hearing him say the words made her skin crawl. "Absolutely not," she said fiercely, but his eyes were unrelenting. She was the first to look away. "God, I hope not," she whispered.

He sat there, waiting, and suddenly she couldn't keep her fear inside for another second.

"Okay, I'm terrified that something might have happened," she admitted. "But she won't talk to me."

"Have you asked her point-blank?"

Her lips curved slightly. "You obviously don't know anything about teenage girls, or at least about my daughter. Confrontation only shuts her down completely.

I've just spent fifteen minutes upstairs trying to get her to tell me why she doesn't want to go on a trip this weekend with Marcie and Caitlyn. I know it has something to do with Evan, but I came at it from every angle I could think of to give her an opportunity to open up, and I got nothing."

"I could try talking to her," he offered. "Unbiased third party. Who knows, she might tell me something she wouldn't tell you."

As annoyed as she was by his sneaky attempt to get the interview he'd been after from the start, she had to chuckle. "Detective, you really, really don't get teenagers, do you?"

A shadow darkened his eyes, but he shook his head. "No," he said, the response and his tone terse.

"Well, trust me, if there's one person they're less likely to open up to than a parent, it's a cop, especially a cop who's trying to put someone they care about in jail." She stood up. "Your ten minutes are up, Detective."

He dutifully stood and Emily thought she was home free. She'd have him out of here with no harm done, not even to her emotional equilibrium. Then his eyes met hers again and this time the warmth and concern she saw was more personal.

"Call me Grady," he said. "I have a feeling you and I are going to get to know each other really well before all this is over."

The tone in his voice made her tremble and she knew it didn't have a thing to do with his attempt to weasel information about Evan from her. She caught sight of his olive-skinned hands and suddenly she could practically feel them on her skin. This wasn't good, she thought, jerking her attention away. This wasn't good at all.

"You okay?" he inquired, a knowing glint in his eyes.

"Just peachy," she said, an edge of sarcasm in her voice.

"You and your daughter will be out of town this weekend?" he asked.

She nodded.

"Then I'll see you again the first of next week." Once again, his eyes locked with hers. "You change your mind about letting me talk to Dani, let me know. If that boy did hurt her and she's keeping it bottled up inside, it can't be good for her."

For once, Emily totally agreed with him, though she didn't intend to give him the satisfaction of telling him that. "You do your job, Detective. I'll worry about my daughter."

"Normally I'd say that's a reasonable request, but unfortunately, in this instance, something tells me the two objectives merge."

Emily was very much afraid he might be right. She turned away before he could see the fear in her eyes. It wasn't until he'd walked away and she heard the front door close quietly behind him that she sank down on a chair and buried her face in her hands.

Was she wrong not to try to force Dani to talk? She thought she was handling it the right way, the only way that had ever worked to get Dani to open up, but maybe this crisis deserved a more aggressive approach. Maybe her questioning needed to be as direct as Detective Rodriguez's had been just now. Dani might not answer, but Emily had learned a lot over the years by reading her daughter's body language. Maybe that would tell her what she needed to know.

Emily was making a halfhearted attempt to fix a chef's salad for dinner, when Dani walked into the kitchen. Her eyes were red rimmed from crying, her cheek imprinted with the pattern from her vintage chenille bedspread that she'd claimed after Emily's mother had died last year.

She bypassed Emily and went straight to the refrigerator and pulled out a can of pop.

"Dinner's almost ready," Emily said. "I thought we'd have a salad. We could eat on the patio. It's a nice night."

"I'd rather eat in my room."

"Not an option," she told her.

"Why not? If we eat together, we're only going to fight."

Emily grinned. "Only if you insist on it. I don't want to argue with you, sweetie. I really don't." She pushed a block of Monterey jack cheese across the counter. "Here, shred this for me."

"You can buy cheese already shredded, you know," Dani grumbled, but she found the shredder in the cabinet and started grating the cheese.

"You can find cheddar and mozzarella shredded," Emily told her. "But you like jack cheese, right?"

"Why don't they shred that? It's dumb."

"I agree, but that's the way it is. Deal with it."

Dani eyed the salad skeptically. "Dinner's not very exciting. Are we gonna have dessert?"

"We have ice cream and some of the brownies Marcie baked. Seems sort of counterproductive after a nice, healthy meal, though."

Dani grinned. "But we're having it, right?"

Emily grinned back, responding to the slight improvement in her daughter's mood. "It would be a shame to let those brownies go to waste. You carry the dishes and drinks outside and I'll bring the salad. You want ranch dressing or Italian?"

"Ranch."

When they were settled at the glass-topped patio table, Dani dove into her salad with enthusiasm. "Who was here before?" she asked, her mouth full of food.

"Dani!" Emily protested, gesturing toward her mouth.

Dani swallowed. "Sorry. Who was it?"

Emily hesitated, not wanting to spoil the moment. Unfortunately, Dani would only persist until she told her. Besides, this might be the opening she'd been hoping for.

"Detective Rodriguez," she said finally.

Dani's eyes narrowed suspiciously. "The guy who's investigating Evan came back again?"

Emily nodded.

"But you'd already talked to him. What did he want this time?"

Emily debated telling her that he'd had a conversation with Josh today that had sent him back here. If she suggested that Josh had pointed the detective in Dani's direction, though, Dani might never forgive her brother. Taking the coward's way out, she shrugged. "You know the police. They always think you know more than you're telling them."

"Was the other cop with him? The woman?"

"Not this time."

Dani's expression brightened unexpectedly. "Really? Are you sure he was here on business, Mom? Maybe he likes you."

Emily felt herself blush. "He has a job to do. That's all."

"You think he's cute, don't you?" Dani gloated. "I can tell."

"Cute isn't the word for Detective Rodriguez," Emily insisted.

"Sexy? Hot?" Dani supplied. "Go for it, Mom. You haven't been on a date since you and Dad got divorced."

"Sweetie, the man has not asked me on a date. He's here for one thing—information."

"Do you flirt with him?"

"Dani!"

"Well, do you? How else will he know you're interested, if you don't flirt a little?"

"Oh, for heaven's sakes, I am not having this conversation with my teenage daughter," Emily sputtered. "I'm going in to get dessert."

"Chicken," Dani called after her. "And bring me two brownies with my ice cream. I'm starved."

If it would distract Dani from the subject of Emily's relationship with the sexy detective, she would give her every brownie left on the plate Marcie had brought over. Sadly, though, she knew her daughter. She was just getting warmed up.

Still, Emily would gladly subject herself to a few more uncomfortable questions if it meant that Dani would keep a smile on her face and a sparkle in her eyes for a while longer. Those had been in short supply around here lately.

For once Marcie had brushed off all of Ken's objections to her taking a trip at this time.

"Caitlyn and I need a break from all the chaos around here," she said flatly. "We're going. Besides, you're totally absorbed with work and spinning this whole mess in Evan's favor. You're hardly ever home anyway."

"But how's it going to look if his mother and his sister take off when he's in the middle of a crisis?" Ken said. "It's going to look as if you're running away because you don't believe in him."

"Then you can be sure to spin that, too. Blame it on the media hounding us, so that we're practically prisoners in our own home. That ought to win us a little sympathy."

Ken glowered at her. "You don't need to get sarcastic. My job pays the bills around here."

"And you're very good at it, that's all I'm saying. Make this trip work for Evan, because Caitlyn and I are going."

"You just don't get how serious this is, do you? Our son could lose everything. His scholarship, his football career, his entire future. He could go to jail, Marcie."

"Believe me, I am well aware of that and it makes me sick. If there was one single thing I could do to prevent any of it, I would," she said. "Me going out of town for a couple of days isn't going to change the outcome of this."

"What about just being here as a supportive mother?"

She gave him a disbelieving stare. "You've seen to it that Evan doesn't give a damn about me or my support," she said heatedly. "I love that boy, but thanks to you, he treats me as if I'm no more important than a cook or housekeeper, so you can both get along without me for one weekend, while I deal with the other casualty of all this—your daughter."

It was the first time she'd ever said any of that aloud and she could tell from the stunned look in Ken's eyes that her comment had hit its mark. "Can't deny it, can you?" she challenged.

He shook his head. "Marcie, I don't understand what's gotten into you. This isn't the time to go around venting your dissatisfaction with Evan—or me, for that matter. Is that what you're planning to do on this trip, spill your guts to Emily about how unappreciated you are around here?"

"Maybe," she said with a touch of defiance that startled them both. "Can you blame me?"

Ken looked as if he might explode, but finally he just shook his head. "I swear to God, I don't even know you anymore."

"Isn't that the sad truth?" she said, and walked away, leaving him staring after her.

She was shaking as she climbed the stairs to pack, but she felt oddly euphoric as well. It was about time she started standing up for herself around here. Past time, most likely.

She could hardly wait to share her epiphany with Emily.

Of course, she'd probably pay for it when she got back. Ken would freeze her out or treat her with even more disdain than usual, but it was a small price to pay for even one glorious moment of putting him on notice that she was running short on patience.

On Friday afternoon Dani piled into her mom's car with Marcie and Caitlyn, determined to be as miserable as possible all weekend long. She stuck the earphones for her iPod in her ears and faced out the window as they drove away from the neighborhood. She felt a tiny twinge of guilt when she saw the hurt look on Caitlyn's face reflected in the glass.

She'd tried twice more to talk her mom into letting her spend the weekend with her dad, but her mother had been adamant that she had to go.

"Stop thinking about yourself and think about Caitlyn and how alone she must be feeling these days," her mom reminded her. "She needs a friend."

Dani knew her mom was right. She knew how badly Caitlyn probably needed to talk about what was going on, but that was the one topic Dani refused to discuss with anyone, especially Caitlyn. Hearing her defend her brother would make Dani hurl.

She felt a tap on her arm and turned to Caitlyn. "What are you listening to?" she mouthed.

Dani mentioned the name of the group and Caitlyn's eyes lit up.

"I love them. Is it the new CD? Can I listen when you're done?"

Her eagerness cut through Dani's defenses. She took out the earphones and handed over the iPod. "You listen now. I can hear them later. I've already played the whole CD about a million times."

As Caitlyn settled back to listen to the music, Dani saw her mom shoot her a grateful look in the rearview mirror. She shrugged. "No biggie," she mouthed, and her mom grinned.

A couple of hours later as they drove across the causeway to Sanibel, Dani felt her spirits start to lift. Even though they lived in Miami and there was water all around, she didn't get to go to the beach that often. Her parents had flat out forbidden her to go to South Beach and hang out there. They were scared to death that there was too much underage drinking going on in the clubs and on the beach. No matter how many times Dani swore she wouldn't touch alcohol and that the clubs wouldn't serve her anyway, they freaked every time she mentioned going to Miami Beach with a group of kids from school. She wondered if they knew that Josh was over there practically every Friday and Saturday night. He was the one they ought to worry about, because Dani

knew for a fact that he had a fake ID. Evan had gotten
it for him.

She honestly didn't care about all the drinking and
stuff that went on over there. She just loved the ocean.
They hadn't gone as a family since she was little, because
her dad didn't like lying around on the hot sand or
swimming in the ocean, when they had a perfectly good
pool in their own backyard.

The last time she'd been to the beach, she, her mom,
Marcie and Caitlyn had come to Sanibel for a girls'
weekend. It had been awesome. She and Caitlyn had
gone swimming until their skin practically shriveled up.
At night the four of them had played cards and Scrabble
till all hours of the night. Marcie always brought enough
food to feed an army, too. And her mom brought lots of
DVDs just in case it rained, but last time it hadn't.

Dani opened the car window and felt the salt air sting
her cheeks as they drove across the blue-green water. The
sun made it sparkle like beads on a necklace. She turned
back to Caitlyn, who'd opened her own window.

"Awesome," she said with a grin.

"Totally," Caitlyn agreed.

The two of them exchanged a high five, the way they
always did when they were in total agreement. Dani sat
back and relaxed for the first time since they'd left
Miami. Maybe this wasn't going to suck, after all.

12

"The girls look like they're having fun, don't they?" Marcie said, her relief evident as she and Emily sat on the beach watching Dani and Caitlyn splashing in the warm waters of the Gulf of Mexico. The air was thick with humidity, the sun hot, but there was a cooling breeze off the water that stirred the palm trees and kept it from being oppressive.

Emily nodded. "It's good to see them getting along so well. They needed this break. I knew once she got here, Dani would be glad she'd come."

As soon as the words left her mouth, Emily knew she'd said the wrong thing.

"Dani didn't want to come?" Marcie studied her with a perplexed look. "Why? Last time we were here, she said it was the best vacation ever."

"I honestly don't know," she said with a shrug, trying to make light of it. "You know how she can be. I couldn't get a straight answer out of her. I imagine it's the stress of this whole situation with Evan. She may feel uncomfortable around you and Caitlyn, not knowing what she should or shouldn't say. I don't always know what to say and I'm an adult. She's only seventeen."

"And she always had a little bit of a crush on Evan," Marcie added, her expression thoughtful. "I guess I hadn't really thought about what his arrest might do to her. I've been totally focused on how it's affecting my family."

"You want to talk about it?" Emily asked.

Marcie hesitated, then shook her head. "Not about Evan, no. I just can't bring myself to discuss it, not even with you. The whole thing is just so horrible, I don't want to think about it for the next couple of days."

Emily picked up the way she'd phrased her response. "Okay, we won't discuss Evan, but there's something else on your mind, isn't there?"

"Ken and I had a fight before I left." For once Marcie didn't sound especially stressed about it. "Not that that's so unusual, but this time I stood my ground."

Emily beamed at her. "Good for you. What did you fight about?"

"He didn't want Caitlyn and me to take this trip."

"Why?"

"Because of how it might look, of course. He didn't care that I've been locked away in the house since all of this started or that Caitlyn's a mess from trying to deal with what everyone's saying about her brother. All he cared about was his precious image. He tried to guilt me into staying by saying people would think I didn't support my own son."

"He didn't!" Emily said, not even trying to hide her shock. That was a low blow, even for Ken.

"Of course, he did. I think he was absolutely stunned when it didn't work." Her lips quirked slightly. "Emily, I can't tell you how good it felt to stand up to him for once. Maybe that will be a first step to changing the way we do things in my house."

Though she applauded Marcie's gumption, Emily was doubtful that it was a real precursor to change. Ken had never struck her as the kind of guy who got the message the first time it was delivered. She sometimes wondered if a sledgehammer would even do the trick.

At her silence, Marcie's expression faltered. "You don't agree?"

Emily chose her words carefully. "That depends on what changes you're hoping for."

"I want the kind of respect I deserve."

"Well, hallelujah!" Emily cheered enthusiastically. "But I'm not sure you can get that by standing your ground one time. This pattern was established a long time ago."

"Believe me, I know that," Marcie said, slathering on another coating of sunscreen. "Leopards don't change their spots overnight." She grinned. "It's taken *me* nearly twenty years to get to this point, after all. I doubt I can turn Ken around in a few weeks."

"But you think it's possible to change his attitude?"

"I have to try. My marriage matters to me. I know all of his flaws—and there are plenty of them—but, God help me, I still love him."

"How long are you willing to try?"

"As long as it takes, I guess."

Emily raised a brow. "That long?"

"Hey, just let me bask in having taken the first step," Marcie said. "My marriage may be far from perfect, but I'm not ready to walk away from it the way you did."

Emily flinched at the implication that she hadn't tried hard enough to save her own. Before she could speak, Marcie regarded her guiltily.

"I am so sorry," Marcie apologized. "I swear I didn't

mean that the way it sounded. I only meant that if I want my relationship with Ken to get better, then I'm the one who's going to have to insist on a change."

Emily relented and picked up a bottle of water from the cooler and held it out. "To the first giant leap," she toasted.

Marcie touched her own drink to Emily's. "To change."

Just then the girls ran across the hot sand and stood dripping all over them.

"What are you guys drinking to?" Caitlyn asked.

"The future," Marcie told her.

"The only future I care about is lunch," Dani said. "What are we having?"

"Whatever you girls go up to the hotel and bring back to us," Emily said.

"Mom!" Dani protested, but Caitlyn nudged her. "Hey, they said it's up to us. That's a good thing. We can pick anything we want."

Dani's eyes brightened. "That's right!"

The two girls took off up the beach.

"Try to remember the basic food groups," Emily called after them, then glanced at Marcie. "Something tells me we're having chips and cookies for lunch."

Marcie, who never served a meal that hadn't been well thought out and artfully arranged, merely shrugged. "Suits me."

Emily stared at her. "My God, you are changing. What have you done with the old Marcie?"

"Given her a sharp poke with a stick to wake her up, I hope. I've recently realized that my priorities have been totally screwed up for years. I was so totally focused on serving gourmet meals in a dust-free, clutter-free environment, that I completely forgot to teach my kids values and respect." Her expression sobered. "I just hope my wake-up call didn't come too late for my son."

"I think you're being too hard on yourself," Emily told her. "You have taught your kids the difference between right and wrong."

"I've said the words," Marcie corrected. "But the way I lived, letting Ken bulldoze right over me most of the time...I'm afraid that's the lesson that stuck, especially with Evan."

When Emily started to respond, Marcie waved her off. "No, it's true and it's time I owned up to it, but that is enough about me and my wimpy ways for one morning. After the girls bring us lunch, I vote we take our credit cards out of hibernation and go on a shopping spree. I don't know about you, but that always improves my outlook on life."

"I could use a new pair of shoes," Emily said.

"Shoes are good," Marcie agreed. "As long as you buy a new outfit to go with them. A spree doesn't count unless you really splurge and buy a few totally useless but greatly desired things as well."

"Such as?"

"Jewelry," Marcie suggested. "That works for me."

"I think I'll stick with the shoes," Emily said, then grinned. "But I might buy two pairs."

"Okay, fine. As long as one pair is totally impractical and sexy as sin, I can live with that," Marcie said.

Suddenly an image of Grady Rodriguez flashed into Emily's mind. She had a hunch a strappy pair of high-heeled sandals would get his attention. Just the thought of an appreciative once-over from his dark brown eyes made her pulse kick up a notch.

Filled with sudden guilt over being attracted to the man intent on putting Evan in jail, she glanced at Marcie who was studying her oddly.

"Have we been in the sun too long?" Marcie asked. "You're turning red."

"That must be it," Emily said, seizing on the excuse. "Maybe we should go back to the suite and have lunch there."

And she could stand under a cold shower until her thoughts cooled down by thirty or forty degrees.

Dani stood in the bedroom she and Caitlyn were sharing and pulled all her new outfits out of their shopping bags. Caitlyn was doing the same thing on her side of the room. Though she'd had her doubts before the trip about being able to spend time with Caitlyn without watching every word she said, they'd had a great time today.

"This is totally awesome," Dani declared. "My mom must be feeling really guilty or something. She never buys me this much stuff at once." She held up a skimpy little halter top. "And she obviously didn't get a good look at this."

Caitlyn grinned. "You think she'll flip out when she sees you wearing it?"

"I know she will," Dani said. "I'll have to wear it under a blouse to get out of the house. After that..." She shrugged. "What she doesn't know won't hurt her."

Caitlyn gave her a troubled look. "Where would you wear it?"

"I don't know exactly."

"You can't get away with it at school. Your mom's right there."

"Definitely not," Dani agreed. "But there are parties almost every weekend."

"But you never go," Caitlyn said. "At least you haven't for a long time now."

Dani frowned. "What makes you say that? I get asked to parties all the time."

"I know that," Caitlyn responded. "But you haven't gone, not since…" Her voice trailed off.

Dani immediately understood. "It's not because of what happened with Evan," she said heatedly.

"Are you sure about that?" Caitlyn asked tentatively. "I know I had my doubts when you told me, but now after this new accusation, I'm starting to wonder if I was wrong."

"You *were* wrong," Dani declared, her voice climbing. "And you should have believed me, instead of just jumping to Evan's defense. How could you do that after all the years we've known each other?"

The door to their room opened and her mom stuck her head in. "Hey, everything okay in here?"

"Fine," Dani said tightly.

Caitlyn regarded her guiltily, then forced a smile for her mom's benefit. "We're great, Mrs. D. We were just arguing about which new CD is better, the one by Eminem or Christina Aguilera's new one."

"For what it's worth, I prefer hers," her mom said. She gave Dani another questioning look, but then she backed off. "Scrabble in fifteen minutes if you girls are up for it."

"Sure," Dani said, eager to do anything that would keep her from having to continue this ridiculous conversation with Caitlyn. She still couldn't believe her best friend had doubted her word for even a second, much less all these months. She wasn't sure she'd ever be able to forgive her for that.

"I'm ready, too," Caitlyn said.

But when Dani started to follow her mom, Caitlyn stepped in front of her.

"Look, I was just trying to be fair," she said, her expression pleading with Dani to try to understand. "Evan is my brother and I had to give him the benefit of the doubt, but I *am* sorry now for doubting you, and I'm sorry if what I said just now about you not going to parties because of Evan upset you."

Dani just wanted the whole conversation to end. It was bringing her down and making it that much harder for her to cover in front of her mom and Mrs. Carter. "No big deal," she said. "Just so you know you're wrong. I haven't been hiding out because of…" She couldn't even say his name, much less refer to what he'd done. "I haven't been hiding out, that's all."

"Okay, fine," Caitlyn said. "Because if you were, it would be really sad. You're finally old enough that your mom would let you date. You've been looking forward to that practically forever."

"I guess there's nobody I'm that excited about going out with." Dani avoided Caitlyn's eyes, because she feared her friend would be able to tell she was lying. She thought of the loneliness she'd felt, shut up in her room for the past few months. The truth was Caitlyn couldn't begin to know just how awful it was not trusting any guy she met, being scared to be around them. If the guy she'd known best and trusted the most could do what Evan had done, then how would she ever be able to go out with another boy?

Late that night, Marcie took a glass of wine out on the patio of their hotel suite. The sky was inky black and dotted with stars. She kicked off her shoes and sat back with a sigh. She was more relaxed than she had been for weeks now, maybe even longer than that. Until recently, she hadn't realized that she was always tense at home, always anticipating some critical remark from Ken, some disparaging comment that would be like a knife to her heart. Once she'd recognized that, she'd known that things had to change. And as she'd told Emily earlier, she was determined they would.

"You feel like company?" Emily asked.

"Sure. Come on out. It's a beautiful night."

Emily sat down beside her with her own glass of wine. She'd brought the rest of the bottle along.

"Did you notice anything going on with the girls when we were playing Scrabble?" Emily asked.

Marcie thought back to the game. "Nothing unusual. Why?"

"Maybe it was my imagination working overtime. Earlier I thought I heard them arguing in their room, but they claimed they were just discussing music. Then while we were playing the game, they seemed a little tense to me."

Marcie grinned. "You know how competitive they are and for once we were really trouncing them."

"Exactly," Emily said. "Because I don't think their minds were on the game."

"Mountain out of a molehill," Marcie said, sounding unconcerned. "If they did have a spat, they'll be over it by morning."

"I hope you're right. They've always been so close. I always assumed they'd turn out like us, friends through thick and thin. I want that for them. I'm not sure people value friendships the way they should."

"Well, we do," Marcie told her.

Emily tapped her wineglass to Marcie's. "Yes, we do, and thank goodness for it."

Marcie glanced over at her friend, who'd drawn her knees up to her chest and was resting her chin on them. "We haven't talked a lot about what's going on with you lately. It's all been about me."

"Because my life is totally boring and predictable," Emily said. "School, dinner with Dani and sometimes Josh, grading papers, then doing it all again the next day."

"When are you going to change that?" Marcie asked. "Isn't it time you found yourself a new man?"

"Where would I do that? In the frozen-food aisle of the supermarket?"

"I'd hang out by the steaks, if I were you. At least find a guy who can cook."

Emily chuckled. "I'm not really looking for a guy. I'm content with things the way they are."

"Really? Then why did you just describe your life as boring and predictable. Those are not words that suggest contentment. Don't you miss feeling that little rush of anticipation when you first see the man you're attracted to?" She grinned. "Don't you miss the sex?"

"Only recently," Emily admitted.

"Why? Just because it's been forever, or did you meet someone who stirred your hormones back into action?"

Emily hesitated for so long Marcie thought she wasn't going to answer.

"Am I getting too personal?" she asked.

"Heavens, no," Emily said. "I just don't have a good answer to your question."

"Either you met someone or you didn't," Marcie said. "It's not complicated."

"Oh, yes, it is," Emily replied.

Marcie gasped. "He's married?"

Again, there was a long hesitation. "You know, I honestly don't know. I don't think so. I certainly hope not."

"Well, well, well, now we're getting somewhere. Tell me more. Who is he? Where'd you meet him?"

Emily actually squirmed uncomfortably and suddenly Marcie recalled the way she'd turned bright red earlier on the beach. She'd attributed her high color to the sun, but that hadn't been it at all. She'd been talking about sexy shoes and Emily had been thinking about this man, whoever he was.

"Em, tell me about him."

"There's nothing to tell, really. We've had a couple of conversations, that's it. But when he looks at me, I feel that rush you were talking about, you know?"

"Oh, I know," Marcie agreed. "What's he look like? Is he a lot like Derek?"

"Not at all," Emily said. "Why would you think that?"

"Just wondering if you have a specific type."

"Apparently not, because they couldn't be more different."

"When can I meet him?"

Emily laughed, though it sounded oddly forced. "Not in the cards, at least not right now. I told you, I hardly know him myself. I'm not going to drag him around to meet my friends."

Marcie studied her. She still looked oddly uneasy, not at all like a woman who was on the verge of falling in love and happy about it. "Is there something you're not telling me?" she asked at last.

For the first time Marcie could recall since the day they'd met, Emily avoided her gaze when she responded.

"No, not a thing," she said.

Marcie sat back in her chair, dismayed. Emily had lied to her. But why? What possible reason could she have for keeping a secret about the man she was interested in? It was the first tiny crack ever in their solid friendship. Ironically, in many ways that hurt more than the fissures in her own marriage.

"You making any progress with Emily Dobbs?" Naomi asked Grady over coffee at Starbucks.

"She still won't let me talk to her daughter," he responded.

"I was thinking more along the lines of getting her to say yes when you asked her out."

Grady scowled at her. "Are you crazy? I haven't asked her out. It would be inappropriate."

"But you want to," Naomi persisted.

"Okay, yeah, it's crossed my mind."

"Was that before, during or after you went over there on your own the other night?"

Grady cringed. "How the hell did you know about that?"

She grinned. "I didn't until just this second. You're entirely too predictable, Rodriguez. So what did you tell yourself, that the visit was personal or professional?"

"Professional, of course. I wanted to try again to get her to see reason about letting me speak to her daughter, especially after what Josh said."

"Did you admit to questioning her son?"

"Of course."

"How'd she take it?"

"She wasn't happy. I thought for a second she was going to break the glass she was holding, but she didn't say a word. She seemed resigned to the fact that there was nothing she could do about it."

"Have you thought about trying to get a court order to talk to the girl?" Naomi asked.

"I've thought about it, but it won't fly. There's not enough evidence to prove she knows anything that would be relevant."

"Just her brother's suspicion," Naomi reminded him.

"And her mother's fear, for that matter. Emily's scared we're right. She pretty much admitted that she's not ready to find out the truth."

"Even if her daughter needs help?"

Grady nodded. "I don't get it either. I think she sees a girl who's functioning okay, no obvious signs of distress, and she doesn't want to rock the boat. Plus, you know how close she is to the Carters. If Evan did hurt Dani, it would rip that relationship apart."

"Still, I just don't see a mother wearing blinders for very long. Dani has to be her first priority."

"She is. I don't question that for a minute," Grady said. "She'll come around. It's just going to take a little longer than I'd prefer."

"You intend to stay on her?"

"Until she's sick of seeing me," he confirmed.

"You sure you want to tick her off? It could ruin this other thing the two of you have going."

Grady chuckled ruefully. "That's only in my dreams."

"Don't be so sure. I thought I saw a little spark in her eyes, too."

To his disgust, he couldn't help jumping on that opening. "Really?"

Naomi laughed. "God, you are pathetic. You may be the nicest, sexiest man I've ever met, but you just don't see it. That ex-wife of yours must have really done a number on you on her way out the door."

Grady stiffened. "Not a word against Kathleen," he said. "Ever."

Naomi flinched at his sharp tone. "Sorry. I didn't know you were so sensitive on the subject. Do you still have a thing for her? Is that why you don't date all that much?"

"No, but none of what happened was her fault. It was all mine. I don't want anyone thinking otherwise. You weren't around back then or you'd know that."

"Sackcloth and ashes don't suit you, Rodriguez. Nothing is ever one person's fault. There's always enough blame to go around."

"Not this time," he said adamantly. "Not this time."

When she would have argued, he held up his hand. "Let's get out of here and catch a bad guy. I need to put somebody behind bars."

For a lot of years now, doing his job and doing it well had been the only thing that gave him any sense of self-worth.

13

For a while now, Emily had been uncomfortably aware that practically every time she turned around, Grady Rodriguez was in her face. Sure, sometimes when he'd been nosing around at the high school, he'd done little more than murmur an amused greeting as she stiffened at the sight of him. Sometimes he'd asked a question or two, most of them innocuous enough to throw her completely off guard. On a few occasions, such as the last time he'd come by the house, the confrontations had been more direct. All of the meetings—whether deliberate or by chance—had been disconcerting.

But on the Monday morning after her trip when he turned up in the bagel shop where she'd stopped to grab breakfast on her way to school, she began to wonder if he was actually following her. Of course, he had been sitting at the counter when she'd walked in, so that might make a case for the argument that she was following him. She had a hunch he'd enjoy turning that around on her, so it was probably for the best to leave it alone.

Still, seeing him here after the way he'd plagued her thoughts while she'd been in Sanibel left her more rattled than usual.

"You again," she muttered as she stood in line to place her order. "I've never seen you in here before."

He gestured toward his coffee and bowl of oatmeal. "My partner's on my case to eat healthier. She considers this place to be a better choice than the Krispy Kreme up the highway, so I decided to give it a try. If you have a couple of minutes, why don't you join me? I'll buy. Then you can vouch for me when Naomi accuses me of eating nothing but doughnuts."

Emily debated whether to accept the invitation. One part of her, the part that had a sexy pair of brand-new high heels in her closet, wanted to stay because of the simmering attraction between them. The part that wanted to be rid of him once and for all hoped that maybe one more conversation would finally put an end to having him pop up on her doorstep and at school. A third and far less vocal part was simply curious. The combination was too much to resist. She sat down gingerly on the stool next to his and ordered coffee and a cinnamon-raisin bagel.

"I'm surprised you let your partner influence your diet," she commented. "What about your wife? What does she have to say?"

"Divorced," he said with no emotion.

"Ah," she said. Her feet, mentally clad in those sexy shoes, danced a little jig.

He grinned, displaying his dimple. "You say that as if it explains a lot."

"Maybe your choice of a striped tie with a checked shirt," she retorted. "Nothing else."

"Gee, and I thought you'd be ecstatic to know I'm available."

"Not so much," she claimed.

He didn't look as if he believed her. "You dating anyone?" he asked.

She frowned at the question. "Is that something you need to know for your investigation?"

"Nope. It's purely personal."

His candor threw her. "Doesn't that cross some kind of ethical line or something?"

"I'll have to check my rule book. I must have a copy of it somewhere."

Surprised by the tone of his bantering, she dared to look at him directly. "Are you flirting with me, Detective?"

"If you have to ask, I must not be doing a very good job of it."

"Or maybe I'm out of practice at being on the receiving end," she said.

His grin spread. "Which must mean you're not seriously involved with someone."

"Sneaky," she said, enjoying herself more than she'd expected to. Usually when she saw Detective Rodriguez, she was immediately on guard. Maybe she'd actually taken Marcie's encouragement to heart, after all, and was ready to open up to new possibilities.

"I am good at what I do," he commented as he pulled money from his wallet and placed it on the counter with their checks. "Something you should probably keep in mind. See you around, Emily."

She stared after him, disconcerted by his abrupt departure after not mentioning Evan even once.

Well, that had been…interesting, she decided. And when was the last time she'd felt that way about a man? The fact that it was Grady Rodriguez, of all people, who'd awakened her hormones out of their slumber was a complication she had no idea how to handle.

* * *

When Emily walked into the teachers' lounge a few minutes after seeing Grady Rodriguez, she was still a little flustered by the encounter.

Paula looked up from the morning paper and murmured a distracted greeting, then took a second look. "What's up with you?"

Emily frowned. "What do you mean?"

"You look a little giddy, like a woman who's just been on a first date."

"At seven o'clock in the morning?"

"Hey, that's the peak of my day," Paula said. "After that it's mostly downhill. So, why are your cheeks so flushed?"

"Maybe I ran in from the parking lot," Emily suggested.

Paula merely rolled her eyes. "Please. I know you. Try the truth."

"Okay, but you can't say a word to another soul," she said.

"Not even Marcie?"

"Especially not Marcie."

Paula looked stunned. "She's your best friend."

"And the last person I can share this with," Emily insisted.

Paula put aside the paper. "Sit. Start at the beginning."

"There really isn't a beginning or a middle," Emily said. "To be honest, I'm not even sure there's anything at all."

"Now I am totally confused."

"Detective Rodriguez," she said succinctly.

Paula looked blank for an instant and then recognition dawned. "Oh, my God, the man who's investigating Evan? I knew it. The first time you mentioned him there was this weird little spark in your eyes and then, when he showed up here, it was there again."

Emily shrugged. "Back then, it was probably annoyance."

"But now it's something else?"

"I don't know, maybe," she admitted. "I feel awful. How can I possibly be attracted to a man who's trying to convict my best friend's son of rape?"

"You forget, I met him, too. I can see exactly how the attraction came about. The man is seriously tall, dark and gorgeous, to say nothing of intense. He has a sense of humor, too. That's a pretty lethal combination." Paula studied her intently. "So, is this attraction mutual?"

"I think it could be." She described their encounter at the bagel shop. "He was flirting with me. He admitted it." She put her hands over her face. "Listen to me. I'm insane. I have to be. I'm forty-two years old and I sound like I'm fourteen, trying to figure out if the boy who teased me in the cafeteria likes me. In Grady's case, it was probably just some new technique to get me to talk."

"You don't believe that," Paula scoffed.

"No, I don't, but this is too complicated for me. I haven't gone out once since Derek and I split up. It just hasn't been worth the hassle. I hate shaving my legs, for one thing."

Paula started to chuckle. "You haven't been dating because you don't want to shave your legs?"

"Well, that's one reason," Emily insisted.

"If you'd ever had all your hair fall out from chemo, believe me, you'd be grateful to have any to shave."

"Okay, I know I sound ridiculous."

"Just a little," Paula agreed. "If you haven't been out, it's because Grady Rodriguez is the first man to come along who appeals to you. Would you shave your legs for him?"

"Oh, yeah," she said with a sigh, then shook her head. "No, I can't even consider going out with him. It's wrong."

"Why is it wrong? You're single. He's single." She frowned. "He is single, isn't he?"

"Divorced."

"Okay, then. I don't see the problem."

"Marcie," Emily said succinctly. "Can you imagine how she'd feel if she found out? Plus, would I ever be able to believe he was actually interested in me and not just trying a more intimate sort of interrogation?"

Paula nodded slowly. "I see the dilemma. Did he ask you anything about Evan this morning?"

"No, that was the really weird part. The conversation was all personal. And if anybody was revealing secrets, it was him, if you count the fact that his partner thinks he needs to cut out doughnuts and stick to oatmeal."

"Now there's something I bet you were dying to know," Paula teased. "You'll know exactly what to feed him after your first overnight."

"Not even a tiny bit amusing," Emily told her.

"Well, I guess you're just going to have to let it play itself out over time. It's not as if you have to make a decision today."

"True. He hasn't asked me out. I don't even know if he's going to. The police department probably has rules about that sort of thing, though when I brought that up this morning, he acted as if he didn't give two figs for the rules."

"How did that sit with Ms. By-the-Book Dobbs?"

"Truthfully?"

"Of course."

"I kind of liked that he would consider breaking them for me."

Paula picked up the paper and fanned herself dramatically. "I really need to get another look at the man who's got you talking about living your life on the edge."

"Oh, stop it," Emily said. "Besides, it will probably never go anywhere at all." The prospect left her feeling more than a little wistful. "The fantasy's pretty amazing, though."

Paula regarded her with a sober expression. "Then maybe you need to stop making excuses for doing nothing and do whatever you can to make sure it becomes reality."

When Emily and Dani got home from school that afternoon, her daughter headed straight up to her room, disgruntled about still being grounded. Emily just shook her head and headed for the kitchen to pour herself a glass of iced tea. To her surprise, she found Josh at the kitchen table, munching on stale cookies and drinking what was probably the last of the milk.

"I wasn't expecting to see you home this early," she said, pulling out a chair across from him. "Don't you have classes this afternoon?"

"I decided to cut. I wanted to talk to you."

"Oh?"

"I'm afraid Evan's going to get away with what he did to that girl, Lauren Brown."

Emily frowned. "What makes you say that?"

"You should hear what's being said on campus.

Everybody's talking about her like she's some big slut," he said angrily. "It's so unfair. They're saying she's accused other guys of the same thing, just to make herself feel important. There's one rumor that she made all this stuff up about Evan because he *wouldn't* have sex with her. It makes me sick."

Truthfully, it made Emily sick, too. "What do you say when you hear things like that?"

"I've tried to tell some of these guys that she's not like that, but they don't want to hear it. The girls are worse. Most of them are so jealous that he asked Lauren out instead of them, they'll believe anything negative that's said about her. They all think I'm a traitor because Evan's supposed to be my friend." He regarded her earnestly. "It's not about that at all, Mom. What Evan and his dad— I know they're behind it—are doing is wrong, almost as wrong as what Evan did in the first place."

Emily was proud of the indignation she saw in her son's eyes. "Is there anything more you could do?"

He shrugged. "I don't know. It's not as if I'm totally credible. I hardly know Lauren, so how can I defend her? I'm just now getting to know her roommate and she is one hundred percent behind Lauren, so I feel like I should be, too, but I'm not sure how to do that."

"Are you still avoiding Evan?"

He nodded. "Mostly. I ran into him the other day and he tried to get me to back him up, to tell people what a great guy he is. He wanted me to say publicly that I've known him for years and he'd never do a thing like this. I told him I couldn't say that, that I believed Lauren."

Emily was impressed with her son's strength. "I am so proud of you for standing up to him, though it breaks my heart that you had to. How did Evan take it?"

"He looked like I'd kicked him in the gut at first. He was really hurt, you know. It made me feel awful."

"I can imagine."

"Then he started getting all arrogant and mean, saying I was backing a loser and he wasn't going to forget about it. He said our friendship was over."

"I'm sure he was just angry. He probably didn't mean it."

"Oh, he meant it," Josh insisted. "If you'd heard him, you'd get that. I can't even repeat some of the stuff he said."

"I'm so sorry," Emily said. "For both of you."

"Yeah, well, it's not like we've been hanging out that much recently, anyway," Josh said with a shrug. "Still, it's all such a mess. I talked to Dad about it over the weekend. He just says I should do whatever I think is right." He regarded her with a helpless expression. "I'm not sure I know what that is."

"It sounds to me as if you're already doing everything you can. You're standing up for Lauren when you hear things that are lies. You're not letting Evan use your friendship to his advantage."

He fell silent, then looked up. "I left out something else. Mr. Carter came over here while you were away. I guess Evan told him I wouldn't go public and back him. Mr. Carter said it was time for me to stand up and be a man and defend Evan. He said only a coward would back down and let a friend face bogus charges like this. He made me feel like slime, or at least he tried to."

Emily's temper flared. "Ken tried to bully you into taking Evan's side?"

Josh nodded. "I told him he could say whatever he wanted about me, but that I wouldn't lie to protect his son. I told him that trying to ruin Lauren's reputation was really low, too."

"Good for you."

"Mom, I get why he's desperate. I know what's at stake for Evan, everything he ever dreamed about, and I feel bad about that. I really do. He's worked hard practically forever to be a big football star and it's all about to go up in smoke." He regarded her earnestly. "But he shouldn't get away with this. I've seen what this did to Lauren. When I was over at their apartment the other day and Jenny introduced me, I held out my hand to shake hers and she jerked away. She was scared, Mom. Of *me*. Think what he must have done to make her feel that way. How does a woman ever get over something like that?"

"I honestly don't know," she told him sorrowfully. "Does she have a good support system?"

"She has Jenny," he said. His expression brightened perceptibly. "And she's pretty amazing."

Emily smiled at his response. "Then one good thing has come out of this. You've met a truly admirable young lady. Maybe you could bring her home sometime. Lauren, too. I'd like to meet them both."

Josh flushed. "Maybe sometime," he said, his tone noncommittal.

"Just so you know they'd be welcome anytime," she said.

"Did you know I'd talked to Detective Rodriguez?" he asked.

She nodded.

"He seems like a pretty decent guy," he said.

"I think so, too."

He studied her anxiously. "Have you let him talk to Dani?"

She shook her head.

"She could know more than she's saying, Mom. I don't want to think about the same thing happening to her, but it could have. Now that I've seen how it affected Lauren, I think we should know if it happened to Dani, too. She's been acting kinda weird since all this started, almost as if she feels guilty about something."

"I've noticed the same thing, and I know you're right. I've tried more than once to get her to open up, but she won't even discuss Evan."

"You want me to try?"

She thought about that. Maybe Dani would open up to her big brother under most circumstances, but not about this. "I don't think so," she said eventually. "I'll try again. If Evan did do anything to her and she's been keeping it to herself, she'll need her mother."

"Okay, but if you change your mind, let me know."

"I will," she promised.

"I guess I should go upstairs and study. Any chance we can order pizza for dinner?"

"Didn't you have pizza every night while I was away?"

He grinned. "What can I say? I love pizza. It's a perfect meal. Just about all the food groups in one."

"Fine, but I'm ordering it with mushrooms and green peppers, so there's at least a smattering of vegetables on it."

He wrinkled his nose. "It already has tomato sauce."

"Tomatoes are a fruit, actually."

"Well, there you go. It's even better than I thought."

He started from the room, then turned back. "Do you think I should contact some of the girls Evan dated in high school? I'll bet anything at least some of them had a problem with him, even if they never talked about it. I have e-mail addresses at college for a lot of them."

Emily gave the offer some thought. She knew whatever Josh found might be invaluable to the police, but the toll it would take on Josh and Evan's friendship—whatever was left of it—would be high. "Do you really want to do that? It's bound to get back to him that you're actively trying to find backup for Lauren. It will sever the friendship forever. Maybe you should just pass the contact information along to Detective Rodriguez."

"You're probably right, but not because of my friendship with Evan. That's pretty much wrecked," he said without any evidence of regret. "I know we were really close when we were kids, but lately…" He shrugged. "He's changed, or maybe I have. I don't know. Is it awful that I can't stand up for him?"

She saw how hard he was struggling to find his way through this quagmire and sought to be reassuring. "No, it's honest, and it shows you're learning that character matters even more than popularity and athletic skill. Lots of people change and grow apart over the years. It's no reflection on either of them."

"But you don't feel the same way, do you? You still think Evan's okay?"

"I'm trying to keep an open mind. I haven't seen him in the same situations you've seen him in, so I trust your judgment about his behavior toward women. I just hate thinking that the sweet boy who spent so much time here could have changed so dramatically. And I feel absolutely awful for what Marcie and Caitlyn are going through."

"Yeah, me, too. It must really suck for them."

"That's why I don't want to do anything to make it

worse, more for their sakes than Evan's." She studied him worriedly. "That's one reason I think you should just give the names and contact information for the girls to Detective Rodriguez. Getting any more deeply involved yourself would really hurt Marcie and Caitlyn."

Josh shook his head. "I get what you're saying, Mom, but the girls might not be as candid with him," he said. "At least I can break the ice for him."

"I'm sure he'd be grateful." She smiled at the young man who was maturing faster than she'd realized. "I imagine Jenny will be, too."

"I'm doing it for Lauren," he insisted.

"Either way, you're doing a good thing for all the right reasons and I'm proud of you."

He looked embarrassed by the praise. "Whatever. I'll be down when the pizza gets here."

Dani had heard her brother talking to her mom downstairs. She couldn't hear what they were saying, but it had to be serious for the conversation to have gone on so long. Usually Josh mumbled a greeting and went straight to his room. She had a funny feeling they'd been talking about Evan again, and maybe her.

She opened the door to her room when she heard Josh on the stairs and went out to wait for him.

"What were you talking to Mom about?" she asked, blocking his way.

"Just some stuff," he said.

"Was it about me?"

He regarded her quizzically. "Why would we be talking about you?"

"Because I know you do it all the time lately. You think I'm hiding something about Evan."

Josh didn't deny it. Instead, he looked her in the eye. "Are you?"

A part of Dani wanted to burst into tears and say yes and then let it all out, every ugly detail, but she simply couldn't get the words past the lump in her throat. Not to the brother she'd always looked up to. He'd never see her the same way again.

"No," she mumbled.

To her surprise, Josh put his hand on her shoulder. "Listen to me, kid. If you do have something to say, you should tell me or Mom. We'd understand. So would Dad."

How could they? Dani thought miserably. They knew she'd had a crush on Evan. They were bound to assume that she'd thrown herself at him, but it hadn't been like that. She'd wanted him to kiss her, sure, but nothing else. None of what had happened after.

Once again, she drew in a deep breath and leveled a defiant look at her brother. "Nothing happened."

Josh didn't look as if he believed her. Oh, he clearly wanted to, but skepticism was written all over his face. Dani backed toward her room.

"When's dinner? Did Mom say?" she asked.

"She's ordering pizza now," he said.

"How'd you talk her into that? She never does it when I ask."

Josh rubbed her head with his knuckles. "She likes me best," he told her. "Always has."

"In your dreams," she retorted, glad that he'd dropped the whole subject of Evan. As annoying as it was when Josh teased her, she still liked it. On his good days, he was the best big brother ever. On the other days, well, she'd gotten used to him being a nuisance.

Even as she thought that, she remembered how close Caitlyn had always been to Evan. No wonder she was struggling with everything that was going on. She loved Evan just as fiercely as Dani loved Josh. If Josh were in trouble—not that he ever would be—Dani wouldn't want to believe the worst about him. Maybe she ought to cut Caitlyn some slack for not being so quick to condemn Evan, even though she had to know the truth about him. Just because Dani had good reason to hate him didn't mean she could expect Caitlyn to. First chance she got, maybe she'd even tell her that.

Though they'd had a good time in Sanibel, they'd both been on the defensive. Dani had missed the way things used to be. With all the trouble going on, maybe they could never have that same easygoing camaraderie again, but she'd like to try. She'd always thought she and Caitlyn would go through life being almost like the sisters neither of them had.

It was wrong to let this whole mess with Evan destroy that, too, she concluded. He shouldn't be allowed to steal one more thing from her. He'd stolen her innocence and her ability to trust, and that was more than enough.

14

Grady's frustration was mounting. Everywhere he went, he and Naomi were running into a wall of silence—the university community, the athletic department, Evan's old high school, the neighborhood. No one wanted to say anything bad about the star athlete, while quite a few were all too eager to disparage Lauren Brown. The tide was shifting, turning Evan into the victim. Grady knew he could thank Ken Carter for that. A well-planted rumor here, a sly innuendo there, and Lauren became the calculating woman who was trying to ruin a boy's life.

Grady was at his desk, trying to figure out what he could do that he hadn't already done when he looked up to see his uncle crossing the squad room. Luis Rodriguez was sixty now, with strong shoulders, a long stride, and salt-and-pepper hair. He ought to be thinking about retirement, but he'd turned down every incentive the City of Miami Police Department had offered him. He liked his beat in the Little Havana neighborhood where he'd been a patrolman for his entire career. He was obviously off today, since he was out of uniform and wearing neatly pressed khakis and a pale blue guayabera shirt.

"Tio Luis," Grady said, walking over to give the older man a hug. "What brings you by?"

"I've been reading the paper, listening to the talk on the radio and on the street. I thought you might need a friendly ear about now. You have time for lunch?"

"I'll make the time," Grady said, calling over to Naomi to let her know he'd be out for an hour.

Naomi grinned at his uncle. "Luis, don't you dare let him near any French fries," she said. "He eats entirely too many."

"We'll stick to good, healthy Cuban food," his uncle promised her.

Naomi frowned. "Are you sure that's not a contradiction in terms?"

"Hey, young lady, you tell me what's wrong with black beans and rice? Complex carbohydrates, yes?" Luis said with indignation. "You know I always take care of my nephew, *sí?*"

"I'm counting on it," Naomi told him.

When Grady and his uncle left the squad room, Luis regarded him solemnly. "She is concerned about you. She is warm, compassionate, not bad to look at. Perhaps you should consider—"

Grady sighed. It wasn't the first time someone in his family had speculated about a romance between him and his partner. The meddling was off base and exasperating, though he should have grown used to it by now. Naomi did a better job than he did of shrugging it off.

"Don't go there," Grady said. "Naomi and I have a working relationship, nothing more."

Luis remained undaunted. "I'm just saying that having such a beautiful woman care about you can't be a bad thing. You need someone special in your life. You've been alone too long."

"You've been talking to my mother again," Grady guessed. His mother wasn't above enlisting her brother-in-law's assistance in fixing his love life.

His uncle shrugged. "She, too, worries about you. It's time to stop blaming yourself for what happened with Kathleen and Megan and move on."

"And I really don't want to go there," Grady warned as he climbed into his uncle's flashy sports car. His aunt had worried that the car was just the beginning of some midlife crisis, but Luis insisted it was nothing of the sort. The car was just the fulfillment of a long-held dream.

"Has Tia Delores ridden in this yet?" he asked his uncle, determined to change the subject to something that would put Luis on the defensive for once.

Luis sighed heavily, his expression sorrowful. "She says she doesn't trust it or me, that we're too old for a car like this. She thinks we should drive a nice, safe sedan."

"You sure she's not sneaking out while you're working and taking it for a spin around the neighborhood?" Grady asked.

"I wish she would," Luis said as he pulled into the parking lot at Versailles, one of the oldest and most popular Cuban restaurants in the heart of Little Havana.

Inside, Luis called out greetings to several of the regulars who were standing at the counter in front ordering Café Cubano, the thick, sweet coffee that came with a real jolt of caffeine and a generous dollop of local gossip spoken in Spanish or, in a very few instances, heavily accented English. He led the way to a table in the back, near one of the ornate, etched mirrors that harked back to the decor of many places in Havana in a happier era before Castro.

When they'd ordered—pork with black beans and rice for Luis, a traditional Cuban *media noche* sandwich with hot pork, ham, cheese and pickles grilled between thick slices of Cuban bread for Grady—Luis studied him. "You look tired."

"I'm not sleeping well."

"Because you are troubled about this boy, am I right?"

Grady nodded. "If I can't find some other women he's done this to, I'm afraid the rest of the evidence— damning as it is—won't hold up. And if he gets off…" He shook his head. "I don't even want to think about what that would do to the young woman he raped."

"On the street, they are saying he has been falsely accused." His uncle gave him a rueful look as he repeated the most outrageous theory of all. "Those who follow football think it is some conspiracy by one of the other colleges to keep him from playing in the fall. One group believes she has ties to Tallahassee, another to Gaines-ville."

"I know," Grady said, not even trying to hide his ex-asperation. "Just imagine what a field day they'd have if *I'd* actually graduated from Florida or Florida State, rather than Miami. I can thank the kid's father for all the speculation. I'll give Ken Carter credit for one thing. He's damn good at what he does. He can spin a story with the best of them."

"Can you blame him? Isn't it what any father would try to do—save his son?"

Grady studied him with dismay. "You're defending him?"

"No, I'm just saying his tactics might be deplorable, but they are understandable."

Grady tried to envision his own father standing behind him in a similar crisis and couldn't. Luis, however, would be there, his loyalty and faith unshakable, so perhaps his attitude made sense, as well. Oh, his father loved him, but he was judgmental and wouldn't tolerate mistakes or flaws, even in his own son.

"That doesn't make it right," Grady groused.

"No," Luis agreed. "And it definitely makes your job harder. Any other prospective witnesses who see what's happening to the victim in this case are far less likely to come forward."

"Exactly." Grady pushed his half-eaten sandwich aside. Suddenly he'd lost his appetite.

His uncle reached across the table and put the meal, including the side of fries, back in front of him. "Eat. Ruining your health won't help this young woman." His dark eyes, so like Grady's own, regarded him with sympathy. "What can I do to help?"

"Just having you listen to me has helped. How did you know I'd hit a wall today?"

"I know you. You are hard on yourself and you take these cases to heart. I knew it would not be easy on you to have people starting to question whether you had done the right thing in arresting that boy."

"I don't give a damn what anybody thinks about me," Grady protested. "I'm only interested in justice for Lauren Brown."

"A noble ideal." His uncle regarded him knowingly. "And I'm well aware than you don't care about public opinion, but it is only a short leap from listening to what's said to doubting yourself. Just look how events in your own life have haunted you for years now. I know you're not convinced of this, but you're a good man, Grady, and a good detective. You have proved that time and again. Your instincts are solid and your heart is on the side of the angels."

Grady appreciated the vote of confidence, but he wasn't so sure he deserved it. He had only to think back ten years to question every action he'd ever taken.

"There, you see, I was right," Luis exclaimed. "I see the doubt in your eyes."

"No," Grady insisted, forcing himself to stay in the present. "I know that boy is guilty. I know in my gut that he's done this before and he needs to be locked away."

"Then you will see that it happens," Luis said with assurance. "Do you have any leads at all?"

"One," Grady said, thinking of Dani Dobbs. "Unfortunately, I'm only speculating. And the girl's underage, so her mother refuses to let me speak to her. At this point, with the little I know, a court would probably support the mother."

"And the girl's father? Surely he would want this man behind bars if his daughter has been harmed."

Grady suddenly realized that he'd never had more than a cursory, preliminary conversation with Derek Dobbs. Even that had been on the phone before he'd become convinced that Dani might hold the key to this case. Maybe because of his personal feelings for Emily, he'd almost blocked the existence of her ex-husband. That alone was proof that he was allowing his emotions to cloud his judgment anytime she was involved. That needed to stop. For now the case had to come first. Whatever there might be between him and Emily had to take a backseat.

"You're a genius," he told Luis, standing up and giving him a smacking kiss on the cheek. "I need to get back to the station. Are you ready?"

Luis tossed him the keys to his beloved car. "Go. I will spend some time in the neighborhood and then call your aunt to pick me up. You can bring the car over tonight and let her feed you dinner. She's missed you."

"I'll be there," Grady promised.

As he headed back to the station in the spiffy little car with the top down and the radio blaring, he felt better than he had in days. The only thing that could possibly improve his mood even more would be having Emily Dobbs riding right here beside him.

He shook his head as he realized how quickly he'd forgotten his resolve to back-burner any wicked, inappropriate thoughts of her for the time being. Still, maybe when things were less complicated and he got up the nerve to ask her on a real date, he'd borrow this car and take her for a spin. She'd say yes and, well, who knew where things would go from there.

Emily was grading papers a few days after her conversation with Josh when the sliding glass door was shoved open and Ken Carter charged into the kitchen, his face red and his eyes dark with fury. For the space of a heartbeat, she felt real fear, but then she reminded herself that this was a man she'd known for years and for all of his demeaning and nasty talk, she'd never known him to become physically violent. If there'd been even a hint about such behavior, she would have pushed Marcie to get away from him at once.

"Where is he?" he demanded, lurching drunkenly. "Where's that lying, rotten son of yours?"

Emily shot to her feet and squared off in front of him. Maybe she was foolish, but nobody spoke to her about Josh that way. *Nobody.*

"Excuse me?" she said softly. "I don't think I heard you correctly, Ken. You just called my son a liar?"

"Damn straight I did. Where is he?"

"Not here, but even if he were, I wouldn't let you near him while you're in this kind of mood. You might get away with bullying your family, but I won't allow you to do the same with mine, especially not when you're obviously drunk. Are we clear?"

To her surprise, he backed down. Pulling a chair away from the table, he sat down heavily. He shoved a hand through his thick, disheveled hair. "I'm sorry, Emily," he said contritely. "I really am. I don't know what got into me. You're not the problem."

Emily didn't entirely buy his sudden transformation, but she was grateful that he'd taken the shouting down a few decibels. She'd been terrified that Dani would hear him. She didn't want her coming downstairs to confront their less-than-sober neighbor spewing his venom.

"Can I get you something to drink?" she asked eventually. "I can make some coffee."

"No, I'm okay," he insisted. He regarded her with a dismayed expression. "I'm just worried sick about Evan, that's all."

"I know you must be," she said, taking pity on him. She might hate his tactics and his behavior in general, but she understood a parent's unconditional love for a child. And in Ken's case, he'd been living vicariously through Evan for years now, pinning all of his own hopes and dreams on Evan becoming a professional football player, some kind of superstar jock. She wasn't sure if it was the money or adulation he craved for his son, but she knew he was desperate for it.

"Why would that girl say such horrible things about Evan?" he asked, sounding genuinely bewildered. "You've known him for years now. Can you imagine him doing the things she accused him of?"

"Honestly, no," she admitted. "But Ken, neither of us were there that night. We don't know what really happened. I have trouble believing that a young woman would make up a story like that. Just look what she's had to go through."

"And what about everything Evan's gone through?" he asked heatedly, growing agitated again. "You saying he deserves that?"

"Not if he's innocent, no."

"But you believe her, don't you?" he demanded, back on his feet and towering over her. "You're as bad as that lying son of yours. Whatever made me think that you would stick by your best friend and her family? God, you people make me sick. You're a bunch of damn hypocrites, nothing but fair-weather friends."

"I am *always* on Marcie's side," she said just as furiously, even though she knew she was wasting her breath. Ken was beyond listening to her. Still, she couldn't help adding, "I want to believe in Evan as desperately as she does, but the evidence—"

"Circumstantial, all of it," Ken claimed, weaving in front of her. "You wait. Once we get into court, Evan's lawyer will prove what a pack of lies that girl has been spouting. She's going to regret the day she made up all that stuff about my boy."

"If you're so certain of that, then why are you so upset by whatever it is you think Josh has done?" she asked him.

"Because he's trying to muddy the damn waters, that's why," he said, then scowled at her. "Why am I even wasting my time talking to you? You don't have any more sense than my wife when it comes to the way the world works."

Before Emily could even think of how to respond to that, Josh burst into the kitchen and threw a punch that caught Ken square in the face. It wasn't a particularly powerful punch, but it was enough to rock the already unsteady Ken back on his heels and to have blood spurting from his nose. He sank back down on a chair, looking dazed, and grabbed for a fistful of napkins to stanch the bleeding.

"Don't you ever talk to my mother that way!" Josh shouted, standing over him. "No real man ever speaks to a woman in that tone of voice."

"Who taught you that, that pansy-assed daddy of yours?" Ken scoffed.

Josh pulled back his arm to throw another punch, but Emily put her hand on the tense muscle in his forearm.

"Josh, it's okay," she said. "Mr. Carter is understandably upset. He doesn't mean what he's saying. There's no harm done."

"No harm done?" Ken said indignantly, waving the bloodied napkins in her direction. "I ought to have the kid arrested for assault."

"Go ahead!" Josh encouraged. "I would love to call Detective Rodriguez and get him over here."

Ken muttered a disparaging remark about the detective's ethnicity that set Emily's teeth on edge.

"I think it's time for you to go home, Ken," she said emphatically. "I'll call Marcie and tell her you're on your way. Shall I tell her to come over and walk with you?"

He struggled up. "Don't bother. The day I need her help getting home, it'll be a sad day in my life."

"I'll see that he gets home, Mom," Josh said, his expression grimly determined.

"Stay away from me," Ken ordered.

"Once you're off our property, believe me, I will," Josh retorted.

A part of Emily knew she ought to remind Josh to respect his elders, but she just couldn't summon up the words. The truth was, she was grateful Josh had shown up when he had and had done what he'd done. She just wished that someone had told the man off years ago.

She flipped on the backyard floodlight and watched as Josh walked along behind Ken, then waited until he'd disappeared into his own yard. She heaved a sigh and sat down, covering her face with her hands.

"Mom?"

She whirled around to find Dani standing hesitantly in the doorway, her complexion pale.

"Are you okay?" Dani asked, worry clouding her eyes. "I heard Mr. Carter shouting and I called Josh. Was that the right thing to do?"

Emily held out her arms and Dani ran into them. "It was exactly the right thing to do."

"I thought about trying to call Dad, but I think he's away on another business trip. Besides, I figured Josh could get here faster. He always drives like a maniac. Thank goodness, he was already on his way home."

"I do not drive like a maniac," Josh said as he joined them. "Why'd you let him in here, Mom?"

"Actually he just walked in. I didn't have the sliding door locked."

Josh regarded her incredulously. "You know you're not supposed to leave it unlocked."

"It's a nice night. I wanted to let in some fresh air. It

never occurred to me that I needed to worry about Ken." She met her son's worried gaze. "What exactly did you do to get him so worked up? That's why he came over here. I assume it's something new and not your failure to back Evan when he asked you to."

"I just did what I told you I was going to do," he said evasively, his attention shifting pointedly to Dani.

Dani regarded him curiously. "Which was?"

Josh hesitated.

"You might as well tell her," Emily told him. "Dani needs to know what's going on."

"I contacted a bunch of girls Evan used to date," Josh explained. "I guess some of them must have reported back to Evan."

Dani looked stricken. "What did you ask them?"

"If Evan had ever gotten too rough with them, if he'd ever forced them to have sex," he said bluntly.

"You didn't," Dani said, obviously upset. "Josh, how could you? That's not the kind of thing you just ask somebody. It's private. It's nobody else's business."

"It is, if there's a pattern to his behavior and it can help Lauren Brown in court."

"That's not your job!" Dani said furiously. "You have to stop asking stuff like that. You have to stop it right now! Promise me."

Emily felt her heart flip over. There was only one reason she could think of for Dani to be this distraught. She was terrified that someone might ask her the same questions. She reached for her daughter's hand.

"Sweetie, it's okay. These are really important questions."

"Then let the police ask them," Dani argued. "It's not our business."

Josh's eyes narrowed. "What would you say if I asked you the same thing?" he asked quietly.

Dani stared at her brother as if she hated him. "I'd tell you to go to hell," she said, and ran from the room.

Emily could barely contain a gasp. Josh looked equally dismayed. In that instant, she knew that Dani had been one of Evan's victims. She knew it as surely as if Dani had admitted it. But how on earth was she going to make her daughter feel safe enough to say the words aloud to her, much less repeat them to Grady Rodriguez or a courtroom full of strangers?

The next day at school, Emily's hand was shaking when she dialed the number Grady had given her. She wasn't sure what she was going to say to him, but she needed to know how the case against Evan was progressing. She wanted to hear that it was solid and didn't need either Dani's testimony or whatever information Josh had unearthed. That would leave her to deal with Dani's trauma on her own timetable, without the pressure of knowing that Evan might walk away from the rape charge.

"This is a surprise," Grady said, sounding pleased. "Have you missed me?"

"No more than I'd miss a splinter once it was removed," she told him dryly.

"You're breaking my heart," he claimed. "Okay, if you're not calling just to hear the sound of my voice, what's going on?"

Emily hesitated.

"Emily, has something happened?" he asked, his tone sobering. "Has Dani opened up to you?"

"No," she said at once. "That's why I was wondering if you've found any other victims?"

"Not so far," he said, sounding frustrated. "But your son called a few minutes ago. He said he might have some leads. You know anything about that?"

"Only that he sent out a few e-mails to girls Evan used to date. It was enough to stir Ken Carter into a frenzy."

"Meaning?"

"He dropped by last night. He had a lot of unpleasant things to say to me and to Josh."

"How bad was it?" Grady asked, instantly sounding on edge. "If that man laid a hand on either one of you—"

She cut him off. "It was just Ken being Ken," she said, downplaying the scene.

"You're sure about that?"

"I'm sure."

"Because I'll back you up if you want a restraining order," he told her.

"Absolutely not. That would only make a bad situation a thousand times worse."

"Well, let me know if you change your mind," he said. "By the way, Josh asked me to come by the house this evening."

"He did?" Emily didn't try to mask her surprise or her dismay.

"You okay with that?"

"To be honest, I'd prefer it if the two of you met elsewhere," she said.

"I can call him and suggest that," he offered. "But I think he had a specific reason for wanting me to come by the house."

Emily was very much afraid she knew exactly what that reason was. Josh was hoping to rattle Dani so that she would finally open up about her own experience with Evan. That was the very same reason she didn't want Grady anywhere near the house.

"Please," she said quietly, "see if you can have that meeting somewhere else, but don't let him know I'm behind the change."

"Emily, what's going on? You sound upset."

"Well, of course, I'm upset. A boy I've loved like another son for ten years is accused of raping a girl and my kids seem to be all caught up in the fallout."

"Are you angry that Josh contacted these young women?"

She sighed. "No, not really. It was something he felt he had to do and I know it was the right thing to do."

"Then it's Dani you're worried about," he concluded.

"I just think it will be incredibly upsetting to her to hear that Evan might have done this to other girls."

"Or, perhaps, it might make her feel less alone," he suggested gently. "After listening to you, I have a feeling that's what your son is hoping for. Or maybe he wants her to spend a little time around me, so she won't feel threatened if I ask her a few questions."

"She's not ready for that," Emily said urgently. "*I'm* not ready for that."

"Okay, I get that, but why don't we leave things the way they are?" Grady said. "I'll come by the house to see Josh and we'll play it by ear. I won't ask your daughter anything about Evan, I promise, but if she brings him up, we'll follow her lead."

Emily knew what he was saying made sense, and it was the way Josh had wanted it, as well. Maybe it would be for the best. "If you're coming, you might as well have dinner with us," she said grudgingly. "It might make things less formal."

Grady chuckled. "I've had more gracious invitations."

"If you think the invitation was halfhearted, wait till you see what I put on the table. Don't count on the gourmet meal of your dreams."

"As long as you don't lace it with arsenic, I'll be happy," he said. "See you around six-thirty. I'll bring a bottle of wine."

"This isn't a date, Detective."

"Maybe it wouldn't hurt to have your daughter think it is," he said mildly.

Emily thought of how eager Dani had been to believe that the detective was interested in her. "Just don't carry the charade too far," she warned. "My daughter has a romantic streak. You could wind up walking down the aisle quicker than you get a straight answer out of her."

"You saying you'd cooperate if she got such an idea?"

Emily sputtered at the outrageous suggestion, unable to form a coherent response.

Grady laughed. "Okay, then, I think it's a chance I should take. I enjoy living on the edge. How about you?"

Something in his tone made Emily's heart do an odd little stutter step. Obviously she hadn't done an especially good job of tamping down her own fantasies where the detective was concerned.

"Not so much," she said. "I think boring and predictable pretty much sum me up."

"Bet I could prove you're wrong," he contradicted. "But we'll leave that for another time. See you around six-thirty."

"See you," Emily said, clutching the phone so tightly her knuckles had turned white.

Despite her own very staunch disclaimer, tonight—

---

set up to share potential evidence in a criminal investigation—suddenly felt very much like a date. What kind of idiot did that make her?

15

"Mom, can we go by the nursery this afternoon?" Dani asked as she and her mother left the school parking lot. "I know I'm still grounded, but couldn't you make an exception for this?"

Her mother regarded her with surprise. "Any particular reason you want to go today?"

Dani wasn't sure she could explain it, at least not so her mom would understand. "I just want to get some flowers, okay? I need to do something besides studying. I can't concentrate, anyway. I'm not asking for money or anything. I still have my allowance."

"You like growing things, don't you?"

Relieved that her mom hadn't said no immediately, Dani nodded. "I know it's probably lame, but yeah, I do. There's something about figuring out what colors look good together, and making sure that they get the right sun and fertilizer and stuff that makes me feel good."

"I'm really glad you have something that you enjoy like that, especially right now," her mom said. "Let's take a detour by the nursery. You want some new containers, too? I'll spring for them."

"Really?" Dani said excitedly. "Last time, when Dad

took me, I saw these really cool ones. They look like
terra-cotta, but they're plastic, so they're not as heavy.
They don't cost much, either. I was thinking I could do
one for either side of the front door. Maybe put in some
vines and some purple and red impatiens. We need some
bright colors out there. It's kinda boring."

"Sounds great!" her mom said. "But we can't take too
long. We're having company for dinner."

Dani shifted to study her mom's face. They never had
company, except for the Carters, and they only came
over on the weekends. This was Wednesday night.
"Who's coming?"

"Grady Rodriguez," her mom said, patches of color
in her cheeks.

Dani took a minute to process that, trying to put a face
with the name. When it came to her, she was stunned.
"That's the detective, right?"

"Yes. I spoke to him earlier."

Dani wasn't sure how she felt about that. It was cool
that her mom finally had a date, and Dani could tell that
she liked this guy, but Dani was uneasy with the idea of
sitting down with a detective who might bring up all sorts
of stuff she didn't want to talk about.

"Maybe the two of you should go out to dinner," she
suggested.

"Why? Will you be uncomfortable having him at the
house? Or do you not like the idea of me dating?"

Dani hated that her mother could see through her so
easily, though she was kinda off the mark this time. "It's
not that," she insisted. "I know you and Dad aren't going
to get back together, and that's okay. But you like the
guy, right? You want to impress him?"

"I never said that."

"But you do. I can tell."

"What does that have to do with going out?"

"Mom, your cooking won't impress anybody."

"Your dad always liked it well enough," she retorted, though she was grinning.

Dani grinned back at her. "Only because half the time he was so distracted that he didn't even know what he was eating. Remember the time I tested him by asking how he liked the roast and he said it was great. We'd had fried chicken that night."

"I do remember, and you have a point," her mom agreed, laughing. "Why don't we stop at the market and pick up one of those ridiculously expensive, ready-for-the-oven gourmet dinners you and Josh like. Maybe lasagna?"

Dani was disappointed she hadn't convinced her mother to go out. "You're going to get dressed up, though, right?"

"I hadn't planned on it."

"Mom, you can't have a date in the same clothes you wore to school. That would be so tacky, like you don't even care what he thinks of you."

"Clean jeans and a T-shirt," her mother countered. "How about that?"

"How about that sundress you bought in Sanibel?"

"I'll think about it," she promised as they pulled into the crowded lot at the nursery. "Don't take too long here, though, or there won't be time for me to pick up dinner, much less change. We'll be reduced to ordering takeout and I won't even have a minute to put on fresh lipstick."

"Ten minutes," Dani said, leaping from the car. "I swear it."

Her mom looked skeptical, but she didn't say a word. Dani leaned back into the car. "Can I drive home?"

For a minute she thought for sure her mom was going to turn her down, but then she nodded.

"You can drive home from the market."

Dani beamed. "Awesome!"

For the first time in what felt like forever, she felt as if everything in her life was okay. Hopefully Detective Rodriguez would be so caught up with making a good impression on her mom that he wouldn't say anything about Evan and ruin Dani's mood.

It was nearly five o'clock when Grady finally caught up with Derek Dobbs after several days of trying. His secretary had said he was away on business, but she hadn't been very specific about when he'd return, so Grady had been forced to call back repeatedly.

"What can I do for you, Detective?" Derek Dobbs asked, sounding distracted.

"Mind if I swing by your office for a couple of minutes? I'd like to talk to you some more about Evan Carter."

"Today's not the best day. I just flew back into town this afternoon and there are a million things I need to catch up on. Can we do this in the morning?"

"I'd really like to do it now," Grady told him. "It involves your daughter, too."

"Dani?" he said, suddenly sounding as if he were giving Grady his full attention. "How does she fit in?"

"I'll explain when I see you. I should be there in ten minutes."

The building that housed the company Dobbs worked for was above an old hotel in the heart of Coral Gables. The pale stucco structure and red-tiled roof had been renovated and the hotel and office complex now towered over the street known as Miracle Mile. Jensen and Landry, which had global interests in everything from manufacturing to real estate, occupied the fourth and fifth floors of the building. The executive offices were on the fifth floor, behind two heavy mahogany doors.

Grady gave his name to the receptionist in the waiting area, which was done in pastel tones that provided a subtle background for the vivid oil paintings of the Florida Everglades that decorated the walls.

Two minutes later an attractive woman in her mid-forties came out to usher him back into Dobbs's office with its panoramic view of Coral Gables and a sliver of the downtown Miami skyline in the distance.

Derek Dobbs, wearing a perfectly pressed suit and pristine shirt that showed no evidence of his travels, stood to greet him. He looked every inch the corporate executive, from his recently trimmed hair to his polished Italian loafers. Despite his own designer shirt and pressed slacks, Grady felt vaguely unkempt in his presence. He had to remind himself that Emily had divorced this man, so he couldn't be as perfect as he seemed.

"Detective." Dobbs greeted him with a handshake and gestured toward a small conference table off to one side. "We'll be more comfortable over there. Would you like some coffee? A drink?"

"Nothing, thanks. This won't take long."

"You said it's about Evan and my daughter."

"Let's start with Evan. When we spoke before, you said he'd always been a decent kid. Since our conversation, have you thought of any instances when his behavior suggested he had a problem with women?"

"Actually, I wasn't entirely truthful when we first

spoke," Dobbs admitted, his expression contrite. "I was trying to protect a kid I'd known for years and I wasn't entirely sure that what I'd observed was truly relevant."

"Understandable," Grady told him. "So, what have you thought of since then?"

"Lately, Evan has started mimicking his dad's attitude toward his mom. Ken Carter is a bully. He's especially demeaning to his wife. He pretty much ignores his daughter altogether. Evan started mouthing off to his mother, being so thoroughly disrespectful that my wife and I commented on the change. We warned our own kids that they were never to speak to an adult like that."

"How about with his sister or your daughter? Was Evan ever disrespectful to either of them in the same way?"

"Not that I noticed. Oh, he teased them both unmercifully, but it never had the edge to it that he had when he spoke to his mother."

"Was he ever a little rough with them in the pool, for instance? A little too intense with the horseplay?"

"Not when I was around," Dobbs said. "He and Josh could get carried away the way guys that age do, but the girls usually steered clear of them when things got out of hand or Emily and I would call them on it."

"Did Evan listen to you?"

"Always," Dobbs said. "And he never said anything the least bit inappropriate to my wife. He never seemed to have the same disdain for either of us that he had for his mother. I figured that was his father's influence." His gaze narrowed. "I know you're after something specific. Mind telling me what it is?"

Grady acknowledged his perceptiveness. "Usually when a young man rapes a girl he's dating, it's not an isolated incident. I have reason to believe that your daughter may know more than she's said to anyone about the kind of person Evan Carter is," Grady told him, phrasing his statement carefully.

Derek Dobbs's expression hardened. "Meaning?" he asked, though it was evident that he'd already guessed exactly what Grady was getting at.

"Look, there's no easy way to say this to a young girl's father, but I think Dani may have been victimized by Carter. Right now it's nothing more than a hunch and I wouldn't come to you with that if I didn't think that getting to the truth is critical, not just for my case, but perhaps for Dani, as well. If that boy hurt her, she has to be dealing with a whole lot of conflicting emotions."

Derek was on his feet at once, pacing, his expression filled with rage. He paused in front of Grady. "You think that boy raped her? That *is* what you're saying?"

Grady nodded. "I can't be one hundred percent certain, because she's not talking to your wife or your son, but they both have their suspicions, as well."

The fury in the eyes of this man Grady would have guessed to be mild mannered was immediate and striking.

"I'll kill him," Dobbs said flatly, wrenching his tie loose as if it were suddenly choking him.

Grady winced at the heartfelt, uncensored response. "Look, I understand how you must feel, but you probably shouldn't say something like that to me, even if you're just blowing off steam."

Dobbs gave him a hard look. "You think that's all it is, that I'm blowing off steam? No, Detective, I'm dead serious. If Evan laid a hand on my daughter—"

Grady held up his hand. "Don't finish that sentence,"

he warned. "Let's talk about a more constructive approach, a way to be sure he's locked up for a good, long time."

"You want Dani to testify," Dobbs concluded, his tone flat.

"If she was a victim, yes, but first I need to establish what went on between the two of them. Did they spend a lot of time alone together?"

"I can't really answer that. I haven't lived in that house for a few years now, but it's entirely possible. None of us would have thought anything about the two of them being alone, any more than we would have worried if Josh was alone with Caitlyn."

"Have you noticed anything unusual about your daughter's moods since this whole investigation began?"

"Again, I'm not around her as much as Emily," he said, clearly frustrated. "She's been quieter than usual, I guess. Why ask me these questions, Detective. Ask her."

"I can't," Grady said. "Your wife is afraid it will be too upsetting for me to question her, and Dani is still a minor. I'd need parental permission."

Dobbs gave him a curt nod of understanding. "I'll speak to Emily. And to Dani, too. They'll cooperate."

"Thank you," Grady said, relieved. "Let's hold off until tomorrow. I'm going by there tonight and this may be a moot point. There's always a chance Dani will say something without you needing to get involved."

"Do you want me to be there?" Dobbs asked.

Grady shook his head, and it had nothing to do with the pseudo-date he and Emily were purporting to have for Dani's benefit. "It's going to be hard enough for her to open up to her mother or to an impersonal third party. Most teenage girls couldn't bear to discuss this in front of their fathers. Right or wrong, they're afraid their dads will be disillusioned with them."

"Even when they know that what happened is not their fault?" Dobbs said incredulously.

"They don't always believe that, no matter how many times they're told that it isn't," Grady said. "If we're right about this, Dani will need your support, no question about it, but let's take this one step at a time. I just needed to know I have your backing, if we need to force the issue."

"You have it," Dobbs said. "But I have to tell you that sitting on the sidelines like this doesn't suit me. Will you let me know what happens?"

"Either I'll call you myself or I'll make sure that Emily does," Grady assured him.

When he walked out of the office, the shattered man he left behind was nothing like the confident, cool corporate executive Grady had met less than a half hour before. Despite whatever rivalry might come up between them, Grady felt bad about that.

Although Grady had seen the formal family photos of Dani Dobbs, they hadn't prepared him for the slender teenager on the front stoop, who was elbow deep in potting soil and surrounded by colorful flowers. She was wearing ragged jeans that had been cut off at mid-thigh, a faded T-shirt, and had her light brown hair pulled up with one of those elasticized bands that girls her age always seemed to have stuck in the depths of their purses. She greeted him with a mischievous smile that made her seem even younger than seventeen.

"Do I need to ask you your intentions toward my mom?" she inquired with an impudent tilt to her mouth.

Grady chuckled. "How do you think she'd feel about it?"

"She'd probably ground me for another week, but I can take it if you'll tell me what I want to know."

"Your mom and I have just met," he said tactfully.

She frowned slightly. "But you like her?"

Grady heard the serious concern in her voice and nodded. "I do." He leaned down and confided, "Don't tell her, though. She's a little skittish."

"Tell me about it."

Grady resisted the urge to bring up Evan. It would blow tonight's cover for his visit and he might never get Dani to trust him. "Since you look as if you're a little busy at the moment, should I walk on in or ring the bell?"

"Go on in. Mom's in the kitchen. Don't worry though, she didn't cook. Dinner will be edible."

Grady laughed again, but when he stepped inside he had to pause to gather his composure. Now that he'd met Dani and been entranced by her exuberance and sense of humor, the thought of Evan Carter harming her infuriated him almost as deeply as it did her dad. He wanted to believe that a girl capable of such teasing couldn't possibly have such a dark secret, but experience had taught him otherwise. Knowing she was the same age Megan would have been made it even worse. He knew that from now on, the two girls would somehow be inextricably linked in his mind. It was going to make staying impartial and clear-eyed about Evan Carter that much more difficult.

He was still standing in the foyer, when Emily came out of the kitchen and gave him a quizzical look. "I thought I heard your voice. Everything okay?"

"Sure," he said, shaking off his mood. "Your daughter's a real handful, isn't she?"

"You have no idea," she said. "Why do you say that, though? What did she do?"

"Let's just say that she's charmingly direct and that she apparently bought into the whole date ruse, hook, line and sinker."

Color bloomed in Emily's cheeks. "I am so sorry."

"Not a problem for me. I'm used to tough interrogations."

"But you're usually on the other side of them," she said.

"True, but I think I held up okay with this one. You need any help with dinner?"

"It's under control. Just lasagna, which I didn't make, by the way, and a salad, which I did."

"So eat the lasagna and avoid the salad," he teased. "Is that what you're suggesting?"

"I see Dani had something to say about my culinary skills, too," she said, her tone resigned.

"Actually you warned me off yourself when we spoke earlier," he said. "Is Josh here yet? Maybe he and I should chat before dinner, get the talk about Evan out of the way before Dani joins us."

She shook her head. "He just called. He's on his way. Why don't we get something to drink and sit in the kitchen? I'd suggest going out by the pool, but I'm not sure it would be a good idea."

"Too visible to the Carters," he concluded.

She looked relieved that he understood. "Exactly. What would you like to drink? I have iced tea, sodas, coffee, wine. There might even be a beer in there."

"You don't strike me as a beer drinker."

"No, but I was away over the weekend and I'm sure some of Josh's friends stopped by. A few of them are old enough to buy it."

He heard a rueful note in her voice. "You don't sound too upset about that."

"He's in college. I'm not blind or naive. The house was cleaner when I got home than it was when I left, proof positive that something went on here. Since none of the neighbors have called to complain about the noise and my son's not in jail, I have to assume it was kept under control."

Grady chuckled. "You'd make a good detective."

"Nope. Just a mom who knows her kids. Now, what can I get you?"

"What are you having?"

"Tea, I think. I need a clear head."

"I'll take a beer, if there is one."

He followed her into the cozy kitchen. He was right behind her at the refrigerator, prepared to accept the beer she was retrieving, when she turned unexpectedly. They were face-to-face, her eyes wide with surprise, her lips parted. It was too tempting to ignore, so Grady brushed a quick kiss across her mouth. When she didn't jerk away or bolt, he dipped his head again and stole another kiss, this time lingering long enough to taste her, to satisfy the curiosity that had been taunting him since they'd met. Knowing they could easily be interrupted by her kids, though, he backed away.

She regarded him with a dazed expression. "Why'd you do that?"

"I could say it was all part of the charade that this is a date," he said, "but it wasn't. I just needed to do it. I've wanted to for a while now. You mad?"

She shook her head, looking more rattled than annoyed.

"Want to do it again?" he teased. "I'm willing. And Dani has given me a tentative stamp of approval."

Amusement danced in her blue eyes. "I warned you she's a romantic. Watch yourself."

"Oh, I think I can hold my own with your daughter," he said. "It's you I'm a little worried about."

"Aren't you forgetting that this date thing is supposed to be just for Dani's benefit?"

"Didn't I mention that I tend to throw myself whole-heartedly into whatever I do?" he responded.

She adopted a tolerant expression. "A convenient lapse of memory, I'm sure."

Grady was still feeling the heat of that kiss. To offset it, he took the beer she continued to clutch and popped the top off the bottle. He noted that Emily couldn't seem to look away as he tilted the bottle for a long, slow drink of the cold beverage. It slaked his thirst, but not the heat.

Emily looked away at last and when she turned back, her regard was steady. "Maybe we shouldn't go too far with this whole make-believe date. I don't want to give either of my kids false expectations."

"You so sure they'd be false?"

She swallowed hard, then blinked and shook her head. "Stop doing that."

"Doing what?" he asked innocently.

"Trying to rattle me."

"I'm not doing it on purpose," he swore. "But when there's something between two people, it's hard to keep it in check."

"Well, try," she said with exasperation, then whirled around. "I need to make sure the lasagna's okay."

Grady had a hunch he could use a few minutes to remind himself that this evening wasn't all about his growing attraction to Emily. He walked over to the sliding glass door and looked toward the Carters' house. For the first time, he noticed the gap in the hedge, a sure sign of the bond between these two families.

"How long has there been a path between your house and the Carters'?" he asked Emily.

"Practically since the Carters moved to the neighborhood. Josh cut it, so he and Evan wouldn't have to run all the way around the block. When the girls were old enough, it became their shortcut, too. Marcie and I have always taken advantage of it, as well."

"Your husbands?"

"They never got along well enough to need easy access," she said candidly. "I used to think that Ken looked up to Derek, but maybe it was more about his tendency to suck up to anyone he thought might be in a position to help him. Derek barely tolerated Ken. From the beginning, he saw through the charm and knew exactly the kind of man he was. Still, for the sake of harmony between the families, he did his best to get along with Ken."

"Then you all spent a lot of time together?"

"Every holiday, birthdays, even a few day trips, though those didn't go so well till we started leaving Ken and Derek at home. Marcie, the kids and I had a better time without the tension of having them scowling at each other half the time." She studied him curiously. "How long were you married?"

"Eight years."

"Whose idea was the divorce?"

"Kathleen's," he admitted. "I didn't contest it. She had grounds."

Her expression turned cautious. "Were you cheating on her?"

He shook his head. "No, it was never anything like that. I loved her, at least as much as I was able to love anyone. I just loved my job more." He was skirting the whole truth by a mile, but it was all he was willing to admit to.

"You still do, don't you?"

"Sure, but not as obsessively. I'd like to think that I've learned something about balance. Did it the hard way, unfortunately. I had to lose the most important people in my life before I got the message."

Emily gave him an odd look. "People?"

Grady never talked about Megan, not even with his own family. Luis mentioned her name from time to time at his own peril, but his parents never uttered it. Still, he knew if he was ever going to have any kind of relationship with this woman, she deserved to know everything, including all the mistakes he'd made, all the regrets that would haunt him till his dying day.

"I'll explain," he said quietly. "Just not tonight, okay?"

She hid whatever disappointment she might be feeling and nodded. "Whenever you're ready," she said easily. Then to his surprise, she gave his hand an understanding squeeze, as if she somehow sensed that whatever he was withholding had damaged his heart so deeply, talking about it simply wasn't bearable.

Ten years earlier

Grady was hoping for the kind of deep, drugging sleep that only came when he was on the verge of sheer exhaustion. He'd worked yet another series of double shifts, determined to get the one last bit of cash he and Kathleen needed so they could buy that car for her without going into debt for it. His body craved rest, not the backyard barbecue that Kathleen wanted to have that evening. He knew she was annoyed with him over his lack of enthusiasm, but tonight he couldn't muster up the energy to appease her.

Sitting outside by the tiny backyard pool that they'd mortgaged themselves to the hilt to have, he took a few sips of beer and his eyes drifted shut. Two or three times he tried to jerk himself awake so he could help Kathleen get the hamburgers on the grill for dinner, but his eyelids were just too heavy, the allure of sleep too tempting. He gave up and sank into it.

A scream jerked him awake. It could have been seconds later or an hour. He had no way of telling, but adrenaline was suddenly pumping through his body as if an alarm had gone off.

"What?" he said, on his feet, looking around, still slightly dazed.

Kathleen's keening wails were coming from the shadowed end of the pool. "Oh, God, no," she kept saying, her sobs finally snapping him back to reality.

"What happened?" he asked, racing toward her, his heart thundering in his chest. "Are you hurt?"

Only when he was practically beside her did he see the inert body of his little girl in her arms. He'd always thought it an exaggeration or an impossibility when someone said their heart stood still, but now he knew otherwise.

On his knees beside them in an instant, his training kicked in. He took Megan from Kathleen and shifted into crisis mode. He started CPR, even as he began automatically snapping out directions at his wife, who was clearly in a state of shock. For the first time, he realized she was soaking wet and shivering in the cool evening breeze.

"Have you called nine-one-one?" he asked.

She shook her head, unable to tear her attention away from their child. "I just found her in the deep end of the pool. She…" She swallowed hard. "She must have hit her head. There was blood in the water. I jumped in and pulled her out," she said. "She wasn't breathing, Grady." She covered her face with her hands. "I didn't know what to do. How could we have a pool when I never learned CPR? All those years of swimming and being around water, and I never learned how to do CPR. What was wrong with me? I counted on you knowing."

She stared at him with such hate that Grady had to look away. "I thought you were watching her," she said. "I told you she was coming outside, that she wanted to go in the water and you needed to go in with her. She's only had a couple of swimming lessons. She still needs supervision. You know that!"

Grady remembered none of that and he was too focused on performing CPR to respond. "Call nine-one-one," he repeated between attempts to breathe life back into his daughter. "Do it, Kathleen. Do it now!"

She finally ran for the portable phone. He could hear her barely coherent plea for help, but he already knew it was too late. Megan wasn't responding. Her body was limp and she had yet to draw in a breath on her own. Her color was changing, too, and her eyes—staring accusingly at him, he thought—were lifeless.

Still, he wouldn't give up. When the EMTs arrived and tried to do what he'd been unable to do, he stood hovering over them. "Breathe, baby," he whispered again and again. "You can do it, sweetheart. I know you can."

When the young man who was working on Megan looked up at him and shook his head, Grady felt as if his world had crashed to a stop. Beside him, Kathleen's sobs had dwindled to nothing.

"No," she protested, her voice almost unrecognizable in its anguish. She turned and started beating on his chest. "This is your fault. You let this happen. You let our baby die."

As harsh as the words were, as filled with anger and hate, they were nothing compared to the loathing Grady turned on himself.

After that awful night, no matter how many times anyone told him that it had been an accident, he reeled from guilt. No matter who reminded him that he'd been asleep when Kathleen had allowed Megan to come outside so that she shared at least some of the blame, Grady heaped it all on himself. He wouldn't allow anyone to direct the blame—not even a portion of it—toward his wife.

They tried for a while to get their marriage back on solid ground—at least he did—but it was a lost cause. Kathleen couldn't forgive or forget.

A few months later, when she finally said she could no longer bear the sight of him or live in the house because of the painful memories of that night, he watched her walk away from their marriage and did absolutely nothing to stop her. Her leaving was just part of the penance he felt he owed for letting his daughter die.

16

Emily was a nervous wreck. Tonight suddenly felt a whole lot more like an actual date than she'd intended. The kiss had been totally unexpected, but not nearly as unwelcome as it should have been. Grady was the first man she'd kissed other than her husband in more than two decades. She'd forgotten the power and hint of mystery that a first kiss could pack. She'd forgotten its ability to awaken the senses and kick all sorts of cravings into high gear.

She was so rattled she could barely get dinner on the table, much less look Grady in the eye. Apparently she wasn't doing a very good job of covering, either, because both Josh and Dani were eyeing her speculatively. Dani, in particular, seemed to be making the connection between Emily's distraction and Grady, thanks to their pretense that this evening was a date. Josh was clueless about the pretense, but clearly aware that there was some sort of tension between Emily and the detective. Hopefully he was still too young and naive to pin a label on it.

Naturally, Dani was the one who couldn't ignore it. "So, Mom, did you and Detective Rodriguez talk about anything interesting before Josh and I came in for dinner?" Dani inquired, her eyes sparkling with mischief.

"Not really," Emily replied, casting a pleading look in Grady's direction for some help. The rat looked almost as amused as her daughter and remained stubbornly silent. To shift the attention away from them, she said, "Why don't you tell us about the flowers you were planting?"

"I don't think Detective Rodriguez cares about my impatiens," Dani replied.

"Why don't you call me Grady?" he suggested. "And I'd love to hear about the flowers. My yard's a mess. Maybe you could give me some ideas."

To Emily's relief, Dani's expression brightened with interest, all thoughts of cross-examining the two of them forgotten, right along with whatever nervousness she'd been feeling about the prospect of having the detective sharing their dinner table with them.

"Really?" she asked excitedly. "Could I see it? I'd love to plan a whole yard from scratch. You wouldn't have to pay me or anything. You'd just have to go with me to pick out the plants and buy them."

"I'm not sure Detective Rodriguez was committing to anything, sweetie," Emily said, trying to put the brakes on Dani's runaway imagination. She'd have his yard looking like a microcosm of Fairchild Tropical Botanic Garden, given the budget and the freedom to indulge her creativity.

"Actually, I'd love to have the help," he corrected, then turned to Dani. "And if you do the work, you get paid for the work. If it's okay with your mom, we'll pick a date and you can look things over." He cast a questioning look in her direction. "Well, Mom?"

"If you're sure," she said. She told herself she was agreeing primarily because it was so wonderful to see Dani excited about something, but the truth was she wasn't nearly as displeased about the idea of spending more time with Grady as she probably should have been.

"Wow, that is so awesome," Dani said. "My first landscaping job. How cool is that, Mom?"

"Very cool," Emily agreed. She glanced at Grady. "Just be sure you give her a budget at the outset. Dani could spend your life's savings at the nursery."

"We'll work it out," Grady said confidently. "Josh, what are you studying at UM?"

"I started out in business, but I'm thinking of switching my major," he said, startling Emily.

"Really?" she said. "I didn't know that."

"I've been thinking about pre-med lately. I asked Dad what he thought, since I'd be in school a lot longer, and he said it was okay with him, if it's what I really want. I'll decide before the end of the semester."

"I think you'd make a wonderful doctor," Emily told him. "You're caring and curious, which would make you a good listener and a good diagnostician, two of the traits I value in a physician. What made you start to think about it?"

"Jenny," he admitted, his cheeks flushing. "She's pre-med and we have that biology class together. We had to dissect this frog and my incision was way neater than hers. She said I'm a natural. My grades are as good as hers, too. At first I thought she was crazy, but then I got to thinking about it. I wouldn't want to be a surgeon, no matter how great my incisions are, but I like the idea of helping people stay well or get well. I think I'd like to provide care for people who can't afford to pay much."

Emily lifted a brow. "More of Jenny's influence?"

"Actually it was my idea, but she liked it, too. Who knows, maybe we could open a clinic in some rural area where there's no decent medical care."

"What a wonderful idea!" Grady told him. "I've read some articles about how difficult it is to get physicians to go into practice in areas like that. There's a huge demand for doctors willing to do that."

Emily studied her son, wondering why she hadn't noticed that his new-found maturity went well beyond the way he was handling the situation with Evan. She was more eager than ever to meet the young woman who was likely responsible for it.

"I don't want to throw a damper on your enthusiasm," she told Josh, "but it's a tough program. I know you have the grades for it, but are you sure you have the commitment and dedication it will require?"

"Absolutely," he said enthusiastically. "I'm up to the challenge, Mom. I really am. Jenny's real focused. She studies all the time, so she'll be on my case if I slack off at all."

"When I met her, I was very impressed with her clear thinking and her ability to remain calm in a crisis," Grady chimed in. He turned to Emily. "Have you met her yet?"

"No, I've encouraged Josh to bring her home sometime. Lauren, too."

"Who's she?" Dani asked, sounding miffed that they were talking about someone she'd never even heard of.

"That's Jenny's roommate," Josh said, his expression guarded.

Emily decided now was as good a time as any to ease into the subject of Evan and the accusation against him. "She's the young woman who filed the charges against

Evan," she said quietly. "I think she's incredibly brave and strong."

"Me, too," Josh said. "I really admire her."

Dani's expression froze. Suddenly she backed away from the table. "Don't bring her here," she said adamantly. "How could you even think about bringing her here, either one of you, when Evan lives right behind us? It would be awful."

Startled by Dani's vehement reaction, Emily couldn't help wondering if she was more worried about Lauren running into the man who'd harmed her or if she simply didn't want his accuser in the house. Of course, there was also the possibility that she didn't want to meet a young woman who'd had the courage to do what Dani herself had been unable to do: hold Evan accountable for his actions. Emily increasingly feared it was the latter.

"Sweetie," she began, but Dani was already pushing back from the table as if she couldn't get away fast enough. Obviously the transition to talking about Evan's case hadn't been nearly as smooth as Emily had hoped. She'd thought that the natural flow of conversation from discussing Josh's girlfriend to mentioning Lauren was subtle, but she'd clearly miscalculated.

"I'm not hungry anymore. I'm going to my room. I've got homework to do."

"Dani, sit down," Emily ordered, but her daughter ignored the command and ran from the kitchen. She turned to Grady apologetically. "I'm sorry. I thought we could ease into the subject and finally get somewhere. Things seemed to be going so well."

"Don't worry about it. I got some good insights into your

daughter tonight." He turned to Josh. "Maybe it's for the best that she's gone upstairs, if you have information for me."

Josh nodded and reached into his pocket. "I have a few names. It's not much, but maybe they'll help."

"At this point, any leads will help."

Emily frowned. "Were there girls from the high school who said Evan had raped them?"

Josh shook his head. "None of them went that far, but there were four who said he didn't know how to take no for an answer, so they'd stopped dating him." He gave Grady a look filled with regret. "I know that's not the same thing."

"It does establish a pattern, though. And maybe if Naomi contacts them, they'll say just how far he pushed things. They might be more forthcoming with her than they would be with you or with me. Girls in this kind of situation respond well to her."

"Naomi's your partner, right?" Josh said. "I saw her talking to Jenny that day you were on campus."

"Right," Grady confirmed.

"Jenny likes her. She says she was really, really good with Lauren."

"I'll tell her you said that," Grady said. "It takes a lot of compassion to be able to do what she does."

Josh gave him a speculative look. "She's pretty hot, too. Is there anything going on between the two of you? Because if there is…" He glanced meaningfully at Emily, proving he hadn't been as oblivious to the under-currents as she had hoped.

"Josh!" she protested, mortified.

Grady grinned. "Message received," he assured Josh. "Naomi and I are partners. We're not involved. It would be too complicated. Besides, she prefers guys who are a whole lot younger and less jaded than I am."

Emily couldn't believe her son felt he had the right to meddle in her love life and ask such an intrusive question. Not that she even had a love life with Grady, or any other man, for that matter. Tonight was the first time since the divorce she'd even seriously considered including a man in her future. Up until that kiss, it had been little more than a fantasy.

And, fantasy or reality, she most certainly didn't want to dwell on it now, not when she was increasingly worried about her daughter's state of mind.

"Look, I hate to cut this short, but I really need to go upstairs and spend some time with Dani. Josh, do you have any more information for Detective Rodriguez? If not, I'll show him out on my way upstairs."

Naturally Grady took note of her suddenly formal tone and the abrupt dismissal and gave her a mocking look. Josh studied the two of them curiously.

"I've already told him what I know," Josh said and drew a rumpled sheet of paper from his pocket. "Here are the names of the girls who answered me, plus their contact information. I really hope it helps."

"Thanks, Josh. I'm sure it will." Grady stood up and his amused gaze locked on Emily. "After you."

Emily led the way to the front door. When she turned back to face him, he was still regarding her with tolerant amusement.

"Can't get me out of here fast enough, can you? Do I make you nervous?"

"Of course not," she lied.

He touched a finger to the tip of her nose. "It's growing, sweetheart. You might want to watch those little white lies. They add up. Next thing you know you'll be like Pinnochio with a nose out to here." He held his hand a foot away from her face.

"Not funny," she said. "I do need to check on Dani."

His expression sobered at once. "I know you do, but I would have happily helped your son clean up the kitchen while you talked to her."

She caught herself smiling. "I think you're giving my son more credit than he deserves. Any cleaning up that goes on around here, I'll be doing."

He frowned at that. "All the more reason to let me stay and help out, maybe encourage him to pitch in."

She shook her head. "I know you really just want to stick around in case I find out anything from Dani."

He shrugged. "That, too."

"There's another reason?"

His gaze caught hers and held, then drifted to her lips. Only after she was all but sizzling with anticipation did he lean down and press a chaste kiss to her forehead.

"I think you know the reason," he chided. "Call me, okay?"

Flustered once again, Emily could only stare. "You mean if Dani says something."

"That would be one reason," he said, his lips twitching. "Or just to say hello and make my day."

"You're a very disconcerting man, Detective."

"And you're a very intriguing woman, Emily," he said just as seriously. Then he winked at her. "Good night. Thanks for dinner and for the company. I like your kids. Tell Dani I'll call to set up an appointment for our landscaping project."

"You don't have to go through with that."

"If you could see my yard, you'd know that I do."

Emily stood in the doorway as he walked down the driveway to his car. A very disconcerting man, indeed. She couldn't quite make up her mind how she felt about that.

On his way home, Grady stopped in Little Havana for some Café Cubano. Sometimes coming to the neighborhood along Eighth Street—*Calle Ocho*—reminded him of what it must have been like for his father and uncle growing up in Havana. The rapid-fire exchanges in Spanish, the businesses catering to Spanish-speaking customers were like a taste of home for the thousands of Cuban exiles who'd fled the island in the sixties and more recently during the Mariel boatlift and other, less organized flights from Castro's rule. The neighborhood had also proved to be a draw for immigrants from El Salvador, Guatemala, Nicaragua and other countries in Central and South America.

After chatting with some of the elderly men playing dominoes in the park across the street from the coffee shop, Grady found an unoccupied bench and dialed Naomi on his cell phone.

"This better be important, Rodriguez," she said, sounding breathless.

"Obviously your date is going better than mine did," he commented dryly. "I'll try to keep this short. You have a pen and paper?"

"You want me to take notes?" she asked incredulously.

"We both know you don't have a head for numbers," Grady retorted. "I have four names, some e-mail addresses and phone numbers for girls who dated Carter in high school and ditched him because he was a little too eager for sex. Interested?"

"Two minutes," she said tersely.

When she came back on the line, she sounded more composed. Grady tried not to imagine the frustrated young stud she'd abandoned in her bed. Instead he gave her the information as briskly as possible.

"Can you get on this right away?"

"In the next half hour," she said firmly.

Grady grinned.

"Stop smirking," she snapped.

"How'd you know I was smirking?"

"Because you always do when you think you know what I'm doing with some guy. The truth is I'm coloring my hair and the stuff has to be washed out in twenty minutes or all my hair will probably fall out. I'll make the calls after that."

Grady choked back a laugh. "I thought—"

"I know what you thought. But I am not the horny broad you think I am." She sighed. "At least not always. Good night, Rodriguez. I'll fill you in first thing tomorrow if I find out anything."

Grady glanced at the tiny but potent cup of coffee in his hand. "Or you could call me at home later. Something tells me I'll be up half the night."

If the coffee didn't keep him awake, the memory of kissing Emily probably would.

Dani retreated to her room the second she got home from school the day after Grady had stayed for dinner. With any luck her mom wouldn't follow her again today as she had the night before. She'd just sat there, asking all sorts of leading questions, a hopeful expression on her face as if she expected Dani to open up and spill her guts about Evan.

Maybe if she'd come right out and asked, Dani would have found some way to say the awful words. Instead, she'd danced all around the subject until Dani had finally claimed a headache and her mom had sighed, then turned out the light and left her alone.

If it had been up to her, she wouldn't have gone to school this morning, but her mom would have freaked if she'd claimed to be sick again. She'd gotten away with it for a couple of days after Evan's arrest, but she knew better than to try for more.

Not that claiming to be ill would have been a total lie. She did feel sick every time she heard something or read an article in the paper calling the girl who'd accused Evan of rape a liar. People had been digging around in her past, making all sorts of ugly claims about her. Dani hadn't believed any of them, not even before she'd heard all the good stuff Grady and her brother had said at dinner. She was smart enough to recognize a deliberate smear campaign when she heard one. She had a hunch that Ken Carter, who was good at selling lies, was behind these. She'd never liked him and she really hated the way he ignored Caitlyn. Dani could tell it hurt her knowing that her dad only cared about Evan.

Chilled by the blasting air-conditioning in her room— or maybe by her mood—she pulled the comforter off her bed and wrapped it around herself as she sat in the chair that Caitlyn usually claimed when she visited. She actually wished she could talk to her about some of this. Keeping it all bottled up inside was making her kind of crazy. Not that she could tell Caitlyn everything, not about this. She'd finally faced the fact that Caitlyn's first loyalty was always going to be to her brother, even if he didn't deserve it. She'd known that the first time she'd even hinted at what Evan had done to her. Caitlyn had called her a liar and fled.

A knock on her door startled her.

"Sweetie, may I come in?" her mom called out.

"I guess so."

Her mom frowned when she saw her. "Are you okay? You're not catching a cold or the flu, are you?"

Dani shook her head, fighting tears. "Nope. I'm fine." She thought she sounded pretty convincing, but her mother continued to study her with concern.

"Don't you want to come down and have a snack? Marcie brought over some brownies."

"She was here?"

"A few minutes ago," her mother confirmed. "She didn't stay long."

Dani swallowed hard, then braced herself to ask. "Is there any news, you know, about Evan's case?"

"No. Actually she was hoping you'd come over and spend some time with Caitlyn."

Dani didn't want to go anywhere near that house, not if there was any possibility Evan might come home. "I'm grounded, remember?"

Her mom smiled. "Of course, I remember, but I thought under the circumstances, it would be okay for you to spend a little time with Caitlyn, if you want to. She needs her best friend. This whole mess with Evan is really hard on her."

Dani stared at her mother incredulously. "Don't you think it's hard on me, too?"

For once her mother didn't get all crazy at her tone. Instead, she said mildly, "I'm sure it is. That's why I thought it might be good for the two of you to get together. She can come over here, if you'd prefer."

More relieved than she wanted to admit, Dani shrugged as if she didn't care one way or another. "Whatever."

"Then I should call and tell Marcie it's okay for Caitlyn to visit? Or do you want to call her yourself?"

"Mom, I'm not two," Dani snapped. "You don't have to arrange my playdates. I'll call."

Her mother's eyes narrowed. "Watch your tone, young lady."

Dani sighed. "Sorry."

"After you call, why don't you go out to the pool to wait for her?"

"Mom!" Dani protested, annoyed by the suggestion that they couldn't plan their own afternoon.

"I'm just saying I think you'll both feel better if you spend some time in the fresh air, instead of closed up inside."

"Whatever."

Her mother looked as if she was about to say something more about Dani's attitude, but instead she turned and left the room.

Dani sighed. She knew she was behaving like a brat, especially since her mom was only trying to help, but she couldn't figure out any other way to handle things.

Suddenly the memory of the way Josh and Detective Rodriguez had talked about Lauren being so brave came back to her and she knew what she had to do. She needed to talk face-to-face to another one of Evan's victims.

She checked the hallway and saw that her mom's door was closed. She eased past it, then headed downstairs and opened the front door.

"Mom, I decided to go to Caitlyn's instead," she called out, then quickly closed the door behind her and ran down the block until she knew she was out of sight of the house. Then she cut through the neighborhood and walked out to U.S. 1 where she could catch a bus to the university. By the time her mom figured out that she'd lied about going to Caitlyn's, Dani hoped to be talking to Lauren Brown.

The University of Miami campus started just west of South Dixie Highway along a street lined with palm trees. Dani didn't know where most of the specific buildings were located, but she figured if she asked the right questions, she could probably find Lauren Brown easily enough. After all, she was the number one topic on campus, according to Josh. Someone was bound to know where she lived.

Then she remembered that Lauren didn't live in a dorm at all. She and Jenny shared an apartment somewhere off-campus. That meant they probably had a phone. Surely every girl in college had a phone just so guys could call to ask them out on dates. And a phone book might even list the address. She wished she'd thought all this through at home, so she could go straight to their apartment, but she hadn't.

Across from the school she actually managed to find a pay phone, an increasing rarity in this cell-phone era, and, miracle of miracles, it had an intact directory. Her heart sank when she couldn't find a listing for Lauren, but then she found it under Jenny's name. Her hands shaking, she used her cell phone to dial the number, but hung up in a panic the minute someone answered.

She double-checked for the address accompanying the phone listing and jotted it down on an old receipt she found in the bottom of her purse. Maybe she should just show up there, see her in person. That way Lauren couldn't slam the phone down the second Dani brought up Evan's name. She convinced herself that made the most sense.

She looked around, got her bearings and started to walk toward Granada Avenue. Her steps slowed as she came to the block of small apartment buildings. Could she really go through with this? Could she tell Lauren Brown that Evan had done the same thing to her? Would it make any difference at all, especially if she wasn't quite ready to tell anyone else? Maybe it would help Lauren just to know that someone else believed her.

Dani was standing outside the apartment building, still debating with herself when someone roughly grabbed her arm and whirled her around.

"What are you doing here?" Evan demanded, regarding her with fury.

Bile rose in Dani's throat. "Take your hand off of me," she commanded, tears stinging her eyes. "I mean it, Evan. Let go right this second."

He released her at once, his expression chagrined. "Sorry. I just didn't expect to see you here."

The tiny victory over his attempt to manhandle her gave her courage. For the first time since the night he'd attacked her, Dani felt in control again. "Why are you anywhere near where Lauren Brown lives?" she asked. "Aren't you in enough trouble?"

Evan shrugged, his cocky demeanor back in place. "It's no big deal, Dani. I can go anywhere I want."

"You're hanging around out here just to intimidate her, aren't you?" she accused.

"Why would I need to do something like that?"

"Because you're scared, Evan, and you should be."

"I am not scared," he said indignantly.

Dani rolled her eyes at the blatant lie. She could see the fear in his eyes. "Whatever. I thought you were suspended from school."

He waved it off. "That's just temporary. This whole bogus mess will be over soon."

"You think so?" she asked doubtfully.

"I know so. Nobody will believe that lying bitch."

Still feeling in control, Dani leveled a look directly into his eyes. "I do."

He laughed at that. "You? You're just a kid."

"A kid who knows exactly what you're capable of doing," she reminded him. "I have to go."

To her satisfaction, he looked bewildered—and maybe just a little scared—by her refusal to back down.

"You don't want to get in the middle of this, Dani."

She nodded. "You're right. I don't." Then, drawing on a strength she was just discovering she possessed, she added, "But if I'm ever going to sleep at night, I may have to."

17

Grady hung up the phone at his desk and muttered an expletive that had Naomi's head snapping up.

"What?" she asked.

"Dani Dobbs just ran into Evan Carter," he said, feeling a desperate urge to punch something.

"I know you think there's a history there, but they live in the same neighborhood. Wasn't it bound to happen sooner or later?"

"He found her in front of Lauren's apartment building just off campus," he said. "You care to count how many ways that scenario sucks?"

"What the hell was he doing anywhere near that apartment?" Naomi asked, her expression alarmed. "Or, for that matter, why was Dani there?"

"My guess is that Carter was there hoping to have a confrontation with Lauren or, at the very least, to intimidate her with his presence. I knew that would happen sooner or later, which is just one of the reasons I've had the police keeping an eye on the building."

"And Dani? What was she doing there?"

"My theory is that she wanted to meet Carter's other victim. When her mom suggested that Josh bring Lauren by the house, Dani reacted pretty heatedly, but I think it made her curious about the girl that Carter assaulted, the one who was brave enough to come forward and file charges."

"You're really convinced that he hurt Dani, too, aren't you? It's gone beyond speculation."

Grady nodded.

"Then hanging around that house isn't all about Emily Dobbs. Wonder how she feels about that?"

"I'm sure she has a whole lot of issues with it, but I am more and more convinced every day that something happened between the Carter kid and Dani," he admitted, popping a Tums in an attempt to fight the acid suddenly swirling in his stomach. "And when Dani's ready to talk, I want to be around." He smiled ruefully. "Not that seeing Emily on a more regular basis poses any kind of hardship."

Naomi rounded her desk and sat on the corner of his. "Do you think maybe you're getting a little too close to the Dobbs family?"

His gaze narrowed. "Are you suggesting I've crossed some kind of line?"

"One way or another, they're all potential witnesses in this case. You're losing your objectivity about them."

Grady couldn't deny that. And with Dani somehow all twisted up in his mind with his own daughter, it had gotten that much more complicated. He hated that she might have been victimized by Evan Carter, hated it with a vehemence that sometimes scared him. When the patrol officer assigned to keep an eye on Lauren had reported seeing Carter grab Dani's arm and jerk her around, Grady had literally seen red. If he'd witnessed it in person, there was no telling what he might have done to the kid. He suspected he would have reacted like a protective parent rather than a cop.

He gave Naomi a plaintive look. "How the hell is it ever possible to remain entirely objective in a case like this? Can you tell me that? You're a woman."

She gave him a wry look. "I thought you preferred to think of me as gender neutral."

Grady rolled his eyes. "You're missing my point. Can you stay objective after listening to any of these victims tell you what the men have done to them?"

"Not entirely, no," she conceded. "But I do the best I can, because the second I get too involved, I can't do my job. I certainly can't go around choking the breath out of these creeps the way I'd like to. That's what you'd like to do right now, isn't it?"

"Maybe. Are you saying you don't think I can do my job when it comes to this case?"

"I'm just saying you're making it a whole lot harder on yourself."

She had no idea, he thought. If she knew that every time he imagined that creep's hands on Dani Dobbs, he envisioned him touching Megan the same way, Naomi would freak out and insist he turn the case over to someone else. She'd probably badger him into seeing the department shrink while she was at it. Thankfully, Naomi had only joined the department a couple of years ago, after all the talk about Megan's death had died down.

Besides, he already knew what a shrink would have to say. He was substituting his inability to protect Megan years ago for a grim determination to find justice for Lauren Brown…and for Dani. The two situations could not be more different, but both involved his ability—or inability, more precisely—to protect a girl he cared about. That same motivation probably drove him on every case, but he was seeing the connection now more clearly than ever before.

"You're not going to rest until you get Dani Dobbs to talk to you, are you?" Naomi asked.

"I can't," he said simply.

Naomi regarded him curiously. "For her sake or yours?"

Grady shrugged. "I'm not entirely sure anymore. I want to believe it's for hers."

"You ever going to tell me what drives you like this?" she asked.

He shook his head. "Nothing I can talk about."

"Can't or won't?"

"It doesn't really matter, does it?"

"I suppose I could find out just by asking around. You've worked with most of these guys for years."

"How do you think they'd feel about you trying to invade my privacy?" he asked.

"Okay, bad idea," she agreed, "but Luis would probably tell me if I asked."

"I doubt it," Grady said. "My uncle may be putty in your hands when it comes to most things, but this is private, Naomi. He'd never betray me."

"Not even if he thought you were in danger of losing perspective on a case?"

"Not even then," he said with conviction, then gave her a halfhearted smile. "Of course, you might succeed in motivating him to beat some sense into me. I hope you won't do that."

She gave him a weary look. "I hope I won't have to."

* * *

An hour later, Grady was too restless to stay in the squad room another second. "I need to get out of here," he told Naomi.

"And go where?" she asked, on her feet at once and striding along beside him.

"To find Evan Carter."

"Grady, you know we can't question him without his lawyer present," she protested.

"I'm not going to question him," Grady replied grimly.

"Oh, shit," she muttered under her breath, but she kept pace with him.

Ten minutes later they were cruising the streets that wound through the campus. Grady kept his eyes peeled for any sign of Carter. Naomi kept her gaze glued to him.

"You could help me look for him," he commented.

"Frankly, I'm not sure I want you to find him," she retorted. "This strikes me as a really bad idea."

"And yet here you are, along for the ride."

"I'm just hoping to keep you from doing something you'll regret."

"I wouldn't regret punching the kid's face in," he said. "But I'm not going to do that. I'm just going to give him a little advice, see how he takes it."

"What kind of advice?"

"I'm going to suggest he stay far, far away from Lauren Brown's apartment. I'm going to remind him that there's a restraining order that says the same thing." He glanced at Naomi. "And then I'm going to tell him that the exact same thing applies to Dani Dobbs."

"Dani doesn't have a restraining order against him."

"Not yet," he agreed. "I just want to gauge his reaction

when I bring up her name. Finding her outside of Lauren's apartment clearly rattled him, according to the officer who called me. I want to see just how unhappy he is about running into her on campus."

"Then this is just a fishing expedition?" Naomi said, clearly relieved.

"Something like that." He grinned at her. "Of course, if he happens to take a swing at me while I'm pushing his buttons, it would make my day."

Emily was surrounded by a huge pile of midterm reports, when Marcie tapped on the kitchen door and stepped inside. "Mind another interruption?"

"Of course not," she said. "What's up?"

"I wanted to talk to you about Dani again. Is she avoiding Caitlyn for some reason? I didn't want to ask earlier and create a problem where there was none, but when she didn't call or show up, I felt I had to ask for Caitlyn's sake. She's really hurt that Dani hasn't been talking to her."

Emily clenched the red pencil she'd been using to grade papers more tightly. "Dani's not at your house now?"

Marcie shook her head. "No. I haven't seen her. Why?"

"After you left here earlier, I spoke to her. She told me she was going over to your house to spend the afternoon with Caitlyn."

"When was that?"

Emily glanced at the clock on the kitchen wall. "About two hours ago," she said.

"And you're sure she's not here, that she didn't just change her mind?" Marcie asked.

"I'll check," she said, praying that Marcie was right

and that Dani was in her room, lost in some homework assignment.

Upstairs, though, she found no sign of her daughter. Her purse was gone, as well, which meant she hadn't simply left the house to take a walk and get some fresh air. She'd deliberately defied her mother. Emily knew a lot of girls Dani's age rebelled and she'd always counted herself fortunate that her daughter wasn't one of them. Today, though, after lying about her destination and sneaking away, she was making up for lost time.

Emily's step was heavy when she returned to the kitchen. She was angry and disillusioned, but most of all, she was scared. "She's not there."

Marcie's expression reflected Emily's gut-wrenching worry. "Where on earth do you think she might have gone?" she asked.

Emily was at a loss. "I have no idea. What could possibly be so important that she'd not only leave home to go somewhere other than your house, but lie to me about it?"

"I can ask Caitlyn if she has any ideas, but I really don't think they've talked that much lately."

Emily agreed. "If she's sneaking around, I doubt she'd tell Caitlyn about it. She wouldn't put her in the position of having to lie for her."

"Not that it would be the first time," Marcie said.

"What?"

"Oh, for goodness' sakes, those two have been covering for each other since they first met. Knowing how they idolized their big brothers back then, they probably copied Josh and Evan and took some kind of blood oath. The stakes might be bigger now, but I doubt the pattern has changed."

"How did I miss that? I'm the cynical teacher who's seen and heard just about everything, especially when it concerns teenagers."

"It's different when it's your own kid," Marcie said. "We all want to believe they're perfect."

Emily thought she heard an edge of weary resignation in Marcie's voice. She wondered if she was coming to accept the possibility that Evan was guilty, after all. It wasn't a question she dared to ask, though. She had a more pressing situation on her hands.

"Could you take a drive, maybe look for her?" she asked Marcie. "I don't want to leave the house in case she turns up back here."

"Absolutely," Marcie said. "I'll take Caitlyn along. Maybe she'll have some ideas about where to look. I'm sorry if I set this in motion when I asked you to give her permission to spend time with Caitlyn. If I hadn't, she'd be in her room."

"This is not your fault," Emily assured her. "My daughter knew exactly what she was doing when she went out the door and flat-out lied to me about her destination. If she thinks being grounded for a few weeks wasn't much fun, just wait till she finds out what's in store for her now. She'll be lucky if she ever speaks to her friends outside of school again."

Marcie leaned down to give her a hug. "I'll call you if I spot her anywhere."

"Thanks. I'm going to start making some calls to some of the kids she hangs out with at school. I'll let you know if I locate her or if she turns up here."

But after Marcie had gone, Emily couldn't seem to make herself dial the first number. She knew she had to get to the bottom of this, but she hated it. She hated that her daughter had lied, hated that she was in the position of having to admit to some of her students that she didn't know where Dani was, hated what all of it said about their deteriorating relationship. She'd always believed that she and Dani were closer than most mothers and daughters, but obviously that was no longer true. Her daughter was clearly in trouble and Emily didn't have the first clue how to go about helping her.

There was still no sign of Dani when Derek showed up unexpectedly. Emily was so frazzled by then, she was tempted to throw herself into his arms and burst into tears, but she didn't.

Instead she took all of her anger and frustration and fear out on him.

"Why didn't you call before coming over here?" she snapped. "You can't just pop up whenever you feel like it. I don't have time to deal with you right now."

Derek looked thoroughly nonplussed by her tone. "I'm picking Josh up. I assumed he'd told you. We're going to dinner."

"Well, Josh isn't home yet."

"So, what? You want me to wait in my car?"

She heard the subtle rebuke behind the question. She bit back another sharp retort and sighed. "No, of course not."

"Want to tell me what put you in this mood?"

She debated getting into this with him, but he was Dani's father. He had a right to know that she'd vanished. And though she'd never given him much credit for his insights into their children, maybe he'd have more objectivity about this than she had.

"It's Dani," she said eventually.

Derek pulled out a chair and sat down. "What's she done now?"

"You know she's been grounded?" she began.

"I've heard it mentioned a time or two, though she never once said you weren't justified in doing it."

"Today I made an exception so she could spend some time with Caitlyn. At first they were going to get together here, but then Dani shouted up to me that she was going over to the Carters?"

Derek looked taken aback by that. "Really? She voluntarily agreed to go over there?"

"Why do you say it like that?"

"We'll get to that in a minute. Finish telling me what happened today."

"She lied to me. She never went over there at all. Derek, I have no idea where she is."

He didn't seem nearly as distressed as she was by that.

"Probably somewhere she knows you wouldn't want her to go," he said.

"Well, that's obvious, don't you think?" she said sarcastically.

"Despite what this behavior suggests, basically Dani's a responsible young woman. I'm sure she's fine, wherever she is." When Emily was about to object, he held up his hand. "I am not excusing what she's done. It's inexcusable. But I don't think you need to worry about her. She'll be back here soon and then you can deal with the consequences for her actions."

"You're really not the least bit upset about this, are you?" she asked incredulously.

"Of course, I'm upset that she lied and broke the rules, but I'm not worried." He frowned slightly when he glanced at the clock. "Not yet, anyway. It's still early."

Oddly, sharing her own concern with Derek had calmed her, as well. She'd forgotten what it was like to share her emotions and fears with another adult, especially with a man who had as great a stake in the situation as she had. For all of his lack of involvement in their upbringing, Derek loved their children as much as she did.

Pushing aside the immediate situation, she said, "Maybe we should get back to your reaction when I mentioned that Dani was supposed to be over at Caitlyn's. Why were you so surprised?"

"Come on, Em, you know the answer to that. She hasn't wanted to be anywhere near Evan since this whole mess started. We both know why, too. Or at least we have our suspicions. Have you let the detective talk to her yet?"

Emily shook her head. "I keep hoping she'll open up to me. I've given her every opportunity, but if she has anything to say, she's not saying it to me."

"Then let Rodriguez or that partner of his speak to her. They know how to handle things like this. I'm sure they'll be sensitive."

She wasn't sure whether she was surprised or dismayed by his reaction. Maybe both. "You're honestly willing to let the police question Dani?"

"I'm not happy about it, but I think we have to. We need to know if anything happened to her. Sticking our heads in the sand won't change the truth."

His attitude surprised her. For one thing he was calmer than he had been when he'd first thought something might have happened between Evan and Dani. There had to be a reason for that and she had a funny feeling she knew what it was. "Has Grady talked to you about all this?"

He nodded. "He didn't tell you he'd come by my office?"

She shook her head, wondering what else the detective had kept from her. He'd gone off to see Josh without mentioning that till after the fact, and now Derek. She wasn't sure how she felt about that. Obviously he had an investigation to handle, but this was her family. If they were getting closer, shouldn't she be kept in the loop? Still, that was a worry for another day. Her relationship, if she even had one, had to be the very last thing on her mind right now.

Just as she was about to ask Derek why he was suddenly so unnaturally calm about everything, she heard the front door ease open. Derek obviously heard it at the same time, because he was on his feet even faster than she was. Since Josh tended to bang doors and announce his presence with some shouted greeting, this had to be Dani.

"Danielle Dobbs, get in here right this second!" he commanded.

To Emily's surprise, Dani appeared in the doorway, her expression wary.

"Dad, what are you doing here? Mom didn't call you, did she?"

"She should have, but no. I arrived to pick up your brother, only to find out you'd gone AWOL." His expression stern, he demanded, "What's that about, young lady? You certainly know better."

Dani avoided Emily, but she dared a look at her father.

"I had something really important to do," she told him, her expression pleading with him to understand.

"So important that it outweighed the fact that you're grounded, that you were bound to worry your mother and that you had to lie to get out of the house?"

Emily stared at her ex-husband in astonishment. When had he learned how to be a real parent, one who took the kids to task when they needed it? He'd always left that to her. Dani looked equally taken aback.

"But, Dad, I swear it was really important, or I wouldn't have done it. Honest."

"Honesty doesn't seem to be a concept you grasp. Try telling both of us what was so important and we'll see if we agree with you."

Dani's expression faltered. "I…I don't want to talk about it," she said.

Derek turned to Emily. "You need to set the ground rules here. I'm not sensing a lot of remorse."

"But, Mom, I *am* sorry I worried you," Dani insisted, finally addressing Emily.

"That doesn't sound like a very complete apology to me," Derek said, his tone unyielding. "Emily?"

Emily thought she saw real fear in her daughter's eyes. She didn't think it had anything to do with whatever punishment she might be facing, either. It had to do with this mysterious mission she'd gone on.

"Sweetie, can't you tell us the truth, please? If wherever you went was so important, we should know about it. You can tell us anything."

Dani shook her head stubbornly. "No. Just ground me or whatever you're going to do and I'll go to my room."

"Dani," Emily pleaded.

"I don't want to talk about this," Dani repeated.

Emily sighed. "Okay, then. Obviously grounding wasn't sending a strong enough message, so we'll try another approach. The computer and the phone are coming out of your room, as are your CD player and the TV."

Dani stared at her in shock. "But what'll I do in there? You're turning it into a prison."

"An apt analogy," Emily said. "Derek, would you help her move those things into the closet in my room? Lock it, while you're up there."

"You're kidding me," Dani said, obviously stunned. "You're going to lock them away?"

"It's apparent you can't be trusted to follow the rules," she said. "I have no choice."

"That is so lame!" Dani said, whirling around and running from the room.

Emily exchanged a look with her ex-husband. "I feel awful about doing that when she's obviously really upset about something."

"And we both know what that something is, don't we?" he said grimly. "I'll go move those things. Who knows, maybe she'll open up to me."

"She's certainly not going to speak to me anytime soon," Emily responded. She gave him a plaintive look. "When did I turn into the bad guy?"

"Unfortunately, you've always had that job," he said, looking wearier than she'd ever seen him. "I was never much help with the discipline around here. I regret that now, more than you'll ever know. I missed out on so much, Em. And I left far too much of the burden on you. I'm sorry."

She saw the genuine remorse in his eyes. Obviously there was more than enough regret to go around. Maybe if she'd insisted on his participation years ago, their marriage wouldn't have gotten so far off track and something could have been salvaged from the wreck. Instead, she'd simply given up.

"I know," she conceded softly. "Go, talk to your

daughter. If you can get through to her now, it will more than make up for anything that's happened in the past."

Sadly, though, she'd seen that closed-down look in Dani's eyes before. She didn't hold out much hope that Derek would learn one single thing that their daughter wasn't absolutely ready to reveal.

And if he didn't, what on earth were they supposed to do next?

"Derek?"

He turned at the sound of her voice.

"What are we going to do if she won't open up to one of us?"

"We'll let Detective Rodriguez or his partner take a stab at it," he said.

"I trust Grady—Detective Rodriguez—but I hate the idea of our little girl being questioned by the police," she said. "I really do."

"I know, but I hate the idea of Evan getting away with hurting her a whole lot more."

The thought was enough to steel her resolve. The time had come for answers, no doubt about it. An image of nine-year-old Evan grinning up at her with a crooked smile made it almost impossible for her to envision him as the kind of young man capable of hurting her daughter, but if he had…God help him. God help all of them.

18

Dani dreaded going to school every day, but she was starting to hate being shut up in her room even more. She had nothing but time to think about running into Evan and the confrontation they'd had. When she'd first felt his hand on her arm, she'd been so scared she'd almost passed out. Somehow, though, she'd found the strength to stand up to him.

It had made her feel better for a little while, but on the bus ride home, she'd started shaking and hadn't been able to stop. When she'd seen her dad's car in the driveway, she'd been relieved. She'd been so sure he would be on her side, but he'd backed up her mom. They'd sounded more like a team than they had in years. If the circumstances had been different, she would have been glad about that.

Sighing, she started on her reading assignment for English. It was another of those boring classics that made her mom go all poetic and crazy. The only reason Dani even bothered to read them, instead of sticking with the Cliffs Notes or online summaries that other kids used, was because she knew her mom would be totally embarrassed if her own daughter sucked at the subject she taught.

A tap on the door dragged her out of the story. "What?" she asked, a cranky tone covering the relief she felt at being interrupted.

"You have a call from Caitlyn," her mother told her. "You can take it downstairs."

"How come?"

"Because she's going through a very hard time and you're the one being punished, not her. Try showing her a little support, instead of using her."

"I never used her," Dani protested, then winced at her mother's skeptical look. "Okay, I said I was going to her house, but I never asked her to lie for me or anything."

"Fair enough," her mom said. "You have five minutes."

Dani ran down the stairs, then heard her mother's footsteps following her. She turned on her. "You're going to listen to my call?"

"Are you actually surprised by that?"

"You're really mean, you know that?"

"Just doing my job, kiddo."

"You mean prison guard?"

"No, being a responsible parent. Anytime you want to change things, all you have to do is talk to me. In the meantime, you're wasting your few precious phone minutes."

"You've already started counting?"

"Yep."

Dani would have flounced right past her and gone back upstairs, but—what was it her mom used to say?— that would be cutting off her nose to spite her face. She ran into the kitchen and grabbed the phone.

"Hey, Caitlyn. How are you?"

"Better than you, I guess," Caitlyn responded sympathetically. "You're in big trouble, huh?"

"Oh, yeah."

"Where'd you go? Or can't you talk right now?"

"You got it."

"I figured," Caitlyn said. "Your mom sounded really mad when she called mine yesterday to say you'd finally shown up at home. We were out looking for you."

Dani felt awful. "I didn't know she'd dragged you into it," she said, shooting a glare in her mother's direction.

"She was worried, that's all. She thought you were with me and then my mom went over there and let it slip that you'd never shown up. Can you blame her for being upset?"

"I guess not. Are you really doing okay?"

Caitlyn heaved a sigh. "It's still really bad at school. The stuff they say about Evan, well, it really stinks. The guys are as bad as the girls."

"Tell me about it. Whatever they're saying around you, I promise you it's worse at my school. The guys even joke like he's some kind of hero or something, because *poor* Evan is in trouble because of all these false accusations. If it wouldn't get me into even more trouble, I swear I'd deck one of them."

Caitlyn giggled. "Now that's something I'd like to see."

"You don't think I can?"

"I *know* you can. Josh taught us both the same self-defense moves, remember?"

Dani wished she'd had sense enough to use a few of them against Evan, but at first she'd been so caught up in the moment that it hadn't occurred to her. By the time she'd wanted to stop him, he'd completely overpowered her. She still shuddered at the memory of how helpless she'd felt.

She sighed. "I remember," she told Caitlyn.

"I wish you could come over," Caitlyn said, her tone wistful. "There's nobody I can talk to the way you and I used to talk."

"I know what you mean."

Caitlyn said something, her voice muffled as if her hand was over the phone.

"Cat, you still there?"

"I'm here," she said, then fell silent, the way she usually did when she was trying to think about how to bring up something touchy. "Dani?"

"Yeah."

She cleared her throat nervously. "Evan said he saw you near campus yesterday when you went missing."

Dani froze. She could feel her mom watching her and knew she was listening to every word, every little nuance in her voice.

"That's true," she said, hoping her tone gave away nothing of the turmoil she was feeling.

"Why were you there?"

"I really couldn't say," she said carefully.

"Because of your mom," Caitlyn guessed, then sighed. "You weren't hoping to see that girl, were you?"

Dani had the strangest feeling in the pit of her stomach. She had the sense that Caitlyn hadn't dreamed up these questions all on her own. That this was what that muffled exchange had been about. Evan had put her up to making this call.

"Cat, is Evan there now?" she asked.

Her friend's silence was answer enough.

"If your brother has something he wants to ask me or say to me, he should be man enough to do it himself, but of course we both know he won't," she said heatedly, no longer caring what her mom heard. "Don't call me again. As far as I'm concerned we're not friends anymore."

Hurt by Caitlyn's betrayal, she slammed the portable phone back into its base.

"What was that about?" her mother asked, her expression dismayed. "I've never heard you speak to Caitlyn like that before. And what did you mean about Evan?"

"He talked her into calling because he wanted to know some stuff. I can't believe Caitlin let Evan use her to do his dirty work," she said. "I can't believe he'd stoop that low or that she'd let him."

"What was Evan trying to find out?"

As upset as she was, she knew better than to tell her mother exactly what had happened. "Nothing," Dani said, trying to shrug it off. "It doesn't matter. That's not even the point."

"If you're this upset, apparently it is the point," her mom contradicted.

Dani decided to put her on the defensive to stop the nagging. "You heard every word I said. Did you hear any devious plans being hatched? That's all you really care about, isn't it?"

"Dani, you know that is not the only thing I care about," her mother protested.

"I don't believe you. And just so you know, we could have been talking in code to throw you off."

Her mother gave her a wry look. "Do you think I'd put that past you?"

Even though she was the one who'd brought up the possibility, it had been in jest. She hadn't expected her mom to take her so seriously. It hurt that she had. "You used to trust me."

"You used to deserve it."

"Mom…" Her voice trailed off.

"What?"

Dani blinked back unexpected tears. "I'm really sorry that things are such a mess."

"So am I," her mother replied. "You can change it anytime."

That was the thing, though, Dani thought as she left the room. She couldn't change what had happened. Not in a million years. So what was the point of talking about it?

Emily sighed heavily as Dani walked out of the kitchen, regretting that once again their conversation had deteriorated into a battle of wills. When the phone rang, she was grateful for the interruption.

"Emily, it's Grady."

Her mood brightened perceptibly. "I hope you're having a better day than I am," she said.

"Why? What's going on?"

"Mostly mother-daughter angst," she said ruefully. "Be grateful you don't have to deal with anything remotely like that."

Her comment was met with silence. "Grady?"

"Sorry. I was distracted for a minute," he said.

As far as she knew it was the first lie he'd ever told her. She knew it the instant he'd uttered the unconvincing words. "Grady, did I say something wrong?"

"Of course not," he said a little too cheerfully.

Emily was so tired of people not being candid lately that she was tempted to press him on it, but then shrugged it off. What difference did it make really? It wasn't as if they had a relationship that she needed to be fighting to preserve.

"Did you call for any particular reason?" she asked in a tone of false cheer meant to match his.

"Actually I was hoping that you and Dani would come by my house for dinner this evening. My mom made a huge pot of picadillo and dropped it off, along with some black beans and rice. I thought after dinner Dani could take a look at my yard, make some recommendations."

"She would love that," Emily said.

"And you?"

She hesitated, then admitted, "I'd love it, too, but Dani's restricted to home and school right now. She took off yesterday, after lying to get out of the house. When she finally turned up, she wouldn't tell me or her father where she'd gone. Since she was already grounded and I'd only given her permission to visit Caitlyn, well, you can imagine how much hot water she was in when she got home."

"I see."

"I'm sorry. Maybe we can do it another time."

"Or I could bring the food over there tonight," he suggested. "I'll take a few pictures of the yard and bring them along, too."

"Is this all about getting a landscape design?"

"Not entirely," he conceded. "I enjoy spending time with you."

"And?"

"And I'm still hoping Dani will start to trust me enough to tell me what happened between her and Carter. The more time she and I spend together, the sooner that might happen."

Since Emily wasn't getting anywhere with Dani on her own, she and Derek had agreed that the time was rapidly approaching when they would have to turn to

Grady for assistance. She might as well help him lay the groundwork for that day.

"What time could you be here?" she asked him.

"How about six-thirty?"

"I'll see you then. We can also chat about how many times you've gone behind my back to talk to members of my family," she said sweetly. "Fair warning, just so you know that the interrogations around here won't be entirely one-sided."

He laughed. "I'll brace myself."

"You should," she warned. "After the way today has gone, I'm ready to go a few rounds with a worthy adversary."

"I promise you one thing," he said, "I won't stonewall you the way your daughter has."

"Well, that will certainly be an improvement. See you soon."

After she'd hung up, she spotted Dani standing in the doorway.

"Who was that?"

"Detective Rodriguez."

"He's coming over?"

She nodded.

"Are you going out with him?"

"Actually he wants to see you," Emily said, watching closely to gauge Dani's reaction. Sure enough, alarm flared in her eyes.

"Why?"

Emily debated using the fear she saw in Dani's eyes as leverage, but couldn't bring herself to do it. "He's bringing pictures of his yard. He thought it would help you to start getting some ideas for the landscaping."

Dani's relief was unmistakable. "That is so cool. I'm

surprised you agreed to that, since it means I'll get to do something I really like doing."

"This was a compromise," Emily admitted. "He wanted us to come to his house for dinner, so you could take a look around in person, but I explained you're confined to the premises."

"You told him I'm grounded?" she asked. "How could you? That is so embarrassing."

"I had to tell him why we couldn't go to his house," she said.

"No, you just wanted him to know that I did something wrong," she accused.

"Why on earth would I want to do that?"

"Just to humiliate me."

Emily sighed. "Sweetie, it is not my life's work to embarrass you. Of course, if you're too humiliated to face him or to take on this job, after all, I can explain to Grady."

"No! I want to do it."

"Then go upstairs and wash up. After that, you can help me set the table."

"What are we having for dinner? Maybe you ought to call Marcie. She could probably send something over."

"Thanks for the vote of confidence," Emily said. "Actually, Grady's bringing dinner. It's Cuban food his mom made."

"Awesome," Dani said. "I'll bet his mom is a great cook."

"And you would know that how?"

"He wouldn't bring us a meal she'd fixed if her food sucked, would he?" she asked reasonably. "He's trying to impress you."

Emily smiled. "You probably have a point. Now

hurry. You don't want him to think that between us we can't even set a decent table, do you? That would really be humiliating."

To her surprise, Dani ran back into the kitchen and hugged her. "Thanks for letting me do this job for Grady, even though you're mad at me."

"I'm not mad at you," Emily corrected. "I'm worried about you."

"You don't need to be. I'm going to figure all of this out. And if I need your help, I'll ask. I promise."

It wasn't much of a concession, but it was a start. Emily supposed it would have to do…for now.

Grady's arrival just as they were pouring the iced tea seemed to improve Dani's mood considerably. Emily watched as she eagerly drew him into the kitchen and took the various bowls he'd brought and set them on the counter.

"Mom, you can heat this up, right?" she said. "Then Grady can show me the pictures of his yard." She looked up at him. "You did bring them?"

"In my pocket," he said, giving Emily a wry look as he let himself be dragged over to the kitchen table.

"You can spread them out right here," Dani told him. "I cleared a space. And I brought down some of my plant books, so I can show you what I think will work. I'm guessing you want it to be really low maintenance, right? You're probably not home a lot. Do you have a sprinkler system?"

"Hey, slow down, kid," he teased. "Why don't you look through the pictures on your own for a moment, while I say hello to your mother."

Dani blinked. "Oh, okay. Sure. Don't take too long, though."

"Yes, ma'am."

Grady crossed the kitchen. "You want any help with that," he asked, sneaking in a quick kiss after he'd determined that Dani was totally absorbed with the photos.

Emily grinned at him. "I'm capable of heating a few things in the microwave," she said. "It all smells delicious."

He glanced toward Dani. "Maybe you should put off heating anything for the time being. It won't take that long and I doubt Dani will want to eat when she's so totally focused on this project."

"Have I thanked you again for providing this distraction for her?"

"I'm not doing it as a favor, Emily. Go take a look at those photos yourself and you'll see how desperate I am."

"Still, it's very nice of you to let her take a shot at it. It's not as if she's a professional."

"Which means she'll suit my budget. Now stop trying to make me into some kind of good guy. This is just a smart business transaction on my part. Besides, I like Dani. She reminds me of someone."

"Who?"

His expression turned sad. "Just someone I used to know," he said.

"But you're not going to tell me any more than that, are you?"

He shook his head. "One day, though. I promise." He studied her for a moment. "You seem more cheerful than you did when we spoke earlier."

"I'm just relieved to see a smile on Dani's face. Those have been few and far between lately."

"Glad to help." His eyes locked with hers. "When are

you going to agree to a real date with me, though? Just the two of us."

Her pulse stumbled. "You haven't actually asked me on one," she pointed out.

He looked startled. "Really? How could that have slipped by me? I know I meant to."

She laughed. "Well, when you get around to it, then we'll have something to discuss, won't we?"

"Of course, there is a lot to be said for coming by here and sharing a home-cooked meal from time to time."

"Even if you have to provide it?"

"Sure. I like seeing you in your element."

"Then you should probably be peeking in the door of my classroom. Something tells me I have a better grasp on teaching than I do on parenting or homemaking."

"And I think you're selling yourself short. This house feels like a home, not a showcase. And if you ask me, your kids have turned out okay."

Emily's attention went to her daughter, who was totally absorbed with jotting notes on a legal pad, several of her plant guides open beside her. "I'm so worried about her," she admitted.

Grady tipped her chin up. "We can talk about it later, if you want. I may not spend as much time with teenage girls as you do, but I'm a pretty good listener."

She saw his compassion and was drawn to it, even more than she was by the heat simmering between them. "I'd like that," she said quietly, then gestured toward Dani. "But I think your consultant is anxious to get started."

"But you and I have a date after dinner," he said. "Right?"

Emily couldn't seem to stop the smile tugging on the

corners of her mouth. "We do," she said. And it promised to be a whole lot nicer and more intimate than dinner and a movie.

At some point during the evening, Josh came home, looked at the gathering in the kitchen, then got a whiff of the Cuban food and immediately sat down at the table.

"Where'd this come from?" he asked, scooping all of the leftovers onto his plate.

"My mother cooked it," Grady told him. "And if you think this is good, you should taste her pork roast or her palomilla steak."

"Count me in," Josh said eagerly. He gave Grady a knowing look. "So, how come you dropped by and brought dinner?"

"I'm here to have a consultation with your sister about my landscaping."

Josh looked dumbfounded, even as Dani preened. "But I thought..."

Grady grinned. "Well, there might be a little more to it," he confided with a pointed glance at Emily that made her blush.

"Okay, that's enough," she said. "Josh, why don't you take that food to your room and finish it? Dani, don't you have homework?"

"Trying to get rid of us, Mom?" Josh teased. "Can't you take a little competition for the man's attention?"

"It is *not* about that," she retorted.

"Then why can't I stay here and talk to Grady some more about his plants?" Dani asked.

"Because you've already overwhelmed him with information. He'll be seeing flowers in his dreams for a month," she told her. "Give him a break."

"Oh, okay," Dani groused, then glanced at Grady. "But we're going to the nursery to buy some stuff soon, right?"

"As soon as your mom says it's okay, which I suspect means you'll need to be on your best behavior for a while," he told her.

Dani rolled her eyes. "It'll probably be months before she lets me out of confinement."

"Nobody to blame but yourself," Emily reminded her. "Now, scoot. Both of you."

After they'd gone, Emily studied the man seated across from her at the kitchen table. He was starting to look awfully darn comfortable there.

"What are you really up to, Detective?"

He gave her an innocent look—or tried to. It wasn't completely successful. "Me?"

"Sounds to me like you're trying to ingratiate yourself with my kids. Any particular reason?"

"You may be the first attractive woman I've ever met who didn't automatically assume that a guy's presence and his attempt to be nice to her kids was all about making inroads with her."

"I'd be flattered if that were true, but I don't entirely trust you. You had an entirely different agenda when we met and I suspect that hasn't changed."

He winced slightly at that. "That's not the best impression I could give you, is it? What's it going to take to turn that around?"

"A few straight answers," she suggested.

He sighed. "Okay, I'll be honest. This is totally confidential though, understood?"

"Of course."

"I'm scared the case against Evan Carter is going to

fall apart, despite the evidence we have. The kid's a fast talker with lots of charm and no priors. He comes from a good family. Lauren's a scholarship student from a lousy neighborhood. Even though her dad's a minister, Ken Carter's found a way to spin that into a negative, too."

"How?" Emily asked.

"Wild child rebelling against all those rules. It's a familiar stereotype and Carter's taking full advantage of it. There's a pretty active smear campaign going on around campus right now. So, that means it's Evan's word against hers and that can go either way in a courtroom."

"Is there anyone who can substantiate the rumors being spread about Lauren?" she asked.

He shook his head. "As far as I can tell, they'd all fall apart under close scrutiny. Doesn't mean the defense can't find some way to get them mentioned in front of the jury, even if the judge turns right around and rules them inadmissible."

Emily saw in his eyes that he genuinely cared about the outcome of the case and finding justice for the victim. "You believe Evan's guilty, don't you?"

"With everything in me. What about you?"

"I don't want to believe it," she admitted. "Our families have always been so close. This is tearing all of us apart."

"What if this had happened to your daughter?" he asked quietly. "Would you want someone to fight for her?"

"Of course."

He kept his regard steady and waited.

"What?" she asked when the silence had gone on too long.

"We both know it may have," he said.

The possibility made her sick inside. "I want to believe I'd know if Evan had done something like that," she said. "But I can't honestly say that I would. Dani's withdrawn. She's acting out in ways she never has before. Something's definitely wrong and it's tied to Evan. I do know that much."

"Did you know Dani paid a visit to campus yesterday looking for the victim?" Grady asked.

Emily stared at him in shock. "Are you sure?"

"We've had the campus police keeping an eye on the girl's apartment. There have been some threats against her. Just talk, we think, but we're trying not to take chances. Dani was spotted there." He paused, then added, "Evan Carter saw her, too. He wasn't happy."

"Oh, God, that's where she went when we couldn't find her and why she was so upset when she got home." Emily felt her heart sink. "And you think that means…"

"That Dani knows something that could help us blow this case wide open. According to the officer who saw them together, Evan was really upset when he found her there. He got right in her face."

"Oh, my God," Emily said, picturing the confrontation.

"Don't worry. Dani held her own this time. But I need to talk to her, Emily. Or I can bring Naomi over here, if you'd prefer that she talk to a woman."

"No," she said fiercely. "I'll talk to her. I'll force the issue now. It's time. This simply can't go on another minute."

To her relief, he didn't try to dissuade her.

"She'll probably deny it," he warned. "If something did happen, she obviously doesn't want you to know."

"She's my daughter," she said, knowing there was a note of desperation in her voice. "She will talk to me."

"Okay, then. You'll tell me what you find out?"

She tried to stare him down, but he didn't waver. Finally she nodded. "I'll tell you."

He stood up then, but instead of heading for the door, he came toward her and bent down, touching his lips to hers. "Just so you know, when it comes to my reason for being here, it's not all about the case. It probably should be, but it isn't."

And then he was gone.

19

The nonstop tension was starting to get to Marcie. Even during the early years of her marriage to Ken, when they had struggled to make ends meet, when Ken had been putting too much pressure on himself to succeed, she had never felt the kind of unrelenting stress that overwhelmed her now. A part of her wanted to crawl into bed, pull the covers up and not emerge until this nightmare was over. Of course, she couldn't. She was all too aware of her responsibilities to her family.

Caitlyn, her beautiful, optimistic child, was an emotional wreck. She could see it in her daughter's eyes every afternoon when she came home from school. Each day she looked a little more miserable, but she stoically denied any problems when Marcie asked, and flatly refused to consider homeschooling until the crisis passed. She tried too hard to become the buffer between Marcie and the outside world. She hid the newspaper when there was an article she thought would be too upsetting for Marcie. She'd even started sitting in the kitchen while Marcie prepared dinner, monitoring the evening news and finding some excuse to switch channels the instant any mention of Evan was made.

Evan barely spoke at all. He still had the cocky swagger that drove Marcie wild and a sharp tongue to go with it, when he did deign to address her. Looking at him, she wondered what had happened to the smiling, agreeable boy he'd once been. Though she loved him unconditionally, sometimes she didn't even recognize this sullen, disrespectful young man.

Worse, she was increasingly fearful that he was guilty of raping that young woman. Even more troubling was her growing concern that he saw absolutely nothing wrong with what he'd done, only with the fact he'd been caught. And he was counting on his father to bail him out of the situation, rather than accepting any of the responsibility himself.

As for Ken, just when they should have been pulling together, he was at odds with her over everything. At first she'd made excuses to Caitlyn for her father's snappish tone and gruff demeanor, but she was losing patience with him. She knew he was feeling the stress even more deeply than she was and she did everything she could think of not to upset him, but nothing she did was right. She knew from experience that snapping back would only make things worse, so she'd bitten her tongue so often lately it was a wonder the tip hadn't fallen off.

Not fifteen minutes ago Ken had taken offense at something she'd said. She had no idea what, since the conversation had been a totally innocuous discussion about dinner. He'd stormed out of the house saying he needed fresh air. Since Caitlyn had retreated to the safety of her room and Evan had gone out earlier without mentioning when he'd be back, she'd been left sitting all alone at their oversize dining room table she'd set for four, her nerves stretched taut, her stomach in knots. It was killing her that she couldn't fix this. Fixing things was what she did, but the whole mess was beyond her. She didn't even know the right starting point.

Slowly she rose and began to carry the virtually untouched food into the kitchen. Annoyed by the waste and even more distraught over the situation, she started jamming the food into the garbage disposal, rather than tucking it into storage containers as she usually did. Ken returned just as she was angrily shoving the last of the vegetables down the disposal.

"What the hell are you doing?" he demanded furiously. "Do you think money grows on trees? I'm spending so much time handling this mess with Evan, I've had to cut back on my paying clients. We can't afford to be throwing away perfectly good food."

She whirled around and glared at him, barely resisting the urge to toss the sponge she was clutching right into his reddened face. "Then you should have eaten it when I put it on the table," she retorted. "As for Evan, maybe you should just let his lawyer do his job and stay the hell out of it!"

"Are you crazy? I swear to God, you don't have the sense—"

"Stop it!" she shouted, the last frayed thread holding her temper in check snapping. "Whatever you were going to say, don't! I've had it up to here with you demeaning me. I'm your *wife,* dammit! Your partner. We're supposed to share things. You're not supposed to treat me as if I'm some second-class citizen or a piece of property that's outgrown its usefulness. You act as if I don't have a brain in my head, as if I have no stake in what happens to our son." She challenged him with a glare. "That's right, *our* son, Ken. You don't have a personal lock on loving him and wanting the best for him. Did it ever once occur to you that I might have some ideas that could help? Or, at the very least, that you ought to discuss your strategy with me, if only so I don't inadvertently say the wrong thing?"

For an instant he looked taken aback by her attack, but then a strange little smirk crossed his lips. "You want to share in Evan's defense? You want me to tell you what's going on? Then let's share this. Your very best friend in the entire world is over there tonight entertaining Detective Rodriguez. Did you know that?"

Shock took the fight right out of her. Marcie sat down hard. Still, she managed to muster a weak argument. "You don't know what you're talking about, Ken. Emily wouldn't do that. He's probably just over there asking more questions. You know he's been talking to everybody in the neighborhood for weeks now."

"Has he been kissing everybody in the neighborhood?" he inquired, his expression smug. "Damn friendly for a cop, if you ask me. Then again, maybe it's some newfangled interrogation technique. Probably pretty effective with a sex-starved divorcée like Emily."

"Don't be vulgar," she snapped. "Emily's not like that."

"Are you sure you know her, Marcie? Has she mentioned anything about her little tête-à-têtes with the detective? This isn't the first time he's spent the evening over there. I've seen his car in the driveway before. And if it's all about business, why isn't that partner of his with him? And how long can it take to ask a couple of questions? Not the hours he's been hanging around, I'll tell you that."

She stared at her husband incredulously, not sure

whether she was more stunned by his twisted take on what was going on or by the fact that he seemed to know so much about what was happening over at Emily's house, in the first place. In the end it was the latter that she found most offensive. In her view, people didn't go around spying on friends. She looked her husband directly in the eye.

"Have you been watching Emily?" she asked, radiating indignation. "For God's sake, Ken, have you no shame?"

He didn't even attempt to look apologetic. "Oh, get off your high horse. Let's face it, who knows this family better than she does? I wanted to keep an eye on her, figure out whose side she's on. I even tried to get her to tell me point-blank where she stood. Well, now I know, and it isn't ours, Marcie. It isn't ours."

"You don't know that," she insisted, needing desperately to believe it. Emily was the one person in the world she'd ever trusted enough to confide in. Emily knew more about her and about her family than anyone else, Ken included. Practically the only thing she hadn't told her was how fearful she was that Lauren Brown had been telling the truth about Evan. She was barely able to stomach thinking such a thing, much less voicing it aloud.

"I saw what I saw," he said, looking thoroughly satisfied at having thrown her so completely.

"You really hate that I have a good friend, while you have no one outside of this family you can really talk to," she accused. "You want to drive a wedge between me and Emily. You always have. That's what this attack is about."

He shrugged indifferently. "I could care less about

Emily Dobbs, except when it comes to her ability to make things harder than they need to be for Evan. He's my only concern right now. He should be your top priority, as well."

"Don't you dare suggest that I don't care what happens to our son," she retorted. "But I have to worry about our daughter, too, or have you forgotten about the toll this is taking on her?"

"Caitlyn will be fine," he said dismissively. "This isn't happening to her."

"It's happening to all of us. Are you blind to everyone in this family except Evan? Nothing's the same for any of us. I can't even walk out the front door. You're obsessed with trying to ruin that girl's credibility. Caitlyn comes home from school looking shattered. She's not even talking to her best friend anymore."

"And none of that compares with the possibility that Evan's life could be ruined forever."

She sighed. "No, I don't suppose it does, but that doesn't mean we're not all feeling the impact of this, and now you want me to distrust Emily, who's stuck by me, who's been there when I needed her for years now."

"All I'm saying is that you might want to consider that her loyalty is an illusion. Ask her about Rodriguez, Marcie. Confront her about that kiss I saw. See what she says. See if she lies. Because if she tells you it never happened, she *will* be lying. I know what I saw. Then you'll need to ask yourself why she'd lie if you two are such good friends."

"Fine," Marcie said, throwing down the sponge she'd been clutching since Ken had walked into the kitchen. "I'll ask her now."

"Go," he said. "And don't come crying to me when you find out what a traitor she is."

Though a part of her didn't want to accept the challenge, she knew she had to. Casting a defiant look at Ken, she slid open the kitchen door with such force it almost jumped out of its track. He had to be wrong. Not just because she couldn't bear the thought of losing her best friend, but, frankly, because the idea of listening to him gloat from now through eternity made her sick.

Emily was still sitting at the kitchen table, her heart aching, when Marcie tapped on the back door, then walked inside, her cheeks red. Clearly upset about something, she looked as if she might burst into tears at any second.

"Are you okay?" Emily asked, dragging herself out of her own misery to try to deal with whatever was going on with Marcie. "Has something else happened?"

"I just had a huge fight with Ken," she began, then waved it off. "Nothing new in that, unless you count the fact that I fought back for once."

Emily hid her surprise. "Sit down. Can I get you some tea? Something stronger?"

"No, but I do need to ask you something." She sat down, her hands reaching for a napkin and twisting it nervously.

"Of course. You can ask me anything."

For several minutes, Marcie seemed to be struggling to work up her courage, but she finally blurted, "Was Detective Rodriguez here tonight?"

Dismayed that Marcie knew about his visit, Emily didn't even consider denying it. She merely nodded.

Marcie looked strangely defeated, as if the response had taken something out of her. "I see."

"Marcie, it's not what you're thinking."

"You can't possibly know what I'm thinking," Marcie retorted in a tone Emily had never heard her use before. "It's not the first time he's been by, is it? Ken says he's been here several times. Why?"

So that's what their fight had been about, Emily thought, resigned to answering more uncomfortable questions. "He's just doing what cops do, asking questions," she said.

"And the kiss? He has kissed you, right?"

Emily's temper stirred. "How on earth do you know about that?"

"Ken saw him kiss you."

"He was spying on us?" she asked indignantly. "You have to be kidding." She stood and picked up the teakettle just to have something to do. She turned on the water so hard it splashed everywhere. She ignored the mess, filled the pot and slammed it down on the stove before facing Marcie again. "Look, I know you and Ken are under a lot of pressure right now. I understand that. I really do. But so help me, Marcie, if I ever catch him over here peeking in windows to see what I'm up to, I will call the cops on him."

"If Rodriguez is here as much as Ken says he is, you won't have to wait long for help, will you?" Marcie said bitterly.

Emily's gaze narrowed. "I think maybe we should end this conversation before we both say some things we can't take back."

"No," Marcie said, surprising her. "I'm not leaving here until I get answers. I want to know why my best friend is chatting up a man who's trying to put my son in jail. Are you so hard up for a man in your life that you'll go to any length to have one?"

Emily froze. "Excuse me?"

Marcie flushed, but she didn't back down. "There must be thousands of available men in Miami. Why would you choose to spend time with this one, when he could destroy us? Obviously you don't give a damn about me or my family."

Stung, Emily stared at her. "It's not like that."

"Really? Ken said you'd turned on us, and you have. I can't believe it. I thought, of all people, I could trust you to be on our side."

"Marcie, you know I love Evan and Caitlyn as if they were my own children, but this is a very serious accusation. The police have to get to the bottom of it. If Evan's innocent—"

"*If?* They're destroying my son with this outrageous accusation," Marcie said heatedly. "And now I find out that you're helping them. Some friend!"

"I've never said a single bad word about Evan to the police or anyone else," Emily insisted. "I've kept an open mind from the beginning."

"Really? An open mind? Not ten seconds ago, you suggested you're no longer convinced that Evan's innocent."

Emily leveled a look at her. "Can you honestly tell me that you haven't had a few doubts yourself?"

"That's not the point. I'm not the one sleeping with the investigating officer."

"Neither am I, dammit!"

"Oh, pardon me. It hasn't gone that far, yet. Fine. Then you're only making out with him not a hundred yards from my house, filling his head with who knows what nonsense about Evan, giving him added ammunition to make him look guilty. For that matter, just letting him visit you puts him in a position to keep a close eye on what's going on over at my house."

"Grady is not the one who's been spying on a neighbor," she retorted angrily, then clamped her mouth shut. She recognized that there was no way to get through to Marcie when she was this worked up. She hated that Marcie had found out about Grady's visits from Ken, who'd obviously given her the news in the most biased way possible.

"I would have told you myself that I was seeing Grady, but honestly, Marcie, it's not that big a deal. He's a really nice guy. We've seen each other a few times, but the situation is complicated. Far more complicated than you can possibly imagine, in fact."

At a loss for how to continue, she fell silent. When she finally looked up at Marcie, she saw the anguish in her tear-filled eyes.

"God, I hate this," Marcie said. "I hate fighting with you. I hate what's happening to my son, to my whole family."

Distraught for her friend, Emily put aside her anger and wrapped her arms around her. "I know. I'm sorry about everything you're going through, and I'm doubly sorry if I've made it worse."

Marcie jerked away and swiped at her tears. "I need to go. I can't talk to you right now."

She whirled around and left before Emily could think of a single thing to say that wouldn't destroy all their years of friendship. She certainly couldn't tell Marcie that Grady wasn't just here because of whatever attraction was simmering between them. She couldn't tell her that he'd been asking questions about Evan's behavior over the years, though Marcie undoubtedly had guessed that much. And there was no way she could possibly admit that Grady believed Marcie's son had raped her daughter.

Of course, if that turned out to be true, their friendship was doomed anyway. She honestly couldn't imagine any way to salvage it.

An hour after Marcie had left, Emily was still reeling from the heated confrontation. She'd had two cups of herbal tea, but all of the chamomile in the universe couldn't calm her rampaging emotions. Worse, there was something she could no longer put off doing.

Filled with dread, she slowly climbed the stairs and knocked on Dani's door. Doubting that she could be heard over the music her daughter was playing at top volume now that she had her CD player back, Emily walked in without waiting for a response and found Dani lying facedown on the bed, her shoulders heaving with sobs.

Emily immediately dropped down beside her and gathered her close. "What is it, baby? What's wrong? Please tell me. Whatever's going on, you can't keep it bottled up inside forever. You'll make yourself sick."

After what seemed like an eternity of silence, Dani finally opened tear-filled eyes. "Everything's such a mess. Evan's going to jail. Caitlyn and I aren't even speaking anymore. Mrs. Carter hates us. I heard what she said to you. I wasn't eavesdropping. I promise. She was really, really loud."

Emily couldn't contradict any of that, so she settled for a platitude. "Things will settle down eventually," she said, though she was no longer nearly as sure of that as she'd once been. "Everyone's very tense right now."

"It won't get better," Dani argued with certainty.

"Time—"

"No," Dani said, her chin thrust out stubbornly. "Don't even try to make me feel better, Mom. It won't get better, because of me."

Emily's pulse seemed to stop. "What do you mean?"

Dani's watery but unwavering gaze met hers. "I want to talk to Detective Rodriguez, Mom. I have to."

So, Grady had been right, Emily thought, her heart sinking. She fought back tears and the desire to stop Dani from saying another word. Once she spoke, there would be no going back.

She knew, though, that silence wasn't an option. If Dani was brave enough to talk—if she had something to say—then Emily had to back her. She couldn't fall apart herself. She owed Dani her strength and her unconditional support.

Struggling to keep her voice calm, she asked, "Sweetie, what is it you want to tell Grady? Can you tell me?"

Dani looked at her. Though she would always be Emily's little girl, there was a new maturity in her eyes. "You know, Mom. I know you don't want to believe it, but you know."

"Evan hurt you," Emily said flatly, nearly choking on the words.

Dani nodded.

Though her anger immediately heated to a boil, she tried to keep her expression neutral. "Tell me what happened."

"I don't want to say the words," Dani said, shuddering in her embrace.

"I know you don't, sweetie, but you need to talk about

it," Emily said with conviction. She'd seen too many teenagers let their emotional wounds fester. It was a dangerous age for not dealing with things. She'd already allowed Dani to avoid facing the truth for too long because of her own misgivings about hearing it. "You'll feel better when you're not in this all alone. Pain is always easier when it's shared with people who love you."

"It's just that it will bring it all back," Dani whispered. "I've tried so hard to forget. For a long time, I thought it was all behind me. I mean I stopped having nightmares. I actually started talking to some of the guys at school again without freaking if they touched me."

Imagining her daughter so fearful that she could overreact to an innocent touch made Emily want to storm over to the Carters' and break every bone in Evan's body herself. He deserved to know what fear was like. Even now, with charges pending against him, it was plain to her that he still didn't get the damage he'd inflicted.

Forcing her vengeful thoughts aside, she asked quietly, "How long ago did it happen?"

Dani didn't answer immediately. She kept her face buried in Emily's shoulder, her tears soaking through the cotton of her blouse. "It was last year," she finally began in a voice that could be barely heard.

She fell silent, her tears unchecked. Emily waited for her to go on.

"I was over there one night when he was the only one home," Dani recounted at last. "It wasn't any different from any other time I'd been over there. We were just watching a video, joking around, you know."

"I know."

"And then he started saying all this stuff about how pretty I was, how he'd always had a thing for me."

Emily knew how much that would have meant to Dani at the time. "And you'd had a crush on him for years, so it was everything you'd been wanting him to say," she said.

Dani nodded. "When he kissed me, I thought I'd died and gone to heaven, Mom. It was amazing. It was everything I imagined it would be. No guy had ever kissed me like that before. We kissed for a long time," she said, then swallowed hard. "Then…then he wanted more. He…he grabbed me." She gestured toward her breast. "It really hurt, Mom. And then he was putting his hand, you know, down here." Her voice faltered.

A fresh batch of tears welled up and spilled down her cheeks. "I told him no, Mom," she said earnestly. "I said it over and over, but he wouldn't listen. I tried to fight him off, but he just laughed and said he knew it was what I wanted, what I'd always wanted." Sobs shook her shoulders. "I didn't want it, Mom. Not then. Not like that."

Emily held her. "Oh, baby, I'm so sorry. Your first time shouldn't have been like that."

"I was so afraid to tell you, so afraid you wouldn't believe that I hadn't asked for it the way he said I did. And I was so scared I'd get pregnant."

It was yet another jolt. Emily had to clutch a fistful of comforter to keep from reaching out to break something. "He didn't use protection?"

Dani shook her head. "So, for weeks, I was worried about that and about getting an STD, because I know he fools around with a lot of girls. I wanted to go to a doctor, but I didn't want to ask, because I knew you'd want to know why and I couldn't think of what to tell you except the truth, and I knew I couldn't do that."

"Oh, sweetie, you could have," Emily insisted, heartbroken that Dani had felt she had to face this whole awful experience all alone. "You can *always* tell me the truth, no matter what. I would have believed you. I know you. So does your dad. We both would have believed you."

Dani stared at her with dismay. "You can't tell Dad," she pleaded. "You can't."

"You know I have to," Emily said firmly. "Josh needs to know, too. They're both going to be on your side, you know that. They're not going to blame you for any of this. It was *not* your fault."

"But they'll look at me differently. I don't know if I can stand that."

"Dad will always look at you as his precious daughter and he'll blame himself for not protecting you. Josh will always see you as his beloved pest of a little sister. That won't change." She brushed Dani's damp hair back from her face. "They have to know. Keeping this a secret from them won't solve anything."

Dani looked worried. "You won't let them do anything crazy, will you? That's what I'm really scared about."

"I'll do my best to keep them in line," Emily promised, not sure how she would accomplish that. She wasn't even sure how she was going to keep herself from taking matters into her own hands and making Evan pay for what he'd done.

"Or maybe Grady could do talk to them," Dani suggested. "Do you think he'd come back over here tonight, even though it's late? I don't know if I'll be brave enough if I have to wait till morning."

"If you want to do this tonight, he'll come," Emily assured her.

Dani looked at her, her expression filled with sorrow and resolve. "I know that girl is telling the truth, Mom, and it's all my fault. If I'd said something sooner, maybe it wouldn't have happened to her."

"Maybe. Maybe not," Emily said. "The important thing is that you want to do what's right now."

"I'm scared," Dani said.

"Of testifying?"

Dani shook her head. "No. Like I said before, I'm scared of what Daddy will do. And Josh. I heard them say they'd kill Evan if he hurt me."

To be honest, Emily was scared to death about that, too. She knew her outrage was mild compared to what Derek and Josh would feel. Still, she needed to give Dani one less thing to worry about.

"Come on, sweetie, you know they were just blowing off steam in the heat of the moment," she said. "They won't go after him. The police and the courts will handle Evan."

"You're sure?"

"I'm sure. Now, will you be okay, if I go downstairs and call your father? I think he and Josh should hear about this from me before I call Grady."

Dani nodded. "I'm okay. But I don't want to see them tonight, okay? I can't talk about all of this with them. I need to tell Grady, and that's all."

"I'll handle it," Emily promised.

She stood up, then leaned down and pressed a kiss to Dani's forehead. "I am so proud of you for wanting to do the right thing. And I'm so terribly sorry that you've been trying to cope with it all alone for so long."

"Don't be proud of me," Dani said. "I should have spoken up a long time ago. I wish I'd been as brave as Lauren has been. She told the truth and she doesn't even have the kind of family around that I do."

"Comparing the situations is a waste of time. You're doing what needs to be done now and that will be a huge help to her case. Concentrate on that. Now let me go call your dad. You get some rest. I'll let you know when Grady gets here."

"Can I talk to him up here, so I don't have to see Dad or Josh?"

"Sweetie, you know your dad's not going to rest until he sees you and tells you how much he loves you. Don't avoid him."

"I won't. Just later, okay?"

Emily nodded. Then, heartsick, she went downstairs to make the calls that would change all their lives even more dramatically than they had been already.

20

Marcie slipped upstairs after her visit to Emily, hoping to avoid another encounter with Ken, who was in his office downstairs. She didn't want to have to admit he'd been right about everything, that Emily was involved somehow with Detective Rodriguez.

She still couldn't get over that. Since the divorce, Emily hadn't shown any interest whatsoever in dating, even though the women in their book club were constantly offering to fix her up with someone. Paula, in fact, had practically made it her mission to get Emily hooked up with a new guy. Marcie wondered if Paula knew that Emily had found her own guy, the worst possible prospect from Marcie's point of view.

After managing to reach the master bedroom undetected, Marcie impulsively grabbed the phone and called Paula. At the sound of her friend's groggy voice, she glanced at the clock and winced. It was nearly eleven, an hour at which she would never have imagined herself calling anyone, especially not a teacher who was usually up at dawn.

"I am so sorry," she said. "You were already asleep. I didn't realize it was so late. I'll call you tomorrow."

"Marcie? No, talk to me. What's wrong? You sound upset."

"Just embarrassed over waking you up."

"It's fine. I was just resting."

Marcie could tell Paula was lying to be polite, but she was desperate enough to take her at her word. "If you're sure you don't mind, I really could use a friendly ear."

"Of course, but why not Emily?" she asked, obviously puzzled.

Marcie sighed. "Because she's the problem," she said bluntly, her anger resurfacing.

"Emily?" Paula sounded incredulous. "What could she possibly have done? She's your best friend."

"I always thought so," Marcie agreed, not even trying to hide her bitterness. "Did you know she's dating Detective Rodriguez, the officer who filed the charges against Evan?"

The silence that greeted her question was answer enough. "You knew," she said flatly.

"I knew there was some kind of attraction there," Paula admitted. "But I didn't know they'd done anything about it."

"Did Emily talk to you about it?"

"Not really. I saw the two of them in the teachers' lounge at school one morning, a couple of days after Evan was arrested, as a matter of fact. There was no mistaking the sparks. I even commented on them, but Emily pretty much ruled out acting on the attraction for a variety of reasons, including her loyalty to you."

"Well, apparently she changed her mind," Marcie said sarcastically. "Ken said he's been hanging around her house a lot and when I confronted her about it tonight, she didn't deny any of it."

"I see."

"How could she do that to me?" she asked indignantly. "How could she be so insensitive to everything that man represents to me and my family? He's a threat to my son."

Paula's silence suggested she didn't see it quite the same way.

"You disagree," Marcie said, her tone flat. "Mind telling me why?"

"I don't think Emily would ever intentionally do anything to betray you," Paula said. "But we can't always choose the people we're attracted to. I think this might have caught her off guard. You know her history, Marcie. Derek was the only man she was ever really involved with, so she didn't have a lot of experience with dating and sexual attraction and that kind of stuff. Along comes this sexy cop who obviously has a thing for her. He has the perfect excuse to spend time with her, because she's a potential witness in his case. Next thing you know, maybe things get personal. It wasn't some big plot to hurt you, Marcie. Please don't make her feel guilty about it."

"I can't help it. I'm really hurt that she would do something like this behind my back. She should have at least mentioned it, so I wouldn't have been blindsided by it, especially by Ken."

"If she didn't say anything, it was because she didn't want to hurt you. I'm sure she didn't want to rub your face in the fact that she was seeing a guy she had to know you view as an enemy. Surely you can see that it was a no-win situation for her."

Calmer now, Marcie tried to examine the situation from Emily's point of view. "I suppose," she admitted grudgingly.

"Look, give it some time. It's not as if she's asking

you to welcome him into your home or something. The exact opposite, in fact. She's trying to keep her personal life and her friendship with you entirely separate."

"How is that possible? Friends are supposed to be able to share everything. Now there will be this huge chunk of her life we can't talk about. And what if they get together and he moves into that house? A day won't go by that I won't run the risk of bumping into the man who charged my son with rape."

"Whoa! Don't you think you're getting way ahead of yourself? I doubt things are that serious. Last I heard, they hadn't even been on an official date."

"Well, if she's willing to betray me for this man, then they could turn out to be serious," Marcie insisted, then sighed. "Bottom line? I'm just not sure I can trust her anymore."

"You know that's not true," Paula chided. "I trust Emily with my life. So can you. She's the most loyal person I know."

"I would have agreed with you a couple of hours ago, but now I have no idea where her loyalty lies…with me or with this cop."

"My hunch is that she's spent a lot of her time with him trying to make him see another side of Evan, the good kid she's known for years," Paula said. "She could be your best ally, someone who can make the detective be more open-minded."

Emily had claimed much the same thing. Marcie tried to let her anger go, but it wasn't possible. "Thanks for listening to me, Paula, especially after I woke you up. You helped. You really did."

"Call anytime," Paula said. "And if there's anything at all I can do to help at any hour, I'm here, understood?"

"Thanks."

Slowly, she replaced the phone in its base, then turned out the light. Maybe she would see things from a different perspective in the morning. In the meantime, she needed to be sound asleep before Ken came upstairs, because one more upsetting encounter tonight would be the last straw.

To her surprise, after talking to her mom, Dani felt better than she had in a long time. Her mother had been right. Getting all this stuff out in the open did make it easier somehow. It felt as if this huge burden had been lifted from her shoulders. She'd gotten so used to toting it around, she hadn't realized how heavy it was until it was gone.

Not that it was all behind her. Far from it. She had a feeling that telling Grady all the stuff she'd told her mom was going to be really, really hard. She was starting to like him, to think maybe he'd make an okay stepdad if he and her mom ever got serious about each other. She'd hate it if he looked at her with disgust or pity. In a way, this was a test. If Grady passed, then maybe she'd be brave enough to face her dad and her brother.

She opened the drawer beside her bed and pulled out her diary. She hadn't opened it for more than a year now, not since the night Evan had raped her. She blinked hard as she mentally used the awful word for what he'd done. She'd gotten used to thinking of it in other ways, using so many innocuous synonyms to make it seem less than the crime it had been. Evan had *raped* her. There was no other word that did justice to what he'd done to her. She had to stop being afraid to admit it.

Fingering the leather diary, she smiled ruefully at the

silly puppy pictured on the front. It was a kid's diary, given to her when she was barely twelve. She hadn't touched it till she turned fifteen, but for a long time after that she'd written in it faithfully, sometimes daily, most often weekly, jotting down all her thoughts and emotions, including the fantasies she'd had about falling in love with Evan.

After drawing in a deep breath, she turned the tiny key in its lock and opened it to the last page on which she'd written. Dated March 12 of the previous year, the entry said only, "I hate him! I hate Evan for what he did to me! *I DID NOT WANT IT!!!!!*" The last words were big and bold and underlined.

Tears spilled out and splashed on the page. She reached for a tissue and blotted them before they could smear the ink. One page out of a whole diary, she thought, but it represented the day her life had changed forever.

And, she prayed, it would be enough to send Evan to jail where he belonged.

In the kitchen Emily sat Derek and Josh down at the table and quietly and succinctly repeated what Dani had told her, then added, "I need the two of you to promise that you'll let the police handle this. Dani doesn't need her brother or her dad taking the law into their own hands. This is going to be hard enough for her as it is."

Derek, the least physically violent man she'd ever known, stood up and kicked his chair halfway across the room and began to pace. Josh jumped up, his expression grim.

"Dad, are you okay?"

"Of course, I'm not okay," Derek shouted.

"Keep your voice down," Emily warned. "You don't want Dani to hear you, do you? More than anything else, she's terrified about how you're both going to react to this."

"Sorry," Derek mumbled. Then, to her shock, he punched his fist through the window beside the back door, shattering the glass.

Emily was on her feet and at his side in an instant. "Josh, get a towel. Derek, what on earth were you thinking? That wasn't like you at all."

"I was imagining Evan's face when I threw that punch," he muttered darkly. "I wish to God I could get my hands on that kid right now."

"Well, you can't," she said, taking the towel from Josh and reaching for Derek's bleeding hand. "Come over here by the sink. Let me get the glass out."

Derek jerked away. "I'm fine. It's just a little blood. Stop making a big deal about it."

"You broke a window, Derek. You put your fist through it. I'd say that qualifies as a big deal. Now, let me see it. There's a lot of blood." She swallowed hard at the sight of it. "You aren't going to faint, are you?"

"No, dammit, I'm not going to faint."

"Mom, you're the one who faints at the sight of blood," Josh commented, grinning. "Want me to bandage Dad's hand?"

"I can do it," she said stubbornly.

Derek scowled at both of them. "Would you stop worrying about my hand and consider what's important. That boy needs to be behind bars. The police need to get him there in a hurry, too, because if I see him, I won't be responsible for my actions."

Josh's expression immediately darkened. "Dad's

right. Is Detective Rodriguez coming over to talk to Dani?"

"I'm going to call Grady in a few minutes," she said. "As soon as I get your father bandaged up and after I speak to Marcie."

Derek stared at her incredulously. "You can't call Marcie."

"I think she has a right to know what's going on. We're talking about her son, Derek. I know what he did was reprehensible and I will never be able to forgive him for it, but Marcie's not responsible. I feel awful when I think about what this is going to do to her and to Caitlyn."

"Forget Marcie. Your focus needs to be on Dani now," Derek said. "What would you say to Marcie anyway? You know she's not going to believe you. More important, there's a good chance she'll warn Ken. As hotheaded and irrational as he is about what's going on, he's liable to pack up Evan and take off."

He sat down at the table and put his head in his hands. When he finally looked up, the rage was gone, replaced by a grim acceptance.

"Maybe we need to think all this through before you call anybody," he suggested slowly.

"There's nothing to think about," Emily responded.

"Yes, there is," Derek contradicted. "I wonder if we should let Dani get mixed up in this at all. Maybe we should just get her whatever help she needs to deal with it."

Emily stared at him incredulously. "What are you suggesting, that she say nothing?"

"That's exactly what I'm saying. Let her put this behind her. Let her heal."

"It doesn't work that way," Emily protested. "Haven't you seen how this has been eating at her? Now that we know the truth, a whole lot of things make more sense. Do you realize she hasn't even talked about wanting to go on a date for months now? I know the kids at school have parties practically every weekend, but she hasn't asked to go to any of them. The few times we've had all the Carters over here this past year, Dani has mysteriously disappeared the second they arrived. I have to admit I was relieved about the dating and the parties and I barely even noticed the way she was avoiding the Carters, but none of that is normal for a kid who was always such a social creature. I should have put two and two together a long time ago, but it was easier to stick my head in the sand."

Derek's jaw set stubbornly. "I still think we should reconsider letting her speak to Rodriguez."

Before she could reply, Josh jumped up and shouted, "Are you crazy, Dad? She has to tell him what she knows. Right now, she's the best witness he has. Evan hasn't gone this far with the girls I've contacted, or at least none of them would admit to it. Dani can make his case. Otherwise Evan's going to get out of this. You know he is. You've seen how the media's made it seem like Lauren's some kind of pathological liar."

"Exactly," Derek said, as if Josh had just validated his point of view, instead of the opposite. "I won't allow them to do the same thing to Dani. She's been through enough."

Emily knew he only wanted to protect their daughter, but she also knew he was a man of deeply held convictions about right and wrong.

She sat down and faced him. "Derek, my every

instinct is to protect Dani, too, but I can't stop thinking about all the other girls who might be hurt if Evan gets off this time. Dani wants to do this. She *needs* to do it. She's feeling guilty enough that it happened to Lauren because she didn't speak up. She'll never be able to live with herself if she stays silent this time, too."

"Mom's right, Dad. You know she is," Josh said earnestly. "It has to stop now."

Derek still didn't look entirely convinced. He faced Josh. "You've hung out with Evan for years. Nobody knows that boy better than you do. What do you believe in your gut about all this? Have there been other times besides your sister and Lauren?"

"None I could prove, but I gave the detective the names of every girl who'd dated him. I've seen how Evan treats women, Dad. It's the same kind of disrespectful garbage he learned from his dad. Has it gone too far? It wouldn't surprise me." He glanced at Emily. "And there was one girl who transferred in the middle of our senior year. Remember, Mom? It was all very sudden and very hush-hush."

Emily regarded him with shock. "You're not talking about Kelly Hernandez, are you? I'd almost forgotten about that."

"I don't get it," Derek said. "Why is that such a big deal? It must happen all the time."

Emily shook her head. "Not like this. No one ever understood why she was in school one day and gone the next. I'm not even sure the principal knew why she left. She seemed as shocked as the rest of us. No kid willingly transfers during senior year, Derek." She turned to Josh. "That had something to do with Evan? You're sure about that?"

Josh nodded. "Almost sure. I would have mentioned it sooner, but I just found out yesterday. One of her friends—Beth Ann Summers—goes to school at Boston College now. She just heard about what was going on here and that I'd been asking questions. She called and told me something had happened when Kelly went out with Evan, but even she didn't know exactly what, only that Kelly didn't ever want to set eyes on him again. The next week her parents sent her away to private school somewhere up north." He looked at his father. "You see, Dad? This has to stop."

Derek closed his eyes, appearing to have aged ten years in the past few minutes. When he opened them again, he said with unmistakable reluctance, "Okay, then. Call Detective Rodriguez."

"Only after I've spoken to Marcie," Emily repeated.

"No," Derek and Josh said in unison.

"Ken will have that boy out of the country tonight if he gets wind that there's more evidence against him," Derek said.

Emily thought of all the years of friendship she and Marcie had shared, all the confidences they'd exchanged. She owed her this warning, especially when Marcie was already convinced that Emily had turned on her. It wouldn't make up for what was about to happen, but maybe in some small way it would show Marcie that she still valued the friendship they'd shared through the years.

But Derek and Josh were right, too. She couldn't take a chance on Evan fleeing.

"I'll get her to stay here till Detective Rodriguez has what he needs," she compromised. "She won't have a chance to warn Ken or Evan."

"At least call Rodriguez first, let him talk to Dani, and then decide what to do about telling Marcie," Derek pleaded. "We can't take a chance on blowing his whole case by letting Evan get away. Can you imagine how Dani would feel about that, if her testimony came too late?"

Emily saw the sense in his suggestion and nodded. "Fair enough."

"I'm going up to see Dani," Derek said, starting from the room.

"No," she said urgently. "She made me promise that you'd wait until after she sees Grady."

"But I just want her to know we're behind her," he said. "And I need to reassure myself that she understands what's coming next, that she's strong enough to deal with it."

"Please, Derek, just take my word that she's ready. I know you need to see her," she said sympathetically. "But she's scared to see you right now. It was really important to her that you wait."

He regarded her with a hurt expression. "Scared to see me? Why?"

"She's afraid you'll be disappointed in her or pity her or look at her differently. She can't take that right now. If you fall apart, I think she's terrified she'll lose her courage and stay silent."

"But—"

Emily cut him off. "We have to let her handle this her way, Derek. She's trying so hard to make the right choices, but none of this is easy on her. Please don't make it harder than it has to be."

He looked as if he wanted to argue, but eventually he sighed. "Fine. I'll wait, but I need a drink. I'll be in the study when the detective gets here. Tell him I want to see him before he speaks to Dani."

Josh moved to his side. "I'll come with you, Dad."

"You don't need to do that."

"Yes, I do. It's too late to start making business calls. You'll go nuts without something to distract you. We can talk about how much medical school is going to cost."

To Emily's relief, a faint smile touched Derek's lips.

"Yes, that will definitely provide a distraction." He held out his hand, which was still wrapped in the towel. "Maybe you'd like to bandage this up for me, see if you can improve on the job your mother did."

"Is that supposed to be some kind of test?" Josh asked suspiciously.

"I just want a bit of evidence that you have what it takes to be a doctor," Derek teased him. "We should probably make sure you don't pass out at the sight of blood the way your mother does."

"Very funny, Dad."

"I thought so."

Emily watched them go, then picked up the phone. Drawing in a deep breath, she dialed Grady's cell phone number.

When he answered, he sounded wide-awake, though it was well after midnight. There was a lot of chatter in the background as well, and it didn't sound as if it was coming from a TV.

"Having a party, Detective?" she inquired innocently. "It's a little late for a weeknight, isn't it?"

"Emily? Hold on. I can barely hear you. I'll go some-place quieter."

She heard some muffled sounds and then the noise of traffic passing by.

"Where are you?" she asked when he finally came back on the line.

"I stopped for Cuban coffee and ran into my uncle and some of his friends. You know Little Havana, this is just the shank of the evening in this neighborhood. What's up? Why are you calling so late?"

"It's Dani," she said quietly. "You need to come over here, Grady."

"Twenty minutes," he said tersely. "You okay?"

Grateful that he understood without her having to say the words, she murmured, "I'm holding it together."

"How's Dani?"

"Stronger than I ever imagined she could be," she said honestly. "Hurry, though."

"Hang on, Emily. I'll be right there. Is Josh home?"

"He's not out trying to hunt down Evan, if that's what you're asking. He and Derek are keeping each other in check for the moment. I can't guarantee that'll last."

"I'll use my flashing lights. That ought to cut a few minutes off the trip," he said.

Emily hung up without another word. However fast he got here, it wouldn't be fast enough to suit her. And sadly, once he was here, the nightmare wouldn't be over. It would be just beginning.

21

Grady made it to Emily's neighborhood in record time, but just down the block he pulled to the curb and cut the engine so he could collect his thoughts. For a few weeks now it had been so clear to him that Dani could be the key to his case against Evan Carter. He'd done everything he could think of to earn her trust, to make sure she knew she could tell him the truth. Now that the time had apparently come, he wasn't sure he was ready to hear it. Like Emily, a part of him wanted to pretend nothing had ever happened to Dani, to keep her out of court, to let her heal. He was thinking less like a cop and more like a protective dad. Naomi had already called him on it and now he could see plain as day that she'd been right.

He reached into his pocket for his billfold and drew out the picture of Megan that was always with him. The picture was worn, the colors fading, but her smile was as bright as ever. All these years after losing her, she was as alive in his memory as if he'd seen her yesterday. The guilt was just as fresh, as well.

Studying her green eyes, he tried to imagine how she'd look today at Dani's age. She would have her mother's long, lithe figure, silky brown hair that fell to her shoulders and that same radiant smile. She'd deserved to grow up, to achieve whatever goals she'd dreamed of, to meet a boy and fall in love, to live happily ever after. Wasn't that what every father's daughter was entitled to?

"I'm so sorry I didn't protect you, baby," he whispered. "I will never forgive myself for that."

He felt a faint whisper of a breeze against his cheek, even though the windows were closed and the air-conditioning was off. It was as soft as the touch of a tiny finger. A thousand times through the years he'd thought he felt that same touch. For a man who dealt in cold hard facts and concrete evidence, the possibility that this was anything more than wishful thinking on his part didn't exist. Tonight, though, he wanted to believe that Megan was there with him, that she understood that his quest for justice for Lauren Brown and for Dani was about her, too.

"Love you, baby," he said quietly before slipping the picture back into his wallet.

He couldn't dwell in the past. Not tonight, when just down the street another young girl needed him. This time he would be there.

Emily had gone out to the front stoop to wait for Grady right after she'd run upstairs to tell Dani that he was on his way. She'd taken along water for the newly planted containers, then remembered belatedly that Dani was adamant about not watering them at night.

"Flowers don't like wet feet overnight," she'd told Emily a dozen times. "They need water in the morning, so they're ready to face the day." She always added dire predictions about what would happen if her edict was violated. Given Emily's black thumb and Dani's green one, she had to concede that sticking to the rule made sense.

Now, as Emily sat on the step to wait, the watering can beside her, she noticed the car pulling to the curb down the block. The lights remained on and the driver stayed inside, even though the engine had been turned off.

Curious, she stood up and walked down the driveway to get a closer look without leaving the relative safety of her own yard, where light spilled from the windows and the front door was cracked open. She clutched the portable phone in her hand, though she doubted the signal would reach that far from the house.

She'd walked only a few yards when she recognized the car that Grady had parked at her house a half-dozen times or so. Why on earth would he be parked down the street now? she wondered. Was he trying to be discreet, hoping Ken Carter wouldn't notice? Even as she considered that possibility, though, she remembered that she hadn't even had a chance to tell him that Ken had been spying on them. That was bound to stir up a ruckus best left for another time.

Needing to see him, she kept on walking. When she reached the car, she tried the door, but it was locked. Seemingly lost in thought, Grady didn't even notice her until she tapped on the window. His head jerked up and he stared at her in shock.

"Open the door," she mouthed.

When the lock clicked, she slid into the passenger seat, then took a long look at him. He looked almost as shaken as Derek had earlier.

"What are you doing walking around by yourself at

this hour?" he asked irritably. "I don't care how safe this area is, it's not smart."

"I saw your car. Why are you parked all the way down here?"

"I just needed a minute to get my thoughts together," he told her.

She saw then that there was a faint sheen of dampness on his cheeks. He'd been crying? Alarmed, she reached out to touch his face, but he pulled away. "Grady? What's wrong?"

A muscle in his jaw worked, but he remained stoically silent for so long she thought he wasn't going to tell her. "Grady, talk to me, please. I'm your friend. You can tell me about whatever's upset you."

He closed his eyes and drew in a deep breath. When he opened his eyes again, he glanced at her, then turned to stare straight ahead. "Remember I told you a while back that there was something in my past that I'd tell you about someday?"

She nodded, then realized he probably couldn't see the motion. "Yes."

"Okay, then, here it is, in all its ugliness. Once I say this, I doubt you'll look at me the same way."

"There is nothing you could say that would change my opinion of you," she insisted.

"We'll see," he said direly. "I had a daughter, a sweet, beautiful child named Megan. If she'd lived, she would be Dani's age now." His voice was flat and measured, reciting facts, but struggling to keep his emotions in check. "She drowned, and it was my fault."

Emily gasped, horrified by the loss, but not accepting his role in it as readily as he apparently had. "Oh, Grady, how awful." She couldn't imagine what that must have done to this sweet, sensitive man she'd grown to care so deeply about. Whatever blame he was heaping on himself, she had a hunch he didn't deserve even half of it. "What happened?"

"Emily, are you really sure you want to hear this now? We should go to Dani."

"Something tells me you need to say this now and a few more minutes won't matter. Dani knows you're on your way. Tell me."

In the same oddly unemotional voice, he described the night that Megan had died after apparently jumping or falling into the deep end of the pool, hitting her head and drowning as he slept nearby. At six she'd had a couple of swimming lessons, but apparently that hadn't been enough. Or maybe she'd been dazed by the blow to her head. She'd panicked. She'd tried to call out, but wound up swallowing water. Inside the house, his wife had heard her cries, but assumed Megan and Grady were playing in the pool. By the time she'd realized something was wrong and run outside, Megan had been underwater for several minutes, an eternity.

"But you didn't even know she was outside," she exclaimed when he'd told her everything.

"I should have known. Kathleen told me she was coming out."

"Did you hear her? Was she standing right there in front of you when she said it? Did she have any idea whether you'd actually heard her?"

"No," he admitted. "Apparently, she hollered out the door when Megan came out. At least that's what she told the police."

"So, she had no idea you were asleep?"

"No."

Emily could only imagine the need of both parents to cast blame. She couldn't judge the woman who'd lost her precious daughter that night. Nor could she accept that the responsibility was totally Grady's.

"Then your wife was at least partially responsible," she said firmly. "She should have made absolutely certain that you knew that Megan was outside, but the truth is, hindsight is twenty-twenty. I'm sure she blamed you out of her own sense of guilt, but the reality is that it was a terrible, tragic accident."

"No!" His tone was emphatic. "I was to blame. There are no excuses for what I allowed to happen."

"Oh, Grady, no," she said softly. Then, suddenly getting it, she said, "Making up for that is what drives you as a cop, isn't it? That's why this case is so personal, why you've been so concerned about Dani. You see your daughter in her, in all the girls who've been victimized."

He nodded, his focus still straight ahead. "It's harder this time, though. I've actually gotten to know Dani. I really do care about her and about you." He finally turned toward her. "I'm probably not the one who ought to be talking to her tonight. I should have called Naomi, let her handle this."

Emily laid a hand over his. "You're the *only* one Dani wants to talk to. She trusts you, Grady. She has faith that you're going to make this right."

"What if I let her down?"

"You won't. With everything that's happened, I may not know much lately, but I do know that."

His lips finally curved slightly. "You're good for me, you know. I don't deserve it."

"You deserve a whole lot more than I've been able to give," she responded. "One of these days, when things get back to whatever passes for the new normal, maybe we can change that. I'd like to try."

His smile spread. "I'd like that, too."

"Let's go see Dani," she said. "Maybe tonight will be a new beginning for her, too. Maybe once she's finally spoken out, she'll start to get her life back."

"I have to warn you that it will get a whole lot messier before it gets better," he said, his expression grim.

"She's ready."

"Are you?"

She thought about it, then nodded. "If my daughter's strong enough to face this, then I have to be."

Grady squeezed her hand. "And you'll have me. I'll do what I can to make it easier. I will do everything I can not to let either of you down. I promise."

She trusted him to keep that promise. In fact, to her surprise, she trusted him completely.

His talk with Emily had given Grady the time he needed to compose himself and the reassurance that together they'd handle whatever came next. Still, it broke his heart listening to Dani sob out the details about the night Evan had taken advantage of her.

They were alone in her room. She hadn't even wanted her mom beside her as she'd told him about the night Evan had raped her.

"I…" She swallowed hard. "I have this," she said, handing him a diary after she'd told him everything that Evan had done to her. "I wrote something that night. Maybe it will help."

Grady flipped through the pages till he came to the final entry and saw the underlined words. *I DID NOT WANT IT!!!* The force of her pen had almost ripped through the page. No jury looking at it would doubt the stress a young girl had been under when she wrote it.

"What's in the rest of the diary?" he asked. "Mind if I look?"

She looked faintly embarrassed. "It's just stuff, about school some of the time, but mostly about Evan. I had this huge crush on him, but there was nobody I could tell. Josh freaked when he kinda guessed. He didn't want me to see Evan, but he wouldn't tell me why. I figured it was just because Evan was older. And Caitlyn acted really weird when she figured it out, so I had to keep stuff mostly to myself."

"Couldn't you have talked to your mom?"

Dani flushed. "I was afraid if she knew she'd keep me from spending so much time over at his house." She regarded him earnestly. "The diary will help, won't it?"

"I hope so," Grady said carefully. He worried that the innocent thoughts she'd put down on those pages might make a jury wonder if she'd been so eager for a relationship that she might have invited what Evan had done after all. "Let me take a quick scan through them, okay?"

Dani nodded.

He glanced at several of the entries and was immediately reassured. They were the words of an inexperienced girl just trying to express what was in her heart. There wasn't a whiff of sexual innuendo or a fantasy that went beyond the hope that someday Evan would kiss her. A prosecutor would have to make the final call, but he thought the diary would be a crucial piece of evidence against Evan. He could show that an experienced young man had taken a young girl's trust and used it to his own advantage.

"You loved him a lot, didn't you?" he asked gently after seeing her heart and soul written onto those pages.

"I thought I did. I thought I knew him, you know. He was here all the time. I knew he liked steak, not fish, and he hated spinach. He could eat a dozen cookies at one sitting. Oatmeal raisin were his favorites. I knew he got straight A's, but the only class he really loved was current events. I even knew that he was lousy at tennis and worse at golf. He was funny, too, and he'd watch a chick flick with me and Caitlyn without moaning and groaning like some guys do." Her expression was stricken. "I thought he was almost perfect, perfect for me, anyway."

Grady's heart ached for her. "I'm so sorry it turned out the way it did."

"Me, too."

"It takes a lot of courage to do what you're doing," he told her.

She shook her head. "Courage would have been telling somebody a year ago, so he could be stopped."

"He'll be stopped now," Grady said grimly. "You want to talk to anybody about this? I know some really good counselors. There's a support group, too."

Dani stared at him, wide-eyed. "There's a whole support group?"

"More than one, unfortunately. This happens too often."

"I thought it had only happened to me, because I was naive and stupid."

"Most girls your age and even older feel that way, which is why the support group can really help. You let me know if you want me to hook you up, okay? Naomi or I can take you by, introduce you."

"Thanks." To his astonishment, she launched herself at him, her arms tight around his shoulders. "I'm so glad you're my friend and that you didn't freak out or get all crazy about this. It made it easier."

"I'm glad. Want me to send your mom in now?"

She shook her head. "I think I'm ready to face my dad. I didn't want to see him before. I was afraid of how he'd act."

Grady understood that kind of fear. He'd seen it many times in rape victims who feared telling the men they were closest to, as if they'd done something wrong. Lauren had only told her own father after the media had gotten all over the case and she'd feared he would see it in the paper. Unfortunately, he hadn't taken it well. He'd blamed her for somehow inviting the attack and accused her of sinning. Derek Dobbs was a far more understanding man.

Grady tried to reassure Dani. "I talked to your dad when I got here. He loves you very much. What happened to you is bound to make him really sad, but he only cares that you're okay. That's all that matters to him."

The worry lines on her forehead deepened. "You're not going to let him go after Evan, are you? I don't want him to do something stupid and go to jail."

"I'll do everything I can to prevent that," Grady promised.

When he left Dani's room, he found Emily standing in the hallway.

"How is she?" she asked.

"She's a strong girl, a lot like her mom, I think."

Emily shook her head. "Not me. I didn't want to face this."

"There aren't many moms who do." He touched his hand to her cheek, wiped away a tear. "It's going to be okay."

"How can you be sure of that?"

"Because no matter what people go through, they do heal."

She gave him a wry look. "You haven't."

"Not entirely, no," he said. "But I'm getting there. Get Derek now. Dani wants to see her dad. And then we all need to sit down and talk about what happens next."

Emily nodded. "I'll meet you in the kitchen."

"I'll pour the coffee. Something tells me none of us is going to get any sleep anyway."

While he waited downstairs, he called Naomi. "I know it's late, but I wanted you to know that I have Dani's testimony, and a diary that pretty much confirms what happened and when."

"Oh, that poor child," Naomi said. "Is she okay?"

"She's doing amazingly well now that everything's out in the open."

"And you? How are you handling this?"

"I'm the tough cop just doing my job," he insisted.

"Don't lie to me, Rodriguez. How are you really?"

"The whole thing makes me sick. I want to go over to the Carters' and beat the crap out of that kid, but I won't. I'm going to trust in the system."

"You've made it that much easier for the system to get it right by getting Dani's statement," she reminded him. "Good work. The chief's going to be ecstatic. The Carter kid might be able to skate away from one charge, but two? Nobody's going to be able to deny he has a problem now. Dani is going to press charges, right?"

"That's what I want to talk to her folks about next," he said. He looked up and saw Emily in the doorway. "I've got to go. See you at the station first thing in the morning. No matter what happens, I'm going to make a call to the local cops and bring the Carter kid in tonight. I think the judge will be thrilled to revoke his bond."

He hung up slowly, watching Emily's face. She'd

gone pale at the mention of Evan losing his bond. "You okay?"

"The implications are just starting to sink in. My daughter is in a position to send my best friend's son to jail."

"To be honest, I'm not sure you've grasped all of them," he said. "I'm recommending that Dani press charges against him. It's your call, and hers, but there are two crimes now, not just the one he committed against Lauren."

She regarded him with dismay. "I thought you just wanted Dani's testimony to establish a pattern."

"Originally that's what I thought, too, but after listening to her, after reading the diary she showed me, there's a strong case to be made that Dani was raped, too. Because of her age, the charge is even more serious, statutory rape. She deserves her own justice."

"I don't know," Emily whispered, stricken. "Grady, how can we ask her to press charges against a boy she's known all her life?"

"How can you not? He belongs in jail for what he did to both of those girls," he said firmly.

"Derek's not going to go along with this," she said. "He tried to talk me out of calling you at all. He didn't want Dani subjected to the same ridicule that's hounded Lauren in the media. Granted, no one's mentioned her name, but her identity is well-known on campus and around town, thanks to Ken. I can't even imagine what he'd do to Dani. The first smarmy comment he leaked would send Derek right over the edge. Josh, too. I just don't know if our family can take that."

"Why don't we get Derek and Dani down here and see what they think?" he suggested. "Bring Josh in on the decision, as well."

She regarded him with unmistakable reluctance. "You're not going to badger them, are you?"

"I hope to be no more than powerfully persuasive," he said.

"Just promise that this will be Dani's call. She has the most at stake. I don't want her pressured to do something she's not comfortable doing. I mean it."

"Of course."

"Okay, fine," she said at last. "I'll get them." She stood up, wobbled slightly and sat back down.

Grady was on his feet at once. "Emily, are you okay?"

"Just shaky. Probably too much caffeine."

"And too many nerves. Believe me, I get how awful this is for you. I really do. And I'm sorry if you think I'm pushing too hard, but I don't want that boy to get away with what he did, not to either of those girls and to who knows how many others."

"I know," she whispered. "I swear if it were any other girl, any other young man, I'd want you to go after him with everything you've got, but this is my baby we're talking about. I'm terrified about what this will do to her."

"Isn't the real issue what Evan has already done to her?" he asked.

"Grady, that's the idealistic notion, but you and I both know that in cases like this, the person reporting the crime is sometimes victimized twice, first by the perpetrator and then by the court system. So far, I've been able to focus on what's best for Dani, but if the media or some defense attorney goes after my daughter, you'll have to put me behind bars to keep them safe."

He smiled at the ferocity in her voice. "I'd like to see that."

"It's not funny."

He sobered at once. "No, seeing someone you love hurt is never funny, but I really believe Dani is strong enough to get through this."

Emily still didn't look convinced, but she stood up again, and this time she remained steady on her feet. "I'll go get the others."

While she was gone, Grady poured more coffee and tried to work out how he was going to convince Derek Dobbs to allow separate charges to be filed on Dani's behalf. He thought he understood where Derek was likely coming from. A big part of him wanted to close his eyes, pretend this had never happened, protect Dani from further trauma. But the cop in him insisted the incident would never be put to rest for Dani until Evan had paid the price for it.

When the family came into the kitchen, Dani was clutching her father's hand. Derek's expression was only fractionally less grim than his son's. Emily couldn't seem to look at them or at him. She busied herself with getting mugs from the cupboard and making hot chocolate for Dani and pouring coffee for the rest of them.

"I wanted to talk to all of you about what happens next," Grady said when they were settled. "Everything Dani told me tonight is very compelling. She'll make a very strong witness in Lauren's case, but I think she deserves justice herself. I'd like to see additional charges filed against Evan for what he did to Dani."

"Go for it," Josh said heatedly. "Lock him away for the rest of his sick life. I swear to God, if I get my hands on him—"

"Hold it, Josh," Grady said, his attention on Dani. "How do you feel about it, Dani?"

"I thought it was too late for me to press charges," she said.

"No, the statute of limitations hasn't run out yet."

"And I'd have to testify either way, right? You want me to go to court to back up Lauren, anyway?"

Grady nodded.

Dani looked to her mother. "Mom, what do you think?"

Grady held his breath. He knew Emily had very mixed feelings about Dani being even more involved in this mess than she would be as a witness in support of Lauren.

"Sweetie, what Evan did to you was a crime. You were only sixteen, a minor." She glanced at Grady. "That's another crime, right?"

He nodded.

"I think you need to weigh this very carefully," Emily told her. "I know you feel you should be loyal to the Carters and Caitlyn, but Evan is old enough to be held accountble for his actions. This wasn't some innocent little mistake. It was a crime."

Dani's eyes welled with tears. "Caitlyn will hate me."

"Possibly," her mother said candidly.

"And the Carters are counting on Evan to be this big superstar jock."

"That's not a reason to back down," Emily told her. "You know right from wrong, sweetie. So did Evan."

Grady turned to Derek. Without him on board, the other opinions would hardly matter. "You've been quiet so far. Do you have an opinion about this?"

Derek's heart was in his eyes when he looked at his daughter. "I just want all of this to be behind her. If the best way for that to happen is for her to bring charges against that boy, then I'm with her a hundred percent." His hand trembled as he brushed her hair away from her face. "What's it going to be, kiddo? You're old enough to make this decision yourself. Mom and I are totally behind you."

"I always thought he was a good guy, you know," she said softly. "Maybe he still can be."

"Then you don't want to press charges?" Derek asked.

Dani hesitated, then sat up a little straighter. "Yes, I do. I want Evan punished for what he did to me and to Lauren," she said. "I don't want him to be able to do it ever again. Maybe then he'll change and be the person I thought he was."

"Then I'll pick him up now and see that his bond's revoked," Grady said at once. It was the outcome he'd hoped for, but oddly it wasn't nearly as satisfying as he'd expected. In the end both of these families were going to be devastated, years of friendship left in tatters.

He was about to stand up, when Emily gave him a pleading look. "Don't go over there yet," she said. "This is going to kill his mother and his sister. I need to warn Marcie. We've been friends for so long, and none of this is her fault. She needs to be prepared for what's going to happen. And, after what happened between the two of us earlier, I want her to hear from me what our role is in it. I owe her that."

Grady gave her an odd look. "What happened earlier?"

"It seems Ken has been spying on me," she said, her cheeks turning pink, her eyes avoiding her ex-husband's as she added, "On us. Marcie believes I've betrayed her by spending time with you. At least if I alert her about this, maybe she'll believe that I'm still trying to be her friend."

Grady wanted to balk, but he understood her dilemma. She was a mother first, but she was a loyal friend, too. And she was right, none of this was Marcie Carter's fault. She'd already had to bear the burden of seeing her son taken away in handcuffs once.

"How about this? I need to contact the police down here about what's happening. That'll take some time. You call and invite her over now. It's the middle of the night. Do you think she'll come? Can you insist on it?"

Emily nodded. "She'll come," she said confidently. "That's what we do when there's any kind of crisis. We show up, no matter the hour."

"Okay, then. I'll wait outside until she's here, then I'll meet up with the local cops and head over to take Evan in. That way, we won't cross paths and she won't have to see me taking her son away a second time. Maybe you should talk her into bringing her daughter with her. This will be hard on her, too."

Emily gave him a grateful look. "You're a thoughtful man," she told him.

That was a new one. No one had suggested he was thoughtful for a long, long time. Maybe ever.

"Could be I have a good teacher," he told her with a wink. "Now, make that call."

As Emily went into the other room to call her friend, he looked around the table at the others. "I doubt this will help, but I am sorry about all of this. Dani, I really wanted to be wrong about Evan hurting you."

"I know," she said.

To his surprise, Derek met his gaze evenly. "You've been a good friend to my family, Detective. I can't tell you how much I appreciate that."

Grady nodded. "I'd better get out of here before

Mrs. Carter and Caitlyn arrive. Dani, you take care of yourself, okay? Maybe we can work on that landscaping this weekend."

Her eyes lit up for the first time in what had been a very long night. "Awesome."

He wanted to tell her how proud he was of her, but with her father sitting right there, Grady felt it wasn't his place. Pride was Derek's right, not his. He just hoped that someday down the road he could claim a few rights as her stepfather. It was a role he'd be honored to have. He just had to convince Emily that there was more between them than an investigation that had ripped her life apart.

22

Marcie was jolted out of a sound sleep by the ringing of the phone. Beside her, Ken was dead to the world. The man could sleep through a category-five hurricane. She was convinced of it.

Rolling her eyes, she reached past him to grab the phone. "Hello."

"Marcie, it's me," Emily said. "I'm really sorry to wake you, but I need you. Can you come over now?"

Even though she hadn't entirely gotten past her earlier anger, she said yes at once. Too many years of habit and loyalty couldn't be broken in a single night, not when there was such urgency in Emily's voice.

"I'll be right there," she responded.

Already out of bed and reaching for her robe, Marcie was about to hang up, when Emily added, "I know it's a lot to ask, but bring Caitlyn, too, okay?"

Marcie had the robe in hand, but Emily's request startled her so badly that she dropped it and left it where it fell. "Why?"

"Trust me, okay? Please bring her."

Marcie sat down on the edge of the bed, careful not to bump into Ken, who was still snoring. "Emily, maybe you should tell me what's going on," she said, keeping her voice low.

"I will, as soon as you get here," she promised. "Hurry."

She recognized the stubborn note in her friend's voice. Emily wasn't going to say any more until they were face-to-face. "Give me ten minutes," she said, resigned to waiting. "You know how hard it is to get Caitlyn moving."

A few minutes later as she waited for Caitlyn to pull herself together and drag on a pair of jeans and a T-shirt, she wondered why she'd agreed so readily to this middle-of-the-night visit. Maybe it was the unexpected command she'd heard in Emily's voice or maybe nothing more than the fact that she'd made the request in the first place. Friends were there for each other, anytime, anyplace. It was an unspoken rule that had served them well practically from the day they'd met. Whether a child's illness, an extremely bad day or even a plumbing crisis, they did whatever they could for each other. Though Emily had frayed that bond by hiding her relationship with Rodriguez, it wasn't yet broken.

"Mom, why are we going over to their house in the middle of the night?" Caitlyn asked sleepily.

"Because Emily said she needs to see us."

"Is somebody sick?"

"She didn't say."

Caitlyn followed her downstairs. "I'll bet it's about Evan," she said direly. "These days everything's about Evan."

"She never once mentioned your brother," Marcie said, though Caitlyn's assessment startled her. Of course, this was about Evan. She should have guessed that herself. No wonder Emily had been so tight-lipped about her reason for wanting Marcie and Caitlyn to come over.

"Would you have gone if she'd said it was about Evan?" Caitlyn asked.

"No," Marcie said at once, then hesitated. "I don't know. Probably." Even on the subjects about which they vehemently disagreed, she and Emily had always found some way to communicate.

Caitlyn fell silent as they went downstairs. When they were about to leave the house, she asked, "Mom, do you think Evan's going to jail?"

Marcie froze. "No," she said fiercely. "He's not going to jail, because he's not guilty."

Caitlyn gave her an unreadable look.

"He's not!" Marcie repeated emphatically. She simply couldn't allow herself to think otherwise.

Switching on the light that lit the backyard and their way through the hedge to Emily's, she stepped outside. The dew on the grass soaked through her thin slippers as she scurried between the two houses. Only as she skirted around the Dobbs's pool did she notice that Emily wasn't waiting in the kitchen alone. Derek was there, too. So were Dani and Josh.

At the sight of them, Marcie was struck by such a sense of impending doom that she almost turned and ran for home.

"Mom," Caitlyn whispered, slipping her hand into Marcie's. "Something's really wrong, isn't it?"

"We don't know that," Marcie said, forcing an upbeat note into her voice.

"Why would Mr. D be here in the middle of the night, if everything was okay?"

"I don't know, sweetie. We'll know soon enough."

As if they'd been watching for her, Derek stood and Emily came to the back door and opened it.

"Thanks for coming," Emily said, giving Marcie a fierce hug that caught her off guard.

Marcie blinked back sudden tears. "What's wrong? Why are you all in the kitchen at this hour?"

"We need to talk to you," Emily said. "There's something you need to hear from us. It's about Evan."

Marcie halted where she was, just inside the door. "No," she said. "I won't have all of you ganging up on me. I won't listen to one word said against my son. It's bad enough what strangers say. I can't listen to it from you."

"I'm so sorry, Marcie, but you need to hear this," Emily insisted. "Caitlyn, too."

Marcie saw the look of utter dismay that flashed across Caitlyn's face. Her daughter whirled on Dani.

"You told, didn't you?" she shouted. "You told them everything! You said you'd never tell."

Dani flushed, but she didn't look away and she didn't deny Caitlyn's accusation.

And in that instant, Marcie knew that her world as she'd known it—already shaken to its foundation by the charges against her son—was about to come tumbling down around her.

Emily knew the exact second when Marcie grasped that Evan's misdeeds were far worse than simply the charges leveled by Lauren Brown. She paled and reached for a chair. Though she looked as if she'd prefer to bolt, she sat down heavily.

"I'll make you some tea," Emily said, giving her shoulder a squeeze as she passed. Now that Marcie was out of her house, so she and Caitlyn wouldn't have to witness Evan being arrested yet again, Emily could take her time telling her what he'd done. She glanced at Caitlyn, who was as pale as her mother, though patches of bright color darkened her cheeks whenever she glared at Dani.

"Sweetie, would you like some hot chocolate?" Emily asked Caitlyn. "That's what Dani's drinking."

"No," Caitlyn snapped, then winced at a warning glance from her mother. "I mean no, thank you."

"It's okay," Emily said. "Let me know if you change your mind or if you'd like something else." She turned to Derek and Josh. "Maybe you two could leave the rest of us to talk. It might make it easier."

Derek nodded. "I'll be in the den if you need me."

Josh stood up, too. "I'll be in with Dad."

Emily studied him with a worried frown. "Shouldn't you get some sleep? You have classes in a few hours."

"I can miss them for one day," Josh said, his expression stubborn. "I'm not leaving. We've got a family crisis and I need to be here."

Emily decided not to waste her breath trying to argue. She made the tea and brought a cup and the china teapot to the table.

"You need to tell me what's going on," Marcie said, her voice flat. "You're scaring me."

"I know," Emily said. "But I don't want to say it, because I know it's going to break your heart."

"Just say it," Marcie snapped. "Whatever lies you plan to say, spit them out."

Dani blinked at her tone, but she sat a little straighter in her chair. "I'll tell her. She'll believe me."

Emily stared at her with dismay. "No, you don't have

to do that. I'll tell her. You've been through enough tonight."

Dani shook her head. "I think she needs to hear it from me," she insisted. "I *want* her to hear it from me."

Emily sighed and relented. "Go ahead, then."

Feeling her child's pain with each word Dani spoke, Emily listened as she once again described the night that Evan had taken advantage of her in Marcie's home.

Looking more horrified with each word that Dani uttered, Marcie leaped to her feet. "And you've told the police this pack of lies? I can't believe you would do such a thing, Dani. What have we ever done to you except treat you as part of our family?"

"*You've* never done anything but love me," Dani said quietly. "And Caitlyn's always been my best friend, but Evan raped me. He did!"

"You're lying," Marcie accused.

"I'm not lying," Dani responded, her expression sad. "Ask Caitlyn."

Marcie seemed to deflate a little as she turned to her daughter. "She's told you about this?"

Caitlyn nodded, tears streaming down her face. "I didn't want to believe her, either, Mom, but…" Her chin rose a notch. "But now I do. Evan's practically admitted it to me. He's been scared for a while now that she was going to tell. He wanted me to help convince her not to say anything."

Marcie stared at both girls with an expression of pure hatred. "You're lying. All of you. Evan would never hurt Dani. He's always thought of her like a sister."

"He did exactly what Dani said he did, Marcie," Emily replied evenly. "You know Dani wouldn't lie about something this important."

Marcie's attention went around the table, from Dani to her own daughter and then to Emily. "Why are you all turning against my son? Why?" she demanded, tears streaming down her cheeks. "All these years I've thought of you as family and now you're conspiring to have my son locked away."

"Oh, Marcie, it's not a conspiracy. You know it isn't," Emily said. "Dani has been in anguish about this for months now. She didn't want to get Evan in trouble. Until this whole business with Lauren Brown happened, she'd convinced herself that what happened was her fault, that she somehow invited Evan to take advantage of her."

"Maybe she did," Marcie said, clearly grasping at straws. "I'll bet that's exactly what happened, Emily. You know how young girls are with their first crush. They'll do just about anything to get a boy's attention. And Evan's only human. He probably took what she was offering and then she had regrets and now she's blaming it all on him."

Dani looked crushed by Marcie's assessment, but before Emily could step in and defend her, Dani spoke up herself. "It wasn't like that. I told him no, Mrs. Carter. I told him lots of times, but he wouldn't stop." Tears cascaded down her cheeks. "No matter what I said, he wouldn't stop."

Emily reached for her hand and gave it an encouraging squeeze. She was so proud of her daughter, so impressed with her strength in the face of Marcie's doubts and accusations.

Even now, Marcie was unwilling to accept the truth. "Evan's not like that. My son was raised to know right from wrong. He's incapable of treating any woman that way, much less a girl he's always thought of as family. How could he do such a thing?"

"Because he's just like Dad," Caitlyn suddenly burst out, stunning them all. "Mom, how can you be so blind? They're just alike. They're both bullies."

Marcie stared at her daughter in shock, but Caitlyn didn't back down. Displaying a strength equal to Dani's, she faced her mother. Eventually Marcie's shoulders sagged in defeat and she finally sat back down.

"Oh, God, what is wrong with me?" she whispered. "How did I let things get so out of control? All I ever wanted was to be a good wife, a good mother."

"Then be one," Caitlyn said, her tone unyielding. She sounded older and far wearier than a fifteen-year-old. "Face the truth about Evan. We both know Dani's not lying about this."

Marcie looked completely at sea. She finally addressed Emily. "I am so sorry." Then she reached for Dani's hand. "Baby, I wish this had never happened to you. I really do. That a boy I've raised could do such a thing…I just can't wrap my mind around that."

"It's not your fault," Dani told her, standing up to move into her embrace. "It's not. Evan did this to me, not you."

"But he's my son. It happened in my house, someplace you should have been safe always. I should have seen…" Her voice trailed off and once more she covered her face. "My God, surely I should have seen something."

"You've always been blind about Evan's behavior and about Dad's," Caitlyn accused.

"Your father—"

"Don't you dare try to excuse him," Caitlin shouted.

"I am so sick of listening to you defend the way he bullies you. It's disgusting."

Emily took pity on Marcie, who looked as if one more word would cause her to unravel completely.

"Let's all calm down and take a deep breath," she encouraged. "I know this is extremely upsetting, but now that everything's out in the open, we can start dealing with what's happened. All of it."

Suddenly Marcie was on her feet, all the color draining from her face. "You said you told the police about this, didn't you? How did I let that slip my mind? Are they at my house now? Is that why you insisted that Caitlyn and I come over? Emily, how could you?"

"I wanted to protect you and Caitlyn," Emily told her. "I didn't want you to have to see him being taken into custody again. And I owed it to you to tell you all of this before anything happened."

"But you kept me from being there for my son," Marcie screamed, her fragile grasp on serenity snapping. "How could you do that?"

"Mom, there's nothing you can do for Evan now," Caitlyn said. "Besides, he has Dad there to fight his battles for him."

"I'm his mother, dammit! I should be there."

"When was the last time Evan gave two hoots about you?" Caitlyn said angrily. Years of pent-up frustration were evident in her voice. "Mom, he treats you the same way Dad does and you just roll over and take it. The worse they are to you, the harder you try. Can't you see how wrong that is?"

"He's still my son and your brother," Marcie said, her expression stubborn. "We need to stick together."

"No, what you need to do is to stop letting Dad and Evan push you around and treat you like dirt."

"They don't..." Marcie began, but stopped as Caitlyn stared at her incredulously. "They don't mean to be disrespectful."

"You are so delusional," Caitlyn retorted.

"Caitlyn!" Emily chided, because she couldn't bear the expression of disbelief and hurt on Marcie's face at being attacked by her own daughter.

"I'm not sorry I said that," Caitlyn said. "Mom, wake up. Get a divorce. Maybe then we'll finally have a life."

As Caitlyn's harsh words sank in, Emily saw the fear in Marcie's eyes. Divorce represented everything she'd always dreaded. It was admitting failure. It would force her to stand up for herself and her daughter. It would throw her financial situation into turmoil. It was probably too late to influence Evan, but there was still hope for Marcie and Caitlyn.

Emily was about to comment, when Marcie spoke up.

"Don't scold her, Emily. Caitlyn's right," she said, a hitch in her voice. "I've made so many mistakes, I can't even begin to count them. I convinced myself I was showing my kids that marriage was meant to be forever, but all I was really doing was showing them that it was okay for a man to bulldoze right over his wife and treat her with a total lack of respect."

"No man will ever get away with that with me," Caitlyn said. "If I ever get involved with a guy, forget being equal partners, he's going to treat me like a queen."

Marcie managed a faint smile. "At least I managed to get one lesson right, albeit in the most misguided way possible."

"Look, whatever you decide to do about your

marriage, the two of you will be fine," Emily told her. "I'll do anything I can to help you get through this."

"Even after what Evan's done?" Marcie asked, her disbelief plain.

"Evan's accountable for that," Emily said. "Not you. We've been friends for years and I can't bring myself to throw that away."

Marcie nodded slowly, then turned to Caitlyn. "If I do this…if I divorce your dad when all this is over—" she regarded Caitlyn with concern "—we'll have to move, live in a smaller house."

"Do you think I care about that?" Caitlyn scoffed. "Come on, Mom. We'll finally be able to do what we want, be whoever we want to be."

"I'm not sure I know what that is," Marcie said.

"But you'll figure it out," Emily assured her. "I did."

"You have a career you care about," Marcie argued. "What do I have?"

"You have a daughter who needs you, a dozen talents that are the envy of all your friends, and you have us. You can lean on us while you figure things out."

Marcie rose to her feet. "Right now, I'm still a mom whose son is in trouble. I need to go home." She leaned down and gave Emily a fierce hug. "This time, though, my eyes will be wide-open."

As she stood, so did Dani. "I'm sorry," Dani whispered.

Marcie blinked back tears and drew her into her arms. "Oh, baby, I'm the one who's sorry about everything, about what Evan did, about doubting you." She touched Dani's cheek. "You're a strong girl and you've got a family who loves you to pieces. And one day I hope you'll be able to forgive me and remember that I love you, too."

"I've always known that," Dani said. "That's one reason this was so hard. I didn't want to hurt you."

Emily faced Marcie. "Caitlyn can stay here, if you want her to."

Marcie nodded. "Thank you for trying to make it seem as if nothing's changed between us."

"It hasn't," Emily said firmly. "Not if you don't want it to. This has been a terrible ordeal for all of us, but we'll get through it. I know we will."

Marcie nodded slowly, her relief plain. "We'll talk later, then. I'll call as soon as I know what's happening at the police station."

"Mom, don't go back home later, no matter what," Caitlyn pleaded. "Make the break now. Come here, if it's okay with Mrs. D." She turned to Emily. "Would it be okay?"

"Of course, if it's what your mom wants."

Marcie gave her a rueful smile. "Sweetie, no matter how messed up things are, I can't abandon your father in the midst of this crisis, but if you don't want to come home and Emily agrees, you can stay over here till everything is sorted out."

Caitlyn regarded Emily intently. "Then is it okay if I stay? Please."

"Of course, you can stay for as long as you need to."

Dani reached for her hand and started to drag her from the room. "It'll be like having a sister. You can help me clean out some drawers and make room in my closet."

After they'd left the room, Marcie gave Emily a grateful look. "Thank you for not turning against her against us."

"Never," Marcie said.

"But what Evan did—"

"Was unconscionable and he'll pay for it," Emily insisted. "Not you and not Caitlyn."

"How did you convince Rodriguez to let you tell me what was going on? I'm sure he objected."

Emily smiled. "He's a reasonable man."

"And he's trying to keep you happy," Marcie guessed.

Emily hesitated, then nodded. "Yes, I suppose he is."

"I'm glad for you. I truly am. You'll have to tell me all about him once things settle down."

"You'll like him once you get to know him under different circumstances," Emily told her.

"I'm not so sure about that," Marcie said. "But for your sake, I'll try."

"That's all we can ever ask of each other, isn't it? Now go, be with your son. He needs you more than ever, whether he admits it or not."

"His father's the one who'll help him fight these charges," Marcie said.

"But you're the one who may be able to make him see that what he did was wrong. Ken won't do that."

Marcie sighed. "No, he won't. How sad is that?"

Emily had no reply for that, so she simply gave her another hug and let her go.

Grady had to stand up and walk away after a few minutes of listening to Evan Carter try to defend what he'd done to Dani. He'd had no business being in the interrogation room in the first place, but when he was about to lose his temper and knock the kid on his butt, he knew it was time to get out.

"You take over in here," he told Naomi. "I need some air."

She gave him a sympathetic look. "I don't think we're getting anywhere anyway. Mr. Carter doesn't seem interested in discussing the error of his ways."

"Not with you, that's for sure."

Grady leaned across the table and got in his face. "Watch your mouth, kid. She's Detective Lansing to you and you'll show her the respect she deserves."

"Or what?" Evan demanded, his expression arrogant. "My dad is going to see that both of you are busted down to patrolmen, assuming you get to stay on the force at all."

Grady bit back another sharp retort. He caught Naomi's eye. "Outside, now."

She followed him into the hallway. "I swear to God that kid needs to have his mouth washed out with soap."

Grady chuckled. "That's your idea of a punishment that befits the crime?"

"For potty mouth, it is," she said. "The jail time he deserves is a whole other issue. How long do you suppose it'll take before his father gets him out on bail?"

"Years, if I have anything to say about it," Grady said, his expression grim. "I don't want him anywhere near Dani Dobbs. I think this time the judge will see it my way, especially when I report his attempts to confront Lauren Brown despite having a restraining order in place to keep him away from her. No judge is going to release him to go home to a house not a hundred yards away from where his underage victim still lives."

"Not even if Daddy promises to keep him on a short leash?" Naomi asked skeptically.

"Not even if Daddy agrees to tie him to a chair," Grady insisted.

Unfortunately Ken Carter overheard him.

"Really?" Carter asked, his tone smug. "When I get through telling the judge how you've bullied and harassed my son, you'll be the one on a short leash, Detective. As for these trumped-up charges about him and Dani, do you honestly think anyone's going to believe that the horny little kid wasn't asking for it? You forget, I've seen how she is around Evan. She's had a thing for him since she hit puberty."

Grady had the man's shirt bunched up in his fist and was about to slam him into a wall when Naomi managed to squeeze between them.

"He's not worth it, Grady," she said quietly. "Let him go."

Grady's grip held firm. "Not until I get my point across," he said tightly. "Don't you ever mention that girl's name again. You see her, you cross the street. If she's outside, you stay in the house. And at the first whiff I get that you're spreading lies about her, I'll see you hauled in here for defamation of character so fast it'll make your head spin. I doubt that'll do much for your PR business, having the world know that you'd spew lies about an innocent young girl just to save your son's sorry hide. Most people who need PR services want someone who deals in positive spin, not mudslinging."

He gave him one last bounce against the wall before releasing him, then walked away and headed straight for the chief's office to tell Mike Miller word for word everything that had just gone down before Carter could put his spin on it with the chief, the mayor and anyone else on his cell phone speed dial.

"And how do you think people will feel when they find out the lead detective is screwing the so-called victim's mother?" Carter shouted after him.

"Don't do it," Naomi said, her grasp on his arm unyielding. "The guy's scum. Don't make a bad situation worse by reacting."

Grady knew she was right, but he really yearned for the satisfaction of connecting his fist with that filthy, lying mouth.

"Grady?" she said urgently. "Are you listening to me?"

"I hear you," he said.

"What are you going to do?"

"I'm going to offer to go on administrative duty until Evan Carter's convicted and locked away," he told her.

Naomi looked shocked. "Why?"

"Because there's no way in hell I'm going to allow my personal involvement with Emily and Dani to muddy the waters once the case goes to trial."

"A judge and jury will see right through that if the defense attorney tries to bring it in," she protested.

"I'm not willing to take the chance." He gave her a weary smile. "Go on back and try to keep those two from wreaking havoc over the place. I need to spend some time with the chief."

"I think I should go with you," she said stubbornly.

He shook his head. "Thanks for wanting to, but this is my situation. Let me handle it."

To his shock, Naomi stood on tiptoe and pressed a kiss to his cheek. "You need backup, all you have to do is shout."

"I know that. Thanks."

Grady watched her go, then drew in a deep breath and walked into the chief's office to face the music.

23

Dani turned her face up to the sun. She knew she'd wind up with freckles or maybe someday even skin cancer if her mom's dire warnings were to be believed, but the warmth felt so good. In some ways she felt as if she'd been locked up inside for the past year. Ever since what she'd started thinking of as "the incident," she'd avoided being outside alone. She hadn't even realized she was doing it until lately. Now that Evan was in jail and the judge had denied bail, she couldn't wait to get outside the minute she came home from school. The choking fear that had kept her from crossing the threshold just weeks ago had vanished.

To her relief, all the containers and patches of flowers she'd planted were thriving now that she was giving them the attention they needed. When her mom had taken over, they'd started to look pretty bedraggled.

"Don't you want to swim?" Caitlyn called out to her from the pool. "You must have pulled every weed by now."

"Pretty much," Dani agreed, sitting on the edge of the pool and letting her feet dangle in the cool, aquamarine water just inches from where Caitlyn was clinging to the pool's side.

Caitlyn looked up at her, her expression wistful. "Dani, do you think things are ever going to feel normal again?"

Dani kicked her feet and splashed Caitlyn. "Come on, Cat, normal's highly overrated," she joked, then sobered. "No, really, I guess one of these days everything will settle down. Reporters have to stop hanging around the neighborhood sooner or later. I mean, we're boring, right? Once the trial's over, we'll be yesterday's news, at least until I win some major international prize in botany and you get one for, what?" She tilted her head quizzically. "What do you want to do once we're grown-up?"

"I think I'm going to be some reclusive writer who lives out in the middle of the Everglades where no one can find me." Caitlyn grinned. "I'll keep a shotgun by the door and wave it at anyone who comes onto my property."

Dani had had her own fantasies about threatening the intrusive reporters, but she couldn't imagine peace-loving Caitlyn actually doing it. "Forget the gun. You'd probably just shoot yourself in the foot."

Caitlyn sighed. "Probably."

"Would you really want to live all alone in the middle of nowhere?"

"After the past few months, it sounds really good to me."

"Then I guess you don't want to go away to college and live in a dorm with me in a few years, or maybe an apartment of our own off-campus," Dani said, surprisingly disappointed. She'd liked having Caitlyn as a temporary roommate. It had been almost as much fun as she'd always imagined it would be to have a sister. With the topic of Evan off-limits, they'd resumed their old friendship.

Caitlyn smiled broadly. "I thought maybe you'd forgotten about that plan we made. We were, what? Ten?"

"You were ten and I'd just turned twelve. And no, I haven't forgotten. I've been counting on it. Once I get to college wherever we decide to go, I'll scope things out and find the absolute best place for when you get there two years later. Can you imagine what it'll be like to be on our own, to do whatever we want?"

"It'll be a blast."

Dani nudged her with her foot. "See. I knew you didn't really want to be a recluse."

"After that," Caitlyn insisted. "If I'm going to be a writer, I do have to have *some* life experiences to draw on."

"If my mom has it right, all the best writers have lived through some sort of trauma or tragedy," Dani said.

"I'd say this whole mess with Evan qualifies," Caitlyn said.

"That's *my* trauma," Dani corrected. "And his, too, I guess. I think *you're* supposed to suffer for your art."

"Please, don't you think I've suffered enough listening to my dad talk down to my mom all these years? And being treated like I don't matter because I can't throw a football? My family brings new meaning to dysfunctional."

"Come on," Dani argued. "Your mom is great! You haven't had it so bad, not like some of the kids we know. Self-pity isn't the same as suffering."

"Maybe not, but I can't wait for the trial to be over," Caitlyn said. "Maybe then my mom will finally get around to telling my dad we're leaving." She regarded Dani with satisfaction. "He's going to freak."

Dani knew all about divorce. Even though her mom and dad still got along okay, she missed what it had been like when they'd all lived here. Now she could call her dad whenever she wanted and they did stuff together— probably even more than they had before, if she was being honest about it—but it wasn't the same as seeing him at dinner every day or being able to go into the den and ask him about stuff. Then, again, maybe she was glorifying the good times, because the truth was he'd been gone a lot even before the divorce.

"Cat, are you really that anxious for your mom and dad to split up?" she asked. "I know you used to idolize your dad and want his approval more than anything."

"And then I woke up and realized I was never going to get it," she said bitterly. "I'm not his precious son. That's my big crime. What's the point in wasting my energy wanting something I'm never going to get?"

"Your dad loves you," Dani said with more hope than conviction. She couldn't imagine feeling her dad didn't care about her. Even when he'd hardly been around at all, she'd known he loved her. It must really suck for Caitlyn not believing that about her dad.

"It doesn't matter," Caitlyn insisted, but her chin wobbled as she said it.

And maybe the dampness on her cheeks was from being in the pool, but Dani didn't think so. She thought she was really, really sad, so she said the only thing she could think of that would get her mind off everything that was going on.

"Who cares about any of that? Your mom sent over more brownies," she reminded Caitlyn. "And we have ice cream and hot-fudge sauce."

Sure enough, Caitlyn's eyes brightened. "Awesome,"

she declared, scrambling out of the pool. "I'll fix 'em, though, because when it comes to food, you're no better in the kitchen than your mom."

Dani grinned as she ran into the house after her. "Maybe not," she said, conceding the point as she surveyed the bright splashes of color around the yard. "But you gotta admit, my garden rocks!"

Emily was a nervous wreck. Not only was today the very first time she and Grady had planned anything close to a real date, but it involved meeting his family, or his mother, anyway. She knew from the way he talked about her and his uncle Luis and the rest of his family that they were all important to him, so she felt the pressure of making a good impression.

"Why do you look as if you've just been caught with your hand in the cookie jar?" Grady inquired, amusement sparkling in his eyes.

"You've been a cop too long. It's not guilt you're seeing on my face, it's fear."

"What are you afraid of?"

She winced self-consciously. "Your mother," she admitted. "Or, rather, meeting her." She rubbed her damp palms on her slacks. "I wonder if this is the way my students feel when they're about to give a book report?"

"You mean terrified enough to hurl?" Dani inquired, bouncing into the kitchen.

"Dani!" she protested.

"Well, that is how they feel," Dani said blithely.

"And how do you know that?" Emily asked, appalled that she was viewed as some sort of terrifying force.

"Mom, kids talk about their teachers all the time. You know that."

"I guess I'm just surprised they'd say stuff about me around you."

Dani grinned. "I ask. Sometimes I even put in a good word for you."

"Gee, thanks."

"Can we go now?" Dani asked Grady. "I can't wait to pick up the stuff for your yard and get to work. There's a lot to do today."

Startled, Emily stared from her to Grady. "Dani's coming along?"

He grinned. "I thought it would be easier if you thought all the attention wouldn't be on you."

"Well, thank goodness for small favors. I just wish you'd told me that before I had my panic attack."

"*That's* your version of a panic attack?" he asked. "Wait until you see my mother. When she's nervous, she cooks. Right about now, my kitchen is probably filled with enough covered dishes to feed me for the next month. And that's just from her first trip over. She'll be back with more later."

"Why would she be nervous?"

"Because you're all I've talked about for a few weeks now. She knows you're important to me."

Emily felt something in her stomach flutter. "You told her that?"

"I didn't have to spell it out. It was the fact that I never shut up about you and Dani and Josh."

She studied him quizzically. "What did you say? Specifically?"

"Now you're just fishing for compliments," he taunted. "Come on. Let's go before the kid here decides to drag us out. She's a little impatient, don't you think?"

"I'm a *lot* impatient," Dani corrected, heading for

Grady's car. "Have you looked at your yard? I could have a whole crew and not get everything done that needs to be done."

"Your mom and I will help," Grady promised.

Dani regarded him with horror. "I don't think so. Mom kills stuff just by looking at it and, from what I've seen, you're not much better."

Grady ruffled her hair. "Careful. I'm the one with the credit card you get to use at the nursery."

As they drove off, Emily watched the interaction between them and marveled. Dani had taken to Grady in a way she'd never anticipated. She'd feared her daughter would always think of him as the man who'd forced her to relive an emotionally painful experience. Instead, Dani seemed almost grateful to him for coaxing the truth into the open.

Listening to the two of them banter, she leaned back in the passenger seat of Grady's car and relaxed. A couple of years ago she would never have imagined herself being this comfortable with a man who wasn't Derek. A few months ago she couldn't have envisioned a future with the man who'd arrested her best friend's son. And only weeks ago, knowing that her attraction to him was deepening with every day that passed, she still wouldn't have given two cents for their chances when he'd forced her to strip away the blinders she'd been wearing about Evan and her daughter. Lately, now that Dani's healing process seemed well underway, it was almost impossible to imagine her life without him.

Stopped at a traffic light, Grady glanced her way, then reached over and took her hand. "You okay?"

"Just thinking about how quickly things change and how many unexpected things can happen."

"Good things?"

She smiled at his serious expression. "Some of them. You, especially," she confessed.

"You know, one of these days we really are going to have to have an honest-to-goodness date," he said. "Think you can handle it?"

"That depends on your idea of a date," she said, her pulse skipping a beat.

"Dinner, maybe some dancing. Believe it or not, I do a pretty mean mambo."

Her eyes widened. "You're kidding, right?"

"Hey, I'm Cuban. We mambo. At least in my house we did. My mother has an entire collection of Celia Cruz CDs. They provided background music for every meal. Drove my dad nuts." He grinned. "Or so he said, but I saw him and my mom dancing more than once after they thought we'd all gone to bed. It was a revelation, since I'd always pegged him as stiff and boring. For an old man, he has some impressive moves."

Emily realized he almost never mentioned his father. "Are you close to your dad?"

A look of regret passed across his face. "We've been at odds most of my life. We're just too different and he's never had much tolerance for people who made choices he didn't agree with. It took a long time for him and my mother to forgive me for Megan's death and for what they viewed as me driving away Kathleen. I'm much closer to my uncle. He may not always agree with my decisions or approve of what I've done, but he listens and he tries to understand. He never judges me. He's the exact opposite of my father. How they came from the same gene pool is beyond me."

Just when Emily was beginning to think she was

finally getting some real insights into this man who'd become so important in her life, Dani cut in excitedly.

"Grady, the nursery's right up there, on the left. See it? Don't miss the turn."

"I'm on it, kid," he said, smiling at her eagerness. He winked at Emily. "To be continued."

Emily couldn't seem to stop herself from smiling. *To be continued*. Funny how words she saw all the time on the bottom of a TV screen and found so incredibly frustrating could be filled with so much promise in real life.

Grady was hot and filthy and tired, but it had been years since he'd felt this much contentment. His seriously neglected yard was coming back to life. The pool, which had been drained and left empty ever since Megan's death, had been scrubbed and painted and filled with crystal-clear water once more.

His lawn had been neatly mowed, old plants ripped out and replaced with bold tropical flowers that suited the Spanish style of the house. The runaway bougainvillea had been trimmed to within an inch of its life, leaving stems that were still bright with splashes of fuchsia and purple flowers. Dani had added orange birds of paradise with their dark green leaves and a dozen other plants he didn't recognize.

The girl worked tirelessly, her arms strong enough to haul the five-gallon containers of plants, her expression serious as she gently patted the soil around their roots.

"She looks happy, doesn't she?" Emily said from the chaise longue next to his. "Almost as if nothing happened."

"She hasn't forgotten," Grady said. "But she's strong enough to start putting it into perspective."

"Do you think it will affect how she thinks of men and dating? I really worry about that. She's been so cautious for months now. I should have guessed it had something to do with Evan."

He knew all too well that the rape could well shape her outlook on dating. "It might," he said candidly. "But with time and the right kind of encouragement, I think she'll get past all of it."

"To be honest, a part of me hopes she won't want to date for another ten years," Emily admitted.

"It would be better for her if she went out next weekend," Grady said. "But I understand where you're coming from."

"When I was Dani's age, parents still screened the boys their daughters went out with," she said. "At the time I thought that was archaic, but once I had Dani I understood the value of it." She gave him a wry look. "In effect, though, I had exactly that chance with Evan. Look how badly I blew that."

"No," Grady said sharply. "You couldn't have predicted anything that happened."

"Josh did," she said.

"Because he was with Evan under different circumstances. He saw how he treated the girls he dated. Stop blaming yourself for not seeing through the polite veneer he worked hard to maintain around you and most other adults."

"But I did see glimpses of that other boy," Emily admitted. "I saw how he treated Marcie."

"And chalked it up to teenage attitude toward parental authority, I imagine," Grady suggested. "You see a lot of that at school."

She sighed. "True."

"Leave the blame where it belongs—on Evan," he told her. "Why don't I pour you a glass of wine and you can relax a little before my mom gets here?"

"I don't think my stomach can take wine right now," she said. "Just the mention of your mother gets it all twisted into knots again."

"Then I'll hurry with my shower so you won't have to face her alone." He leaned down and brushed a lingering kiss across her lips until the color returned to her cheeks. "That's better," he said with satisfaction.

She smiled. "Indeed, it is." Then her attention went to Dani. "She probably needs to clean up too."

"Not unless she wants to."

"But she'll make a terrible impression looking like that," Emily protested.

"Trust me, all my mother will notice is what she's done with this yard of mine." He gestured toward the pool. "And what she's motivated me to do. Most of all, she'll think that Dani will make a beautiful, industrious granddaughter."

Emily's eyes widened with alarm.

"Not to worry, *querida*. She's not going to hold a shotgun to your back till we head down the aisle. She's just anticipating."

"Too much, perhaps," Emily said.

He touched a finger to her lush mouth. "Not really."

Not if he had anything to say about it.

The petite dynamo who'd taken over Grady's kitchen was the most fascinating woman Emily had ever met. She'd exuberantly hugged Dani, oblivious to the dirt that covered her and the sweat running down her face and arms. Then she'd embraced Emily just as enthusiastically, chattering happily in Spanish until Grady had reminded her that their guests spoke only English.

When she'd switched to English with a quick apology, her words were barely accented and her excitement unabated. There was no mistaking the fact that she already had high expectations for this new woman in her son's life. Emily feared she was going to be disappointed. All the signs were pointing in the right direction, but she and Grady had just walked a few feet on a long and sometimes difficult road.

"Come," she'd commanded a few minutes earlier. "You can help me with dinner. We will get to know each other."

"I'll set the table," Emily offered. "You don't want me ruining all this wonderful food you've brought." Grady had been right. There was enough here to feed an entire army, not just the four of them.

"You don't cook?" Mrs. Rodriguez asked, looking stunned.

"Not like this," Emily replied, gesturing at the display on the counter and the kitchen table.

"Not to worry. I like to do it. You concentrate on teaching children. I will see that you and my son don't starve."

"Mrs. Rodriguez, you might have gotten the wrong idea. Grady and I are friends. We're just getting to know each other."

"My son has *friends,*" she said dismissively. "He needs a woman in his life. He wants you. That is enough for me."

"But—"

"Here is silverware," Mrs. Rodriguez said, cutting off her protest before it could be formed. "We'll eat in the dining room. This is a special occasion, *sí?*"

"Yes," Emily said, biting back a sigh. "Yes, it is."

When Josh showed up a few minutes later, she felt as if she were being hurried toward a future she hadn't yet embraced.

"I didn't know you were coming," she told Josh, regarding Grady with a frown as she said it.

"He told me his mother was cooking. Where else would I be?" He impulsively gave the older woman a kiss on the cheek. "Your picadillo was the best I ever had."

Mrs. Rodriguez beamed at him approvingly. "Smart boy. I like you. Now finish setting the table. Your mama can watch me add a few spices to my arroz con pollo."

Josh gaped and Dani, who'd just come inside, giggled.

"You might not want to let her anywhere near the stove," Dani said with some urgency.

"Nonsense," Mrs. Rodriguez said. "Come."

Emily went, too intimidated not to. After all, she was only going to observe, not touch anything or add anything.

Unfortunately, a container of something was shoved into her hand at once.

"One pinch," Mrs. Rodriguez said. "Like so." She demonstrated, then waited.

"I don't know," Emily said.

Grady grinned at her. "Give in, sweetheart. It'll be painless."

"But will the food be edible?" she asked warily.

"It's one pinch," Mrs. Rodriguez scolded. "How hard can that be?"

Emily sighed and opened the lid of the container. She dumped what to her looked like a pinch into her palm, only to have Mrs. Rodriguez gasp and jerk her hand away from the pot.

"Too much! A pinch is like so." Again, she demon-strated, then glanced at Grady. "The two of you, outside. I will finish in here. *Los niños* can help me." She cast a disapproving look at Dani's filthy hands. "After you have washed up." When Josh started to move to her side, she frowned. "You, too."

"But I wasn't digging in the dirt," he protested.

"Wash!"

He grinned. "Yes, ma'am."

Dismissed, Emily followed Grady outside. "They actually listened to her."

"My mother's pretty formidable. People tend to listen."

"I could use that skill in my classroom," she said, unable to keep a wistful note out of her voice.

Before she could sit down, Grady beat her to the chaise longue and pulled her down beside him. She tried to ignore all those muscles and all that masculine heat, but it was a losing proposition.

"You forget I've seen you in your classroom," he said. "My mother has nothing on you. If you ask me, you're two peas in a pod."

"Except she can cook."

"I can get a good meal anywhere," he consoled her. "You, I've only found once."

Suddenly, ridiculously, she felt the sting of tears in her eyes. Grady looked alarmed.

"What did I say?" he asked.

She brushed impatiently at the tears. "The sweetest thing anyone's ever said to me."

He looked entirely too pleased with himself. "That was just the beginning. Give me a few weeks to warm up."

That was what scared Emily more than anything. He had her right here, right now. She didn't need to wait for any encores.

24

Marcie didn't think she could bear sitting through her son's trials, especially not the one in which he'd be facing Dani's accusations. As much as she hadn't wanted to believe her son capable of such a crime, she'd looked into Dani's anguished face and known she was telling the truth. She suspected she'd feel the same awful, sinking sensation in the pit of her stomach if she heard Lauren Brown's testimony.

Two weeks before the court date for Evan's first trial, she made several phone calls, including one to Evan's attorney, then insisted that Ken sit down across from her in their kitchen. Determined not to be put off, she overrode his objections that he didn't have time to waste chatting.

"Make the time," she said flatly. "This is important, Ken. It's probably the most important conversation we'll ever have."

"More important than saving our son?"

"This may be the only way to save him," she responded quietly.

"You're not going to bring up that crap about a plea bargain again, are you?"

She ignored the jeering note in his voice. "Yes, I am. And I'm going to keep bringing it up until you actually hear me."

"How can you even suggest that Evan spend one minute behind bars for a crime he didn't commit?"

"Crimes," she said emphatically. "He didn't do this once, Ken. There are two young women who've made these charges, one of them a girl we've known practically all her life."

"That doesn't mean she's not a liar," he said stubbornly.

She looked into his eyes. "You know better."

"I know our son," he countered.

"So do I, and as much as I hate believing it, he is capable of doing this. I've looked him in the eye and asked for the truth. He mocks me. That is not the reaction of an innocent young man. It's the reaction of someone who can't deny his own guilt."

"How can you say that? He's our son, dammit! What has gotten into you? He deserves our unconditional support."

"Not unconditional, Ken. Not when it comes to this. I've had to face the truth. In fact, I've had to face a lot of truths over the past few months. Our marriage is in shambles. It has been for years. I've just been too scared to admit it. Our son has adopted your attitude toward women. It started with me and, sadly, it's taken an awful twist with young girls his own age. I blame myself for that, as much as I do you." When Ken opened his mouth, his face contorted with outrage, she held up a hand. "Don't contradict me or belittle my opinion. You've done that enough and for the last time."

"So this is all my fault?" he demanded. "I made Evan into the kind of boy who could commit rape?"

She winced at the harsh word, but it was accurate. "As usual, you didn't really listen to what I said. I accepted my share of responsibility. I never stood up to you. I never called you on your behavior, partly because I loved you and partly to keep the peace, because that's what I thought made a good wife. I was wrong, more wrong than I could possibly have imagined. I taught Evan that it's okay to show utter disrespect for a woman, that we don't deserve better than that, especially from someone who's supposed to love us."

Tears welled up in her eyes and fell, unchecked. "Together, we set the example, Ken. Together, we made Evan into the kind of young man who thought it was okay to take advantage of a woman because she didn't deserve respect or consideration or even being heard. Maybe it even goes all the way back to childhood when no never meant no with Evan, because we always gave in."

"Have you been watching that guy on TV again? What's his name? Dr. Phil? Cut all the psychological mumbo-jumbo. Our boy is perfectly normal."

Could Ken be that delusional? she wondered. "It is not normal to bring a sixteen-year-old girl into this house and force her to have sex when she repeatedly told him no. It is not normal to take a young college girl into her apartment and force her to do the same thing, even though she'd rejected him."

"He never—"

"Yes, he did," she said flatly. "You know it, and the sooner you stop denying it, the better off Evan will be. He needs help, Ken. He doesn't need his daddy to get him out of another jam, so he never learns that actions have consequences. That stops now." He opened his mouth, but before he could speak, she said, "I've spoken to Evan's attorney and he agrees with me. Remember, he's seen the evidence. He understands the likely impact on the jury, not only of the physical evidence, but the testimony of these two young women. We both believe that the plea arrangement offered by the prosecution is Evan's best chance to get the help he needs, rather than spending years in jail."

She looked him directly in the eye. "Years," she repeated. "He won't get off with a slap on the wrist if he's convicted, but if he's willing to plead guilty to lesser charges and the two girls agree, he can serve a minimal amount of time and then get probation. His attorney believes the prosecution and judge will accept the deal because he has no other criminal history and has always been a good student and otherwise a model kid. They want justice for Dani and Lauren. They don't want to destroy Evan. This needs to happen, Ken. It's the only way to save him. You and Evan both need to face facts. He's not going to walk away from this. If God is merciful, Lauren and Dani will agree."

The fight suddenly seemed to drain out of her husband, a man she'd loved for most of her adult life but no longer respected.

"You shouldn't have called the attorney," he said, but there was little fire in his voice. "I was handling everything just fine."

"You were trying to," she agreed. "But this can't be *handled,* Ken. It needs to be faced head-on. If those girls say yes, I want Evan to take the deal and save himself from an even worse punishment if he's convicted in both of those cases."

"*If,* Marcie. That's a big *if.*"

She shook her head. "If Evan's own mother, me,

believed what Dani said, then a jury will, too. Every word coming out of that child's mouth is God's honest truth. There's not a doubt in my mind about that, not one shred of reasonable doubt. Worse, Evan admitted as much to Caitlyn. Do you want her dragged into this, forced to testify against her own brother?"

"Our attorney is good," he countered. "The best. He can make a saint sound like a sinner."

She regarded him with disgust. "And you would let that happen? You would let him try to harass those girls and tarnish their reputations? You would put your own daughter through this?"

"To save Evan? Yes, without the slightest qualm."

"Well, I won't allow it," she said, shaking but determined. "I can't. It goes against every shred of decency in me. As a mother, I hate the thought of Evan pleading guilty, but also as a mother, I have to imagine what it's like for those girls he victimized. And unlike you, I care about what it would do to Caitlyn if she were forced to testify."

"You've let Emily influence you," he charged. "You've listened to her whining about poor Dani and you're willing to throw your own child to the wolves to save her."

"I haven't discussed this with Emily. She has no idea what I intend to recommend."

"Oh, please, you didn't dream this up on your own," he jeered. He tried to stare her down, his scowl meant to intimidate, but she held firm.

"Evan wants to fight," he reminded her. "He wants to clear his name."

"Because you've convinced him that's possible. He wants desperately to believe you because it'll be the easy way out of all this. I intend to sit him down with his attorney and explain a few facts to him."

Ken seemed stunned by her refusal to back down. "You've changed," he said at last. It didn't sound like a compliment.

"Yes, I have, thank God. It's taken me far too long."

"Evan will never forgive you for forcing him to do this," he said.

She sighed then. "I can't force him to do anything. I wish I could. Maybe, though, if he follows my advice for once, he will get a tiny glimmer of what it's like to do the right thing. If so, I can live with having him hate me. Thanks to you, he's not all that fond of me as it is."

She was about to stand up and make the call to the attorney, when Ken stopped her. "Wait."

She sat back down.

"This will be the end of our marriage, you know." He said it as if he meant it to be a threat.

Marcie nodded. "That's a given."

He seemed startled by her easy acquiescence. "It's been over for a long time, hasn't it?"

Unable to speak, she merely nodded.

For the longest time, his gaze held hers, but he was the first to look away. "I'm sorry."

She reached across the table and touched his hand. It was ice-cold. "Me, too," she said, filled with dismay and just the first, faint hint of relief. "Me, too."

Emily was surprised to find Grady waiting for her in the parking lot at school.

"What are you doing here?"

"I came to see my two best girls," he said. "Where's Dani?"

Something in his voice set off an alarm. His good cheer sounded forced. "What's wrong?"

"Nothing, really, but there's something you both need to know."

"Tell me first," she insisted.

He looked as if he wanted to argue, then shrugged. "Evan's attorney wants to make a deal with the court. If it works out, neither case would go to trial."

Emily stared at him incredulously. She couldn't believe that after all Evan had put Dani and Lauren through, they wouldn't have their day in court. "He made a deal?" she demanded, her voice escalating. "You have to be kidding me. What's he getting? Some kind of slap on the wrist? What the hell kind of justice is that?" She poked Grady in the chest. "It's wrong. You know it's wrong."

He captured her hands. "Hey, calm down. It's definitely more than a slap on the wrist. He'll serve some time, get some serious counseling, then be on probation for a good long time."

Since she didn't know quite where to direct her anger, she chose to aim it at Grady since he was right here in front of her. "Why wasn't I told about this? Why didn't we have any say?"

"Actually I'm telling you about it now and you can have your say. This will all be finalized in court tomorrow. You and Dani will have a chance to speak, if you want to. Lauren will, as well." He touched her cheek. "What those girls want will count, but I believe this is for the best, Emily."

She frowned at that. "How can you say that? Dani deserves a chance to confront Evan, the satisfaction of having him proved guilty and sent to jail."

"And she'll have her chance. She just won't have to relive every second of the crime. Evan is being punished. In the end, isn't that what we all wanted?"

She gave him a rueful look. "I wanted to see him hang," she admitted.

He smiled slightly at her ferocity. "No, you didn't. I know you, *querida*. A part of you still thinks of that boy as a son."

"Okay, a tiny part," she admitted. "I do want to believe there's a chance for him to get his life back on track eventually."

"This will give him that chance."

"Does Marcie know?"

"Actually she fought for it. She ganged up with Evan's attorney and together they convinced Ken and Evan this was the way to go. She wanted it over for Dani's sake and for Lauren's, and she wanted Evan to acknowledge what he'd done and get help."

"God, it must be killing her that he's going to spend even one second behind bars."

"I spoke to her earlier. She knows this is the best solution for everyone."

"I need to go over there," she began, then stopped. She hadn't set foot in Marcie's house in weeks now, first because Marcie hadn't wanted her there and then because she was afraid she'd envision too clearly what had happened to Dani. "God, I'm such a coward. You're still able to live in the house where your child died and I can't face walking into Marcie's even for a visit."

"I stayed in that house as penance," Grady said. "And finally, with your help and Dani's, I'm starting to make peace with what happened there. You'll make your own peace eventually. In the meantime, call Marcie, invite her over. I know she's anxious to see you and tell you her plans."

"Plans?"

"She and Caitlyn are moving out. They've found a smaller house in Coral Gables. Caitlyn's going to private school. Ken's paying for it. He's putting the house in your neighborhood on the market and they'll split the money."

"Are they getting a divorce?"

He nodded. "I don't know her as well as you do, of course, but she seems content with that, eager to move on."

"How about Ken?"

"She says he's angry about all of it. Something tells me he's basically a very angry man. He could use some help dealing with his issues, too, but I doubt he'll get it. I feel sorry for him. He had this terrific family, a job he's really good at, and a wonderful home and he's thrown it all away just because he didn't know how to show his appreciation for any of it."

"Don't you dare feel sorry for him," she said angrily. "He set the example for Evan. It's because of him that all of this happened."

Grady reached for her.

"No," she said, jerking away. "I can't talk to you right now."

He regarded her with bewilderment. "What did I do? I'm only the messenger here."

"Yes, well, you know what happens to messengers when they bring bad news. They're the ones who get killed. I need to go."

"Emily, come on. Let's talk about this. You have to know this is the best thing for everyone."

"No, I don't know that," she contradicted. "I'll talk to

you later. I have to go someplace alone and think this through."

"Couldn't we talk it through together?"

"I don't think so. Right now, I view you as part of the system and I'm not very happy with the system." She yanked open her car door, got in and turned the key impatiently. The second the ignition caught, she had the car in Reverse and shot past Grady, who was still regarding her with confusion.

She didn't know exactly why she was so furious, especially with him, but just thinking about Evan getting away with what he'd done made her crazy. If Evan had been home, rather than safely tucked away in jail, she might have marched into Marcie's and taken justice into her own hands.

Even as the fantasy played out, she sighed. She knew that if Evan had been home, she wouldn't have done it. She wouldn't turn into the kind of person who took the law into her own hands, but she wanted to. Oh, how she wanted to!

Calmer now, she turned onto her own street, into her own driveway.

Inside, she mechanically went about making tea, then sat down at the kitchen table and thought about all the times she would have gone running to Marcie after a day as monumentally bad as this one. She could have told her about blaming Grady for something he'd had no part in. She could have discussed the fury that made her want to hurt the young man who'd hurt her child. But that young man was Marcie's son, so how could she?

Tears welled up as she thought about the months it had taken to get to the truth, the weeks of torment she and Derek and Dani had gone through preparing to go to trial. And now it was all going to be over with a flick of some judge's pen. It didn't seem right or fair or just.

Grady had insisted it was for the best, but how could it be? Anything that ended with Evan getting one second less than the maximum sentence possible wasn't for the best. How could she be with a man who thought it was?

And how was she going to tell her daughter that the system that was supposed to protect her, that the man who'd promised her justice, had failed her?

Grady stood in the hallway outside of the courtroom where Evan's hearing had been held. Lauren and Dani had both spoken passionately about what had happened to them and about the effect it had had on their lives, but in the end both had agreed to the deal that would give Evan another chance.

Based on their testimony and compassion, the judge had agreed to the plea to lesser charges. He'd sentenced him to serve time in a minimum-security prison for a year, then added years of probation on the condition that he successfully undergo psychological counseling and change his behavior around women. Any misstep would send him back to prison.

Grady had thought it a fair deal, but one look at Emily's seething expression told him she disagreed. She wouldn't even look at him, as if she somehow blamed him for the case being resolved with a plea bargain rather than a trial.

As he waited for her to emerge from the courtroom, Naomi joined him. "Dani's mom doesn't look too happy about this," she commented.

"She's not."

"Even though Dani agreed?"

"She seems to think Dani's being too easy on a boy she once cared about."

"Is Emily taking it out on you?"

He shrugged. "Looks that way."

"Well, you know what I think? I think she blames herself for not seeing what was happening right under her nose and seeing Evan sent to prison for years and years was going to be her way of making up for not protecting Dani."

Grady regarded her with surprise. "I hadn't looked at it that way."

"Because you're not a woman. Give her some time. She'll come around and see that this was the best solution for everyone."

Just then Emily, Derek, Josh and Dani came through the doorway. Derek gave him a curt nod. Josh came over and shook his hand. But when Dani started toward him, Emily halted her.

"Dani, we need to go," she said tersely.

"But—"

"Now," Emily said, not looking at him at all.

Beside him, Naomi gave a dramatic shiver. "Now that was just plain cold," she said.

"I don't need you to do a play-by-play," he said. "I got the message. She's still unhappy with me."

"What are you going to do about it?"

"I wish to hell I knew," he said. Regretting that he desperately needed the advice, he glanced at Naomi. "Flowers?"

"No way."

"Chocolates?"

"Not enough in the world."

"What, then?"

"Time," she said, then grinned. "And maybe some heavy-duty groveling."

"But I didn't do anything," he protested.

"Do you want to be right or do you want to make things right?" she inquired.

He sighed heavily. "I'll get back to you on that."

"When are you going to give in and call the man?" Paula demanded a few weeks after Evan's hearing and Emily's breakup with Grady. "He's left at least one message every day since Evan's sentencing."

Emily stared morosely at the stack of term papers in front of her and tried to work up some enthusiasm for grading them. "I'm not going to call him. That's why I tore up all the messages."

"Maybe you should explain to me again why you're so mad at him."

"Because he let Dani down," she said tersely. "What happened in court wasn't justice, not for Dani or Lauren."

"None of that was Grady's call. Why are you blaming him?"

"Because he's convenient," she admitted. "And because he went along with it as if it were just another case to get crossed off his list."

"I doubt he saw it that way. I know how hard that man worked to make sure that Evan could be successfully prosecuted. So do you."

"I suppose," Emily said, though she didn't want to concede even that much. It was easier to blame Grady than to admit that she was the one who'd truly let Dani down by not intervening before her crush on Evan had had such disastrous consequences.

Paula studied her. "Can I ask you something?"

"Of course."

"Are you really angry with Grady—or yourself?"

Startled that Paula had read her so easily, she sighed. "Myself," she admitted in a small voice.

"And don't you think that's just as ridiculous as blaming him?"

"It's not!" she insisted. "We both let Dani down."

"Is Dani mad at either one of you?"

"No. In fact she's been pestering me every since we left court to call Grady so she can go over to his house and check on her landscaping. She's relieved that all of this is behind her."

"Then apparently she's forgiven both of you. Or, perhaps, she understands that there's nothing to be forgiven."

"I failed her."

"She doesn't seem to think so," Paula said reasonably. "Call Grady. Try being as grown up as your daughter and let him off the hook."

"I'll think about it," she promised. "That's the best I can do."

Since eating crow wasn't in her nature, it was just as well that she found Grady waiting for her in the parking lot that afternoon. He was leaning against her car, wearing faded jeans, a tight T-shirt and aviator sunglasses that prevented her from reading his expression. She wanted to snuggle up to all that hard masculinity and beg him to forgive her for being a stubborn idiot, but of course, she didn't.

"Finding you loitering in the school parking lot is getting to be a habit," she said, trying to keep her voice steady. "Should I report you for suspicious behavior?"

His lips curved slightly. "I wish you wouldn't."

"What are you doing here?"

"Naomi suggested for the thousandth time that it was time for me to start groveling. I got tired of the nagging."

Emily had to fight the smile tugging at her lips. "Really? I wouldn't mind seeing you grovel. Are you any good at it?"

"I doubt it. And I'm not entirely sure where to start, since I don't have a fix on exactly what I did wrong. Maybe you could help me out."

She'd thought about little else for weeks now, but she still didn't have a reply that made a lot of sense. She offered the best she had. "You crossed the mother hen in me," she said. "And made me feel a thousand times guiltier for not doing more to prevent what happened. If I'd been on the job, Evan would never have been alone with my infatuated daughter."

"You do know it wasn't your fault, right?"

"I want to believe that."

"Well, believe it."

"So, where do we go from here?" she asked, her heart in her throat. Surely the fact that he was here meant he hadn't given up on them.

"Your place?" he inquired, grinning. "Or mine?"

It was time to seize the moment, but she couldn't seem to get the words out.

"Come on, Em. Say something. I do okay on body language, but I can't read your mind."

She reached up and removed his sunglasses. "You sure about that, Detective? Take a guess. What am I saying?"

He moaned. "Don't look at me like that, not here in the school parking lot. I've been waiting for a while to see a spark like that in your eyes. Your timing sucks."

"Did I mention that Dani is staying after school for cheerleading tryouts for next year?"

His expression brightened at once. "No, you didn't. You're sure she's not coming home right away?"

"She's been really, really looking forward to these tryouts," Emily said. "They usually take hours. And I know she's anxious to talk to you about how your yard is doing without her constant monitoring. That gives us hours to kill doing, well, whatever we can think of to do."

"Then it makes perfect sense for the two of us to go home to wait for her, right?" he inquired hopefully.

"Perfect sense," she agreed. "You going to meet me there?"

"No, I'm taking you with me. I can use the siren and flasher."

"Isn't that illegal or something?"

"Don't ask."

"Who knew you harbored the soul of a break-the-rules kind of guy?"

"Yeah, who knew?" he said. "Now, will you please hurry?"

He didn't have to ask twice.

When Emily came home from work a month after Evan's sentencing and after the Carters had moved away, Grady was in the backyard with a shovel. She admired the view of his bare shoulders for several minutes before crossing the lawn to drop a kiss on his cheek.

"What are you up to?"

"Josh and I thought we'd have this done before you got home," he said, linking her hand with his, then pressing a kiss to her knuckles.

"Have what done?"

"This," Josh said, rounding a corner of the house with a huge fuchsia bougainvillea that he placed in front of the gap in the hedge. "We're mending fences."

"Moving on," Grady added. "Okay with you?"

She thought of all the good memories that would be left behind with the bad. "So many years," she said with regret.

"You don't have to forget everything," he reminded her. "And we'll make new memories."

She thought of the promise she'd made to Marcie right before she and Caitlyn had driven away. The two of them would come back for visits. They were only moving across town, after all. They would make fresh memories together. Good ones.

Dani joined them just then and linked her fingers through Emily's.

"Do it," Dani said softly. "It's time, Mom."

Emily blinked back tears. Her daughter was so incredibly strong, and she was smart enough to see that the present and the future meant more than a past that couldn't be changed.

"Yes," she agreed, her eyes locking with Grady's even as she gave Dani's hand a squeeze. "It's time."

* * * * *